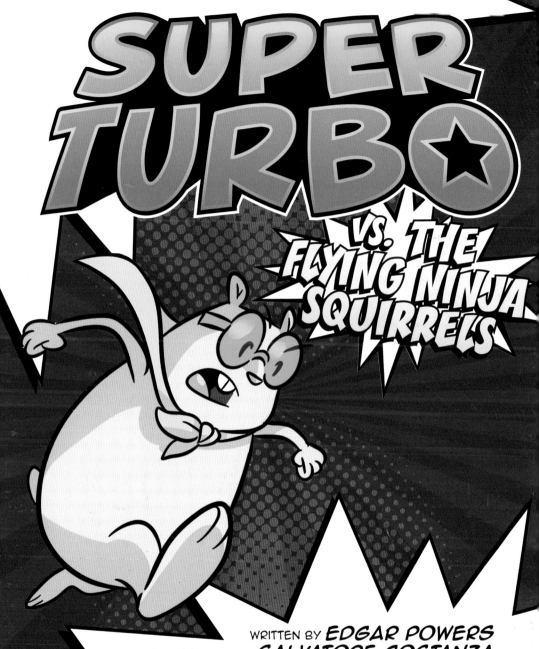

SUPER TURBO ★

VS. THE FLYING NINJA SQUIRRELS

WRITTEN BY **EDGAR POWERS**
ILLUSTRATED BY **SALVATORE COSTANZA**
AT GLASS HOUSE GRAPHICS

LITTLE SIMON
NEW YORK   LONDON   TORONTO   SYDNEY   NEW DELHI

LITTLE SIMON

AN IMPRINT OF SIMON & SCHUSTER CHILDREN'S PUBLISHING DIVISION 1230 AVENUE OF THE AMERICAS, NEW YORK, NEW YORK 10020 FIRST LITTLE SIMON EDITION FEBRUARY 2021 * COPYRIGHT © 2021 BY SIMON & SCHUSTER, INC. ALL RIGHTS RESERVED, INCLUDING THE RIGHT OF REPRODUCTION IN WHOLE OR IN PART IN ANY FORM. LITTLE SIMON IS A REGISTERED TRADEMARK OF SIMON & SCHUSTER, INC., AND ASSOCIATED COLOPHON IS A TRADEMARK OF SIMON & SCHUSTER, INC. FOR INFORMATION ABOUT SPECIAL DISCOUNTS FOR BULK PURCHASES, PLEASE CONTACT SIMON & SCHUSTER SPECIAL SALES AT 1-866-506-1949 OR BUSINESS@SIMONANDSCHUSTER.COM. THE SIMON & SCHUSTER SPEAKERS BUREAU CAN BRING AUTHORS TO YOUR LIVE EVENT. FOR MORE INFORMATION OR TO BOOK AN EVENT CONTACT THE SIMON & SCHUSTER SPEAKERS BUREAU AT 1-866-248-3049 OR VISIT OUR WEBSITE AT WWW.SIMONSPEAKERS.COM. DESIGNED BY NICHOLAS SCIACCA * ART SERVICES BY GLASS HOUSE GRAPHICS * ART, COLORS, AND COVER BY SALVATORE COSTANZA * COLOR ASSISTANT: FRANCESCA INGRASSIA * LETTERING BY GIOVANNI SPATARO/GRAFIMATED CARTOON * SUPERVISION BY SALVATORE DI MARCO/GRAFIMATED CARTOON * MANUFACTURED IN CHINA 1120 SCP * 2 4 6 8 10 9 7 5 3 1 * LIBRARY OF CONGRESS CATALOGING-IN-PUBLICATION DATA NAMES: POWERS, EDGAR J., AUTHOR. | GLASS HOUSE GRAPHICS, ILLUSTRATOR. TITLE: SUPER TURBO VS. THE FLYING NINJA SQUIRRELS / BY EDGAR POWERS ; ILLUSTRATED BY GLASS HOUSE GRAPHICS. DESCRIPTION: FIRST LITTLE SIMON EDITION. | NEW YORK : LITTLE SIMON, 2021. | SERIES: SUPER TURBO, THE GRAPHIC NOVEL ; BOOK 2 | AUDIENCE: AGES 5-9 | AUDIENCE: GRADES 2-3 | SUMMARY: "FRESH OFF THEIR VICTORY AGAINST WHISKERFACE, THE SUPERHERO PETS OF SUNNYVIEW ELEMENTARY FACE OFF AGAINST A FIERCE NEW FOE: FLYING NINJA SQUIRRELS!"— PROVIDED BY PUBLISHER. IDENTIFIERS: LCCN 2020024907 (PRINT) | LCCN 2020024908 (EBOOK) | ISBN 9781534474499 (PAPERBACK) | ISBN 9781534474505 (HARDCOVER) | ISBN 9781534474512 (EBOOK) SUBJECTS: LCSH: GRAPHIC NOVELS. | CYAC: GRAPHIC NOVELS. | SUPERHEROES—FICTION. | HAMSTERS—FICTION. | PETS—FICTION. | NINJA—FICTION. | ELEMENTARY SCHOOLS—FICTION. | SCHOOLS—FICTION. CLASSIFICATION: LCC PZ7.7.P7 SV 2021 (PRINT) | LCC PZ7.7.P7 (EBOOK) | DDC 741.5/973—DC23 LC RECORD AVAILABLE AT HTTPS://LCCN.LOC.GOV/2020024907 LC EBOOK RECORD AVAILABLE AT HTTPS://LCCN.LOC.GOV/2020024908

CONTENTS

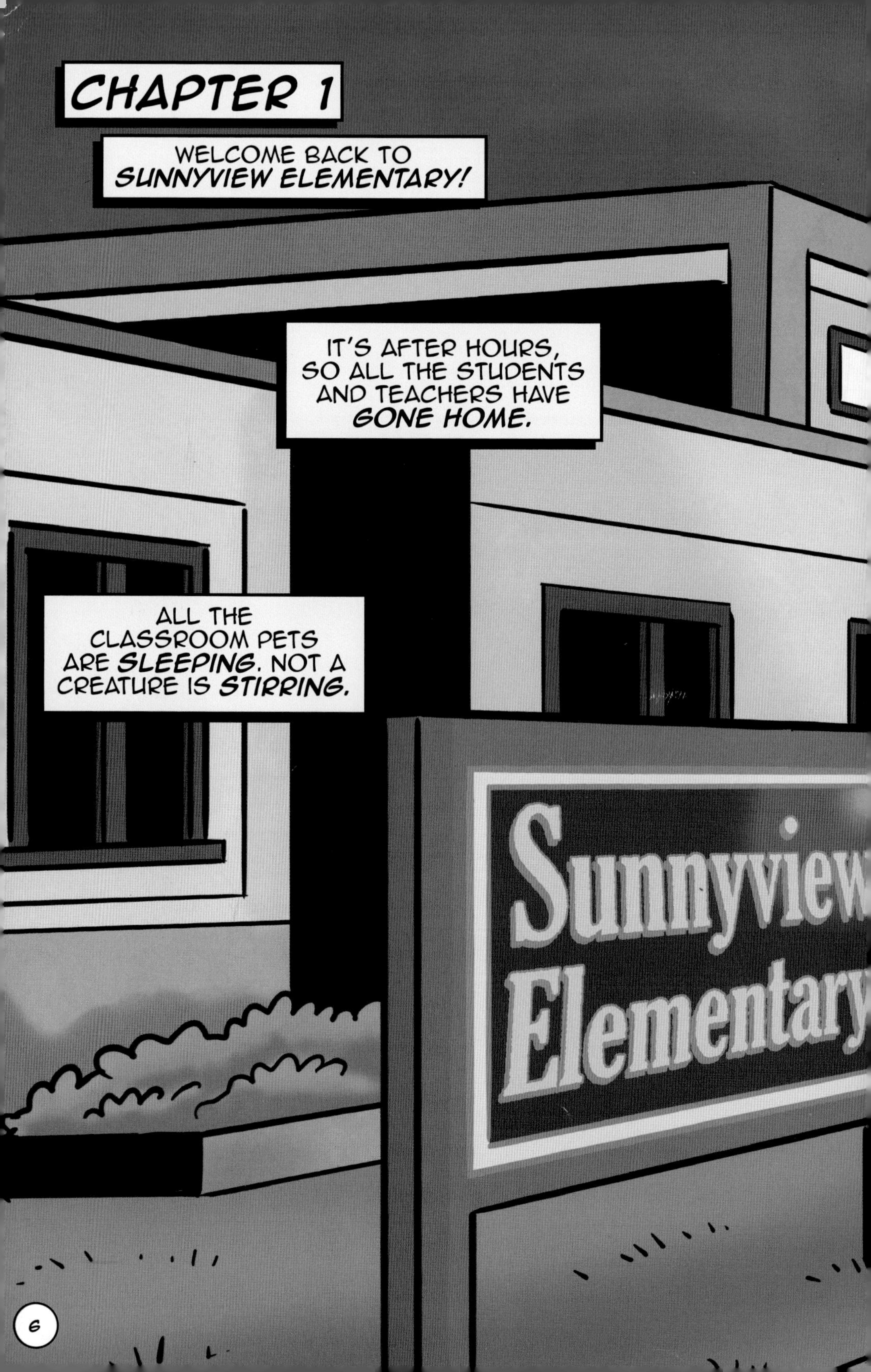
CHAPTER 1
WELCOME BACK TO SUNNYVIEW ELEMENTARY!
IT'S AFTER HOURS, SO ALL THE STUDENTS AND TEACHERS HAVE GONE HOME.
ALL THE CLASSROOM PETS ARE SLEEPING. NOT A CREATURE IS STIRRING.
Sunnyview Elementary

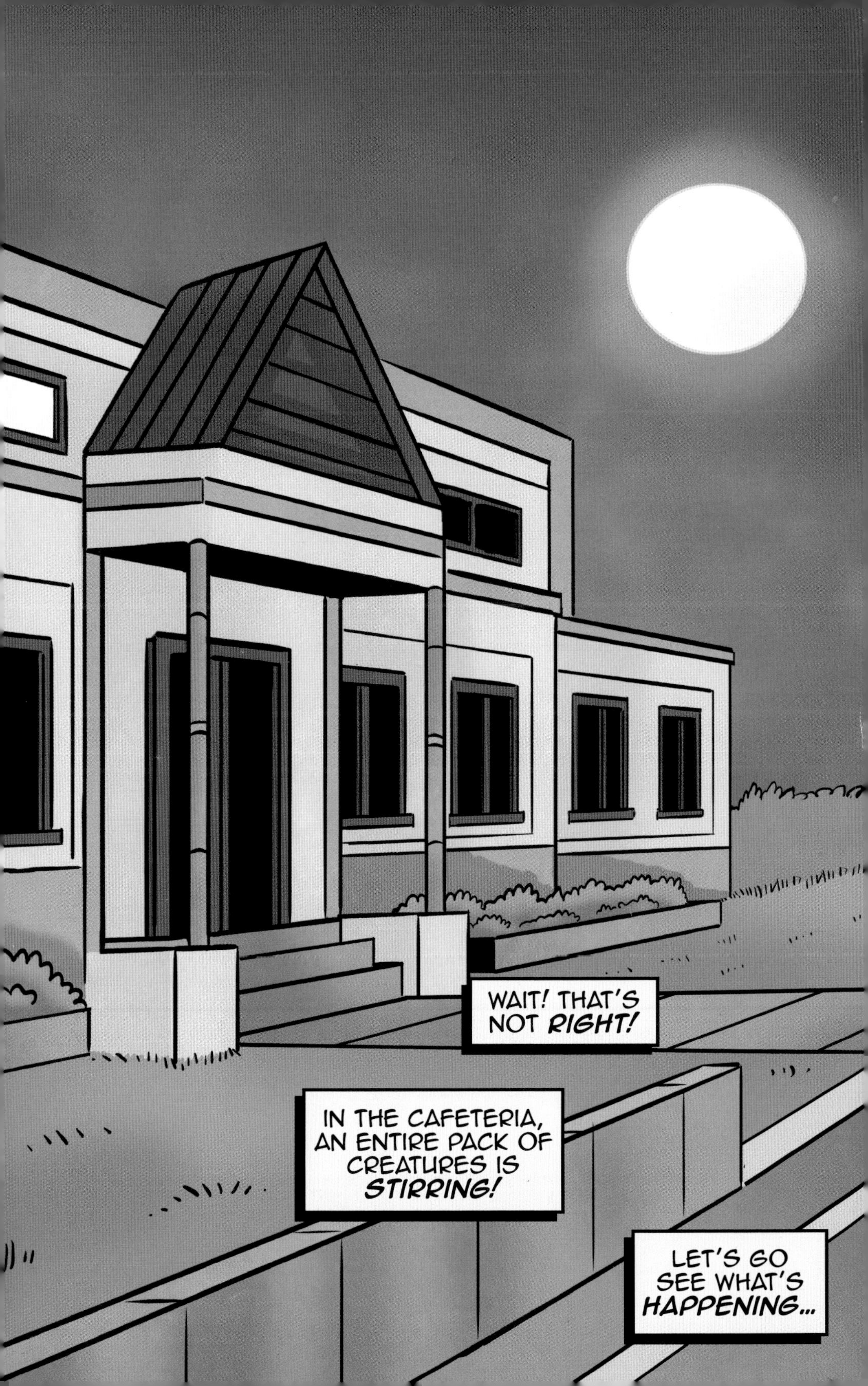
WAIT! THAT'S NOT RIGHT!
IN THE CAFETERIA, AN ENTIRE PACK OF CREATURES IS STIRRING!
LET'S GO SEE WHAT'S HAPPENING...

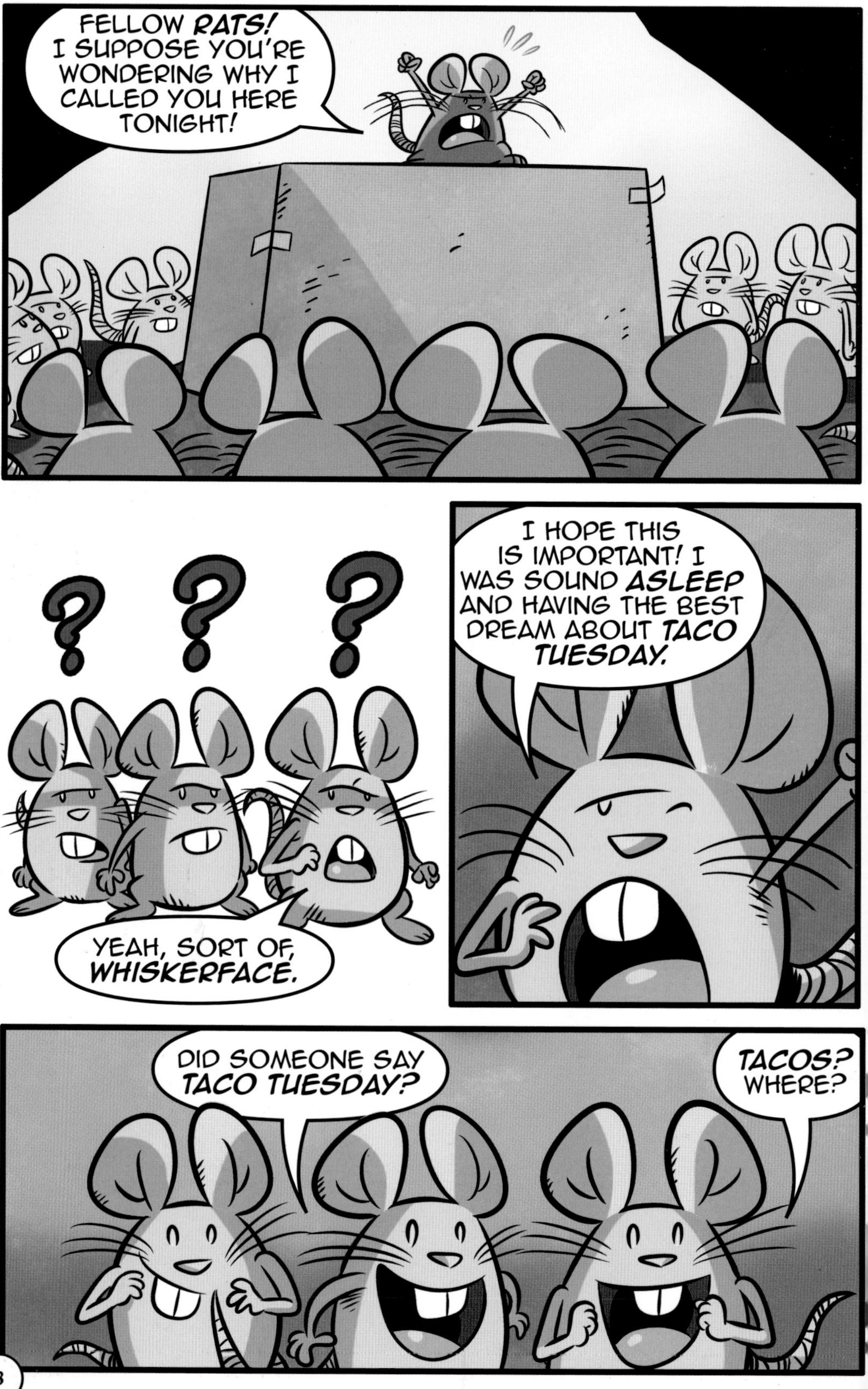
FELLOW RATS! I SUPPOSE YOU'RE WONDERING WHY I CALLED YOU HERE TONIGHT!
YEAH, SORT OF, WHISKERFACE.
I HOPE THIS IS IMPORTANT! I WAS SOUND ASLEEP AND HAVING THE BEST DREAM ABOUT TACO TUESDAY.
DID SOMEONE SAY TACO TUESDAY?
TACOS? WHERE?

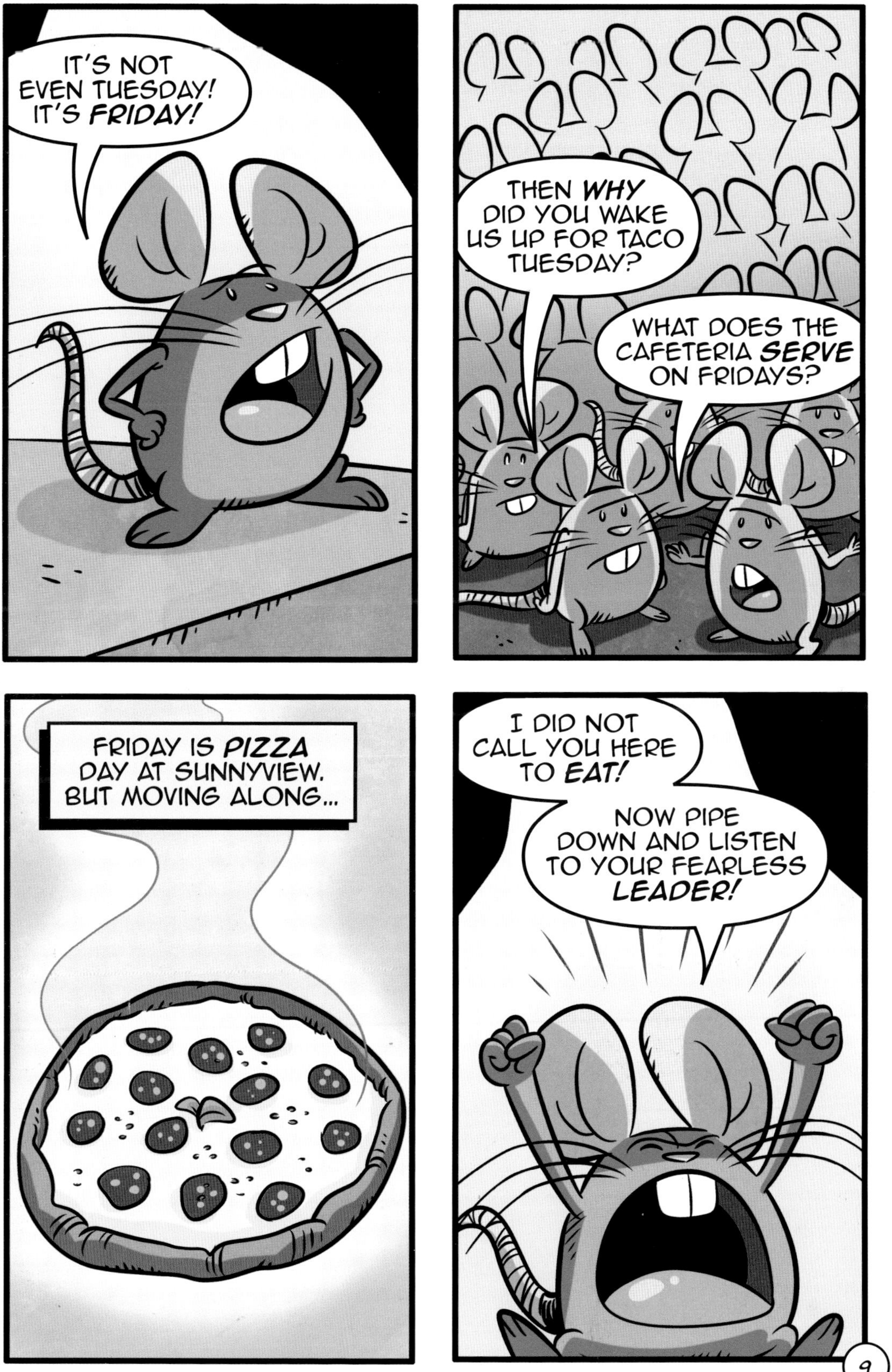
IT'S NOT EVEN TUESDAY! IT'S FRIDAY!
THEN WHY DID YOU WAKE US UP FOR TACO TUESDAY?
WHAT DOES THE CAFETERIA SERVE ON FRIDAYS?
FRIDAY IS PIZZA DAY AT SUNNYVIEW. BUT MOVING ALONG...
I DID NOT CALL YOU HERE TO EAT!
NOW PIPE DOWN AND LISTEN TO YOUR FEARLESS LEADER!

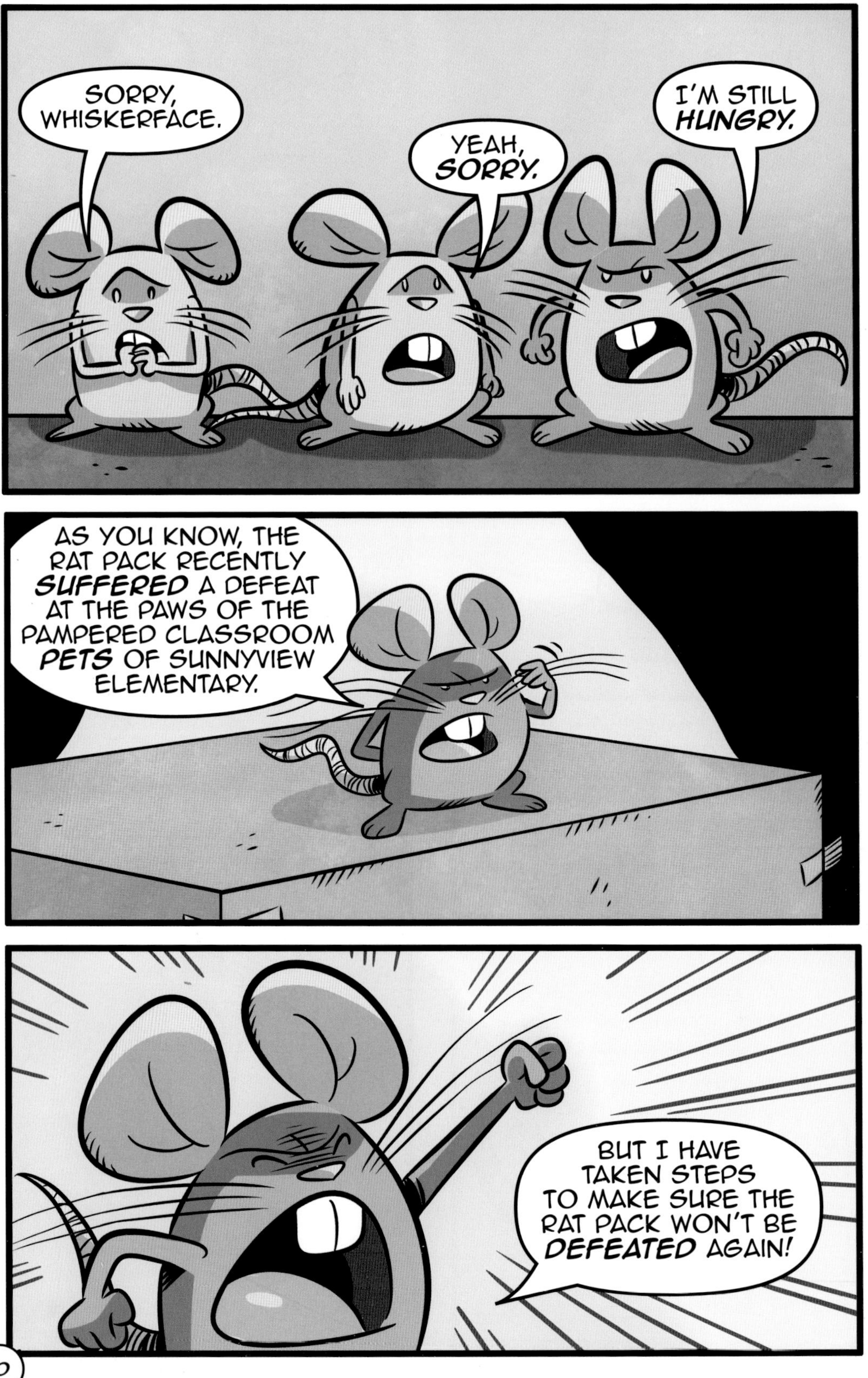
SORRY, WHISKERFACE.
YEAH, SORRY.
I'M STILL HUNGRY.
AS YOU KNOW, THE RAT PACK RECENTLY SUFFERED A DEFEAT AT THE PAWS OF THE PAMPERED CLASSROOM PETS OF SUNNYVIEW ELEMENTARY.
BUT I HAVE TAKEN STEPS TO MAKE SURE THE RAT PACK WON'T BE DEFEATED AGAIN!

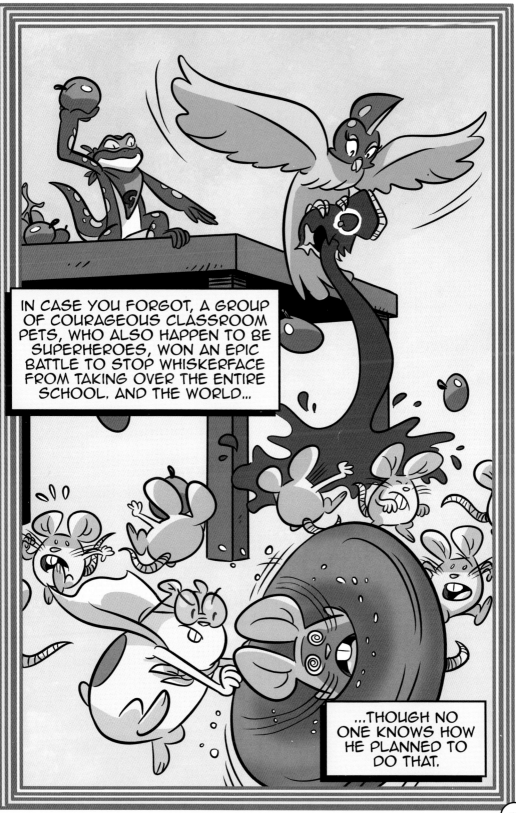

IN CASE YOU FORGOT, A GROUP OF COURAGEOUS CLASSROOM PETS, WHO ALSO HAPPEN TO BE SUPERHEROES, WON AN EPIC BATTLE TO STOP WHISKERFACE FROM TAKING OVER THE ENTIRE SCHOOL. AND THE WORLD...

...THOUGH NO ONE KNOWS HOW HE PLANNED TO DO THAT.

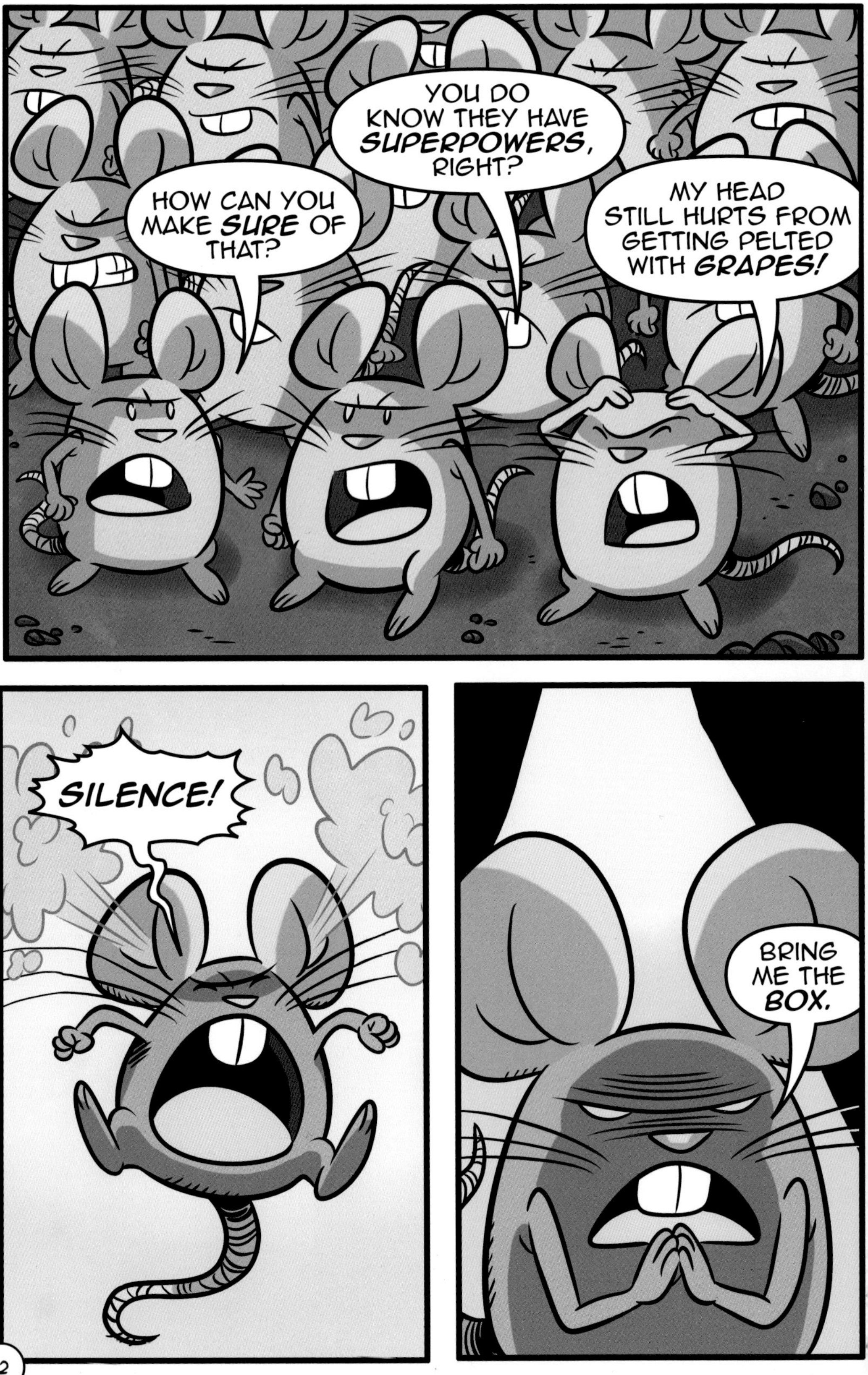
HOW CAN YOU MAKE SURE OF THAT?
YOU DO KNOW THEY HAVE SUPERPOWERS, RIGHT?
MY HEAD STILL HURTS FROM GETTING PELTED WITH GRAPES!
SILENCE!
BRING ME THE BOX.

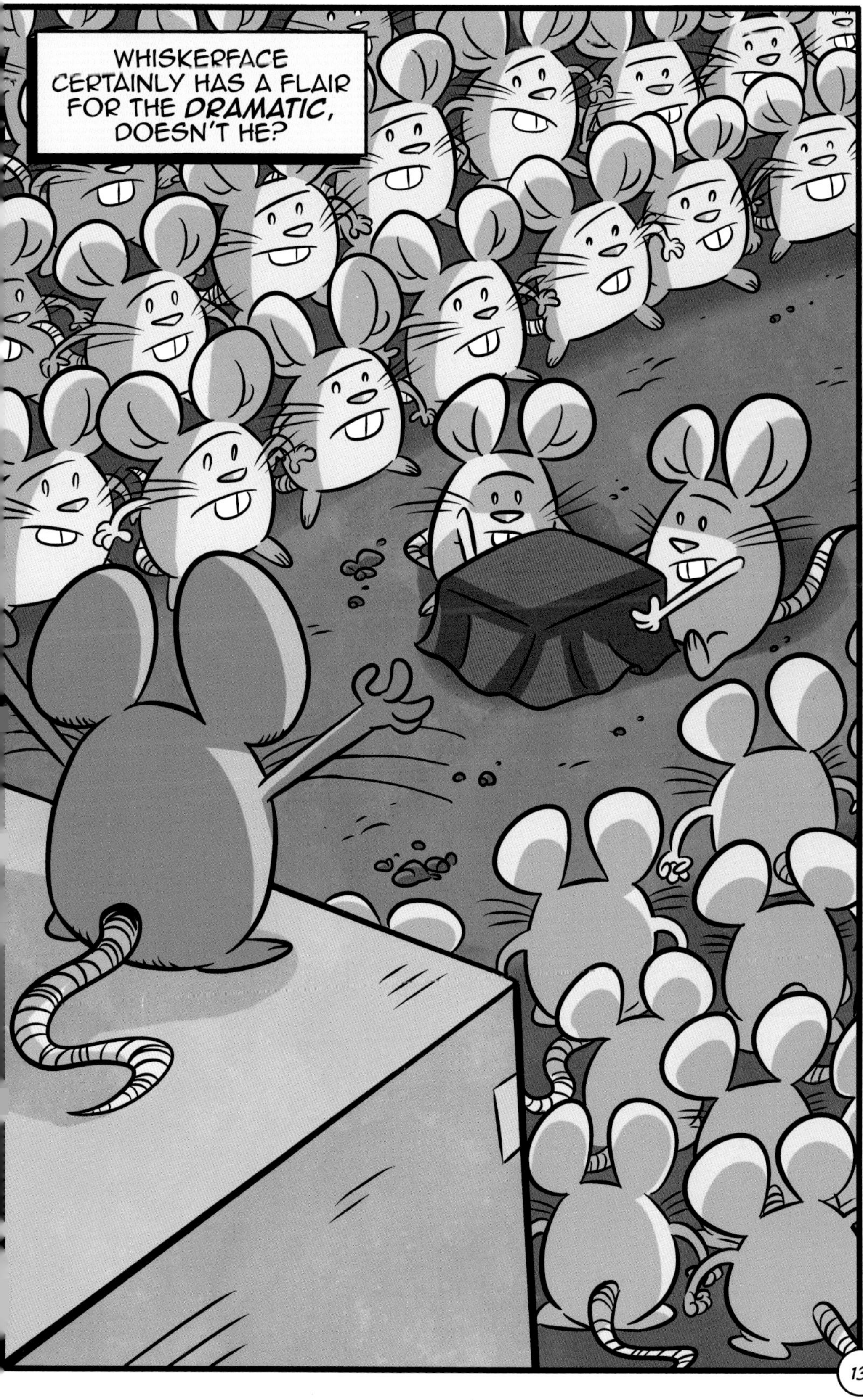
WHISKERFACE CERTAINLY HAS A FLAIR FOR THE *DRAMATIC*, DOESN'T HE?

HAVE YOU ALL HEARD OF THE *GOLDEN ACORN?*

THAT'S THE SACRED SYMBOL OF NUTKIN AND HER FLYING *NINJA SQUIRRELS!*

CORRECT! AND I NOW POSSESS IT! I DEFEATED THE NINJA SQUIRRELS IN COMBAT!

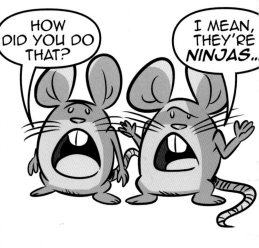

HOW DID YOU DO THAT?

I MEAN, THEY'RE *NINJAS...*

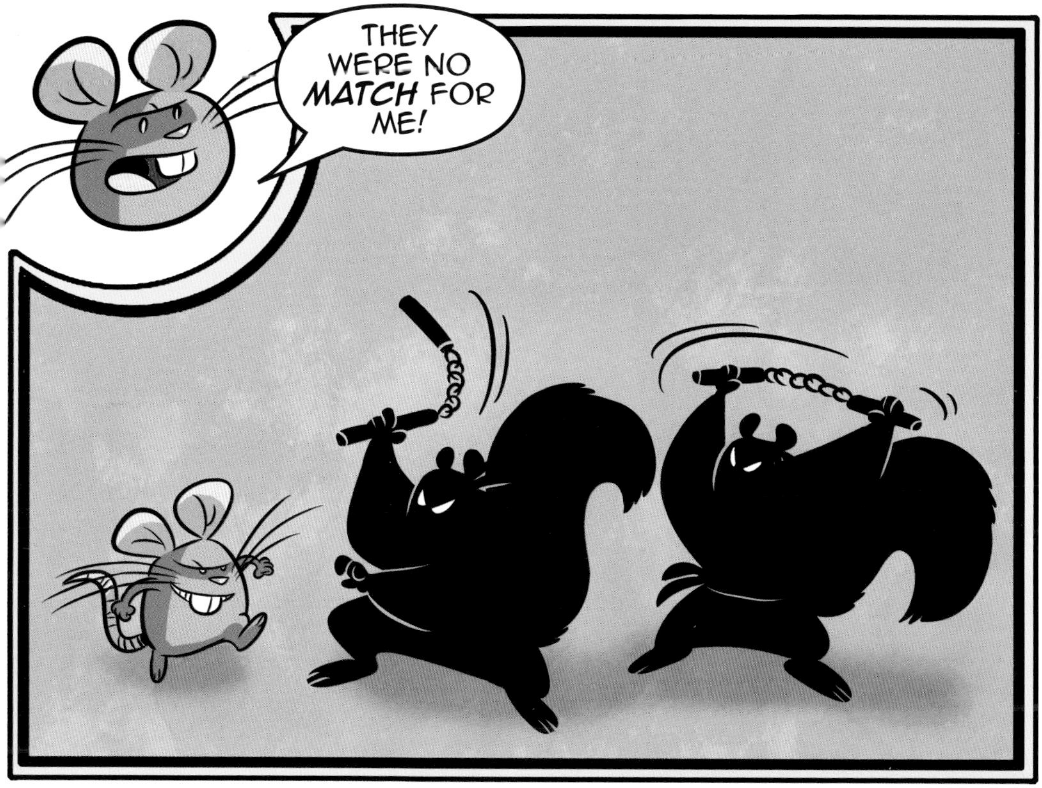
THEY WERE NO MATCH FOR ME!

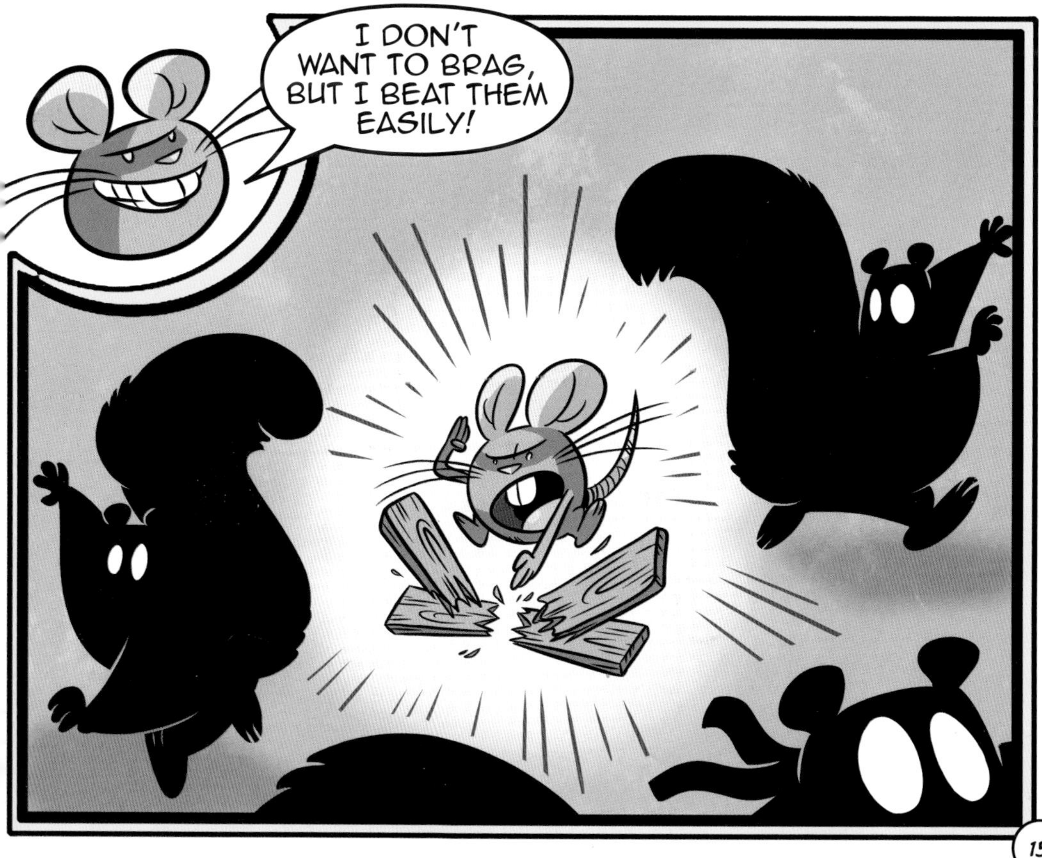
I DON'T WANT TO BRAG, BUT I BEAT THEM EASILY!

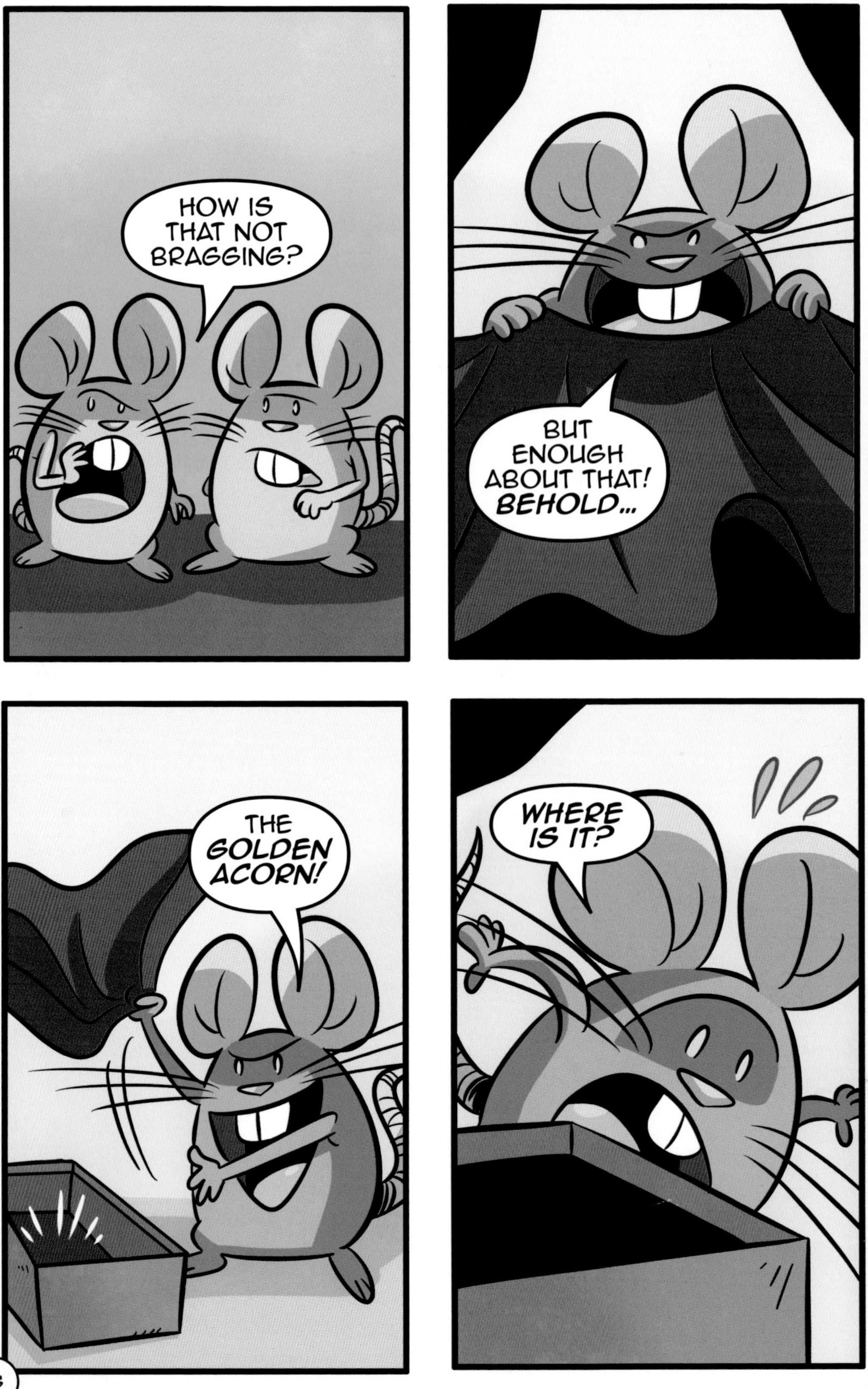
HOW IS THAT NOT BRAGGING?
BUT ENOUGH ABOUT THAT! *BEHOLD...*
THE GOLDEN ACORN!
WHERE IS IT?

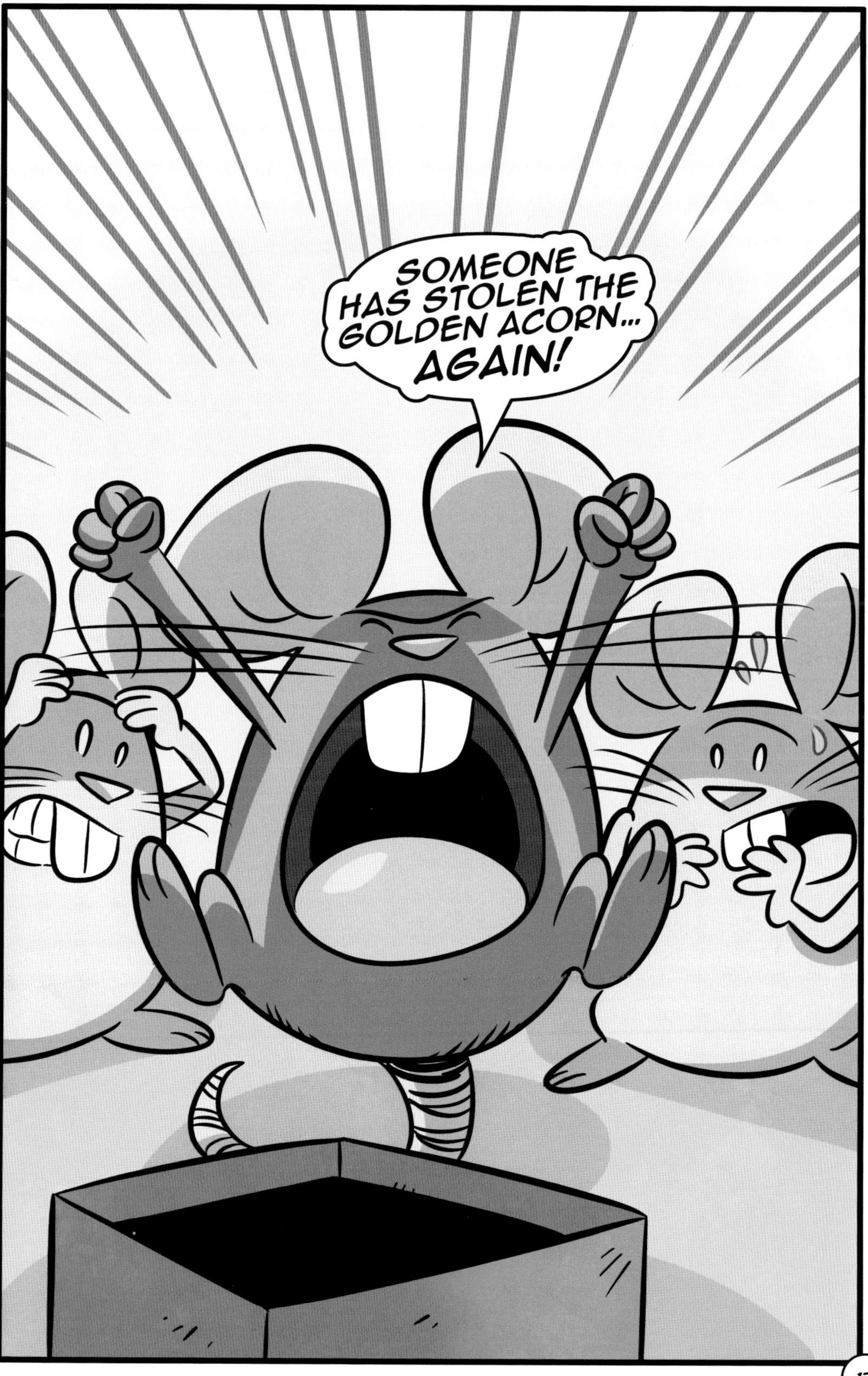
SOMEONE HAS STOLEN THE GOLDEN ACORN... AGAIN!

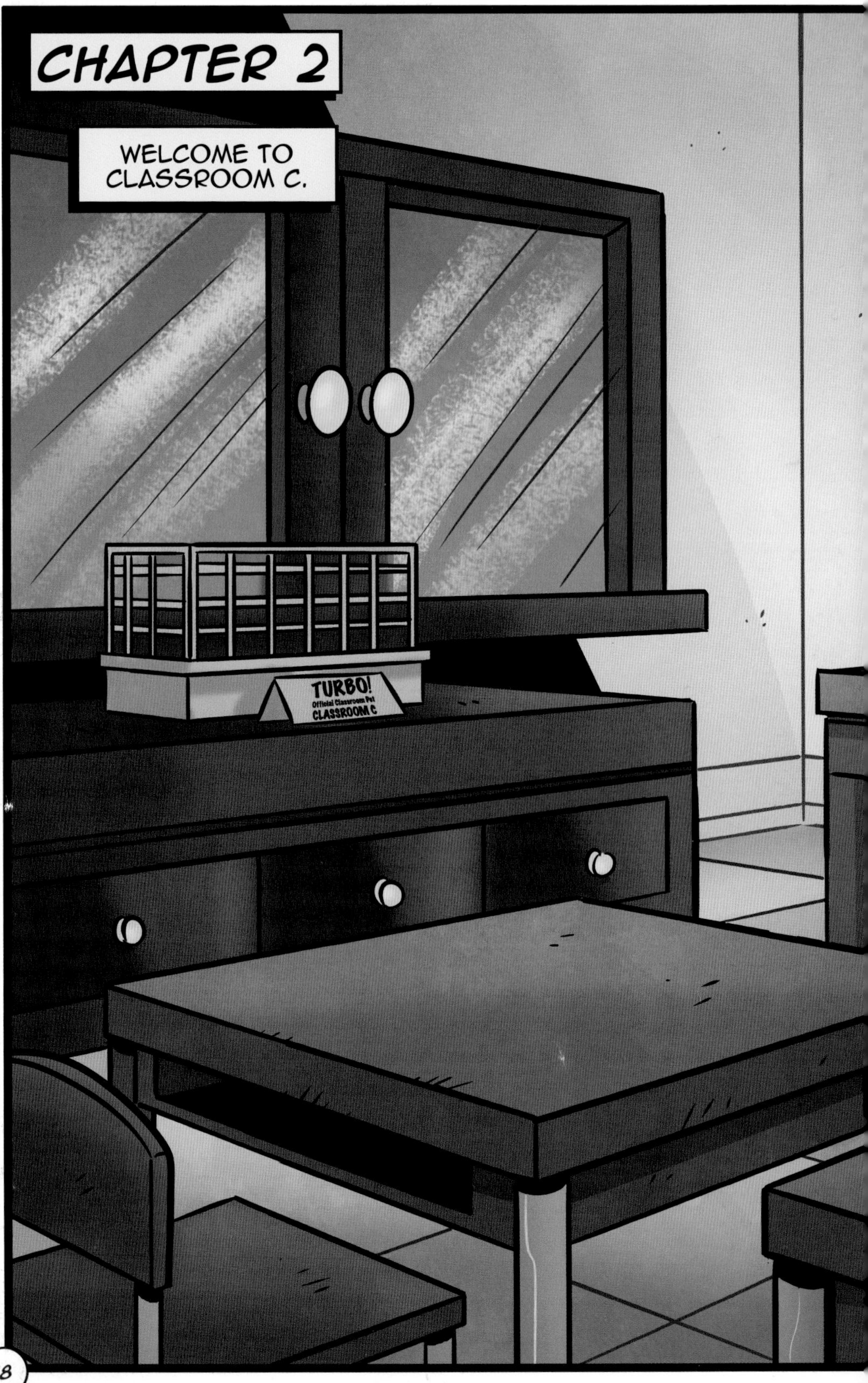
CHAPTER 2
WELCOME TO CLASSROOM C.
TURBO!
Official Classroom Pet
CLASSROOM C

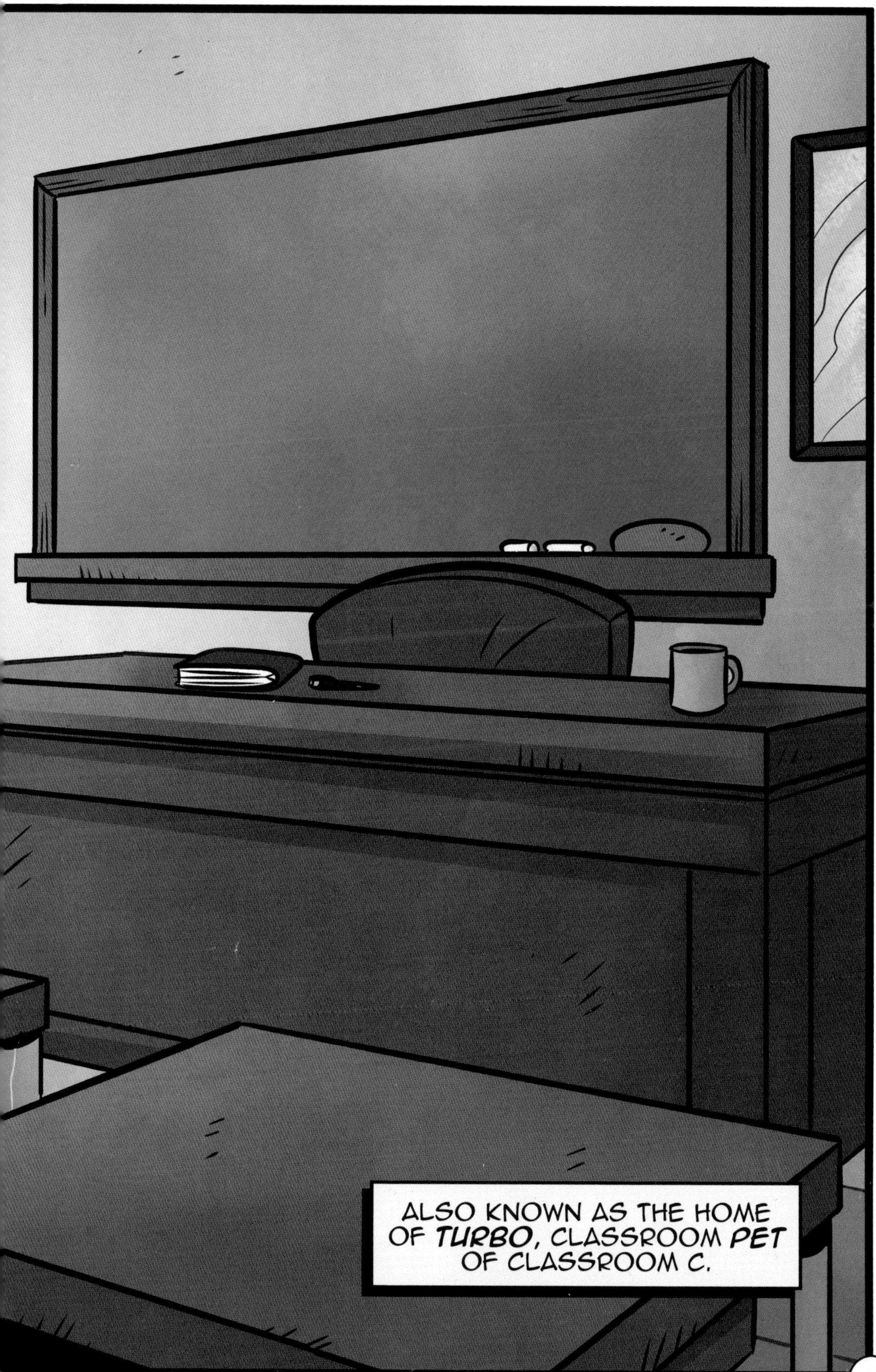
ALSO KNOWN AS THE HOME OF TURBO, CLASSROOM PET OF CLASSROOM C.

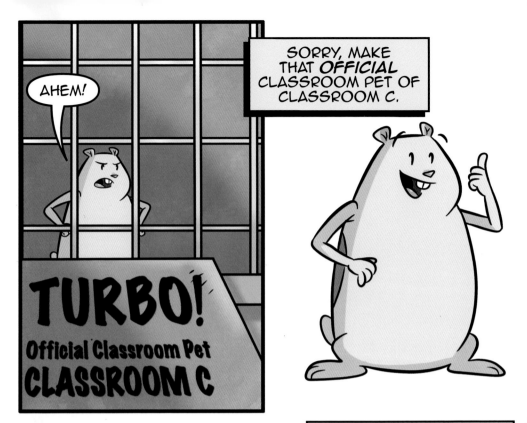

AHEM!

SORRY, MAKE THAT *OFFICIAL* CLASSROOM PET OF CLASSROOM C.

TURBO!
Official Classroom Pet
CLASSROOM C

TURBO MAY LOOK LIKE AN ORDINARY *HAMSTER...*

WHO ARE YOU CALLING *ORDINARY?*

AS I WAS SAYING, TURBO MAY *LOOK* LIKE AN ORDINARY HAMSTER. BUT HE'S *NOT!*

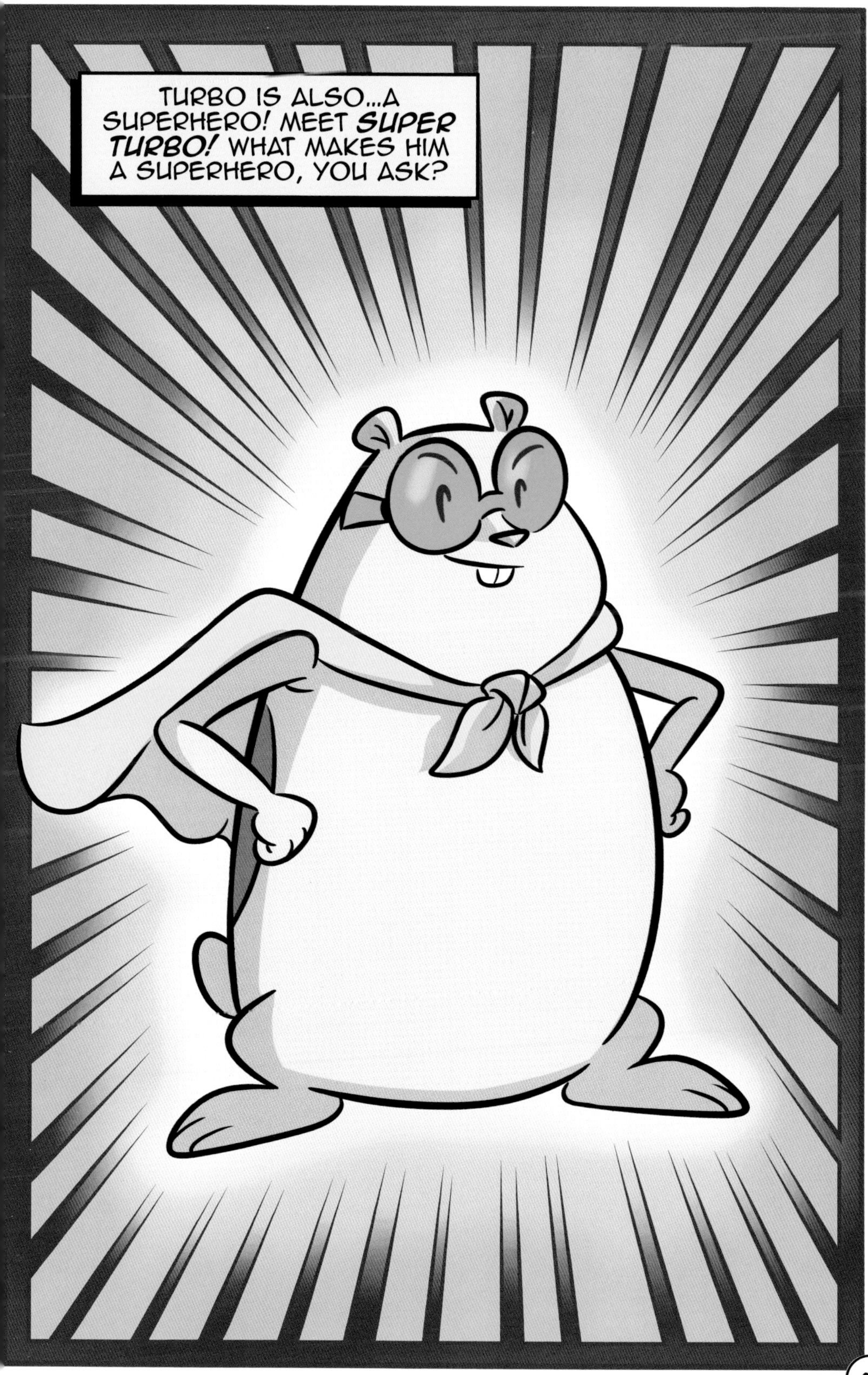
TURBO IS ALSO...A SUPERHERO! MEET *SUPER TURBO!* WHAT MAKES HIM A SUPERHERO, YOU ASK?

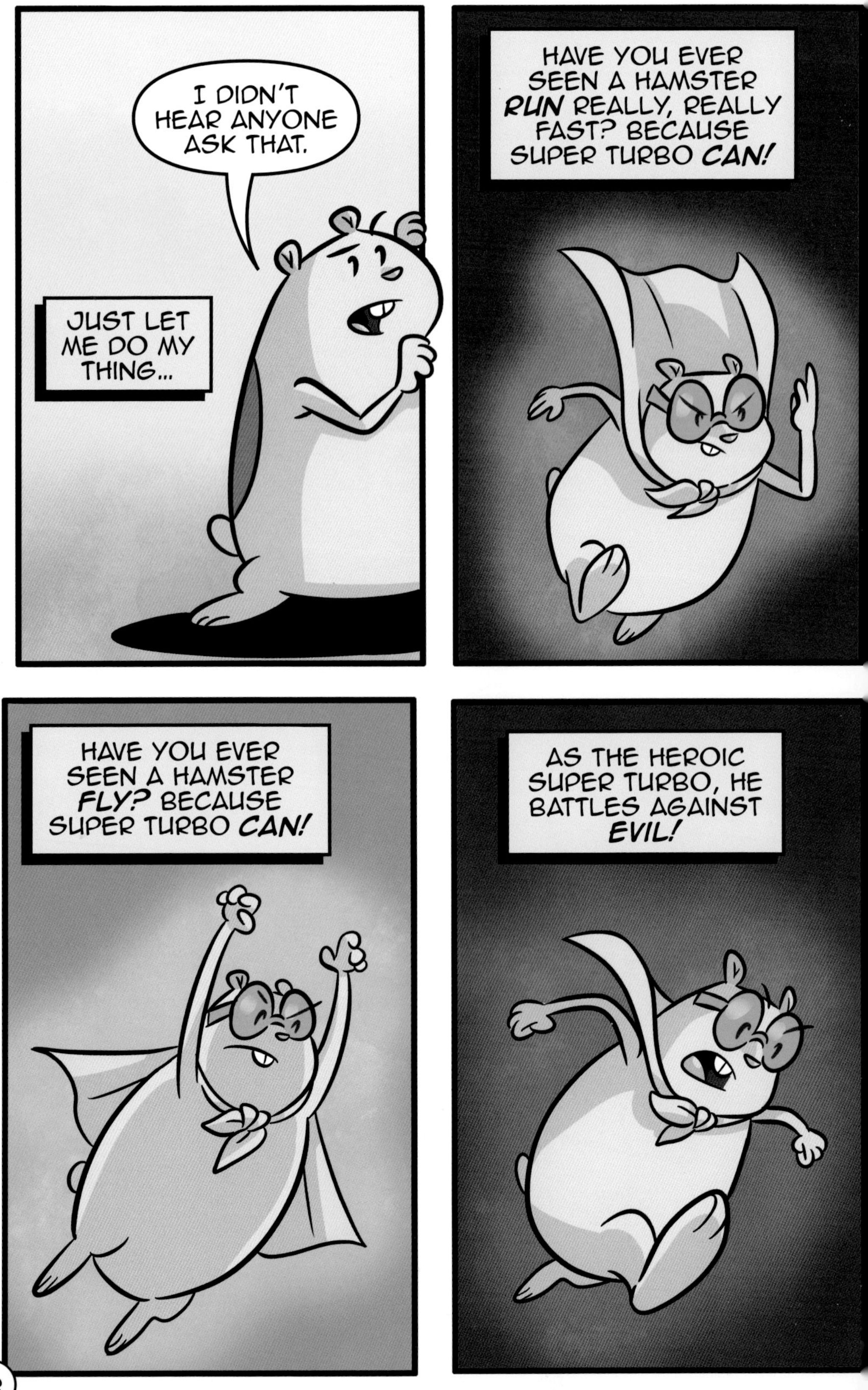
I DIDN'T HEAR ANYONE ASK THAT.
JUST LET ME DO MY THING...
HAVE YOU EVER SEEN A HAMSTER RUN REALLY, REALLY FAST? BECAUSE SUPER TURBO CAN!
HAVE YOU EVER SEEN A HAMSTER FLY? BECAUSE SUPER TURBO CAN!
AS THE HEROIC SUPER TURBO, HE BATTLES AGAINST EVIL!

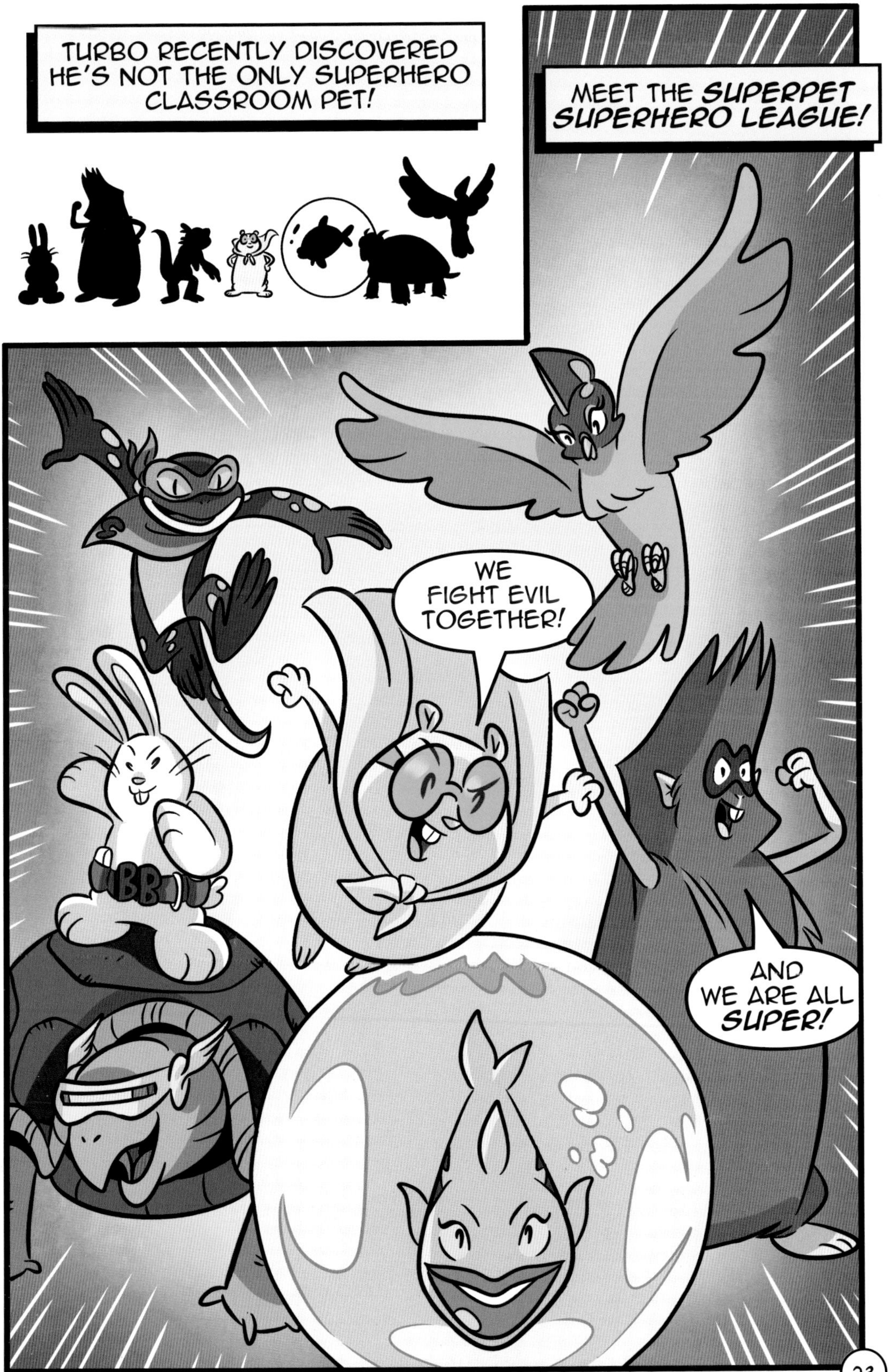

TURBO RECENTLY DISCOVERED HE'S NOT THE ONLY SUPERHERO CLASSROOM PET!
MEET THE SUPERPET SUPERHERO LEAGUE!
WE FIGHT EVIL TOGETHER!
BB
AND WE ARE ALL SUPER!

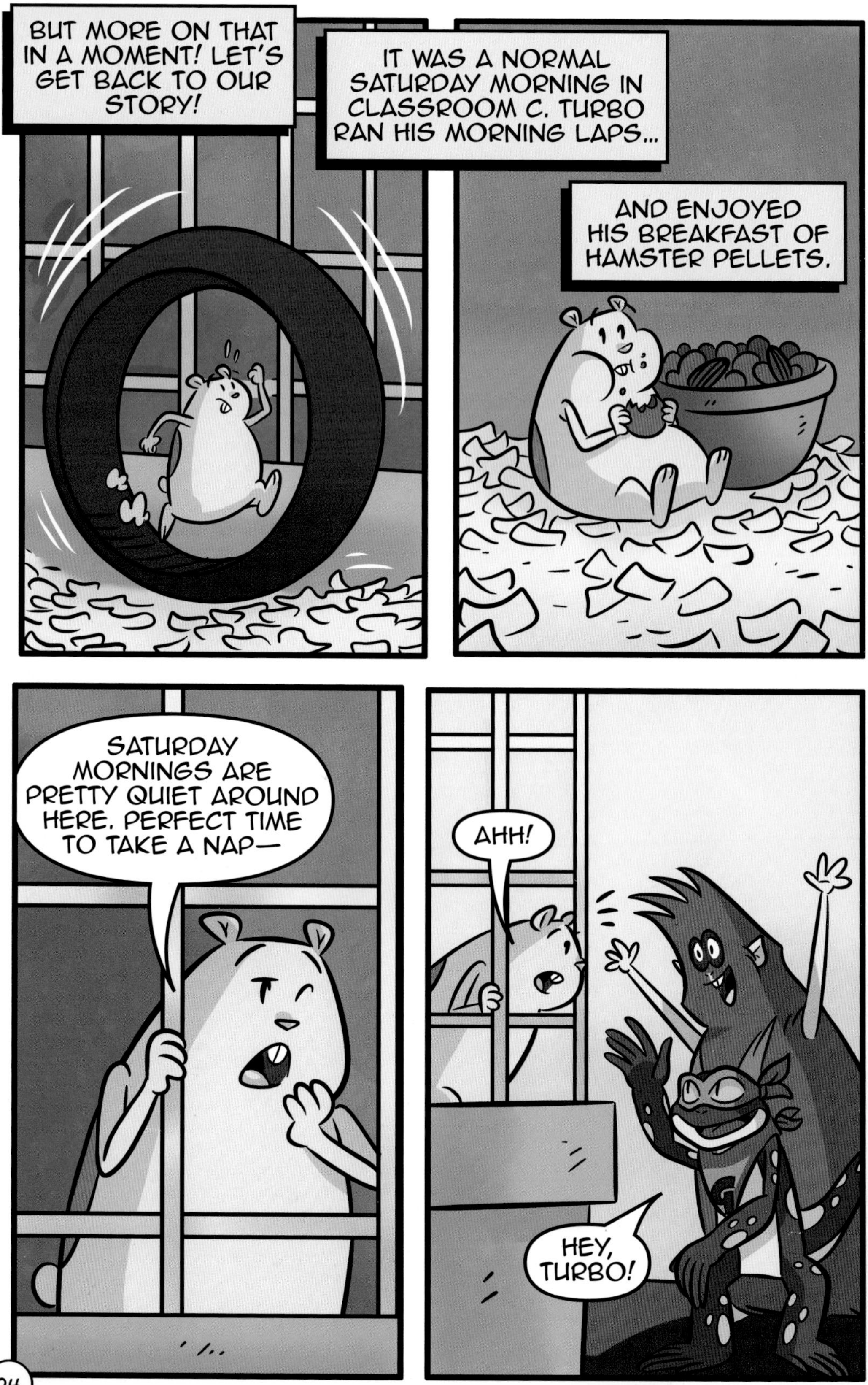
BUT MORE ON THAT IN A MOMENT! LET'S GET BACK TO OUR STORY!
IT WAS A NORMAL SATURDAY MORNING IN CLASSROOM C. TURBO RAN HIS MORNING LAPS...
AND ENJOYED HIS BREAKFAST OF HAMSTER PELLETS.
SATURDAY MORNINGS ARE PRETTY QUIET AROUND HERE. PERFECT TIME TO TAKE A NAP—
AHH!
HEY, TURBO!

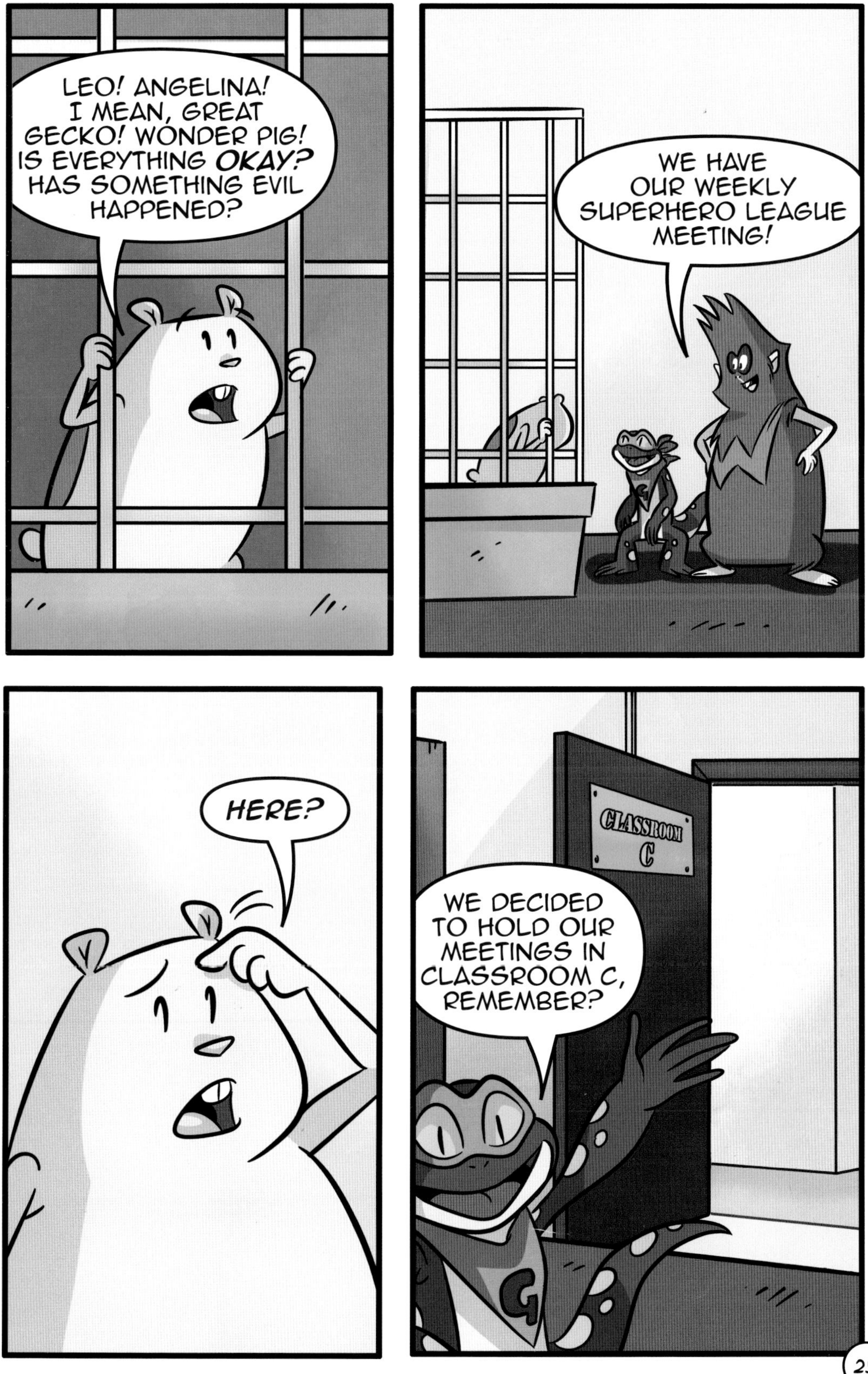
LEO! ANGELINA! I MEAN, GREAT GECKO! WONDER PIG! IS EVERYTHING OKAY? HAS SOMETHING EVIL HAPPENED?
WE HAVE OUR WEEKLY SUPERHERO LEAGUE MEETING!
HERE?
CLASSROOM C
WE DECIDED TO HOLD OUR MEETINGS IN CLASSROOM C, REMEMBER?

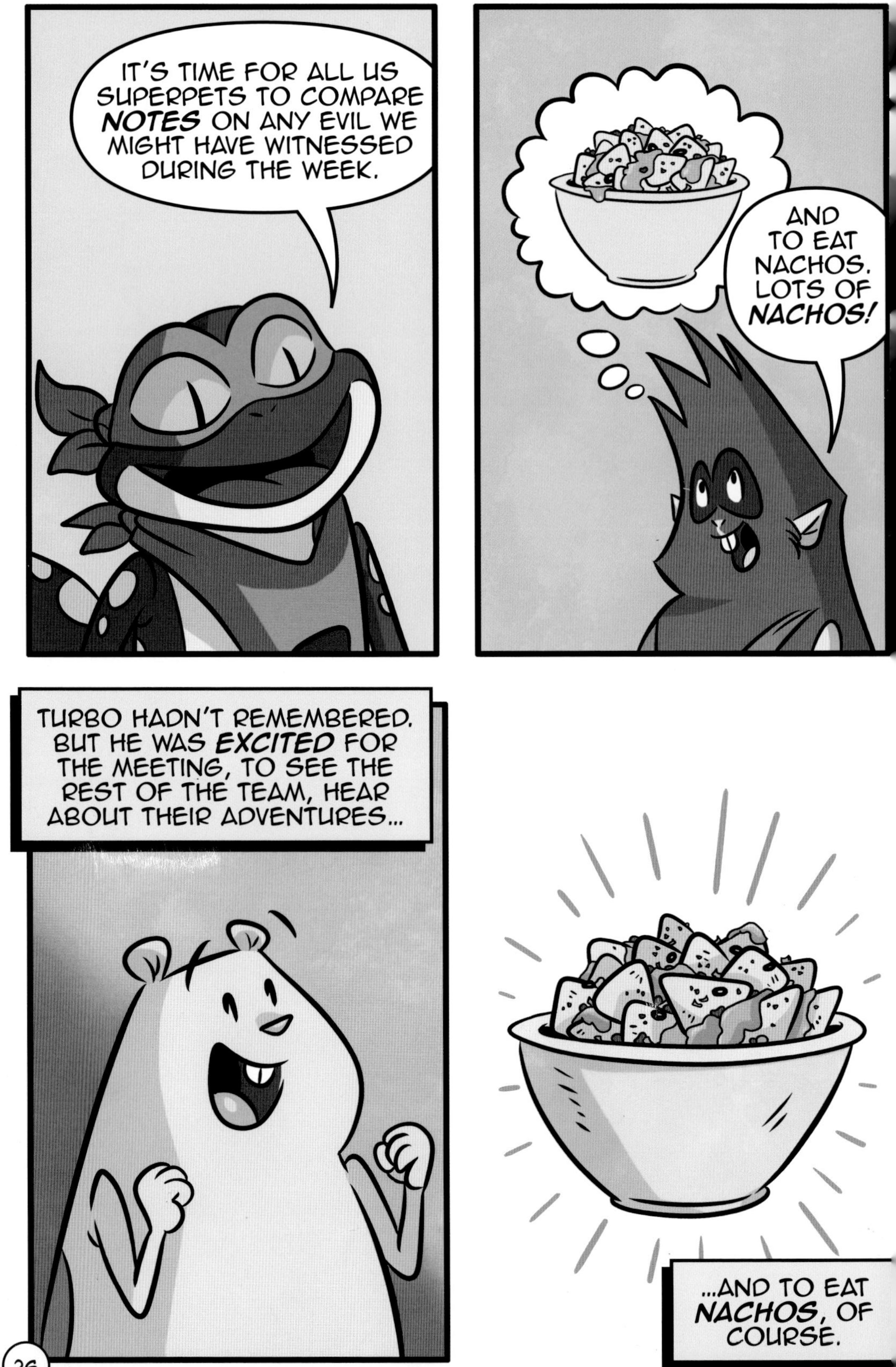
IT'S TIME FOR ALL US SUPERPETS TO COMPARE *NOTES* ON ANY EVIL WE MIGHT HAVE WITNESSED DURING THE WEEK.
AND TO EAT NACHOS. LOTS OF *NACHOS!*
TURBO HADN'T REMEMBERED. BUT HE WAS *EXCITED* FOR THE MEETING, TO SEE THE REST OF THE TEAM, HEAR ABOUT THEIR ADVENTURES...
...AND TO EAT *NACHOS*, OF COURSE.

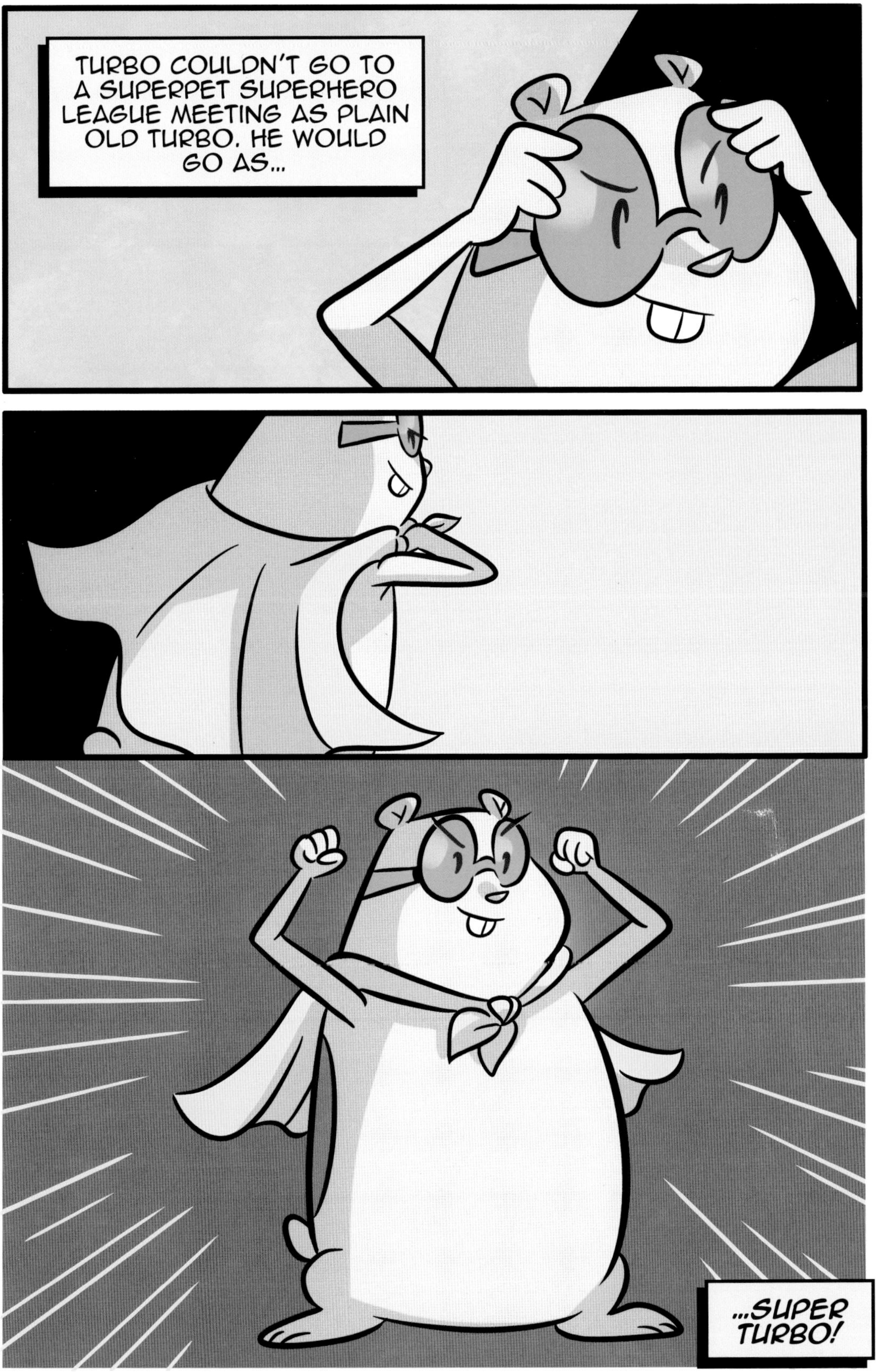
TURBO COULDN'T GO TO A SUPERPET SUPERHERO LEAGUE MEETING AS PLAIN OLD TURBO. HE WOULD GO AS...
...SUPER TURBO!

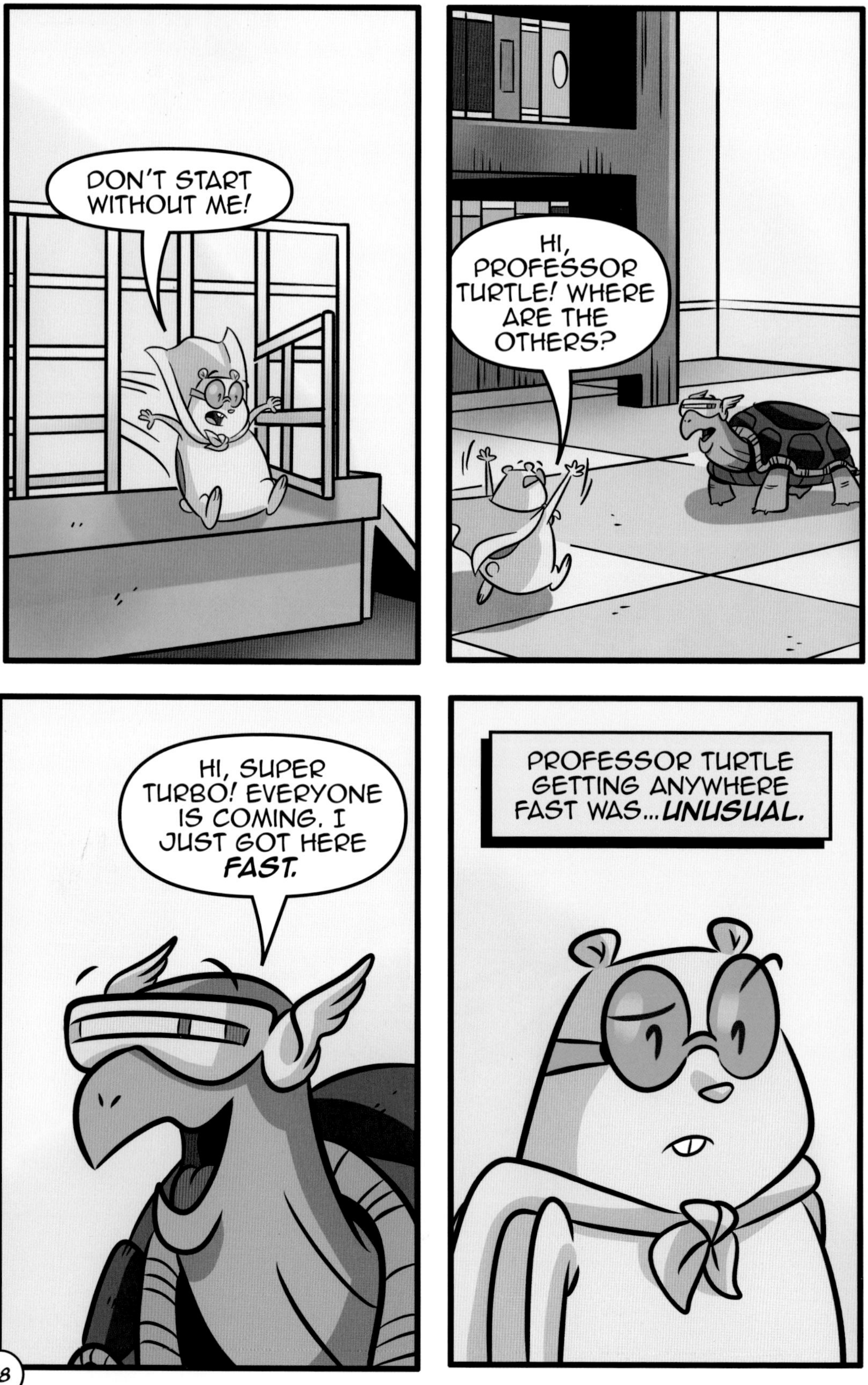
DON'T START WITHOUT ME!
HI, PROFESSOR TURTLE! WHERE ARE THE OTHERS?
HI, SUPER TURBO! EVERYONE IS COMING. I JUST GOT HERE FAST.
PROFESSOR TURTLE GETTING ANYWHERE FAST WAS...UNUSUAL.

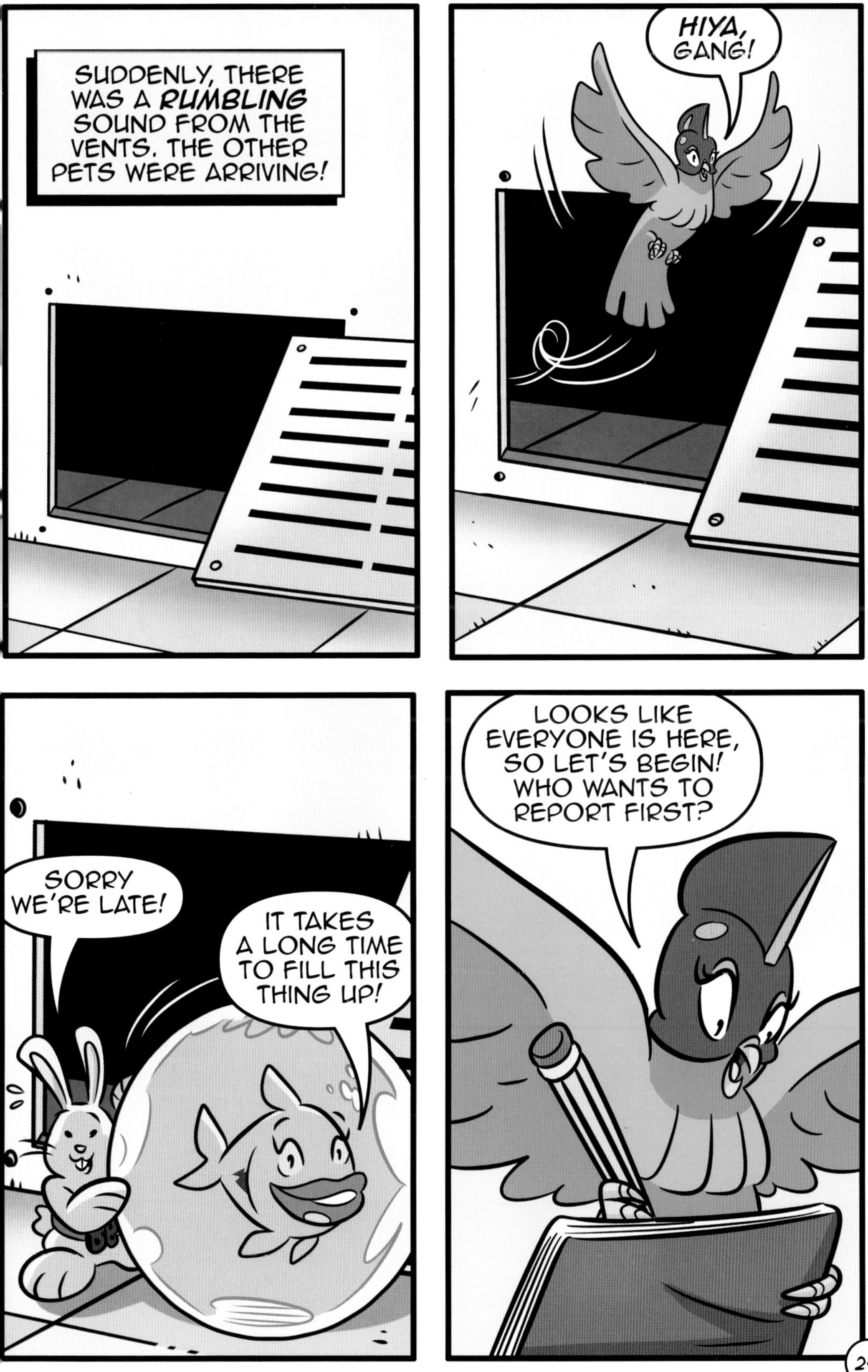
SUDDENLY, THERE WAS A *RUMBLING* SOUND FROM THE VENTS. THE OTHER PETS WERE ARRIVING!
HIYA, GANG!
SORRY WE'RE LATE!
IT TAKES A LONG TIME TO FILL THIS THING UP!
LOOKS LIKE EVERYONE IS HERE, SO LET'S BEGIN! WHO WANTS TO REPORT FIRST?

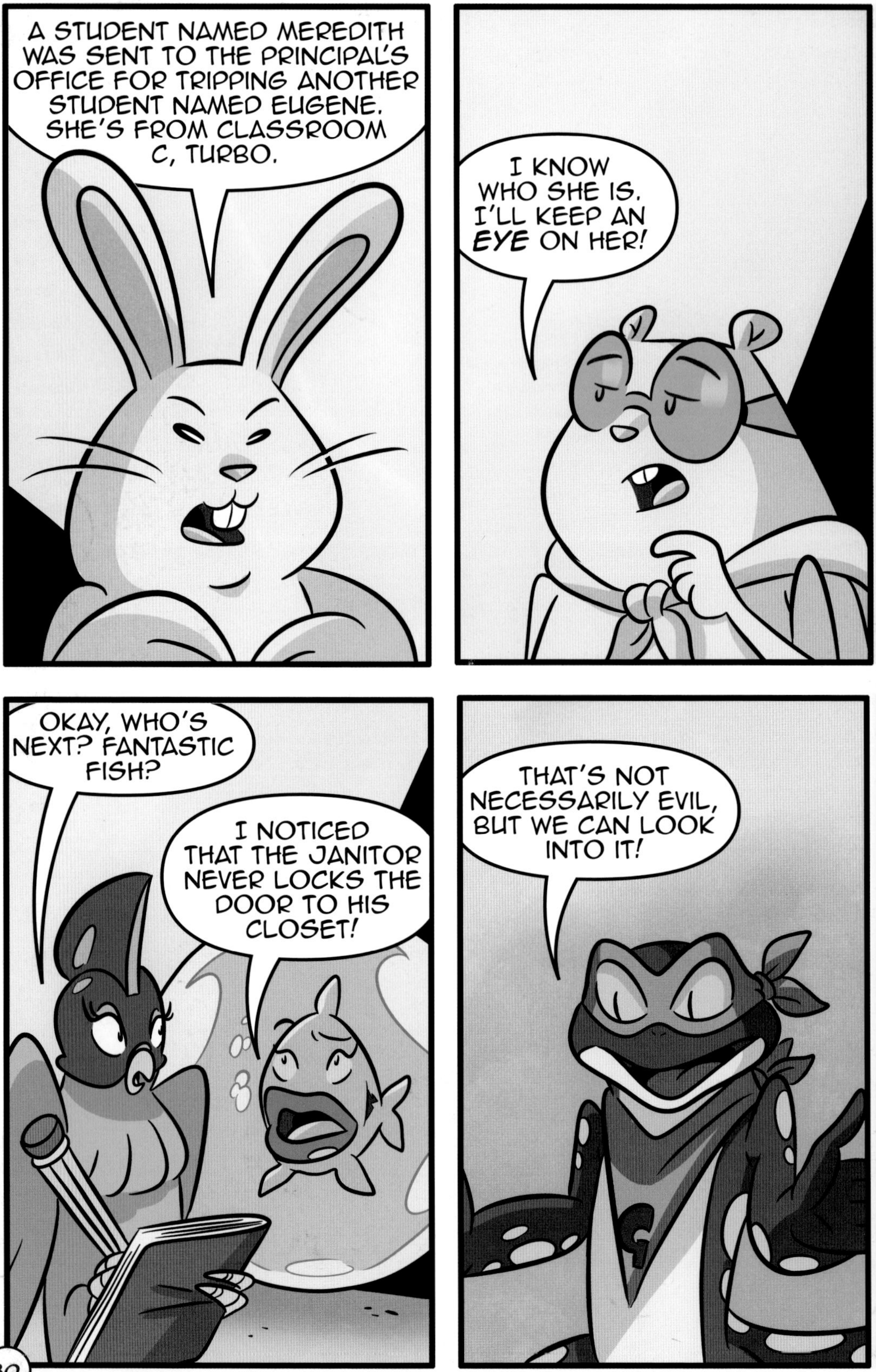
A STUDENT NAMED MEREDITH WAS SENT TO THE PRINCIPAL'S OFFICE FOR TRIPPING ANOTHER STUDENT NAMED EUGENE. SHE'S FROM CLASSROOM C, TURBO.
I KNOW WHO SHE IS. I'LL KEEP AN *EYE* ON HER!
OKAY, WHO'S NEXT? FANTASTIC FISH?
I NOTICED THAT THE JANITOR NEVER LOCKS THE DOOR TO HIS CLOSET!
THAT'S NOT NECESSARILY EVIL, BUT WE CAN LOOK INTO IT!

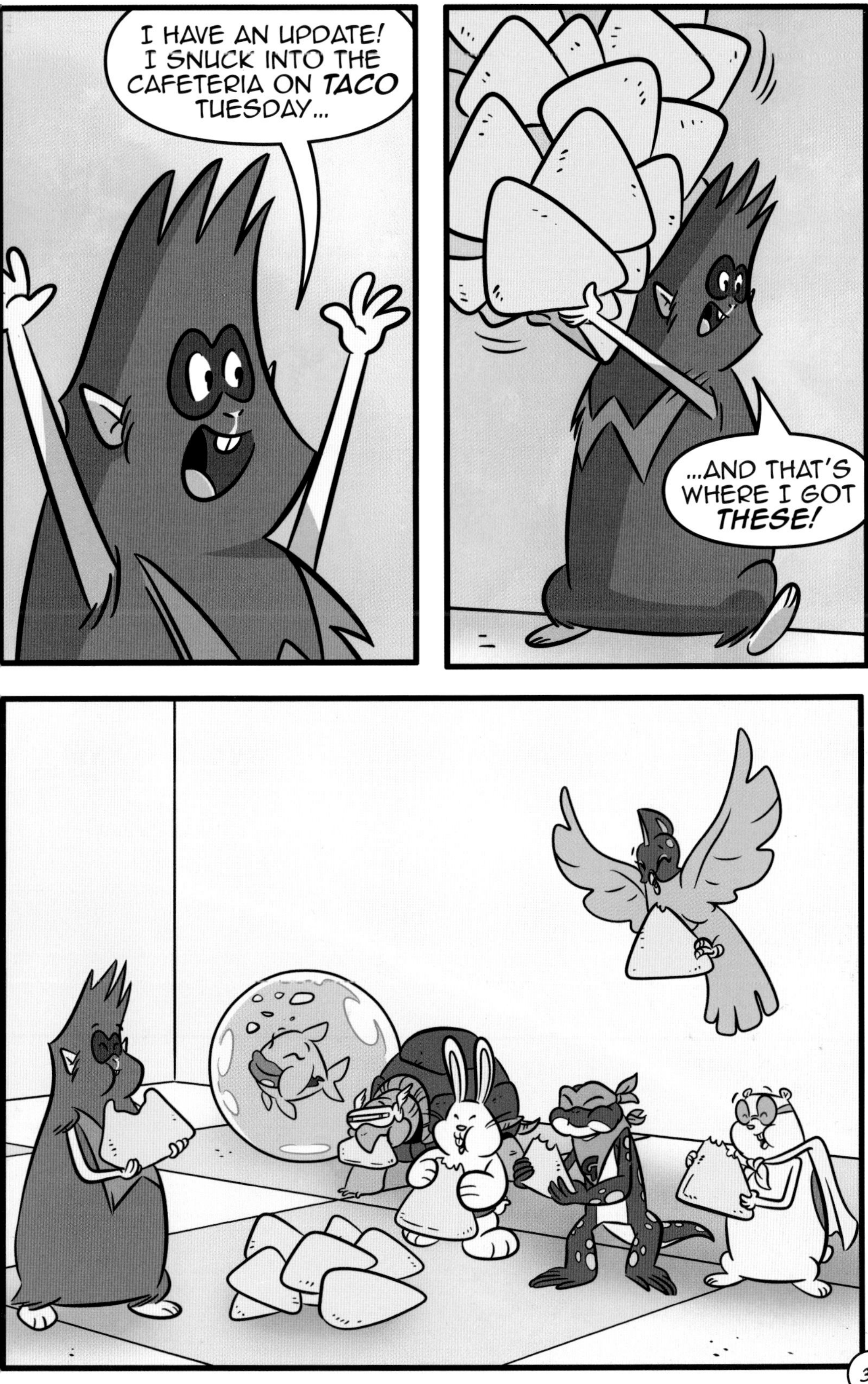
I HAVE AN UPDATE! I SNUCK INTO THE CAFETERIA ON *TACO* TUESDAY...
...AND THAT'S WHERE I GOT *THESE!*

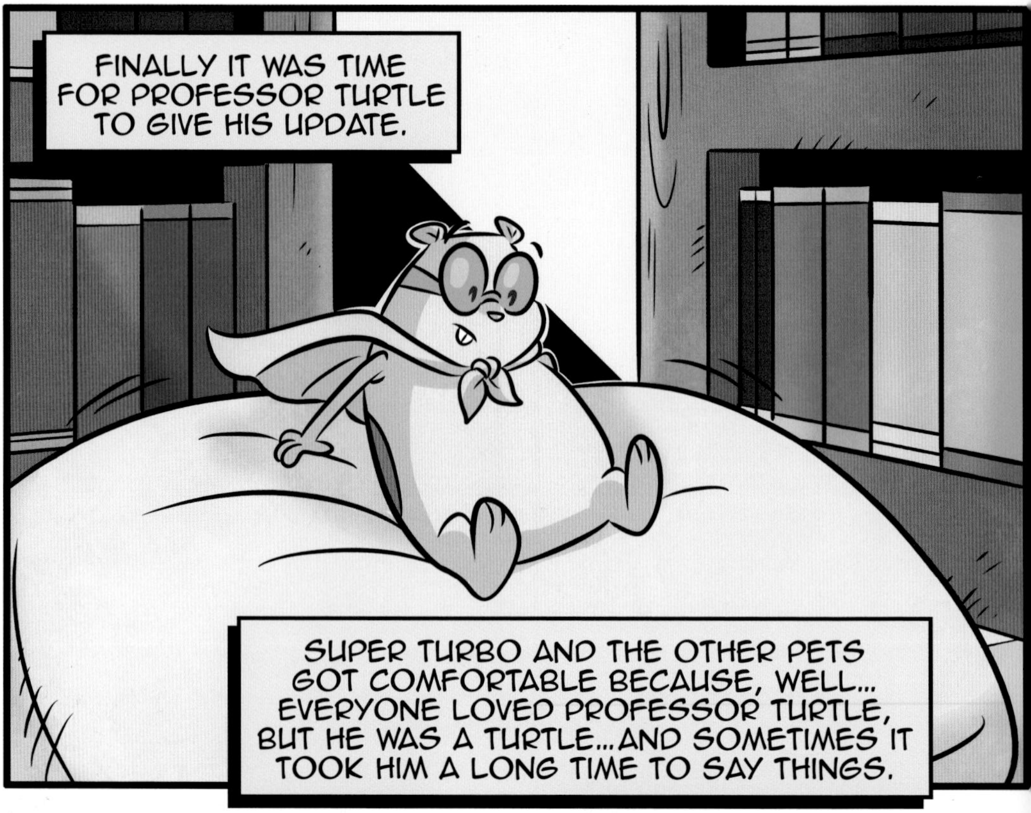
FINALLY IT WAS TIME FOR PROFESSOR TURTLE TO GIVE HIS UPDATE.
SUPER TURBO AND THE OTHER PETS GOT COMFORTABLE BECAUSE, WELL... EVERYONE LOVED PROFESSOR TURTLE, BUT HE WAS A TURTLE...AND SOMETIMES IT TOOK HIM A LONG TIME TO SAY THINGS.

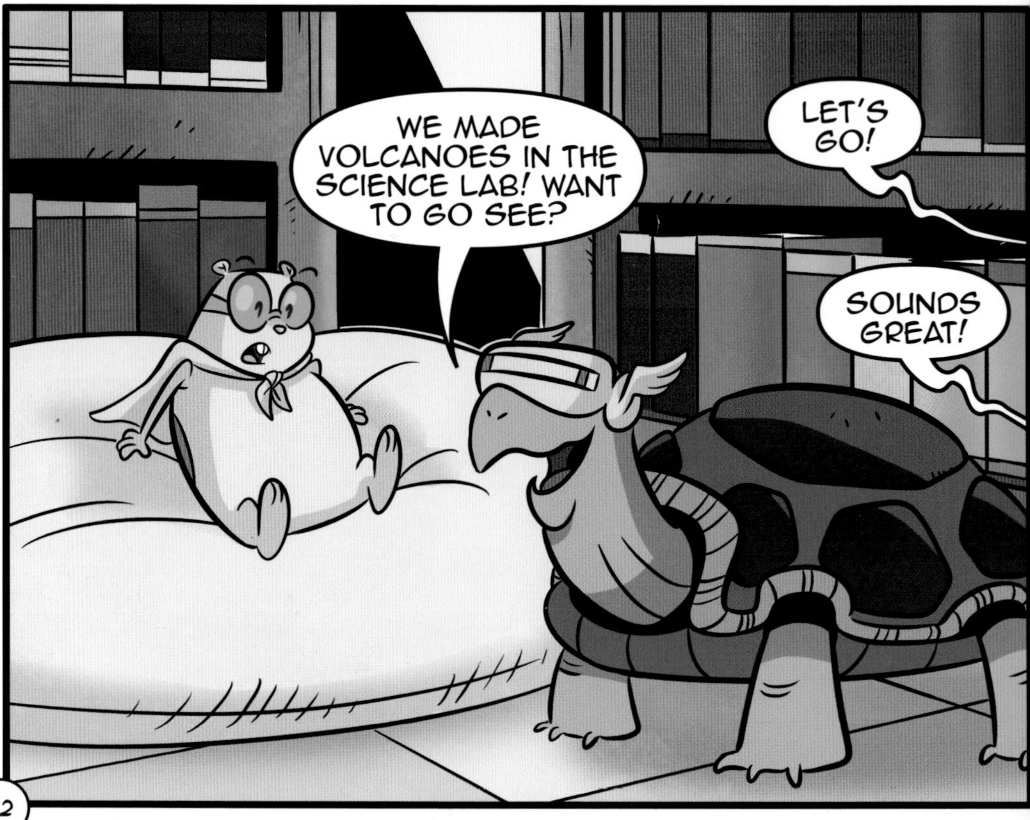
WE MADE VOLCANOES IN THE SCIENCE LAB! WANT TO GO SEE?
LET'S GO!
SOUNDS GREAT!

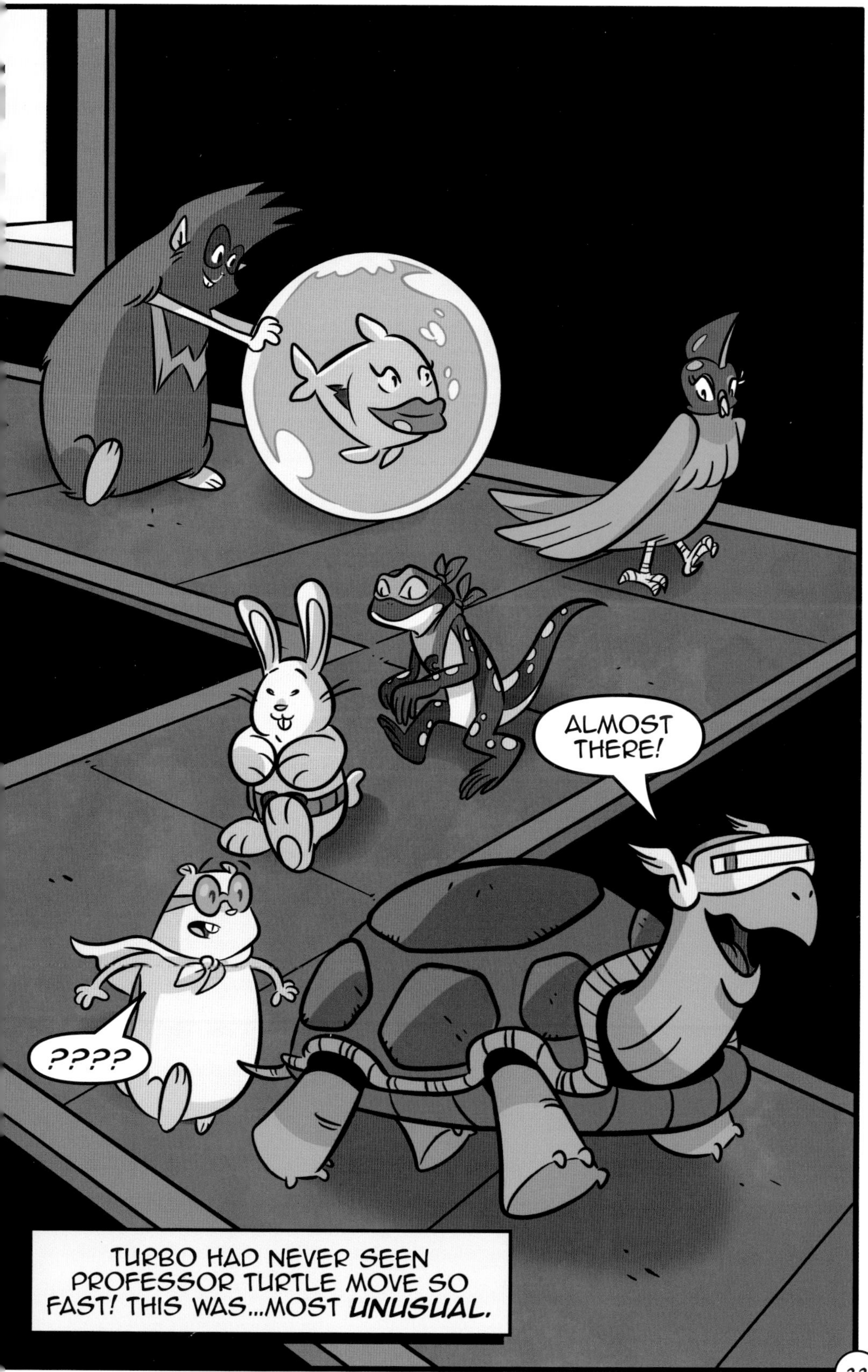
ALMOST THERE!
????
TURBO HAD NEVER SEEN PROFESSOR TURTLE MOVE SO FAST! THIS WAS...MOST *UNUSUAL.*

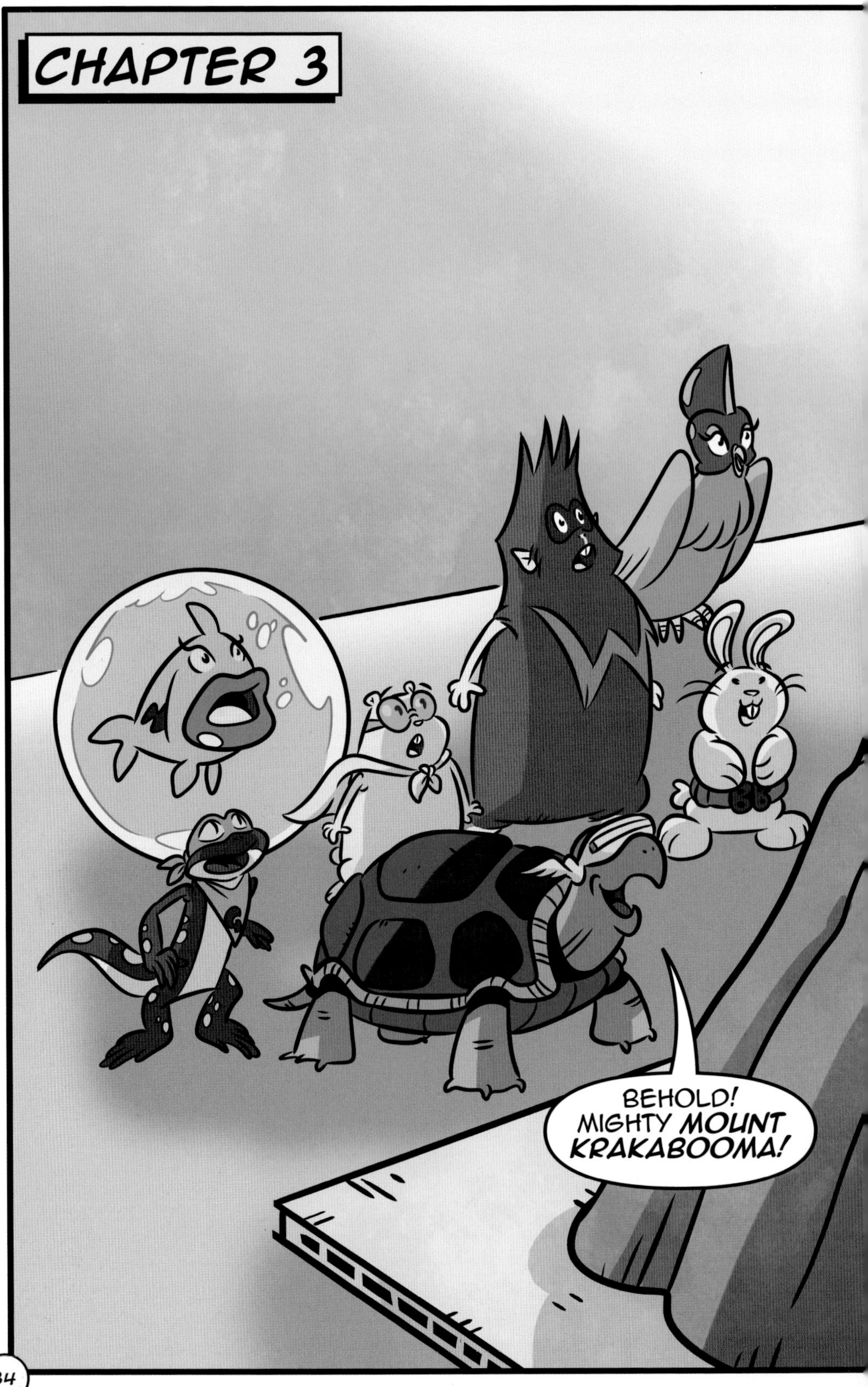
CHAPTER 3
BEHOLD! MIGHTY MOUNT KRAKABOOMA!

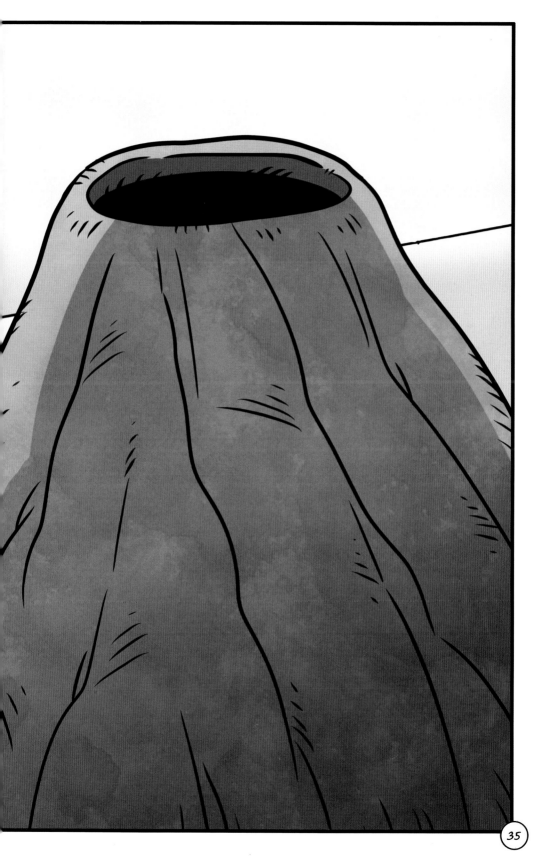

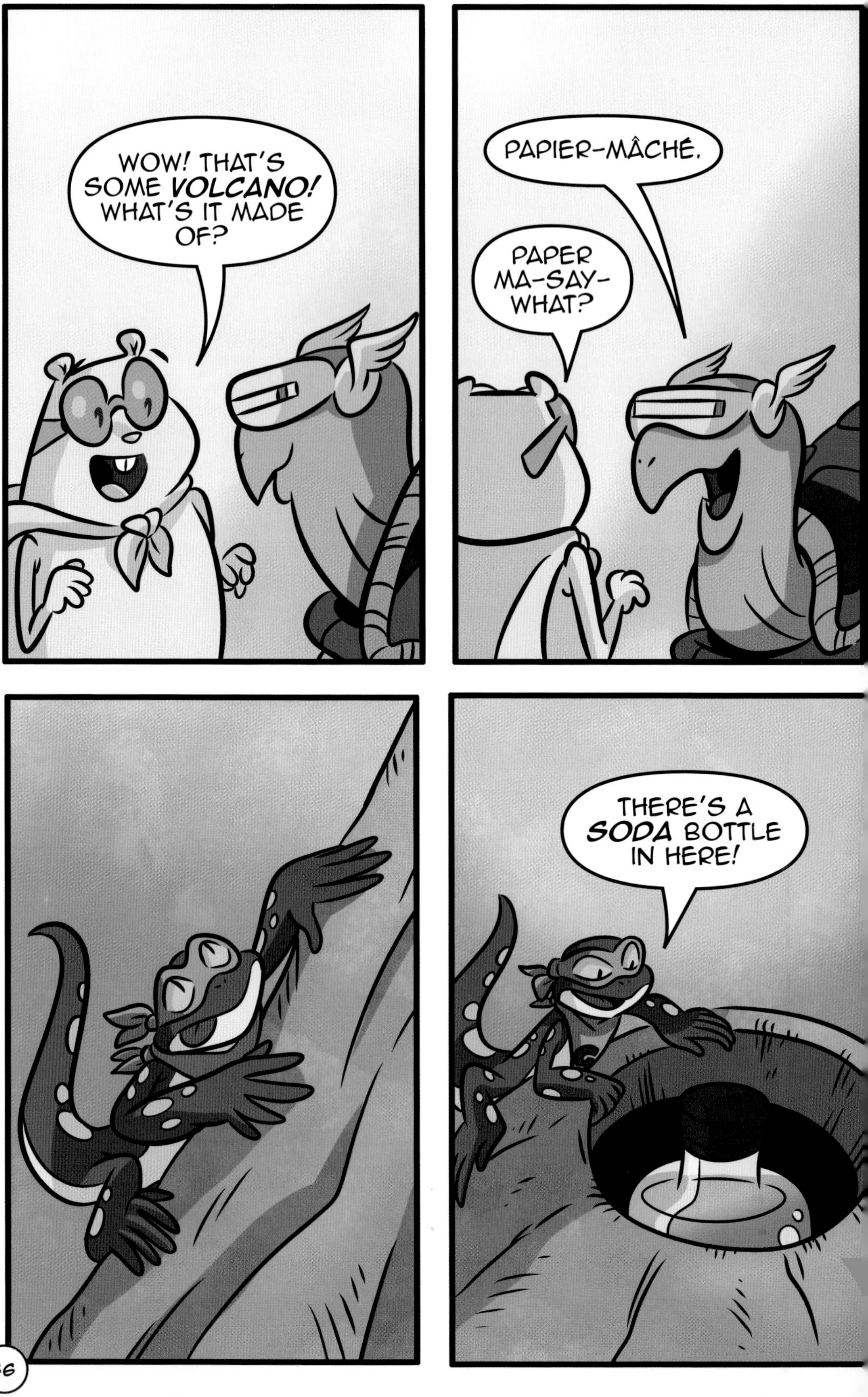
WOW! THAT'S SOME VOLCANO! WHAT'S IT MADE OF?
PAPIER-MÂCHÉ.
PAPER MA-SAY-WHAT?
THERE'S A SODA BOTTLE IN HERE!

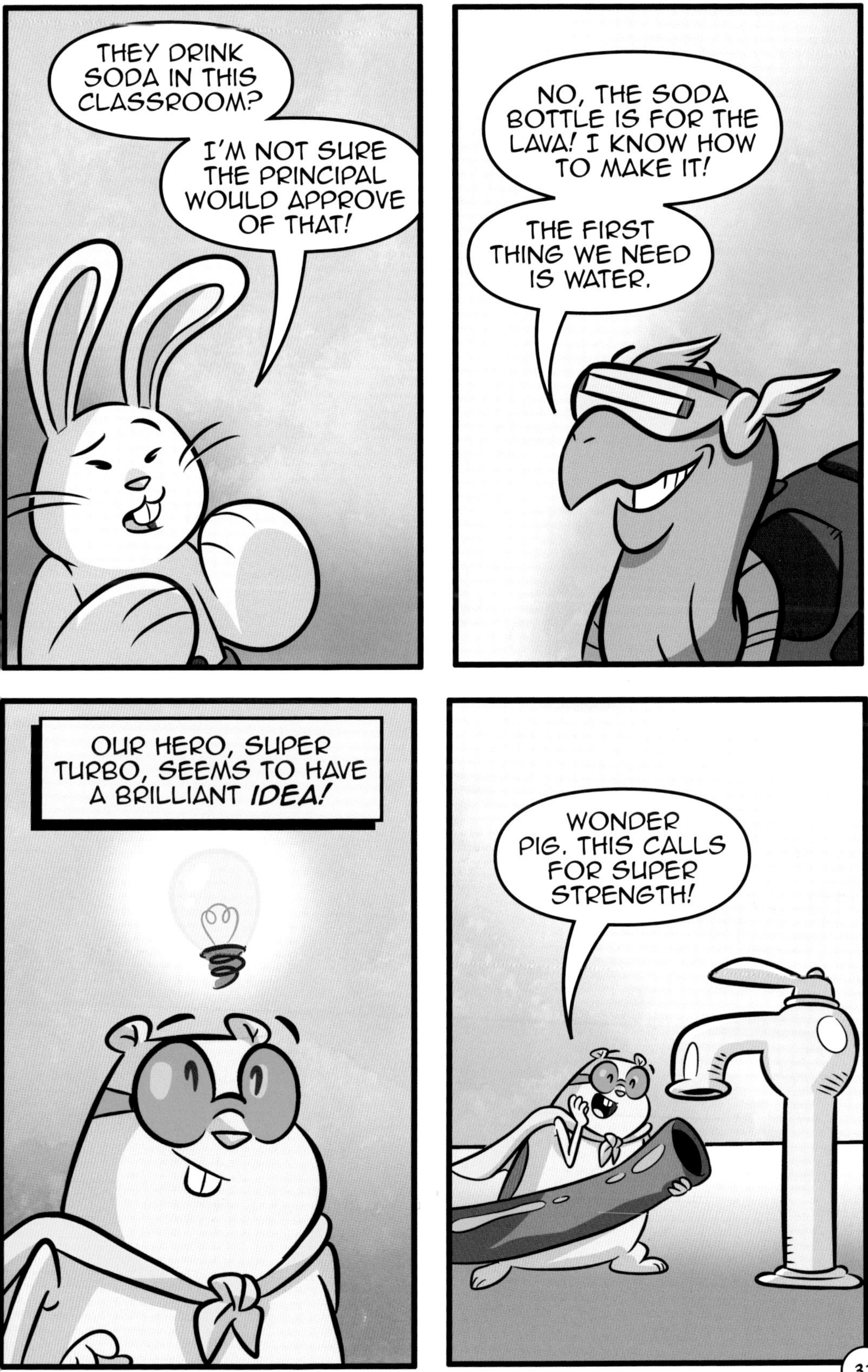
THEY DRINK SODA IN THIS CLASSROOM?
I'M NOT SURE THE PRINCIPAL WOULD APPROVE OF THAT!
NO, THE SODA BOTTLE IS FOR THE LAVA! I KNOW HOW TO MAKE IT!
THE FIRST THING WE NEED IS WATER.
OUR HERO, SUPER TURBO, SEEMS TO HAVE A BRILLIANT *IDEA!*
WONDER PIG. THIS CALLS FOR SUPER STRENGTH!

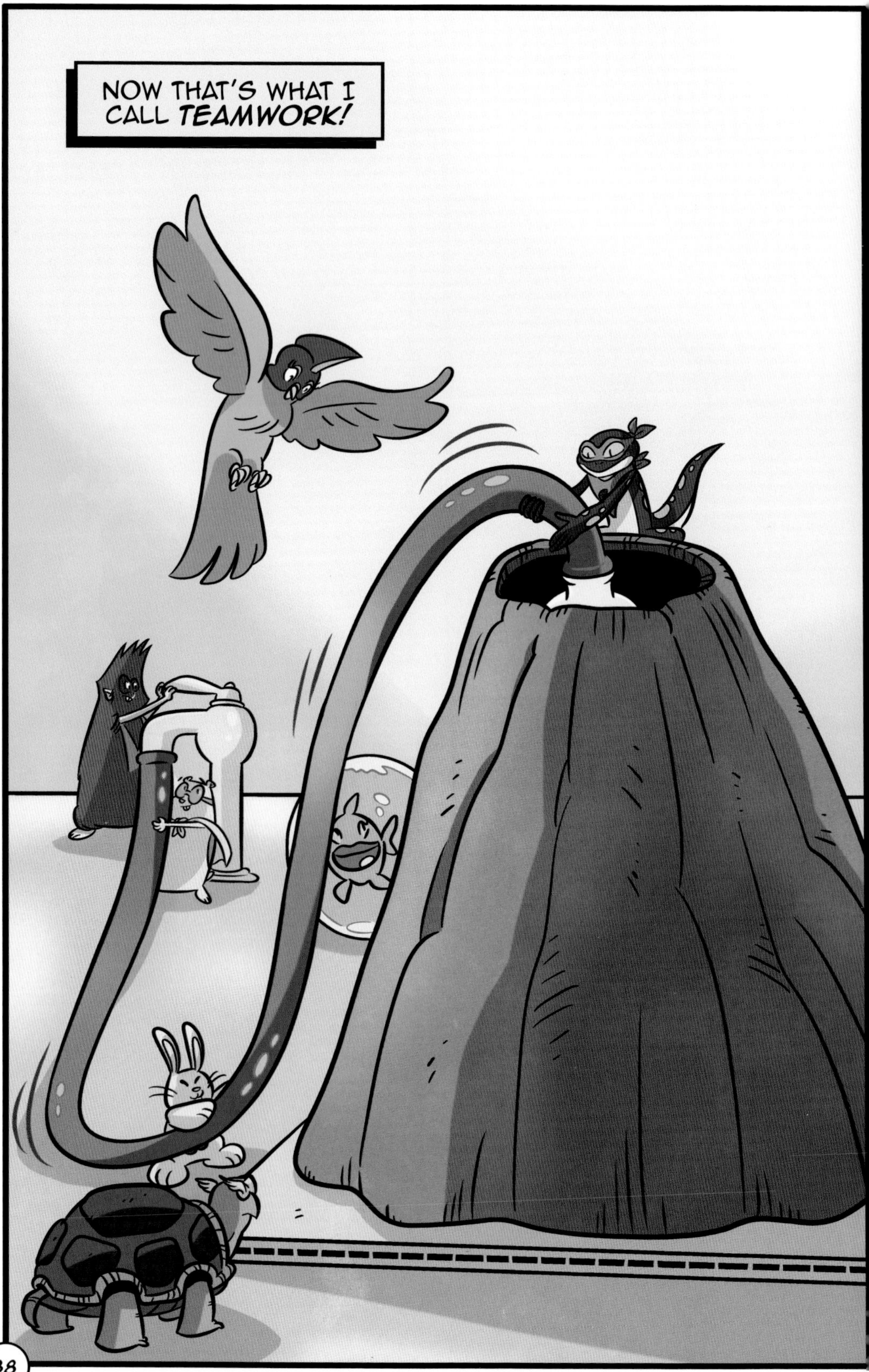
NOW THAT'S WHAT I CALL TEAMWORK!

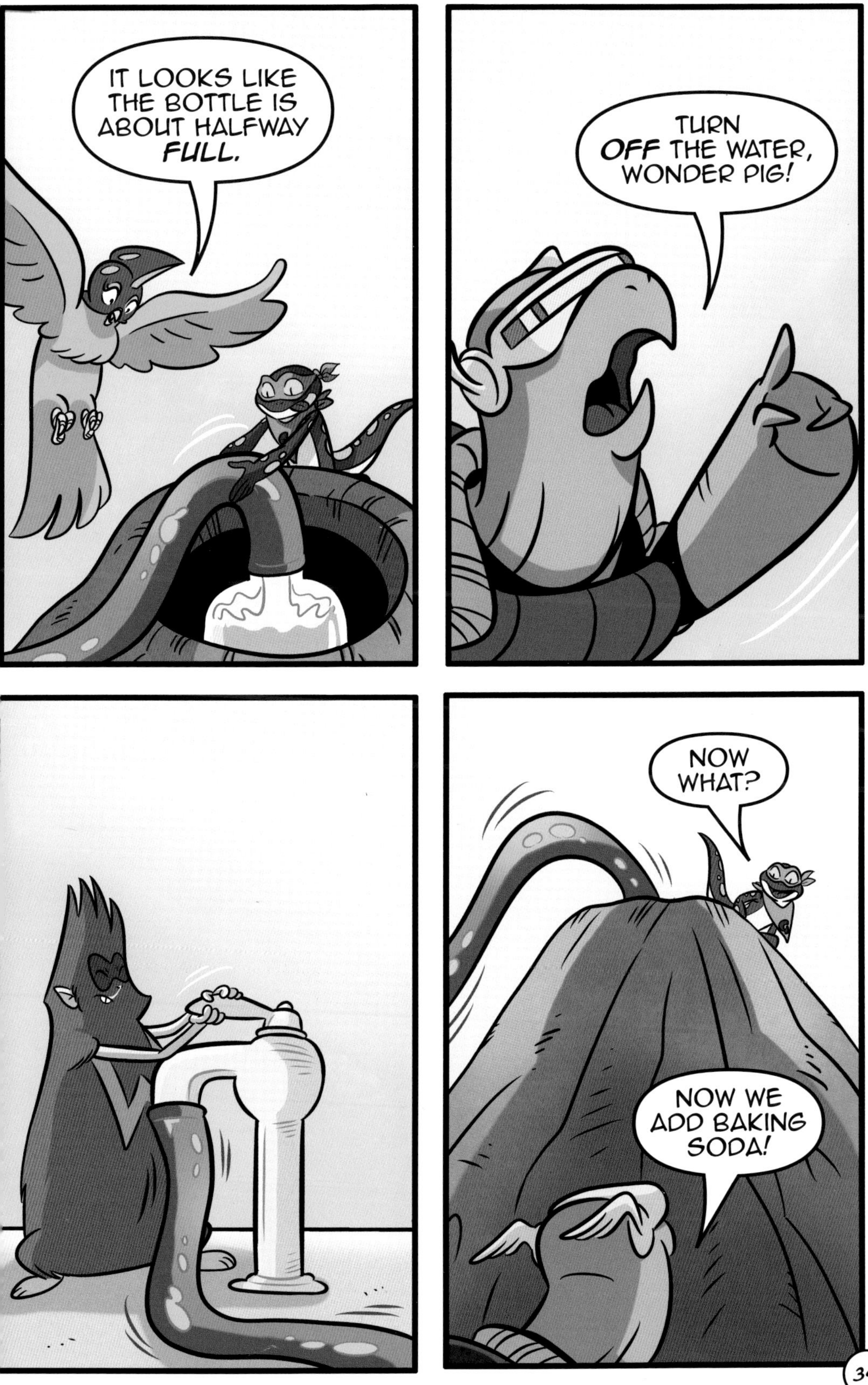
IT LOOKS LIKE THE BOTTLE IS ABOUT HALFWAY FULL.
TURN OFF THE WATER, WONDER PIG!
NOW WHAT?
NOW WE ADD BAKING SODA!

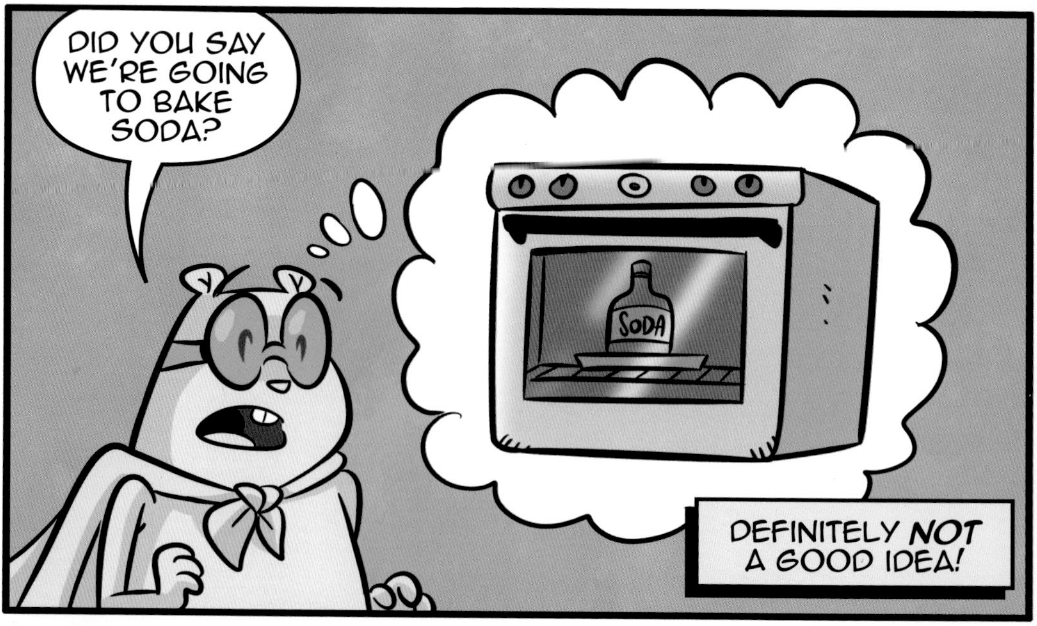
DID YOU SAY WE'RE GOING TO BAKE SODA?
SODA
DEFINITELY **NOT** A GOOD IDEA!

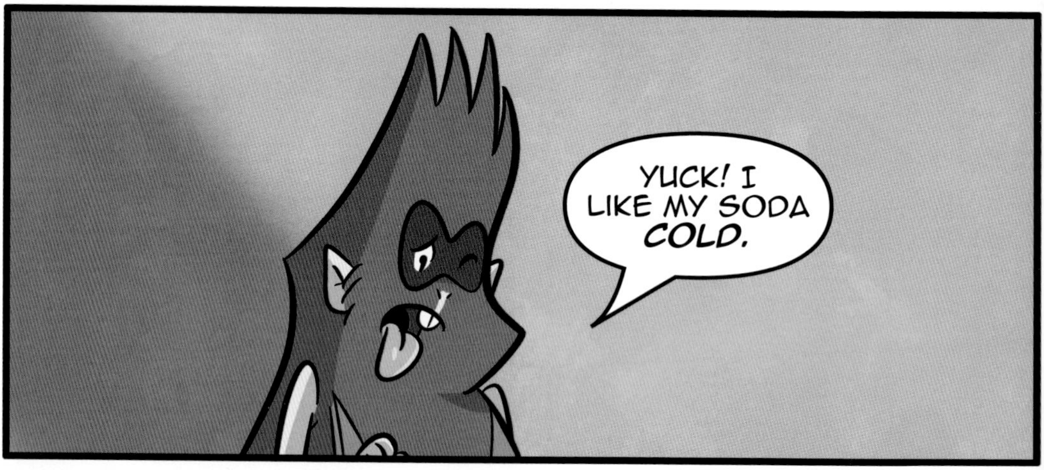
YUCK! I LIKE MY SODA **COLD.**

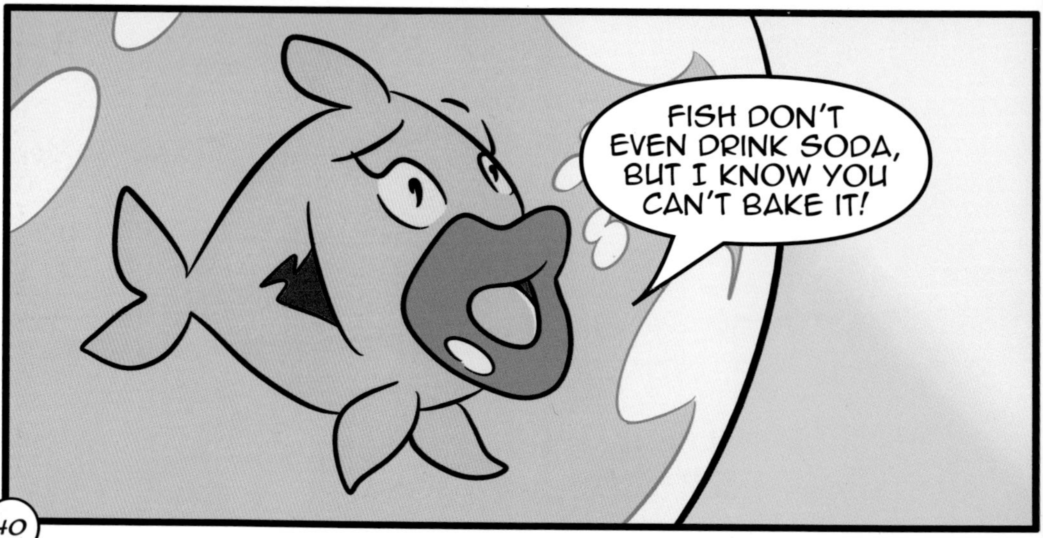
FISH DON'T EVEN DRINK SODA, BUT I KNOW YOU CAN'T BAKE IT!

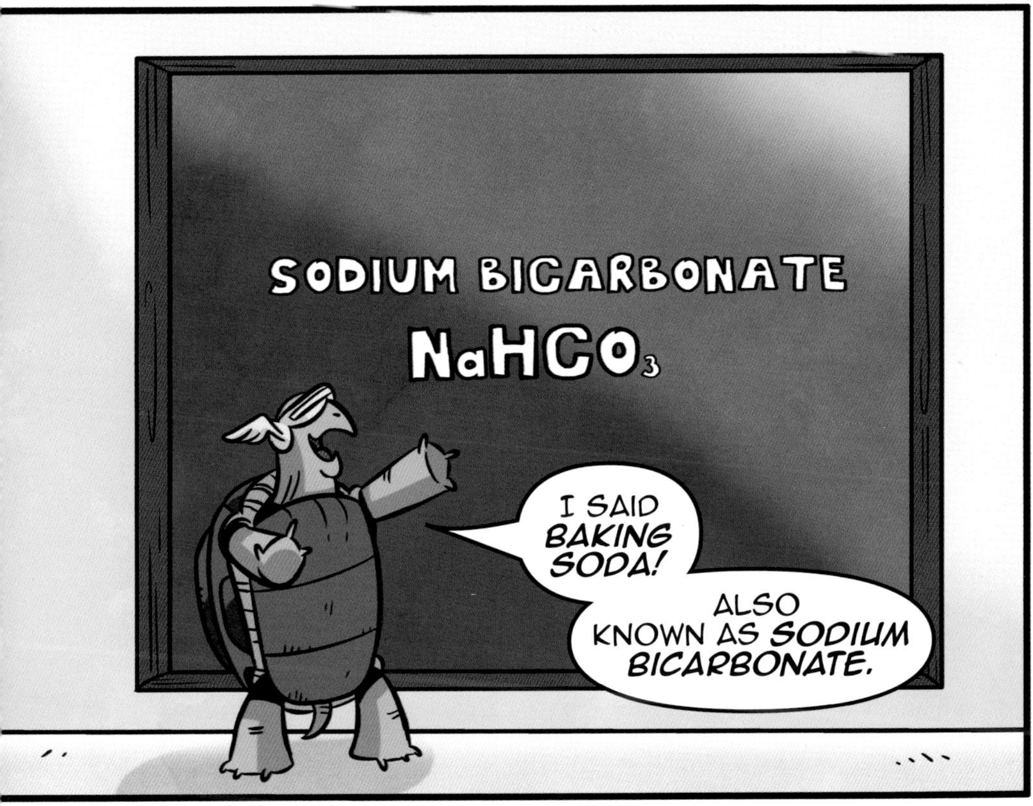
SODIUM BICARBONATE
NaHCO3
I SAID BAKING SODA!
ALSO KNOWN AS SODIUM BICARBONATE.

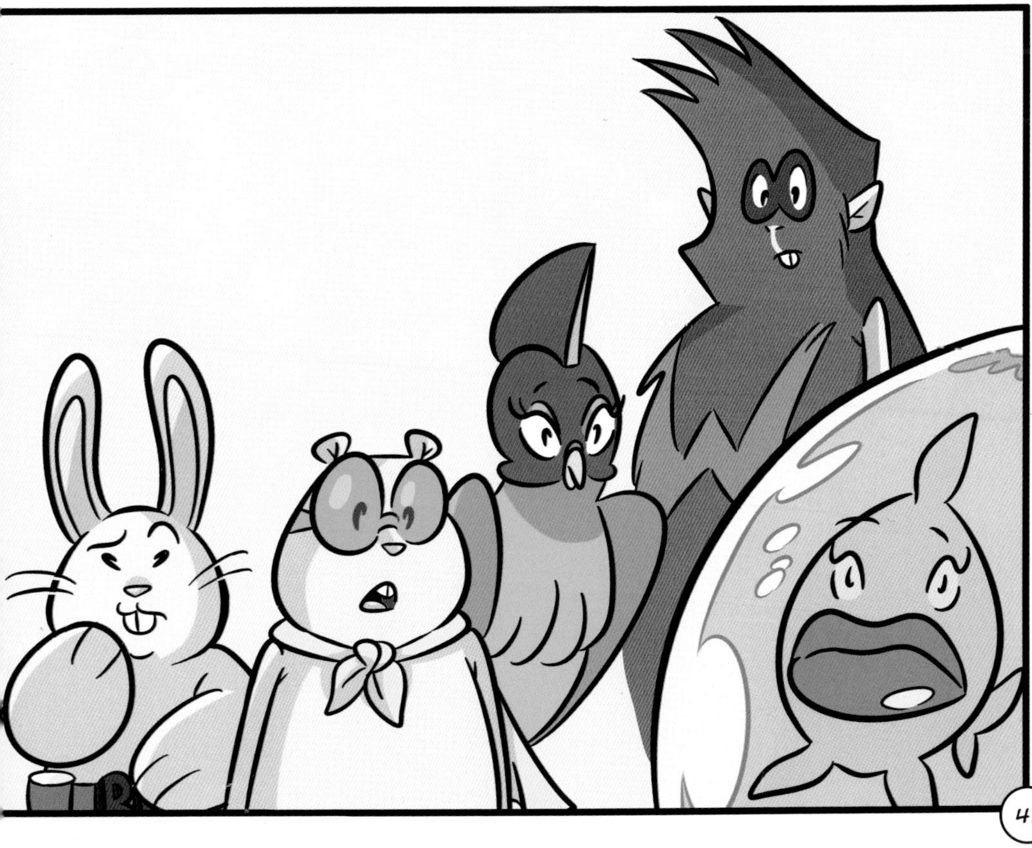

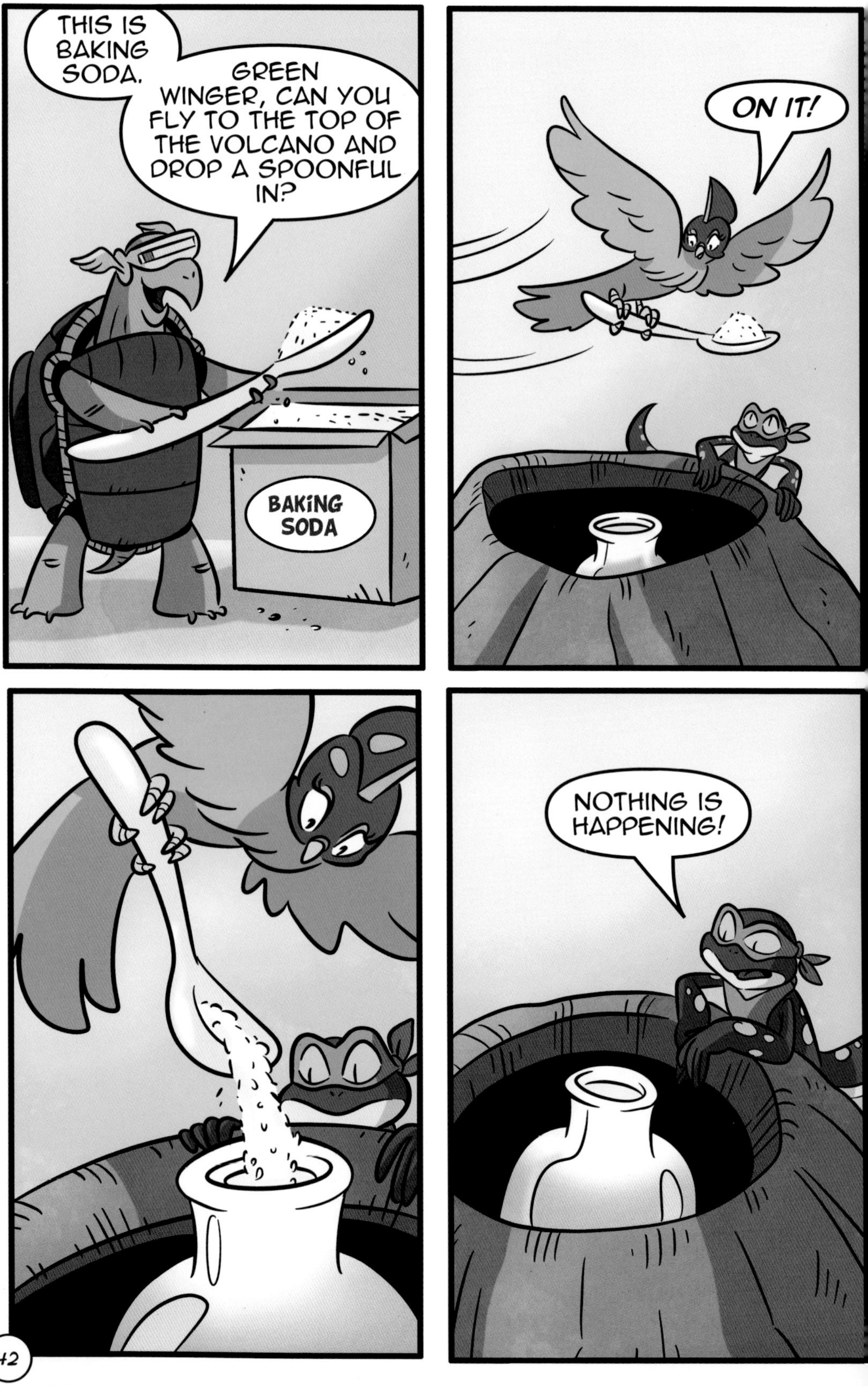
THIS IS BAKING SODA.
GREEN WINGER, CAN YOU FLY TO THE TOP OF THE VOLCANO AND DROP A SPOONFUL IN?
BAKING SODA
ON IT!
NOTHING IS HAPPENING!

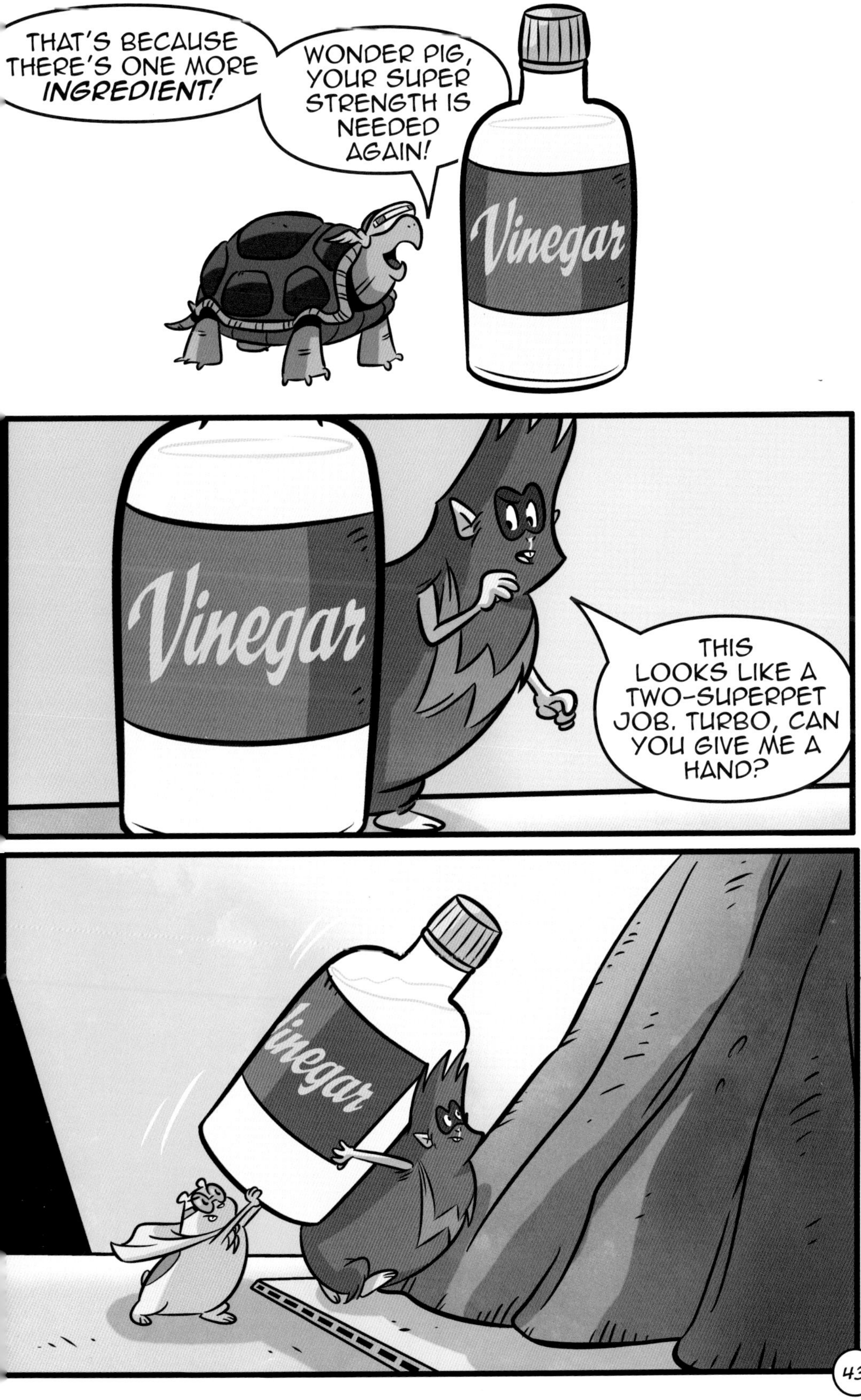
THAT'S BECAUSE THERE'S ONE MORE *INGREDIENT!*
WONDER PIG, YOUR SUPER STRENGTH IS NEEDED AGAIN!
Vinegar
Vinegar
THIS LOOKS LIKE A TWO-SUPERPET JOB. TURBO, CAN YOU GIVE ME A HAND?
inegar

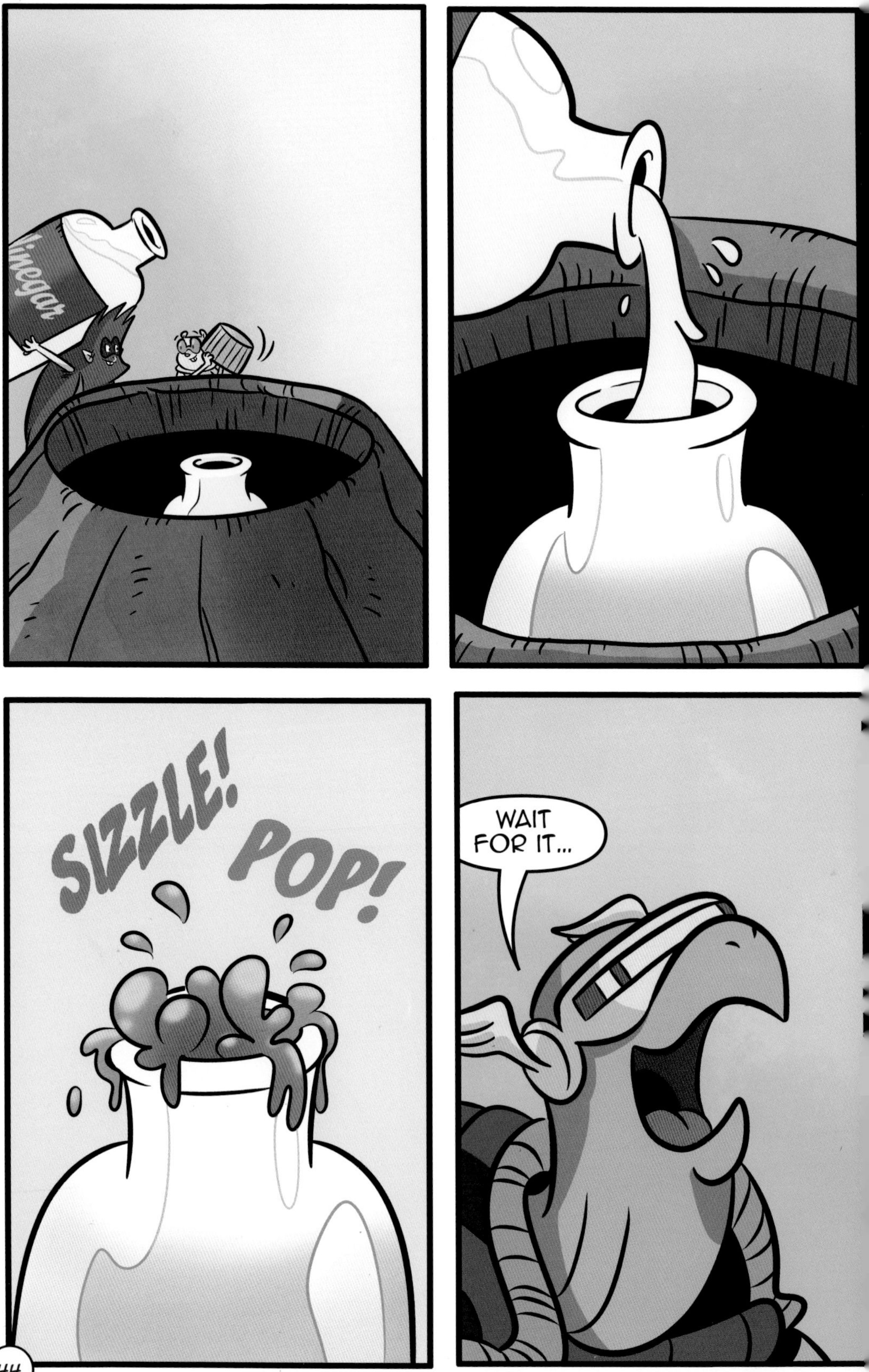
Vinegar
SIZZLE!
POP!
WAIT FOR IT...

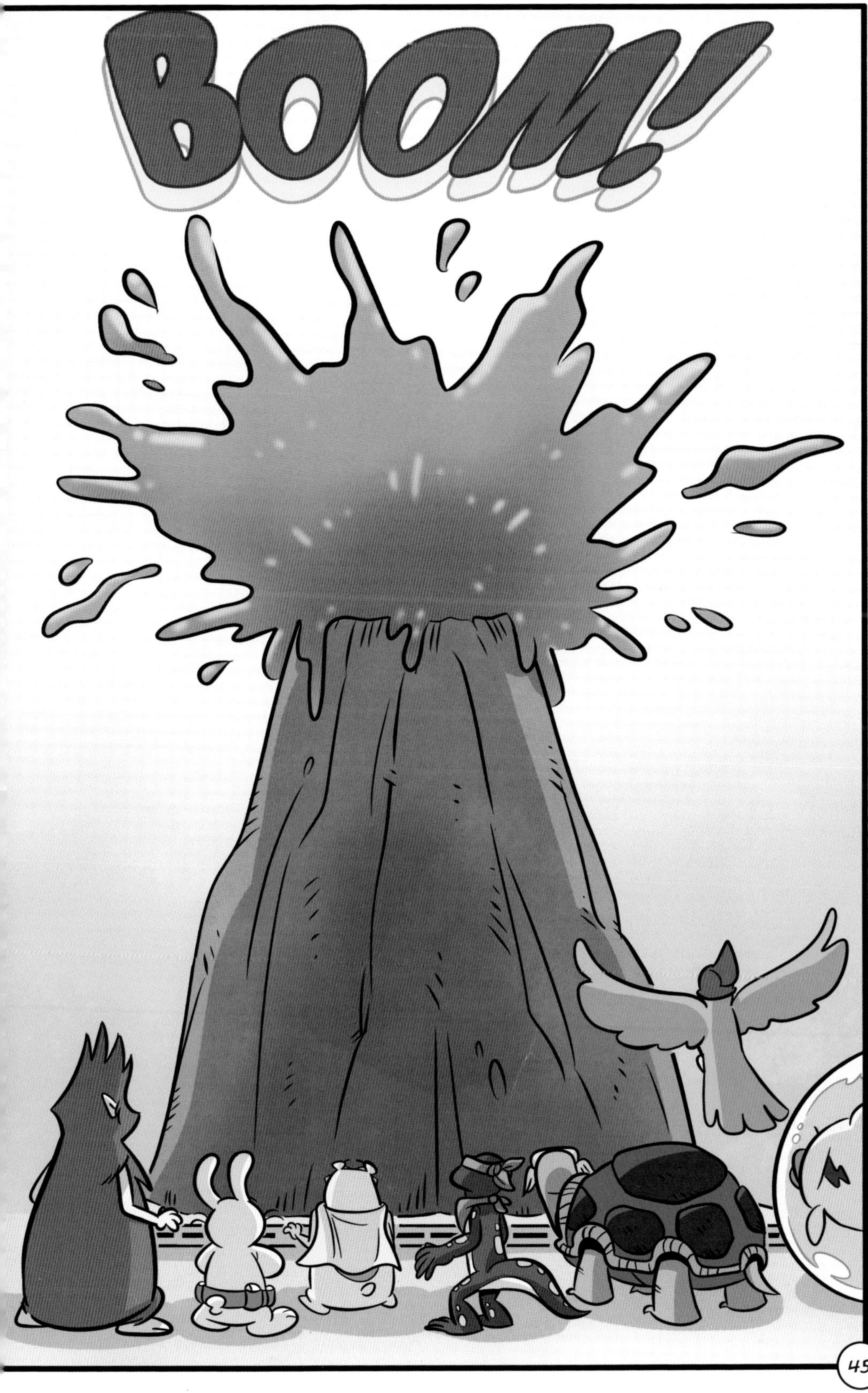
BOOM!

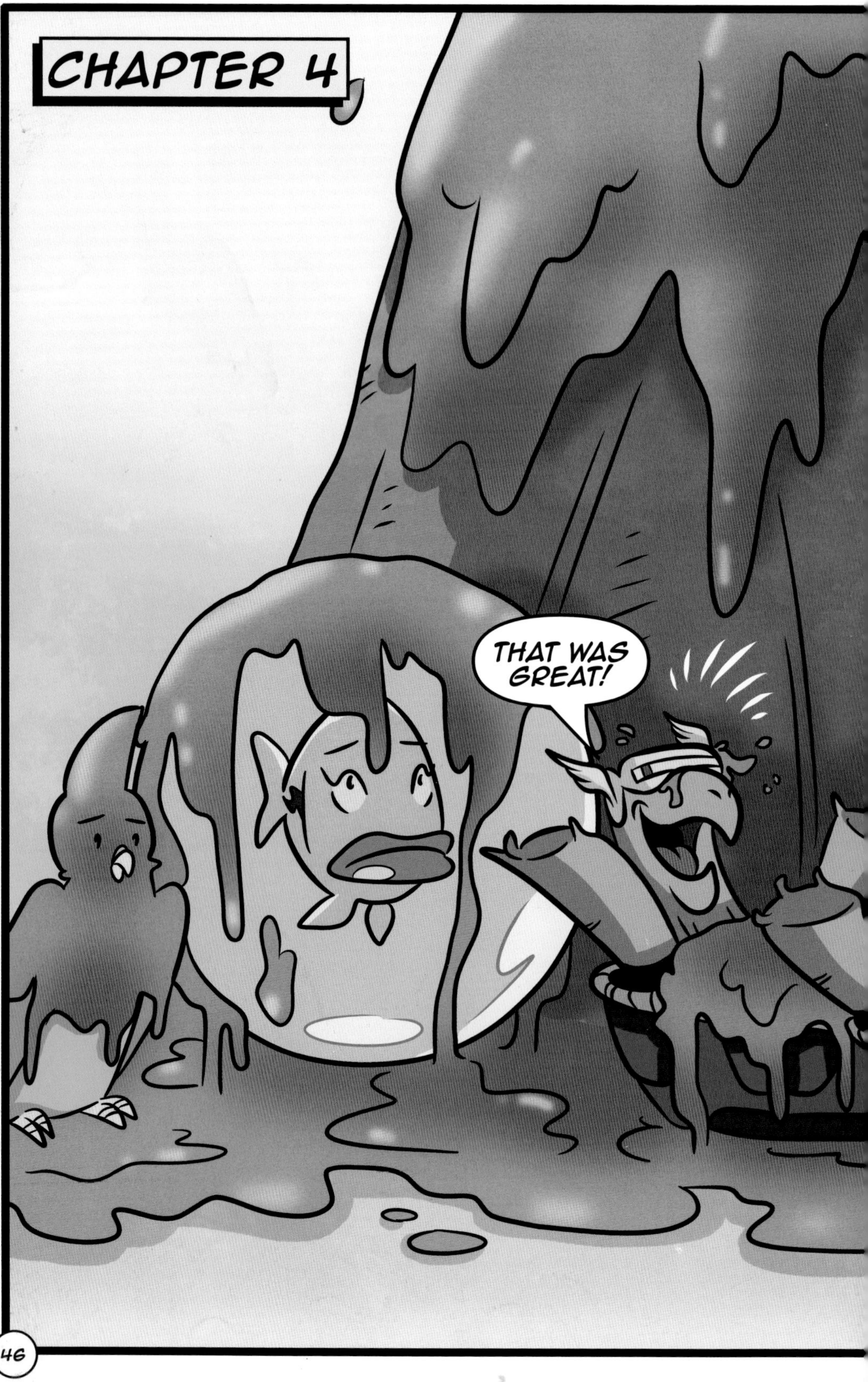
CHAPTER 4
THAT WAS GREAT!

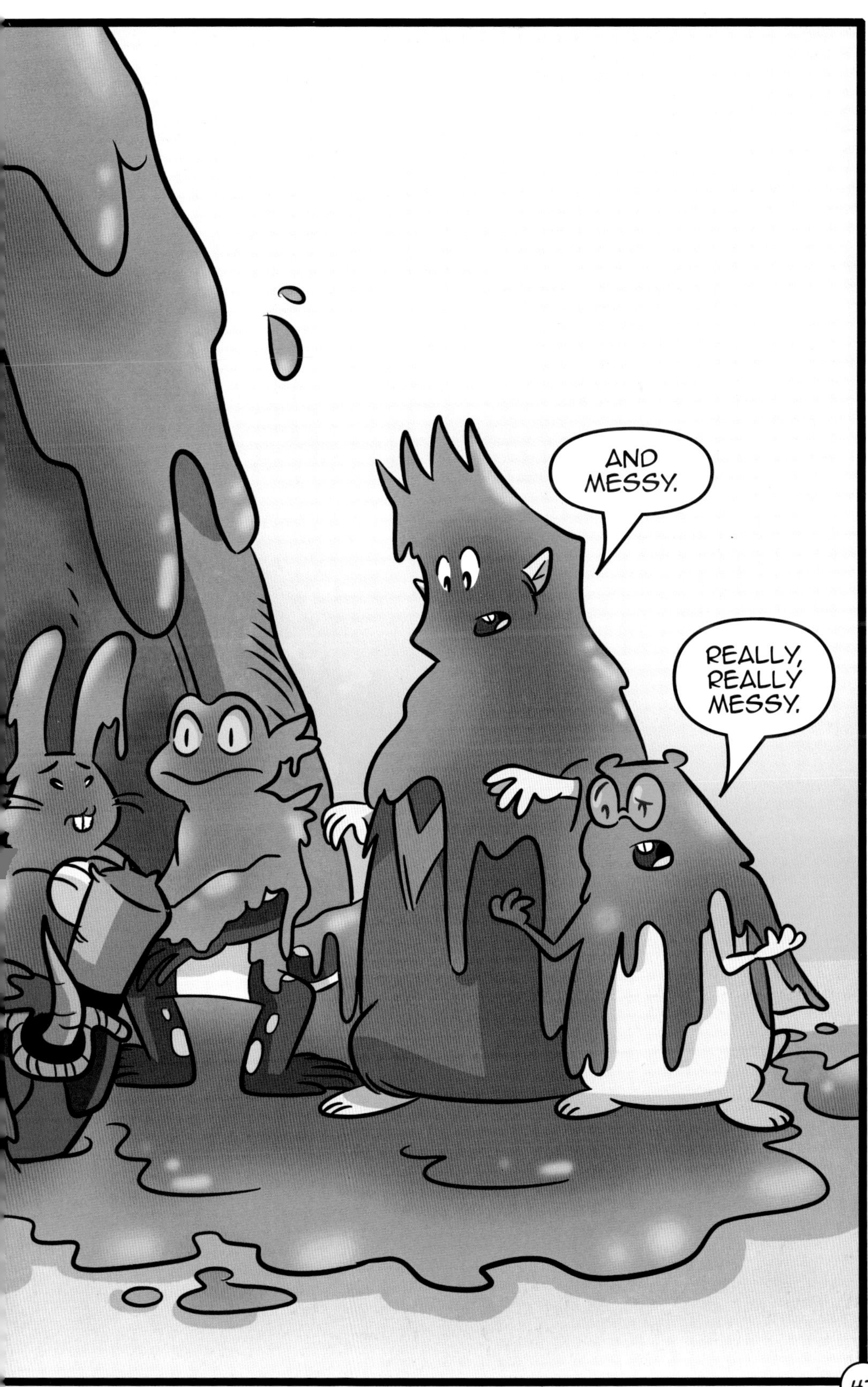
AND MESSY.
REALLY, REALLY MESSY.

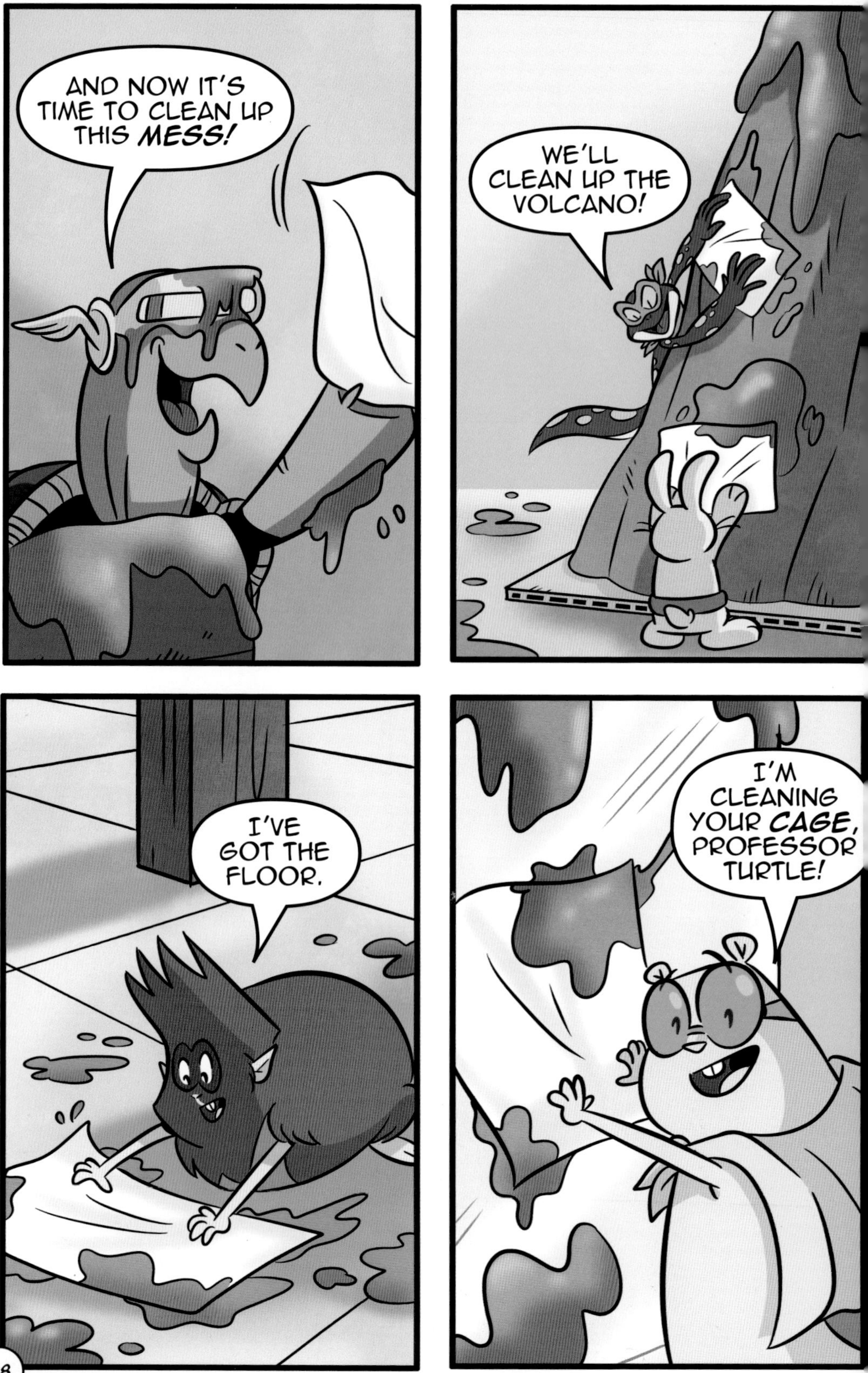
AND NOW IT'S TIME TO CLEAN UP THIS MESS!
WE'LL CLEAN UP THE VOLCANO!
I'VE GOT THE FLOOR.
I'M CLEANING YOUR CAGE, PROFESSOR TURTLE!

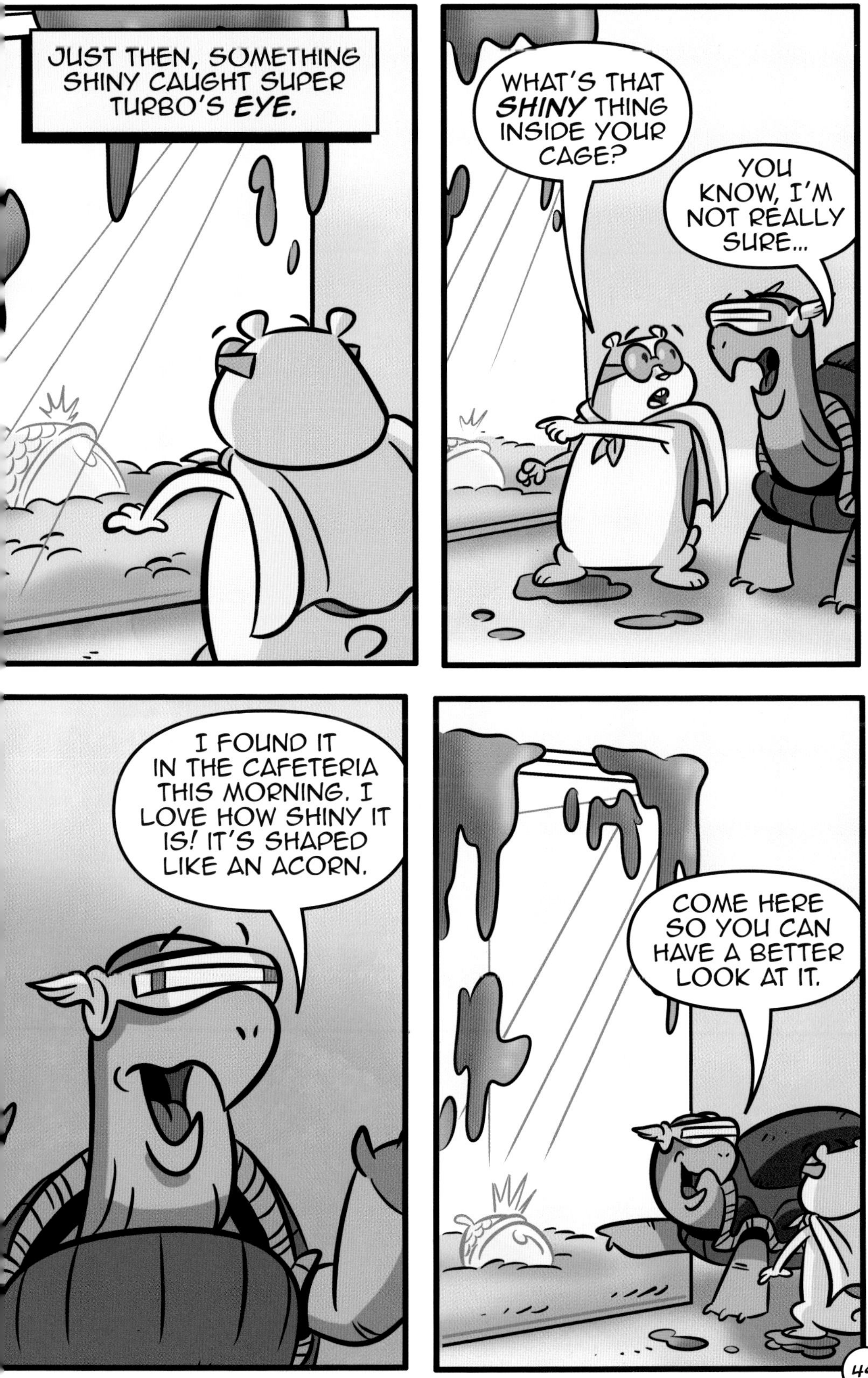
JUST THEN, SOMETHING SHINY CAUGHT SUPER TURBO'S *EYE.*
WHAT'S THAT *SHINY* THING INSIDE YOUR CAGE?
YOU KNOW, I'M NOT REALLY SURE...
I FOUND IT IN THE CAFETERIA THIS MORNING. I LOVE HOW SHINY IT IS! IT'S SHAPED LIKE AN ACORN.
COME HERE SO YOU CAN HAVE A BETTER LOOK AT IT.

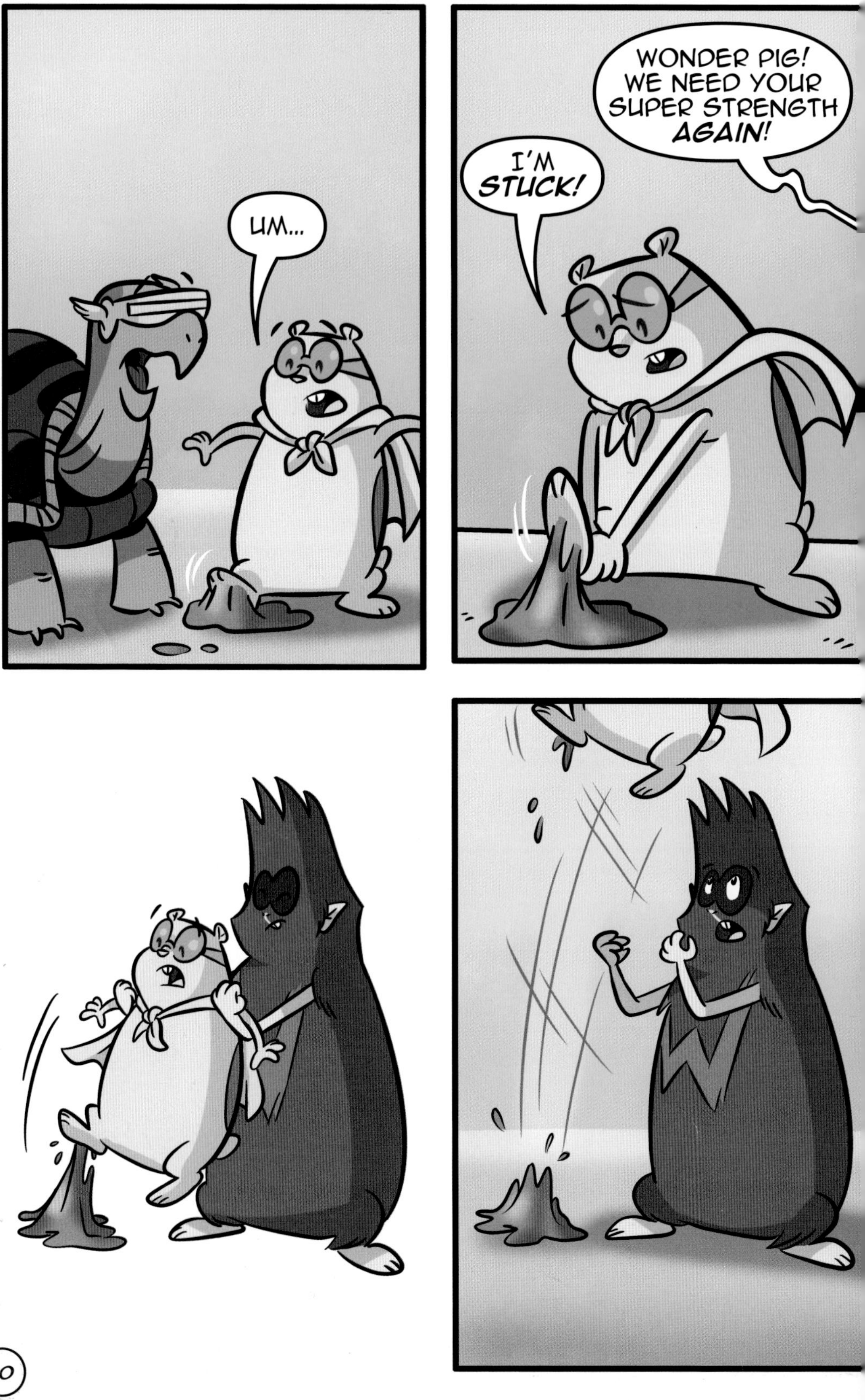
UM...
WONDER PIG! WE NEED YOUR SUPER STRENGTH AGAIN!
I'M STUCK!

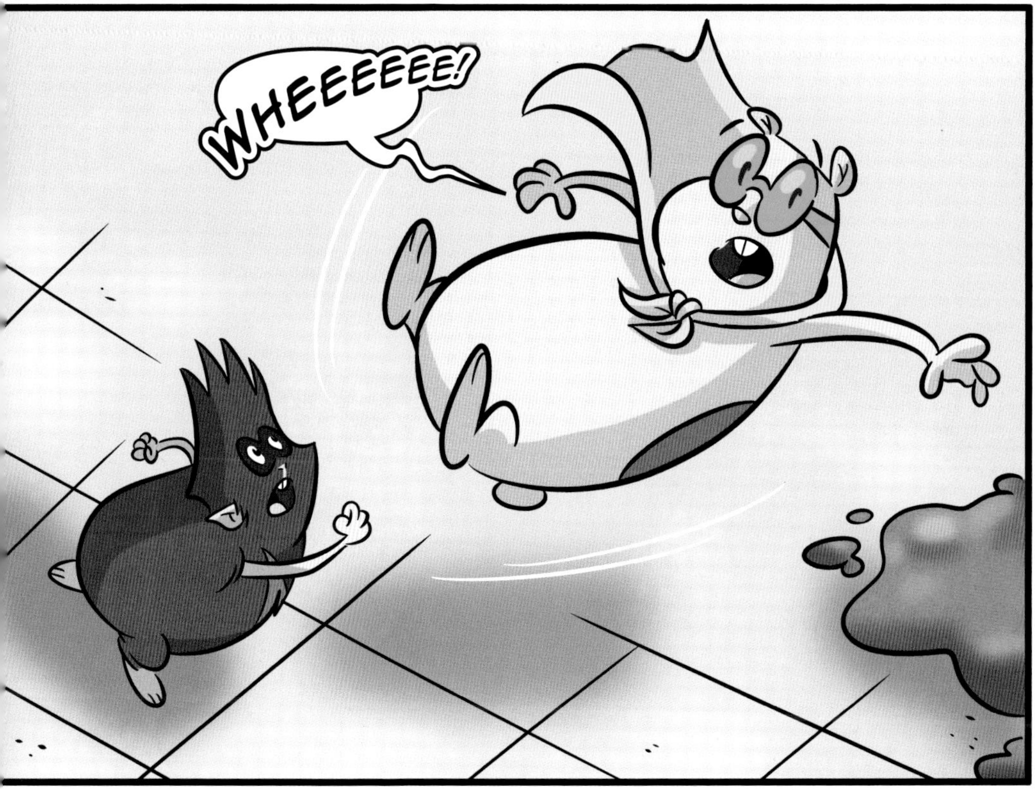
WHEEEEEEE!

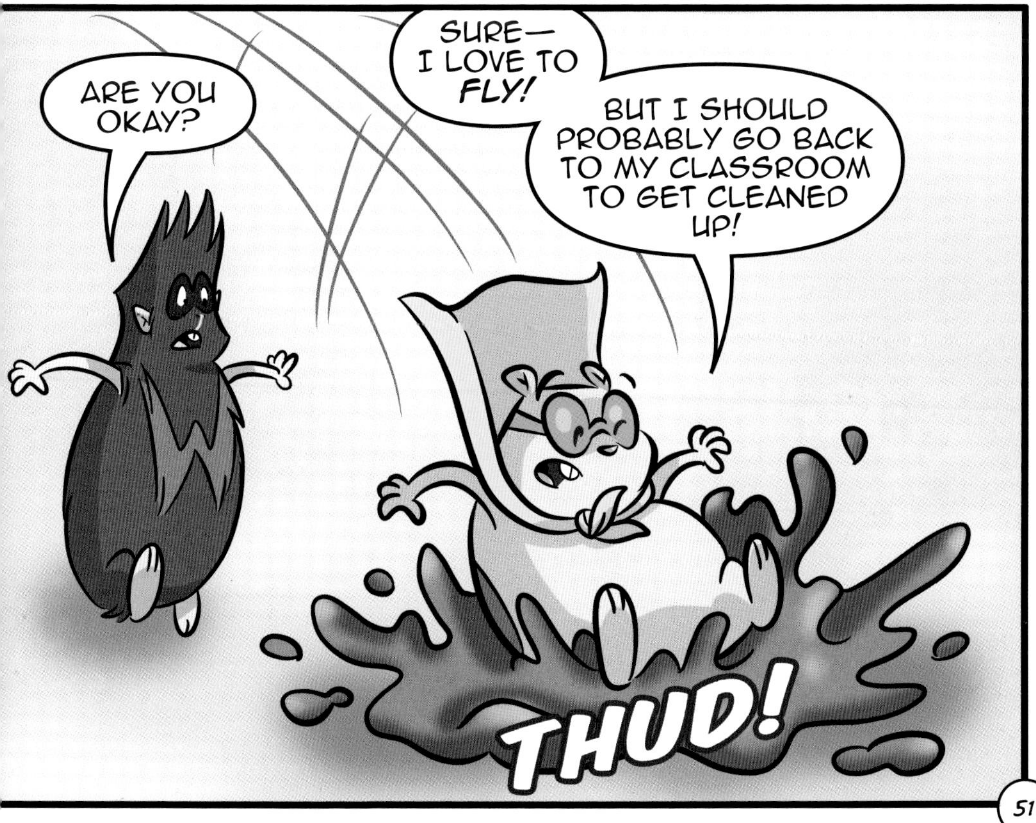
ARE YOU OKAY?
SURE— I LOVE TO *FLY!*
BUT I SHOULD PROBABLY GO BACK TO MY CLASSROOM TO GET CLEANED UP!
THUD!

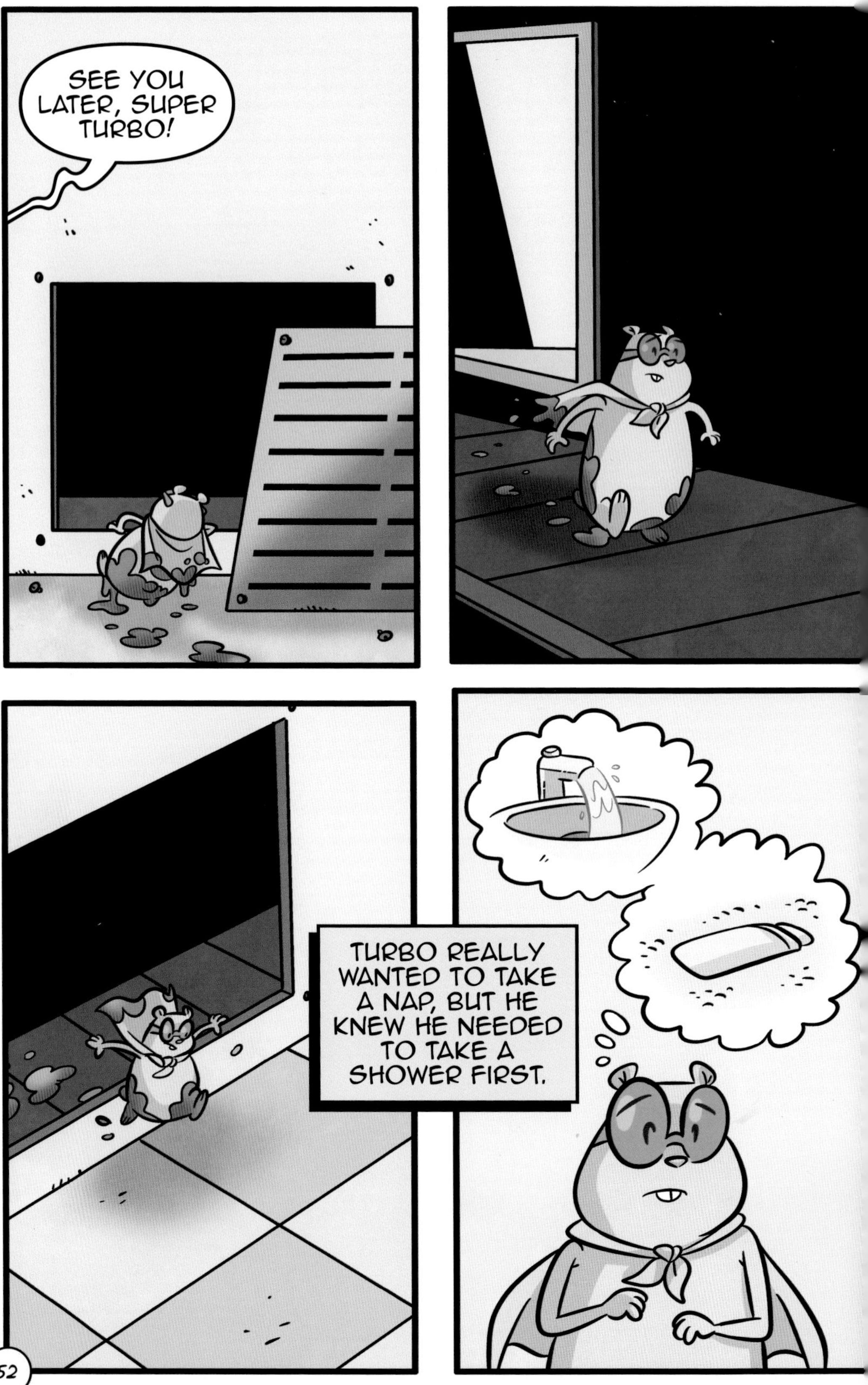
SEE YOU LATER, SUPER TURBO!
TURBO REALLY WANTED TO TAKE A NAP, BUT HE KNEW HE NEEDED TO TAKE A SHOWER FIRST.

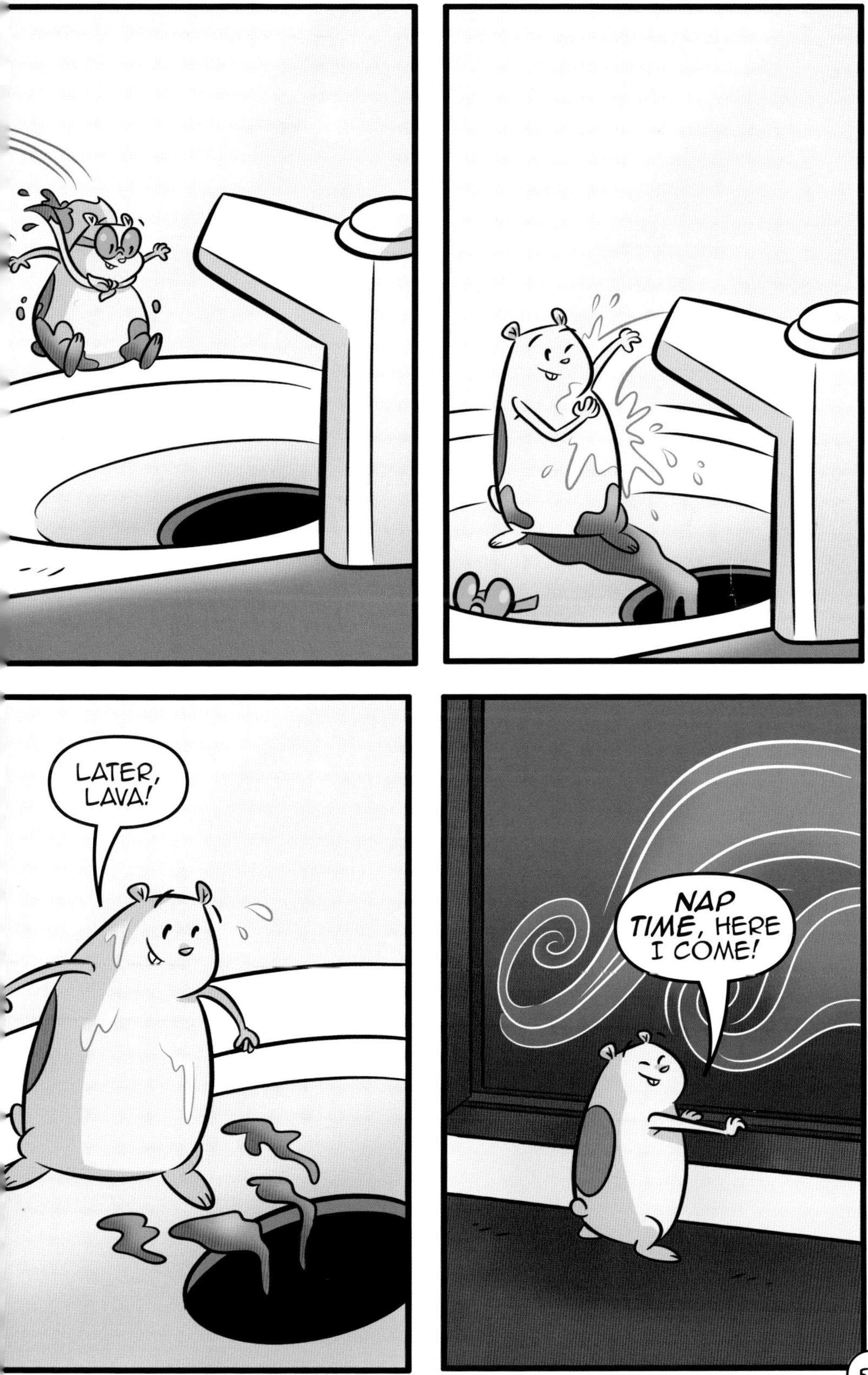
LATER, LAVA!
NAP TIME, HERE I COME!

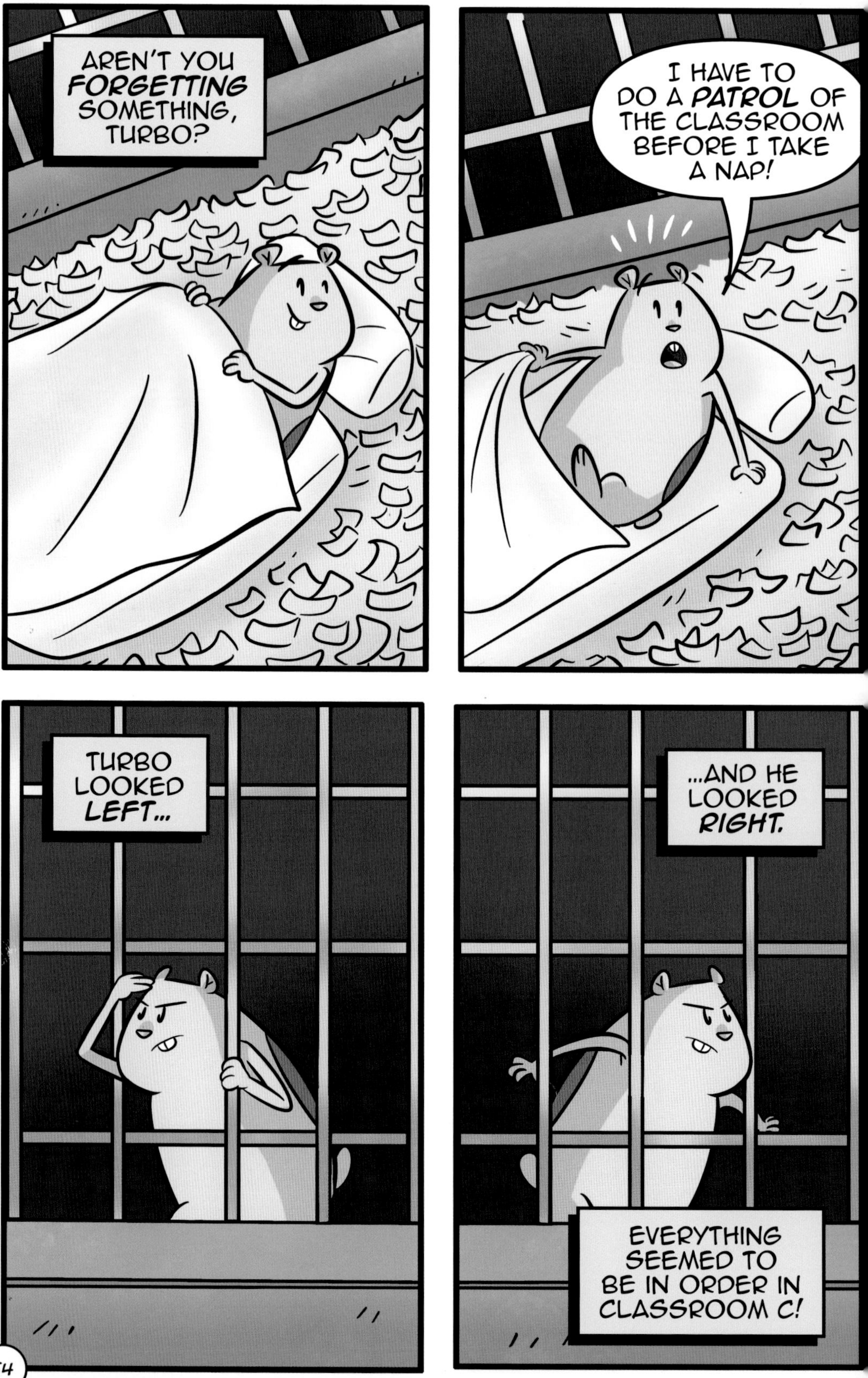
AREN'T YOU FORGETTING SOMETHING, TURBO?
I HAVE TO DO A PATROL OF THE CLASSROOM BEFORE I TAKE A NAP!
TURBO LOOKED LEFT...
...AND HE LOOKED RIGHT.
EVERYTHING SEEMED TO BE IN ORDER IN CLASSROOM C!

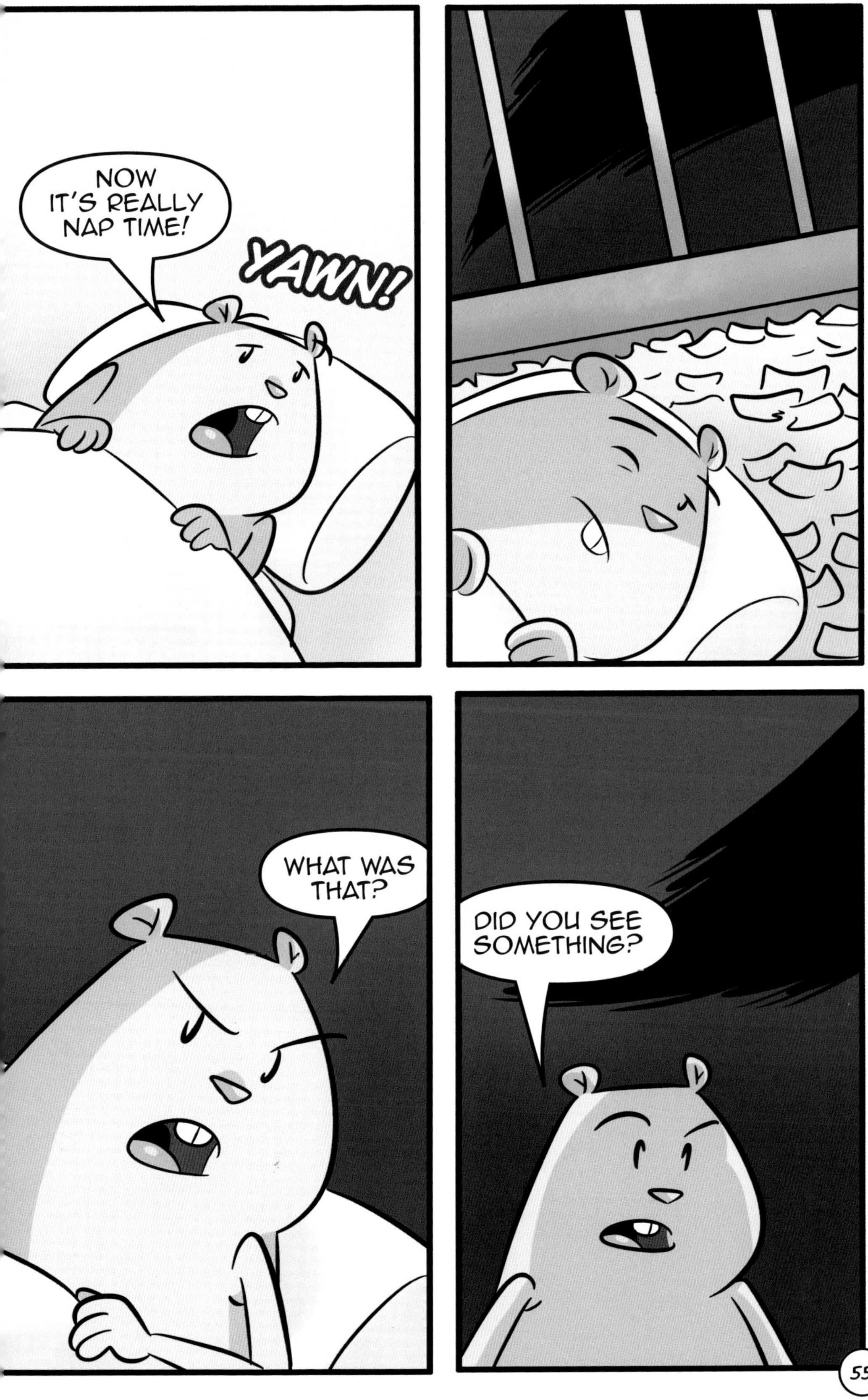
NOW IT'S REALLY NAP TIME!
YAWN!
WHAT WAS THAT?
DID YOU SEE SOMETHING?

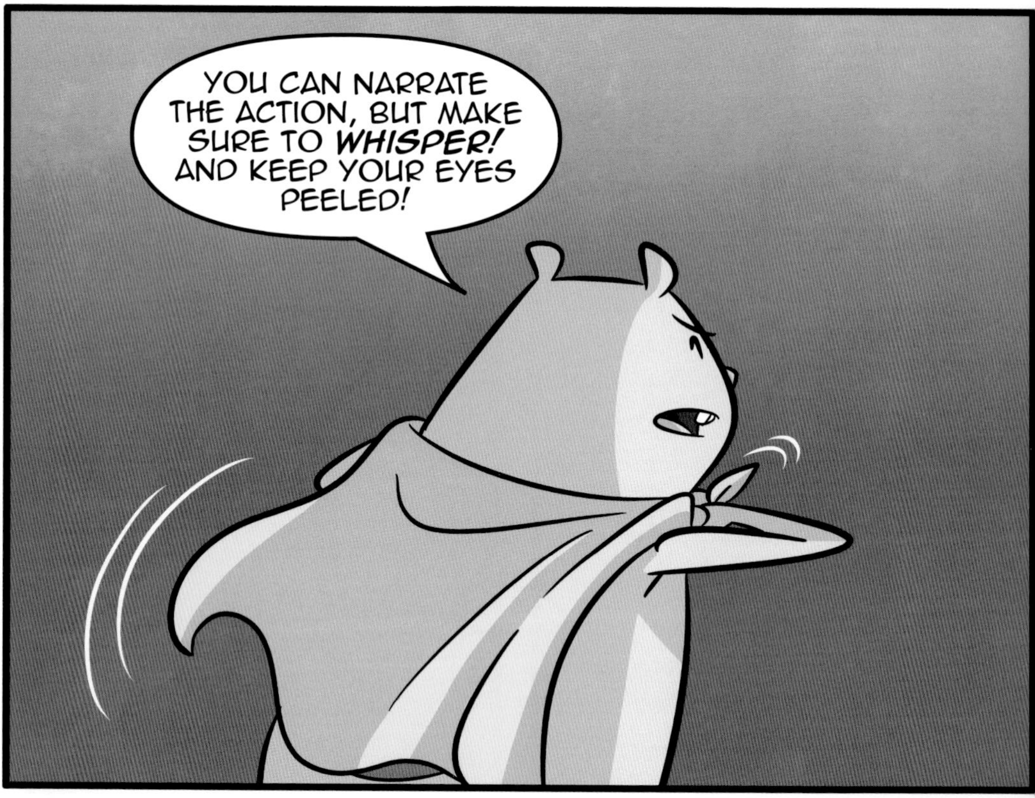
YOU CAN NARRATE THE ACTION, BUT MAKE SURE TO **WHISPER!** AND KEEP YOUR EYES PEELED!

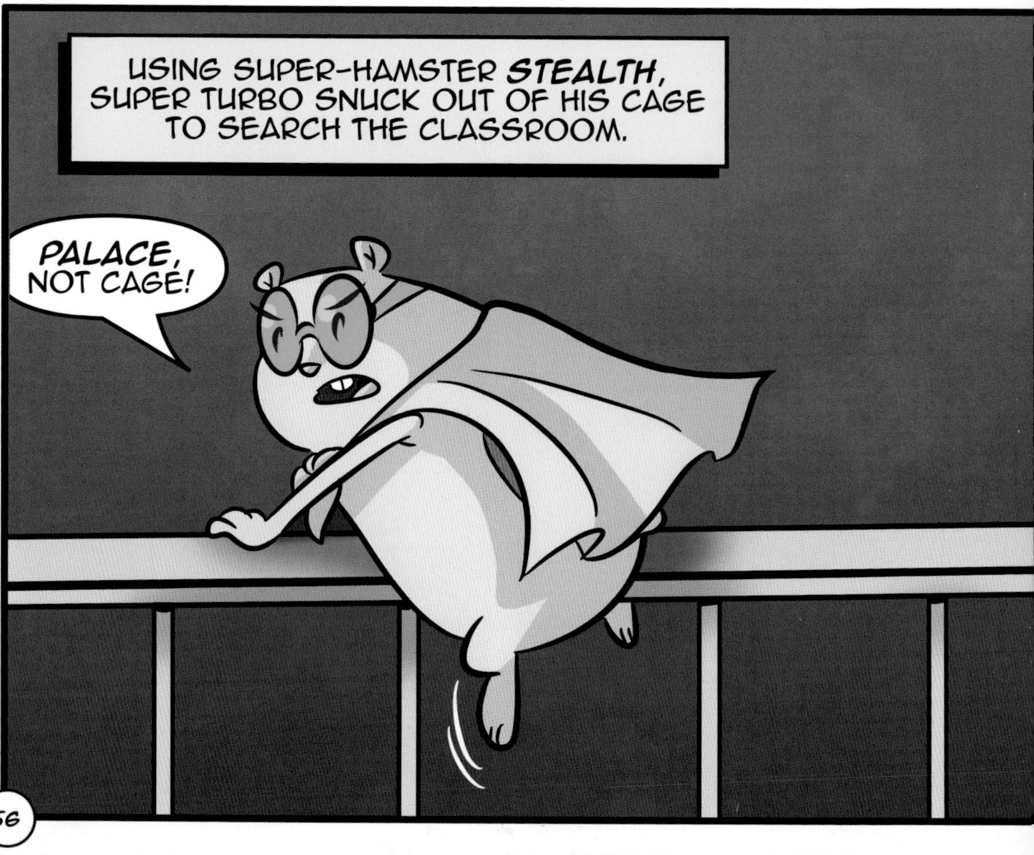
USING SUPER-HAMSTER **STEALTH**, SUPER TURBO SNUCK OUT OF HIS CAGE TO SEARCH THE CLASSROOM.
PALACE, NOT CAGE!

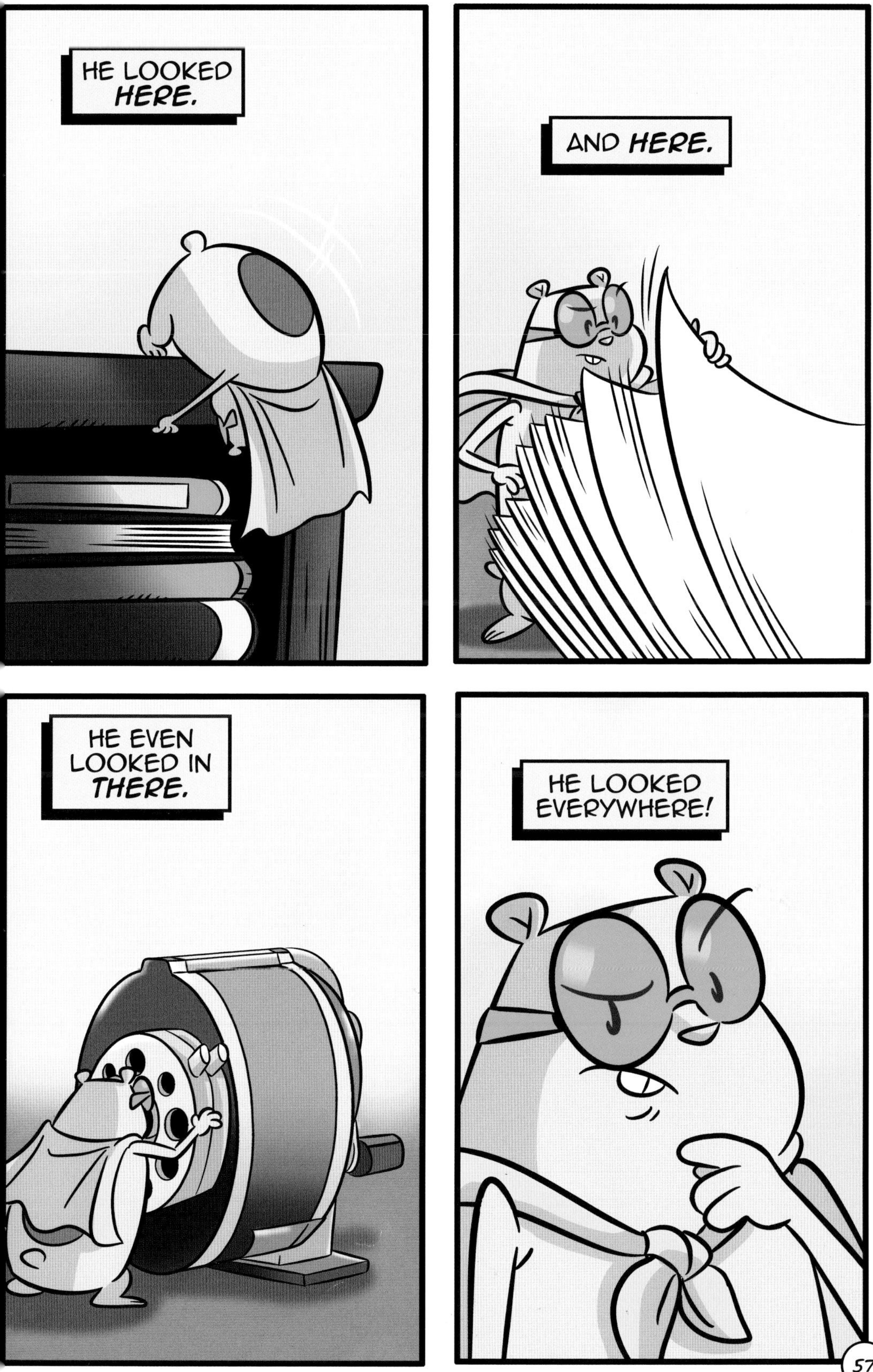
HE LOOKED HERE.
AND HERE.
HE EVEN LOOKED IN THERE.
HE LOOKED EVERYWHERE!

TURBO DECIDED HE MUST HAVE IMAGINED THE SHADOW WHEN SUDDENLY...

...SOMETHING, OR SOMEONE, ZIPPED BY HIM.

REALLY, REALLY *FAST.*

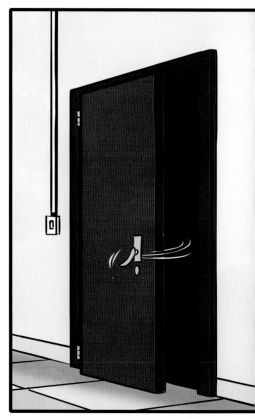

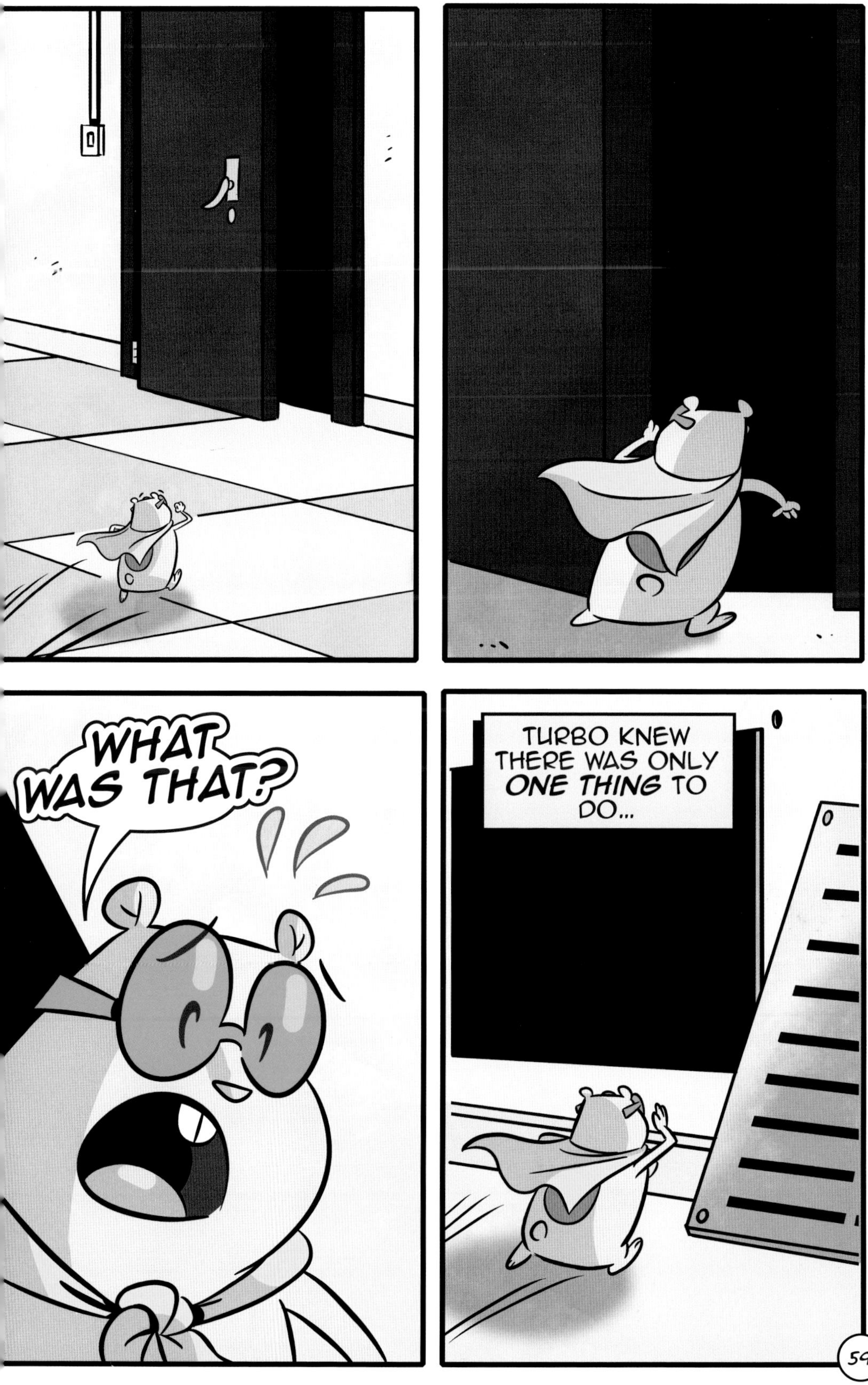
WHAT WAS THAT?
TURBO KNEW THERE WAS ONLY *ONE THING* TO DO...

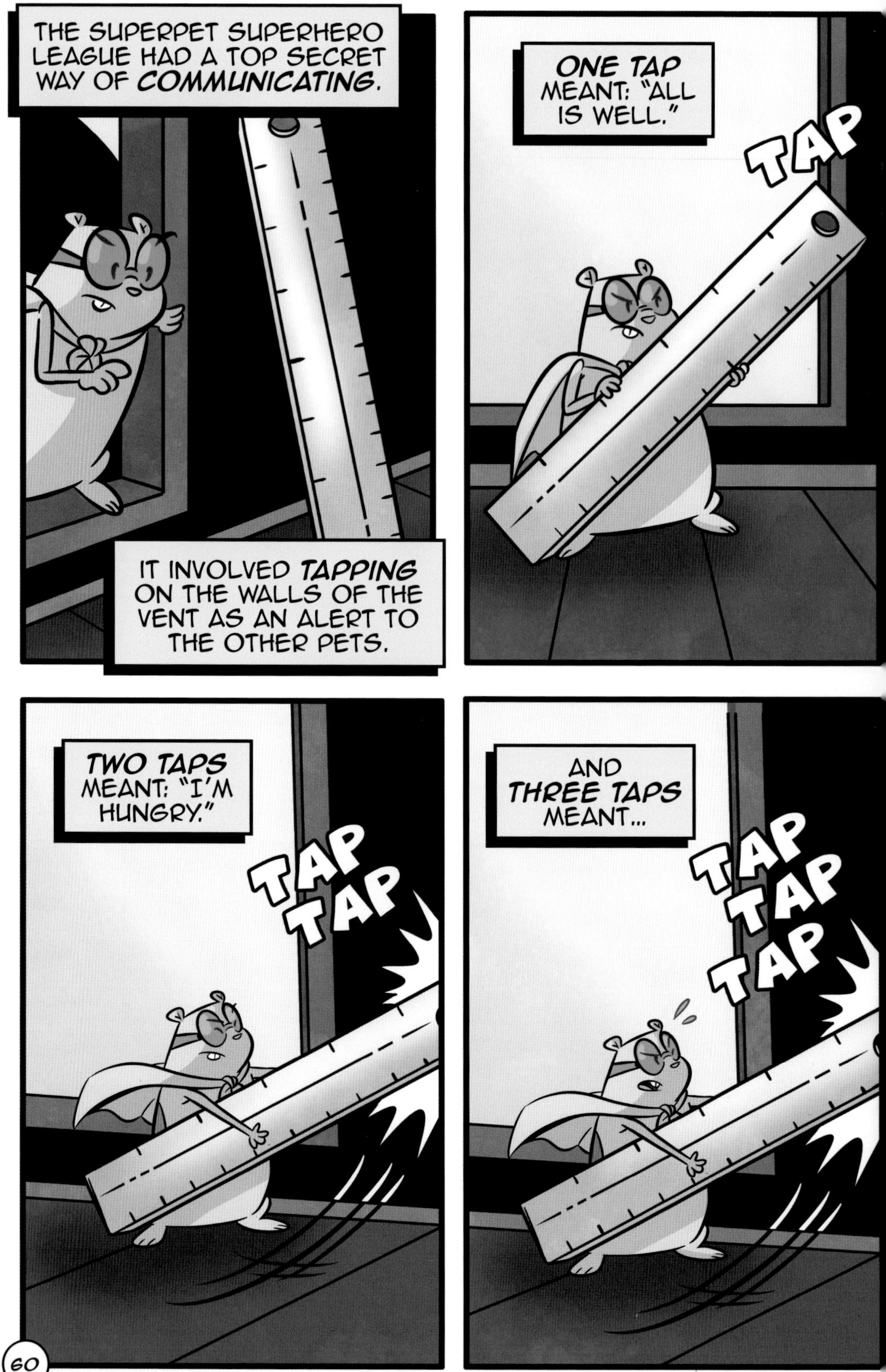
THE SUPERPET SUPERHERO LEAGUE HAD A TOP SECRET WAY OF *COMMUNICATING*.
IT INVOLVED *TAPPING* ON THE WALLS OF THE VENT AS AN ALERT TO THE OTHER PETS.
ONE TAP MEANT: "ALL IS WELL."
TAP
TWO TAPS MEANT: "I'M HUNGRY."
TAP TAP
AND *THREE TAPS* MEANT...
TAP TAP TAP

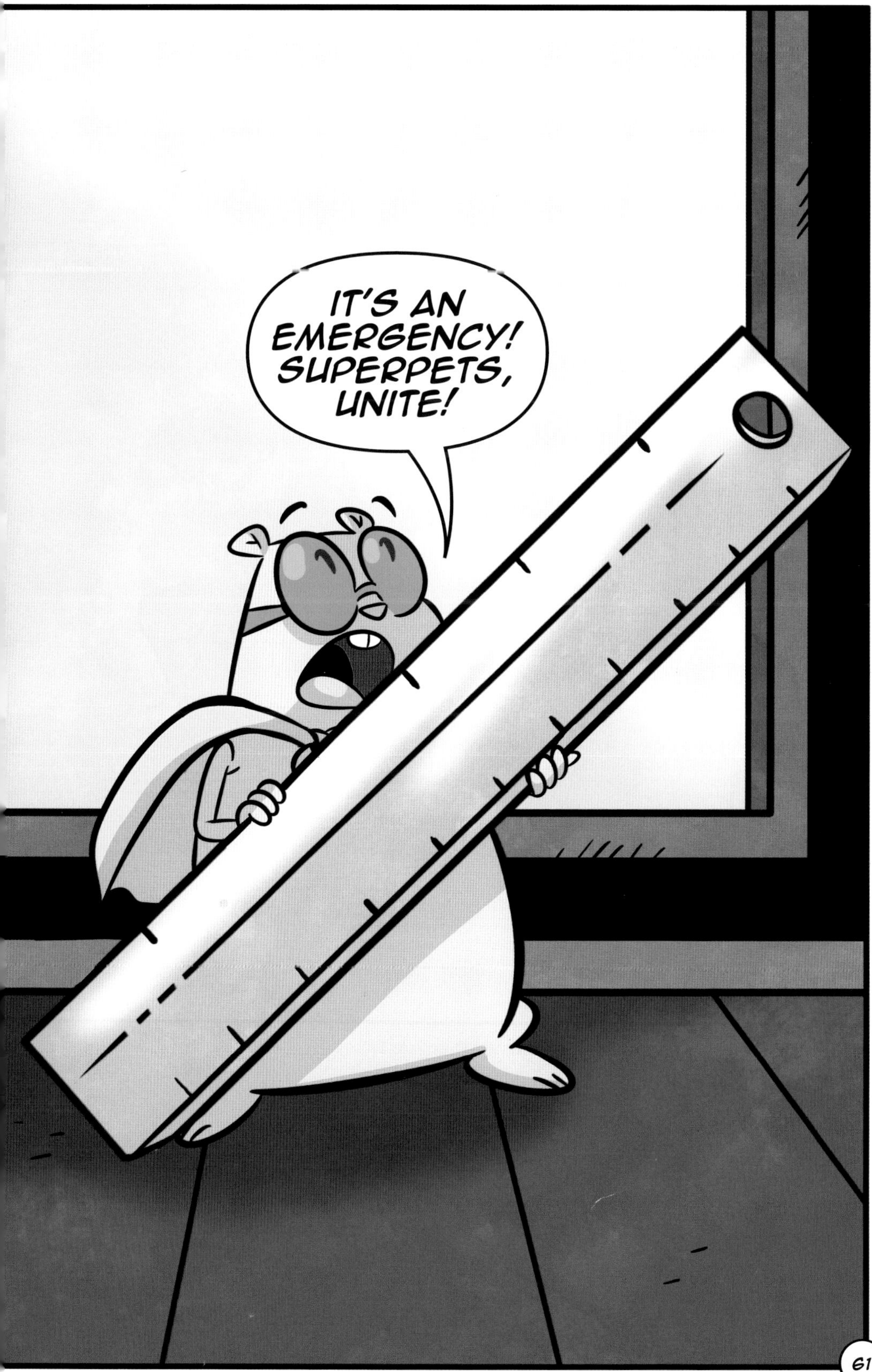
IT'S AN EMERGENCY! SUPERPETS, UNITE!

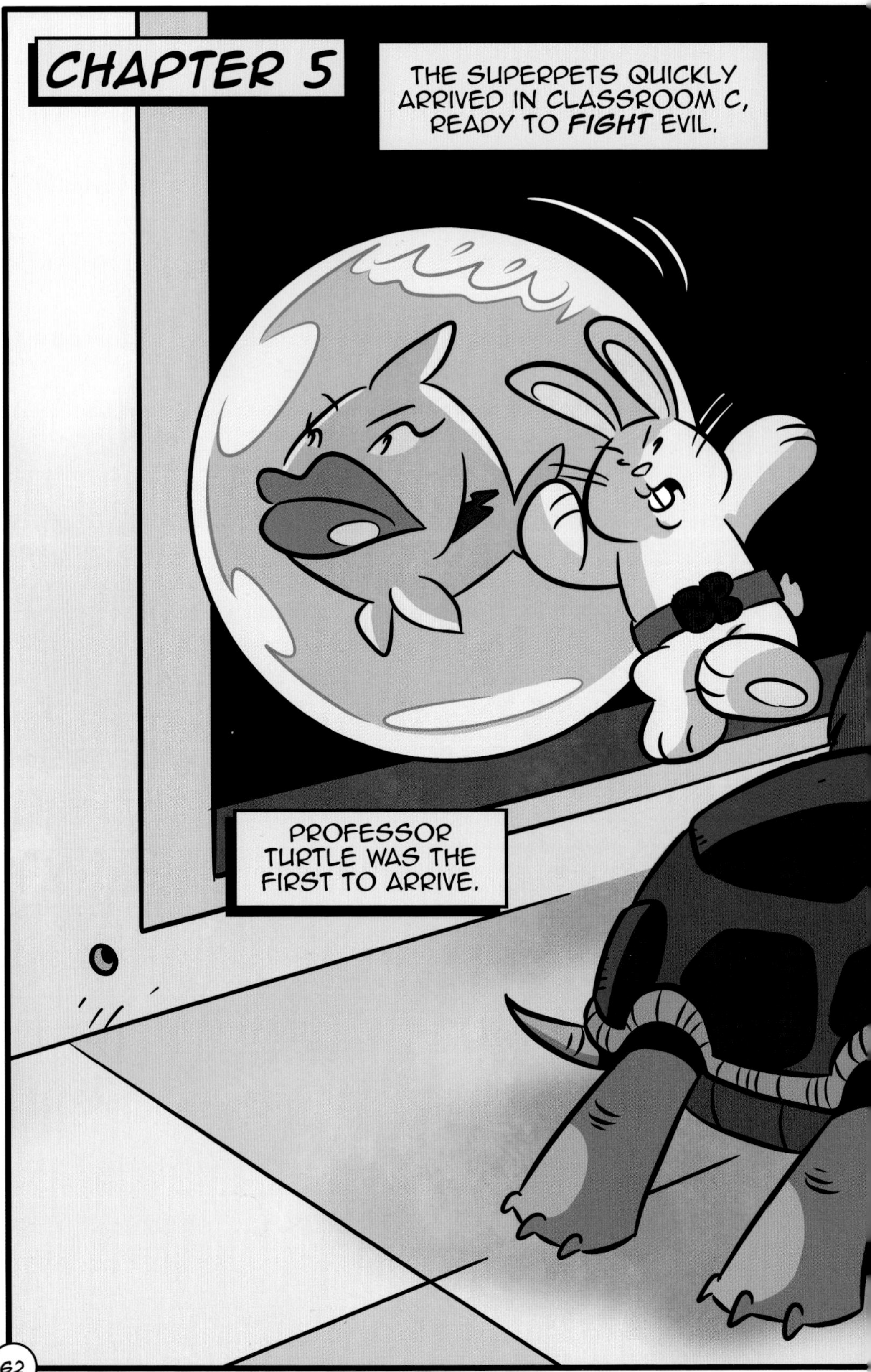
CHAPTER 5
THE SUPERPETS QUICKLY ARRIVED IN CLASSROOM C, READY TO FIGHT EVIL.
PROFESSOR TURTLE WAS THE FIRST TO ARRIVE.

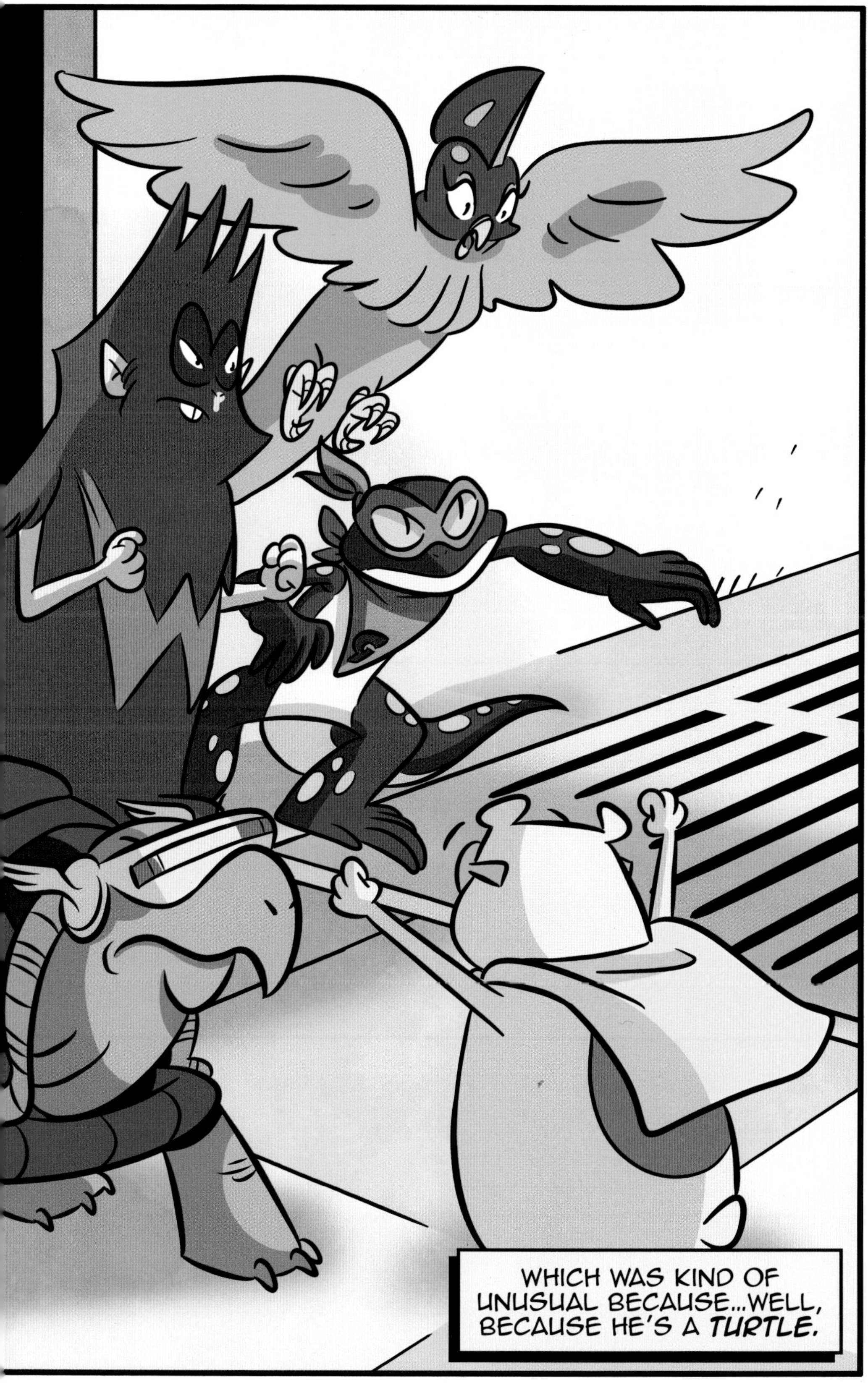
WHICH WAS KIND OF UNUSUAL BECAUSE...WELL, BECAUSE HE'S A *TURTLE.*

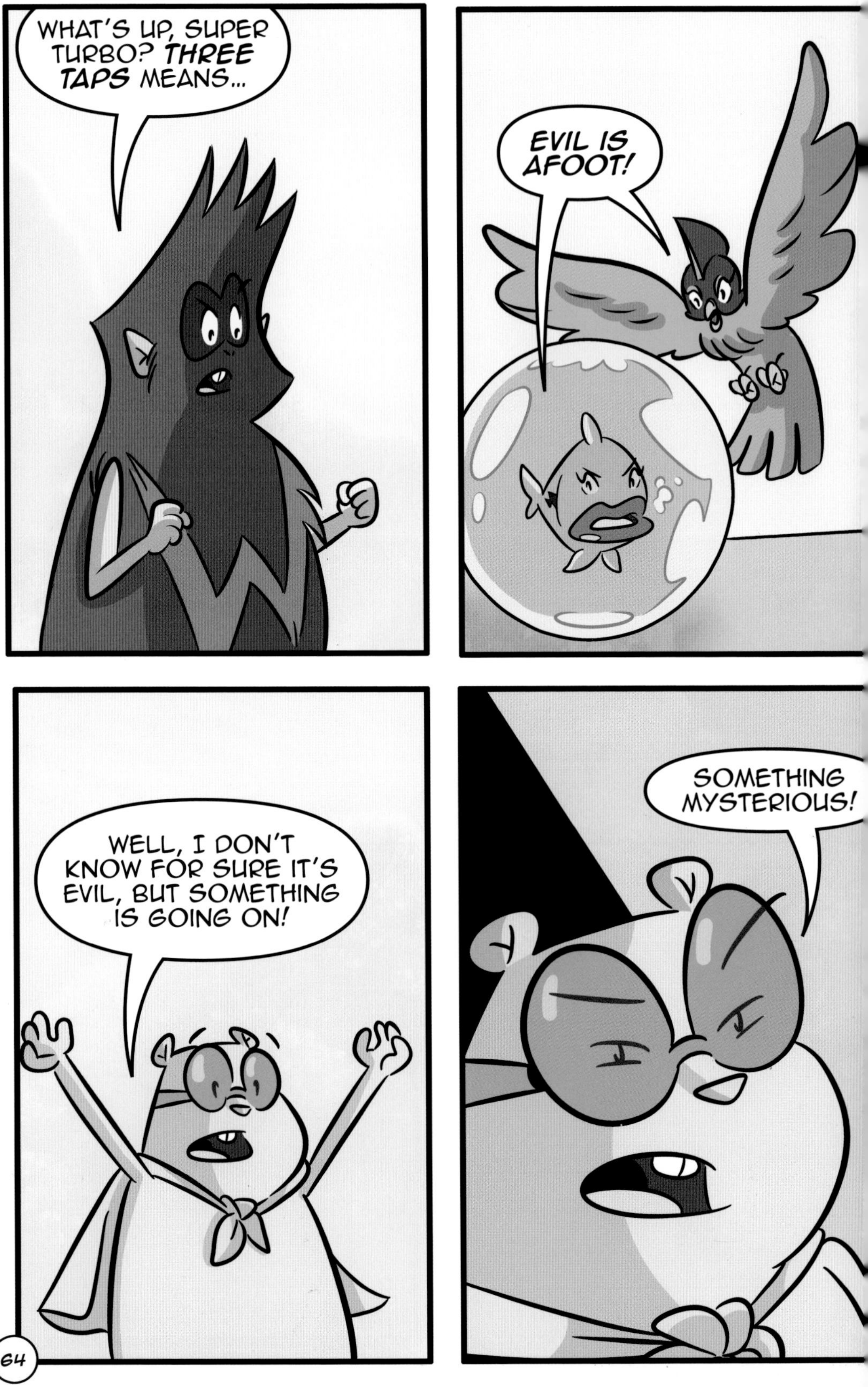
WHAT'S UP, SUPER TURBO? THREE TAPS MEANS...
EVIL IS AFOOT!
WELL, I DON'T KNOW FOR SURE IT'S EVIL, BUT SOMETHING IS GOING ON!
SOMETHING MYSTERIOUS!

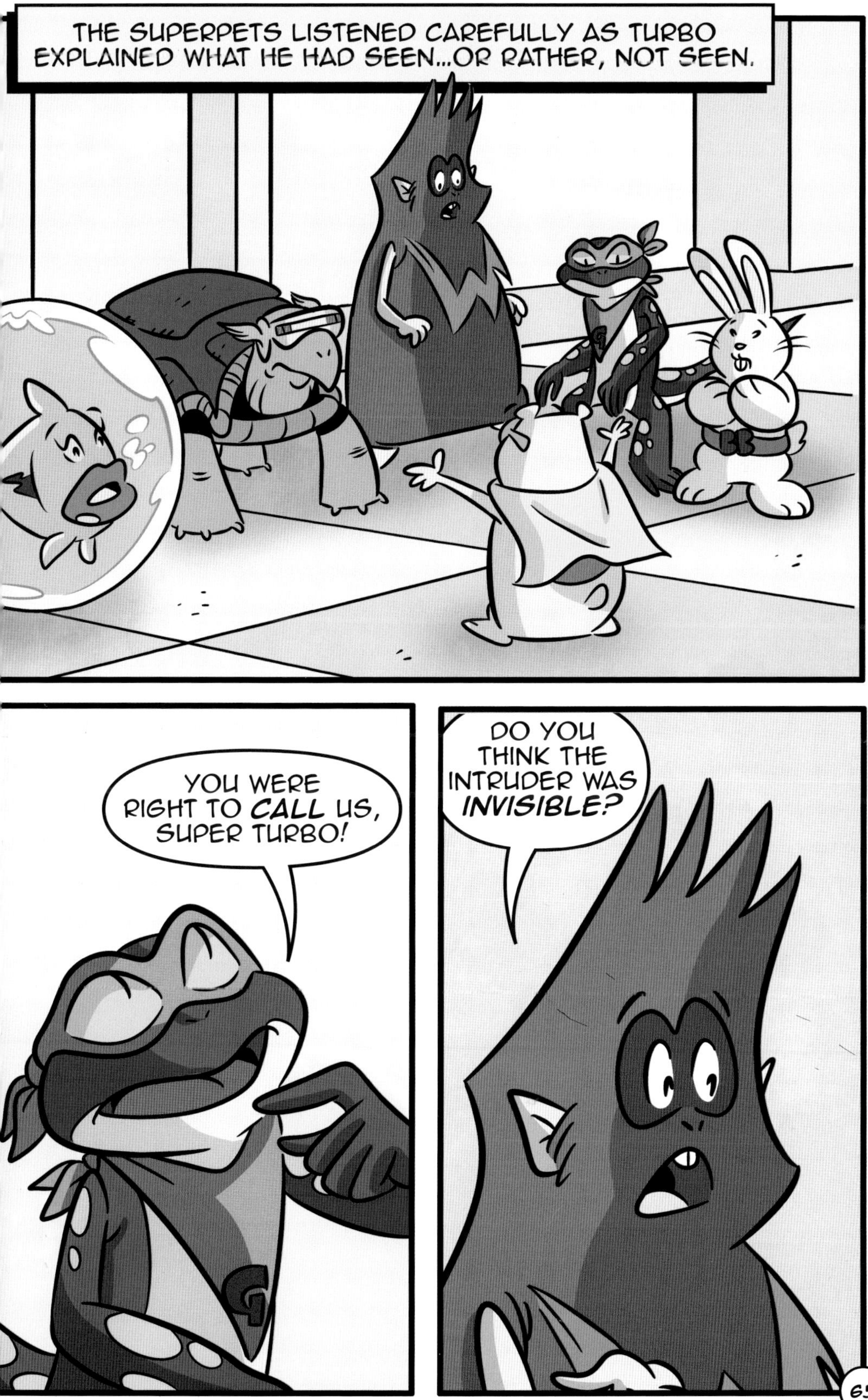
THE SUPERPETS LISTENED CAREFULLY AS TURBO EXPLAINED WHAT HE HAD SEEN...OR RATHER, NOT SEEN.
YOU WERE RIGHT TO *CALL* US, SUPER TURBO!
DO YOU THINK THE INTRUDER WAS *INVISIBLE?*

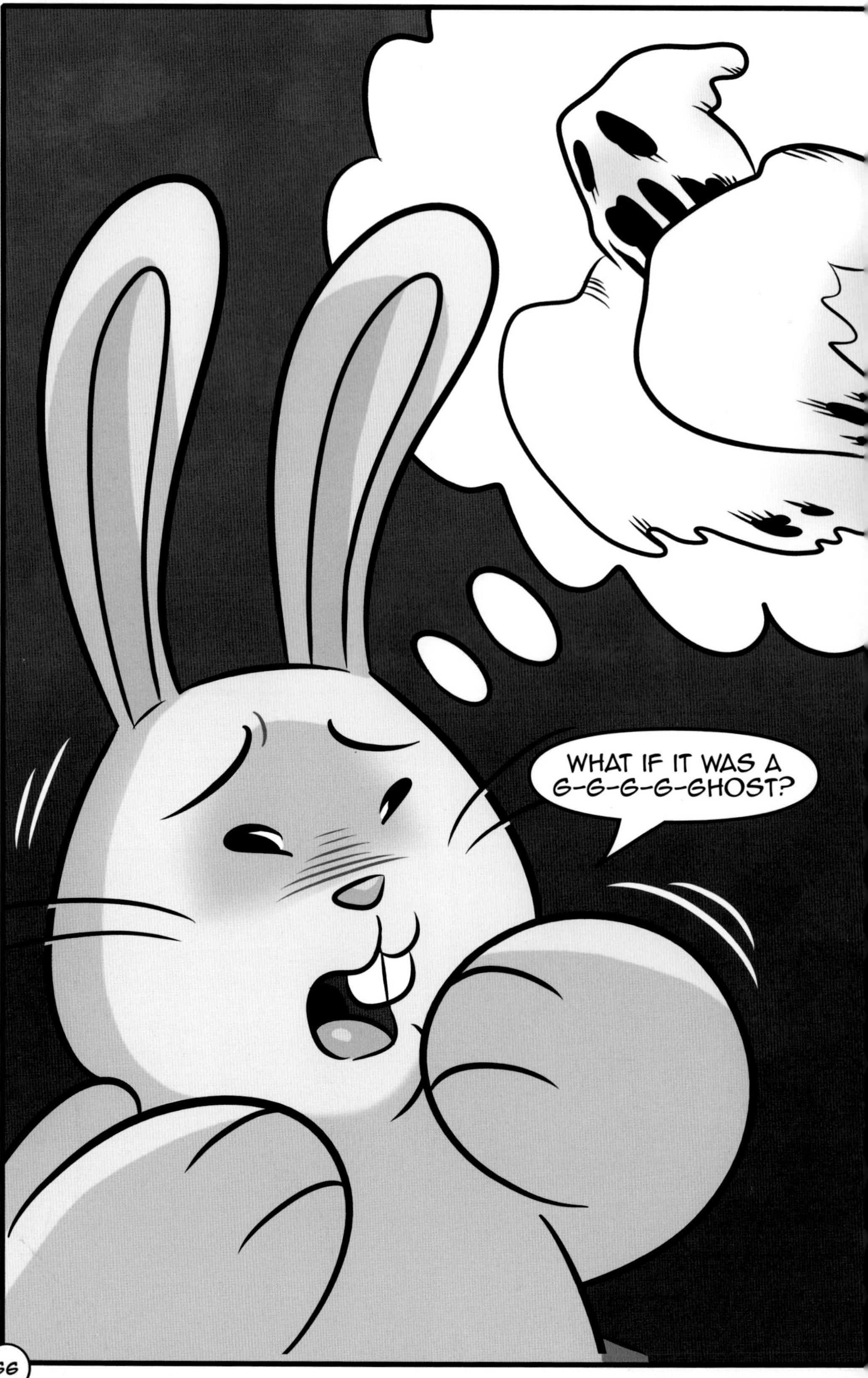
WHAT IF IT WAS A G-G-G-G-GHOST?

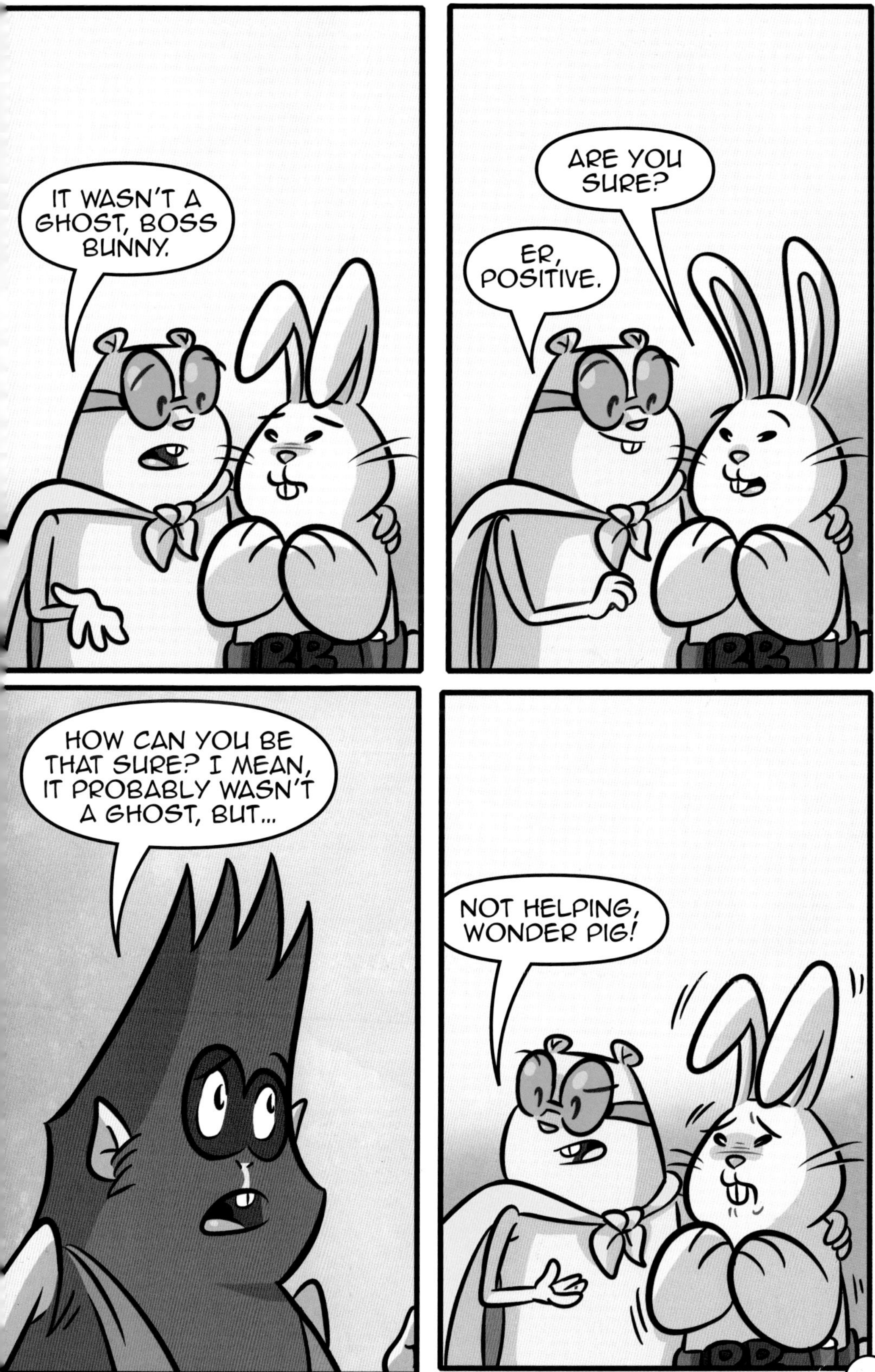
IT WASN'T A GHOST, BOSS BUNNY.
ER, POSITIVE.
ARE YOU SURE?
HOW CAN YOU BE THAT SURE? I MEAN, IT PROBABLY WASN'T A GHOST, BUT...
NOT HELPING, WONDER PIG!

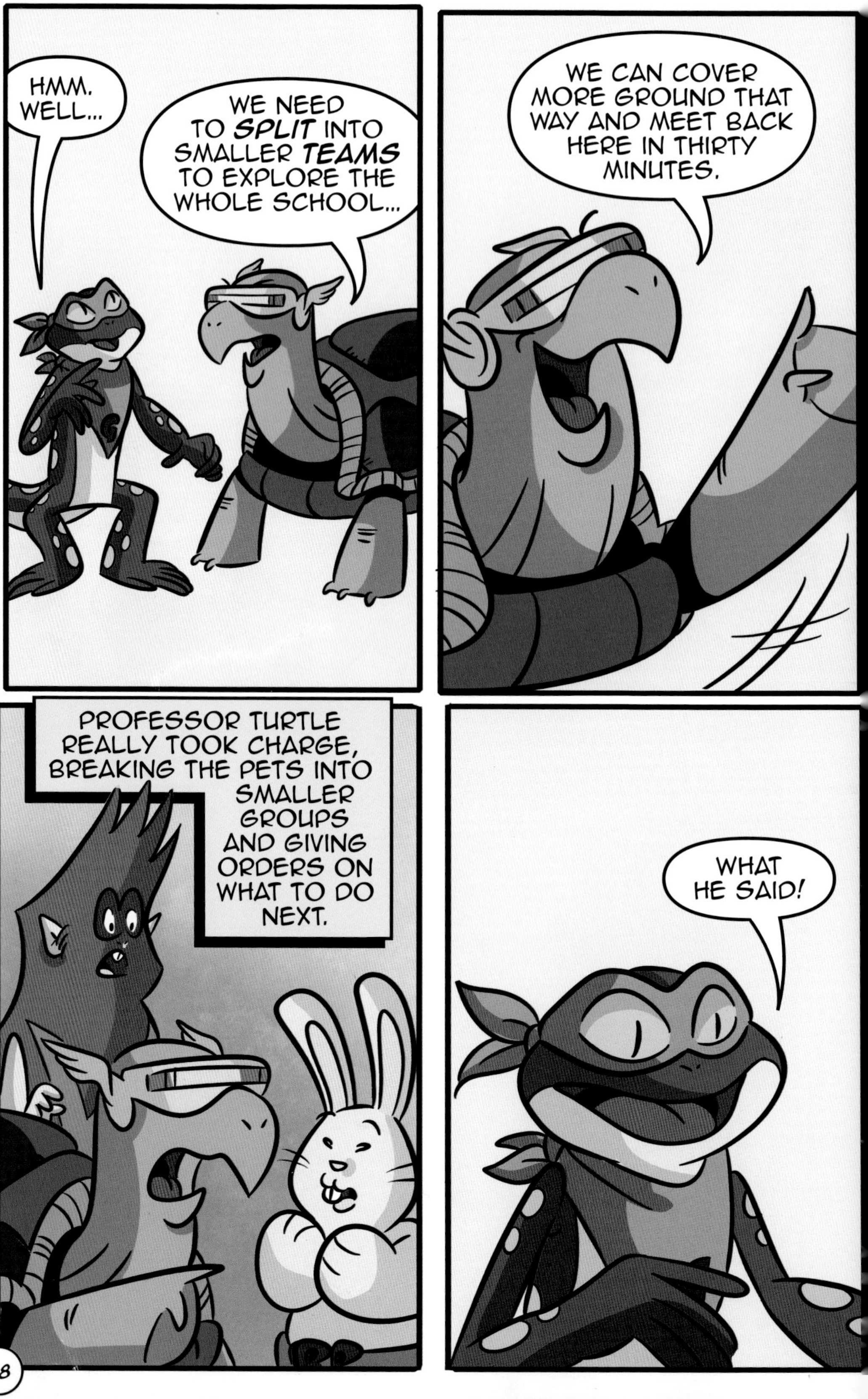
HMM. WELL...
WE NEED TO SPLIT INTO SMALLER TEAMS TO EXPLORE THE WHOLE SCHOOL...
WE CAN COVER MORE GROUND THAT WAY AND MEET BACK HERE IN THIRTY MINUTES.
PROFESSOR TURTLE REALLY TOOK CHARGE, BREAKING THE PETS INTO SMALLER GROUPS AND GIVING ORDERS ON WHAT TO DO NEXT.
WHAT HE SAID!

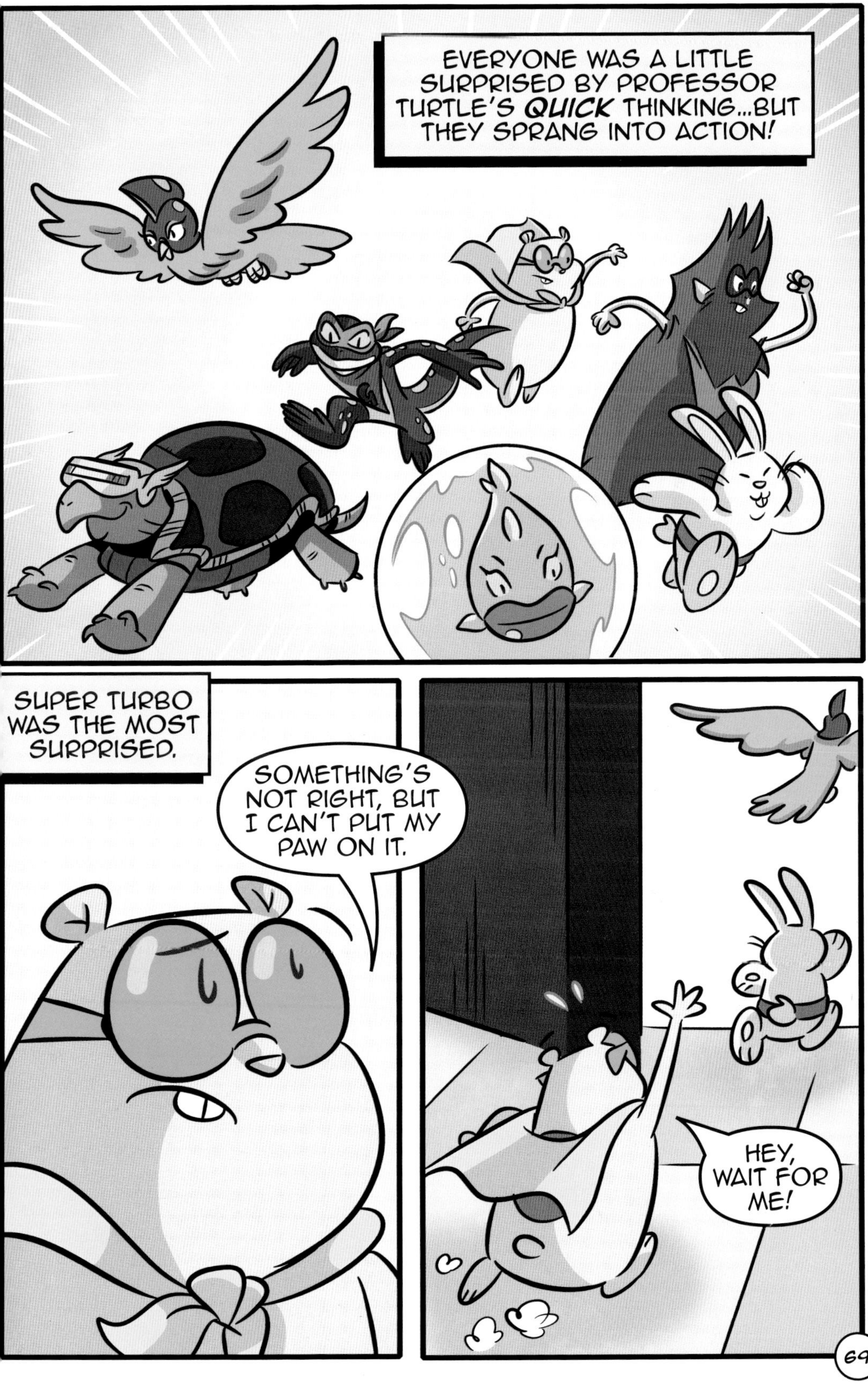
EVERYONE WAS A LITTLE SURPRISED BY PROFESSOR TURTLE'S QUICK THINKING...BUT THEY SPRANG INTO ACTION!
SUPER TURBO WAS THE MOST SURPRISED.
SOMETHING'S NOT RIGHT, BUT I CAN'T PUT MY PAW ON IT.
HEY, WAIT FOR ME!

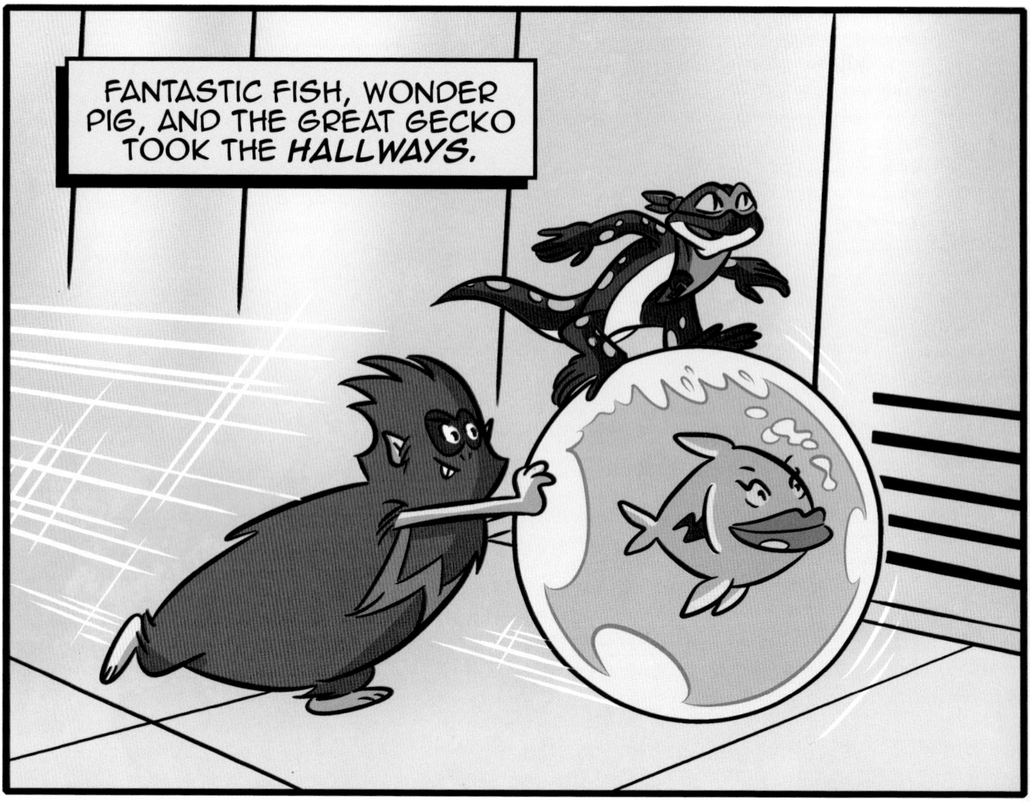
FANTASTIC FISH, WONDER PIG, AND THE GREAT GECKO TOOK THE *HALLWAYS.*

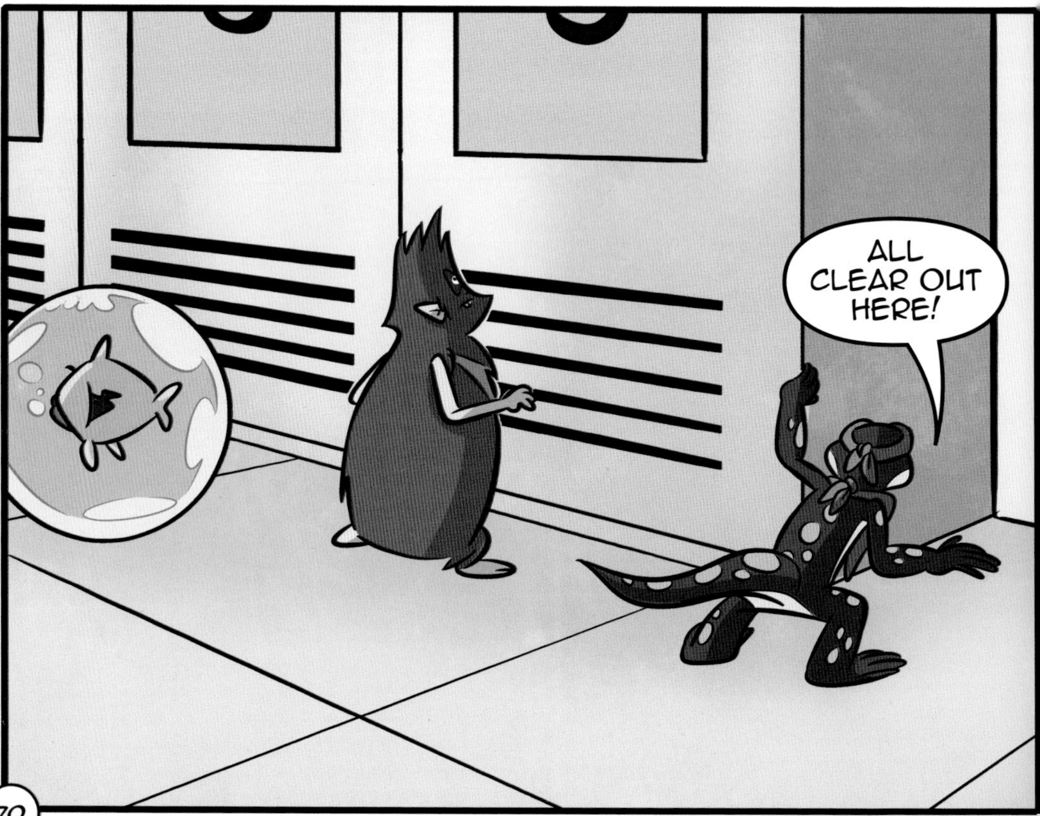
ALL CLEAR OUT HERE!

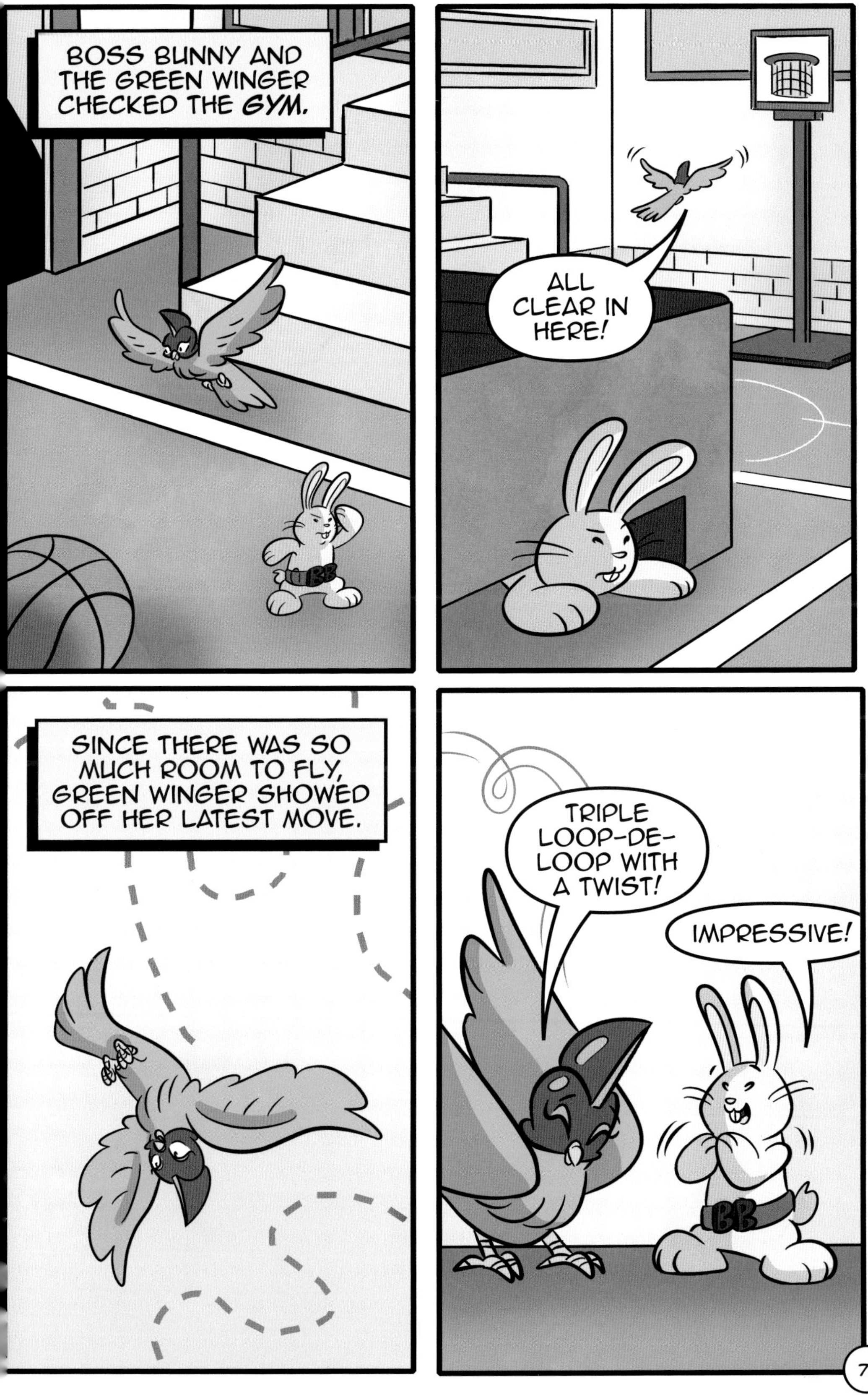
BOSS BUNNY AND THE GREEN WINGER CHECKED THE GYM.
ALL CLEAR IN HERE!
SINCE THERE WAS SO MUCH ROOM TO FLY, GREEN WINGER SHOWED OFF HER LATEST MOVE.
TRIPLE LOOP-DE-LOOP WITH A TWIST!
IMPRESSIVE!

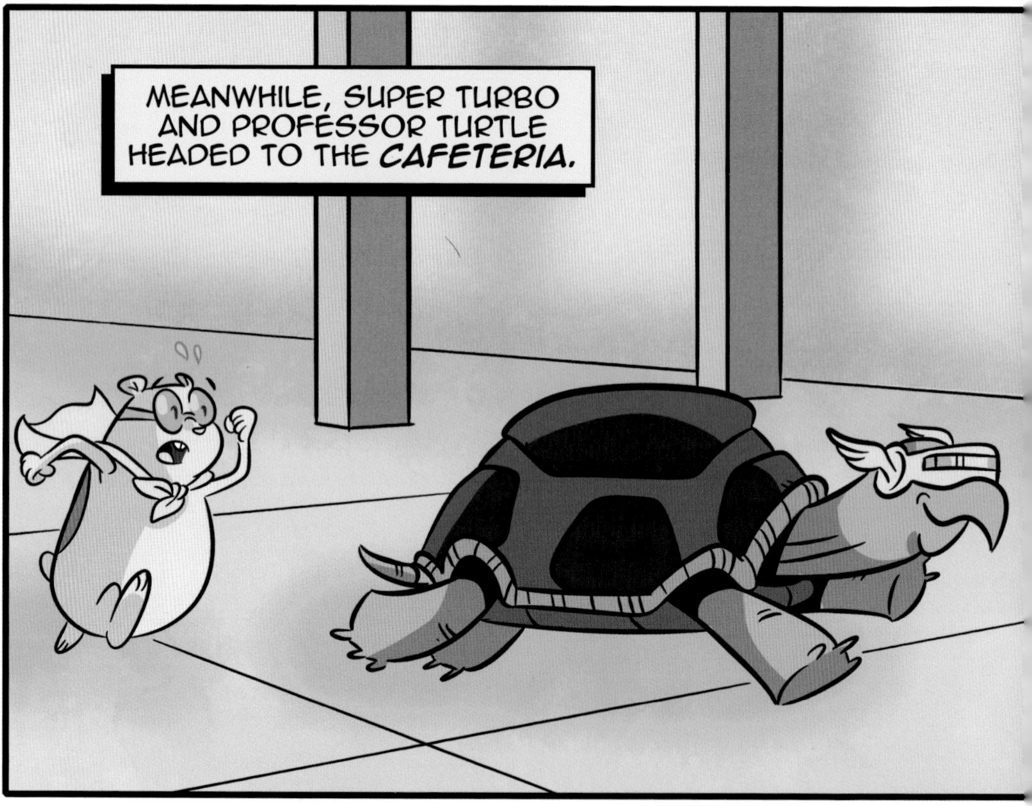
MEANWHILE, SUPER TURBO AND PROFESSOR TURTLE HEADED TO THE CAFETERIA.

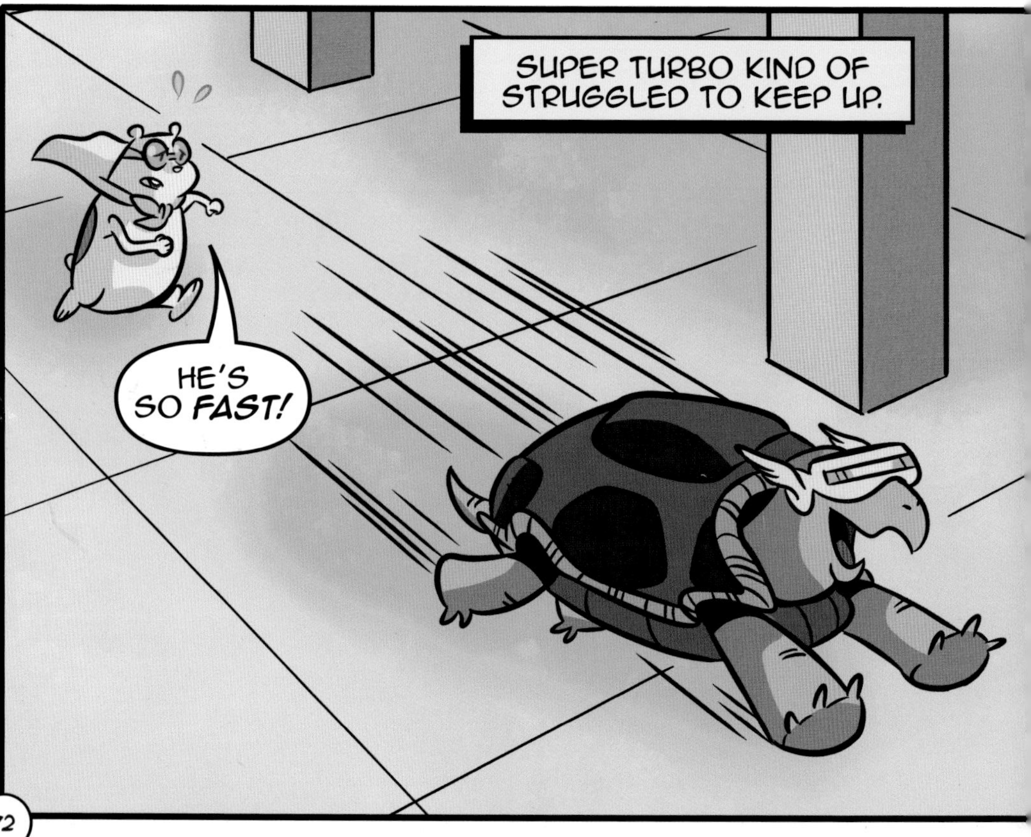
SUPER TURBO KIND OF STRUGGLED TO KEEP UP.
HE'S SO FAST!

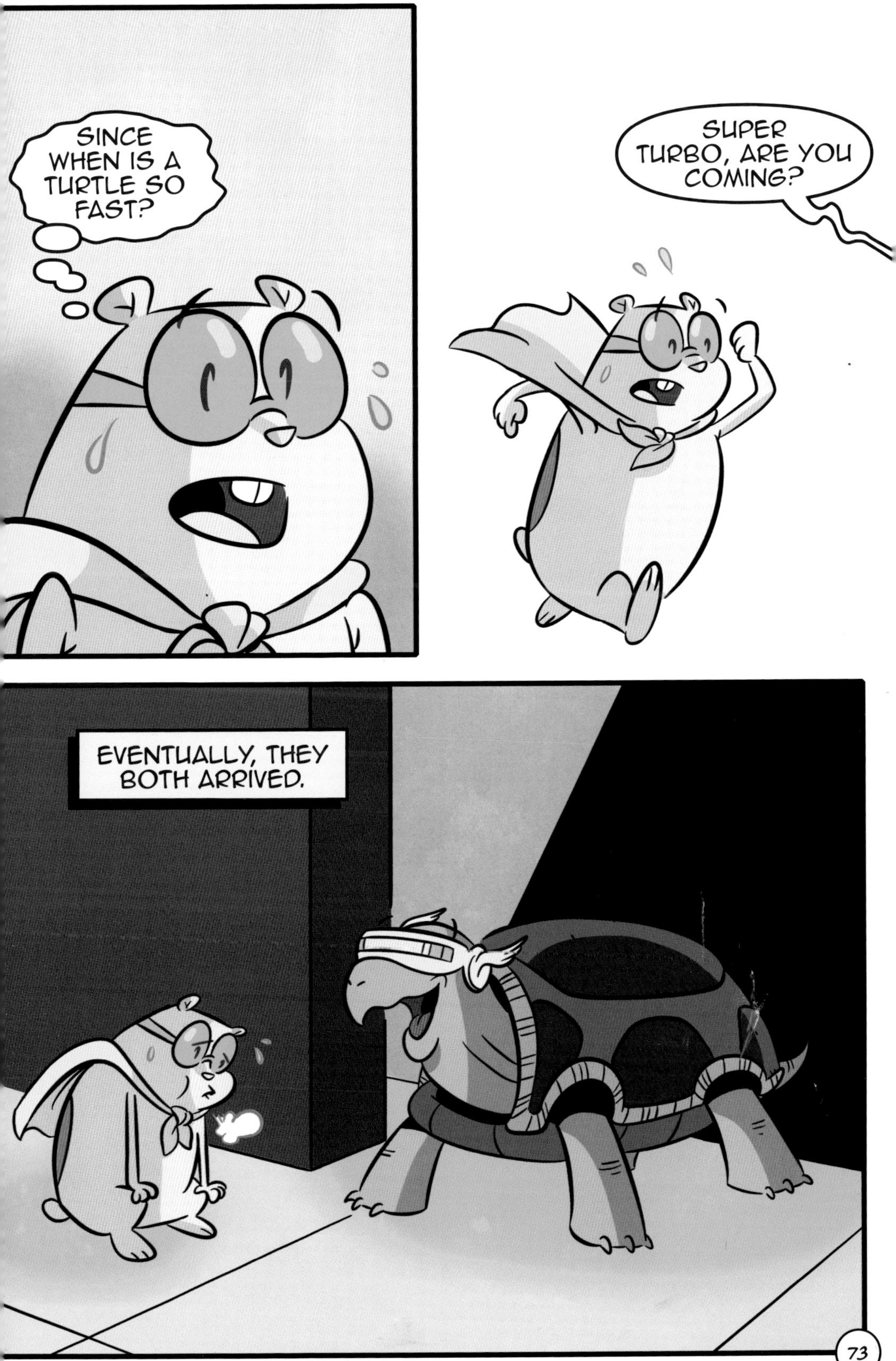
SINCE WHEN IS A TURTLE SO FAST?
SUPER TURBO, ARE YOU COMING?
EVENTUALLY, THEY BOTH ARRIVED.

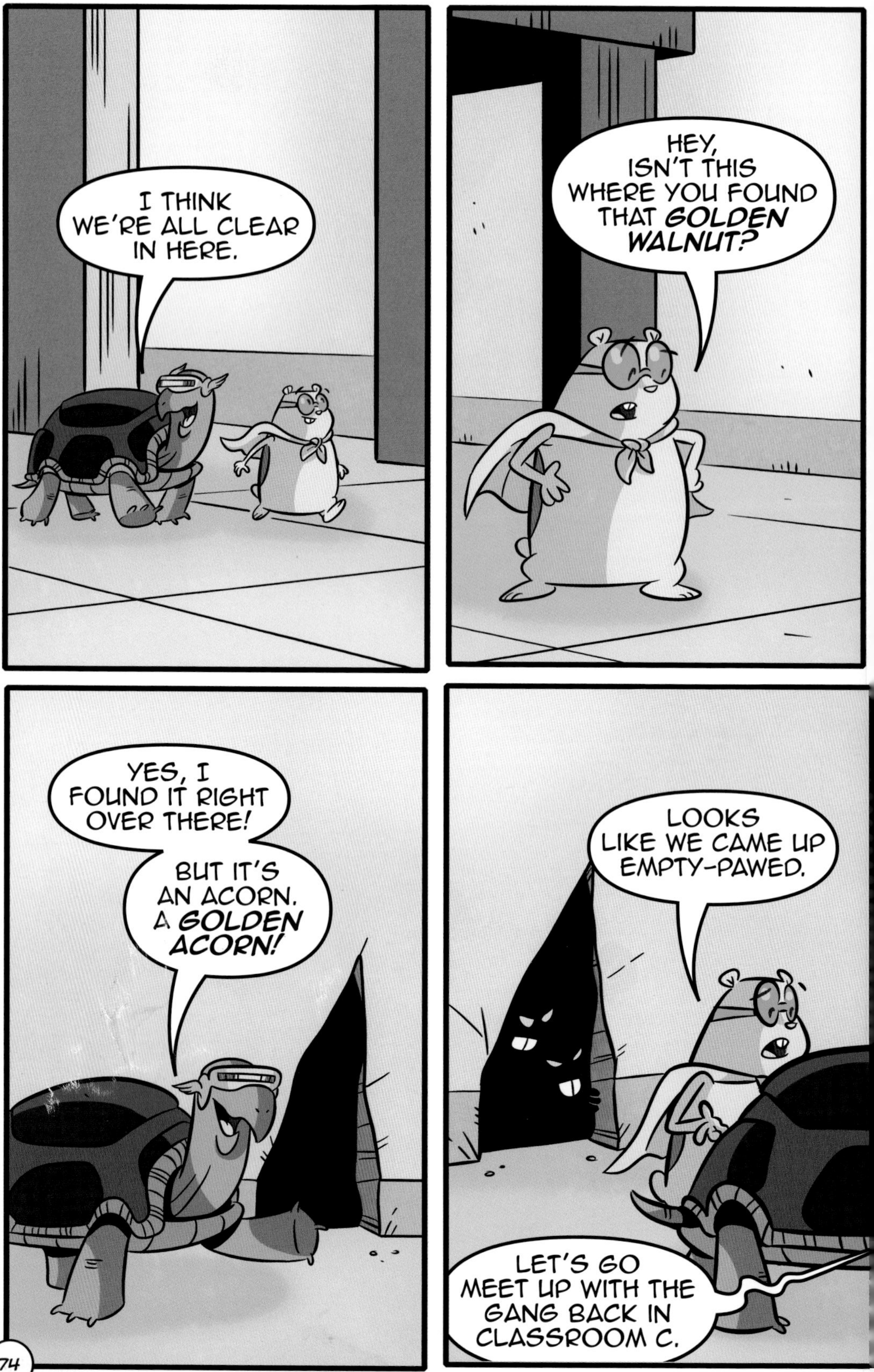
I THINK WE'RE ALL CLEAR IN HERE.
HEY, ISN'T THIS WHERE YOU FOUND THAT *GOLDEN WALNUT?*
YES, I FOUND IT RIGHT OVER THERE!
BUT IT'S AN ACORN. A *GOLDEN ACORN!*
LOOKS LIKE WE CAME UP EMPTY-PAWED.
LET'S GO MEET UP WITH THE GANG BACK IN CLASSROOM C.

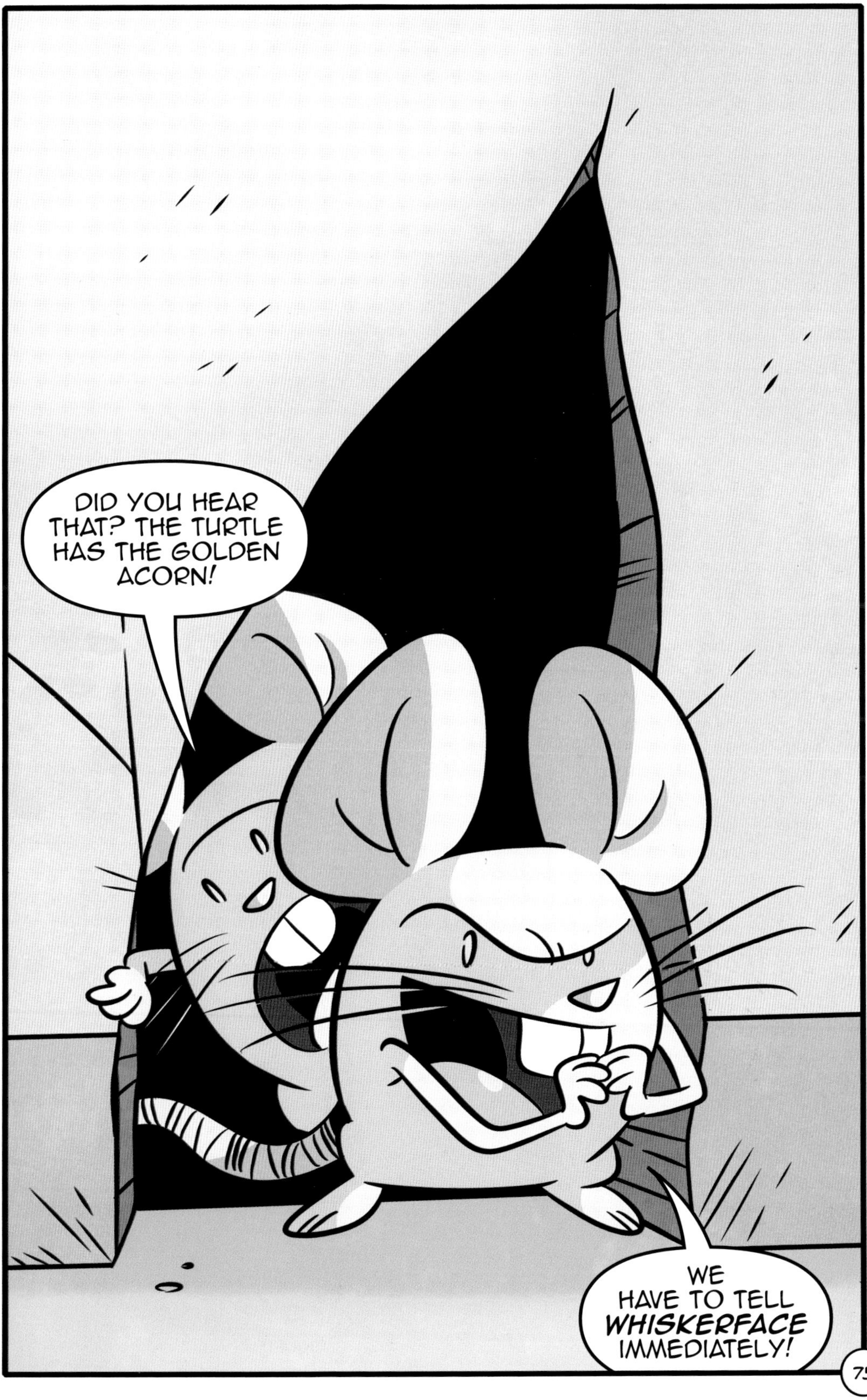
DID YOU HEAR THAT? THE TURTLE HAS THE GOLDEN ACORN!
WE HAVE TO TELL *WHISKERFACE* IMMEDIATELY!

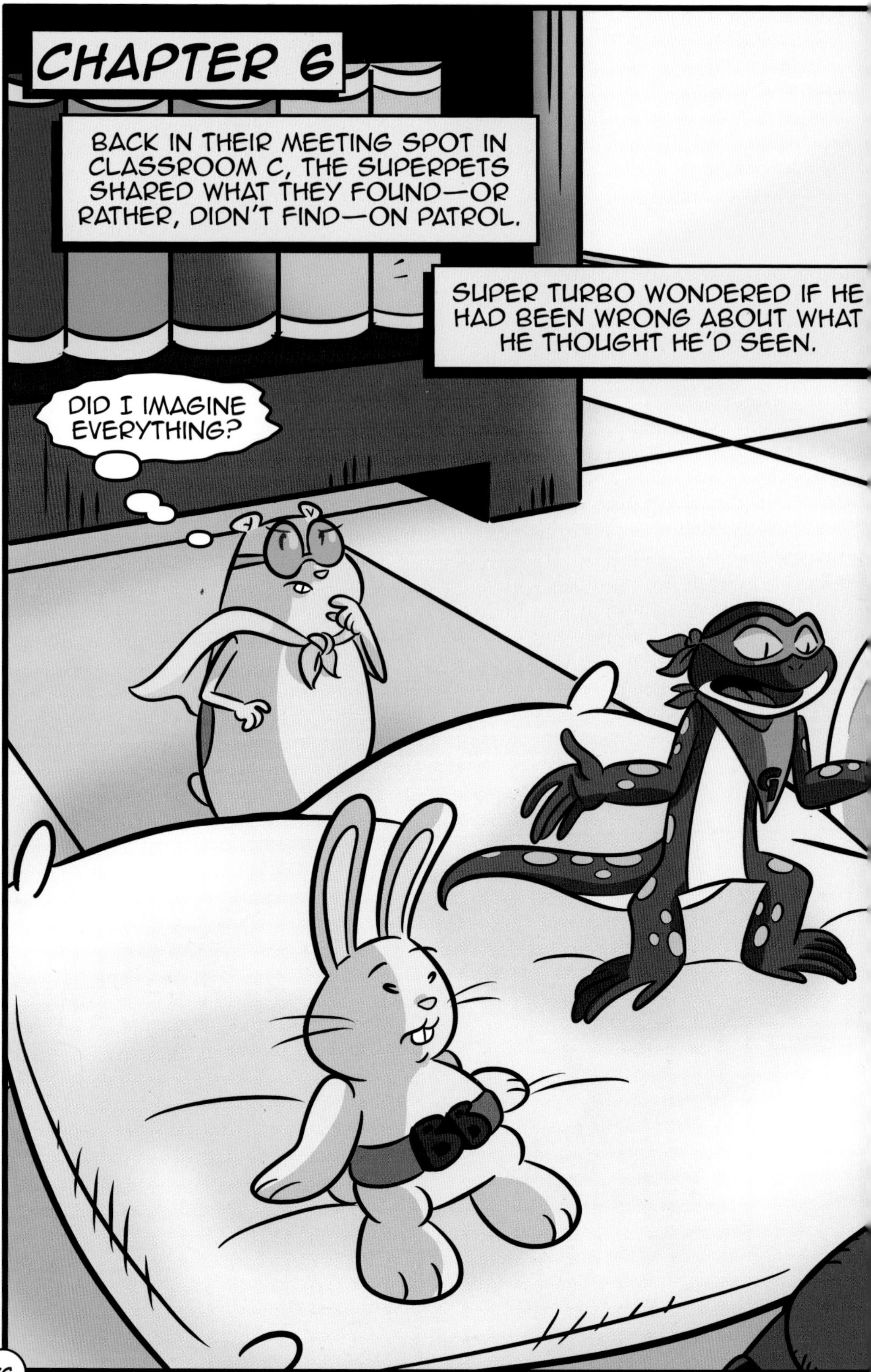
CHAPTER 6
BACK IN THEIR MEETING SPOT IN CLASSROOM C, THE SUPERPETS SHARED WHAT THEY FOUND—OR RATHER, DIDN'T FIND—ON PATROL.
SUPER TURBO WONDERED IF HE HAD BEEN WRONG ABOUT WHAT HE THOUGHT HE'D SEEN.
DID I IMAGINE EVERYTHING?

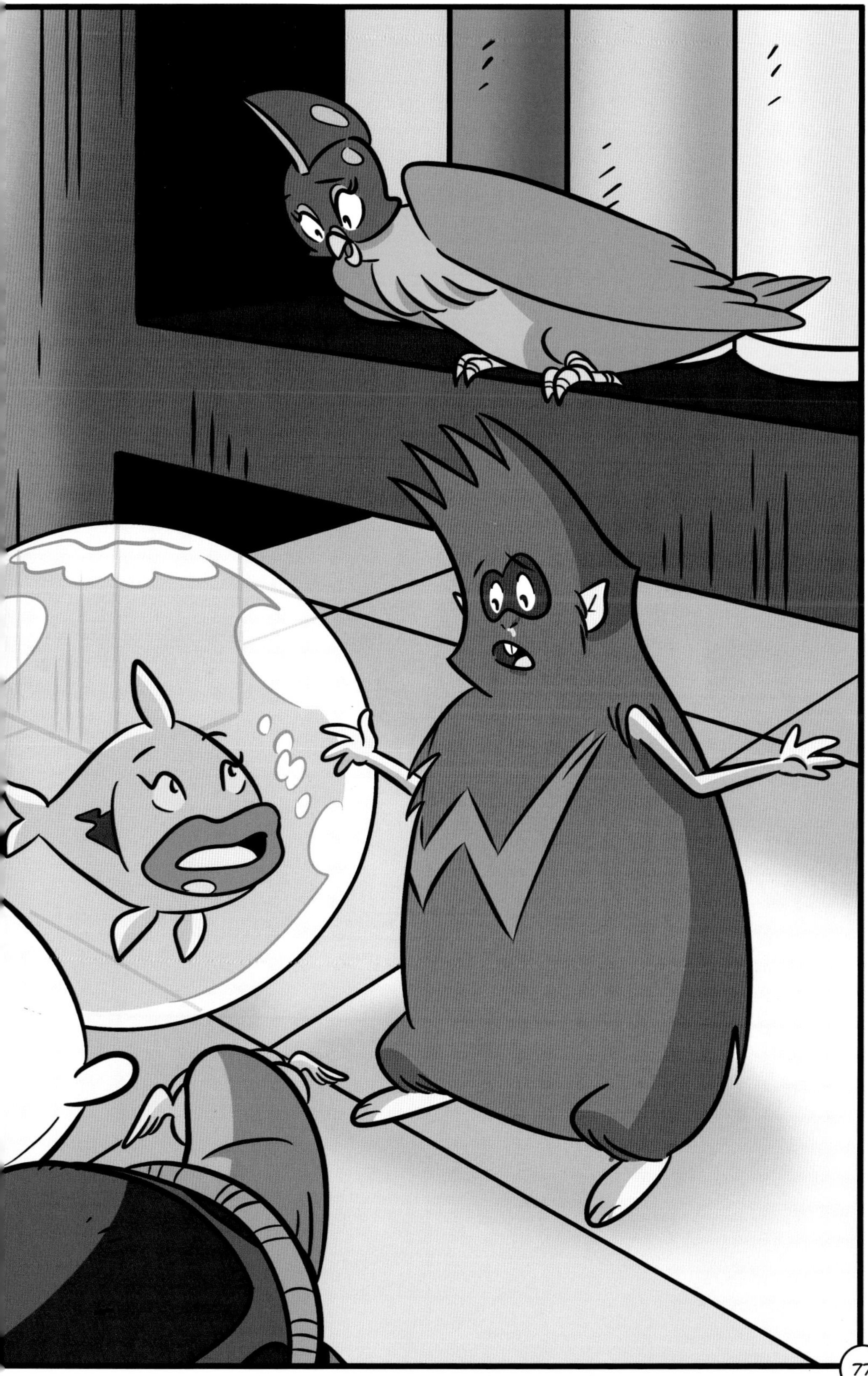

BUT THEN SOMETHING HAPPENED.

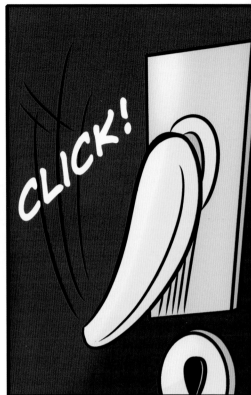

CLICK!

LOOK!

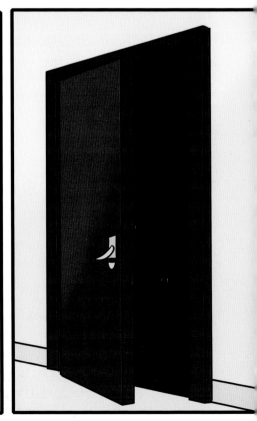

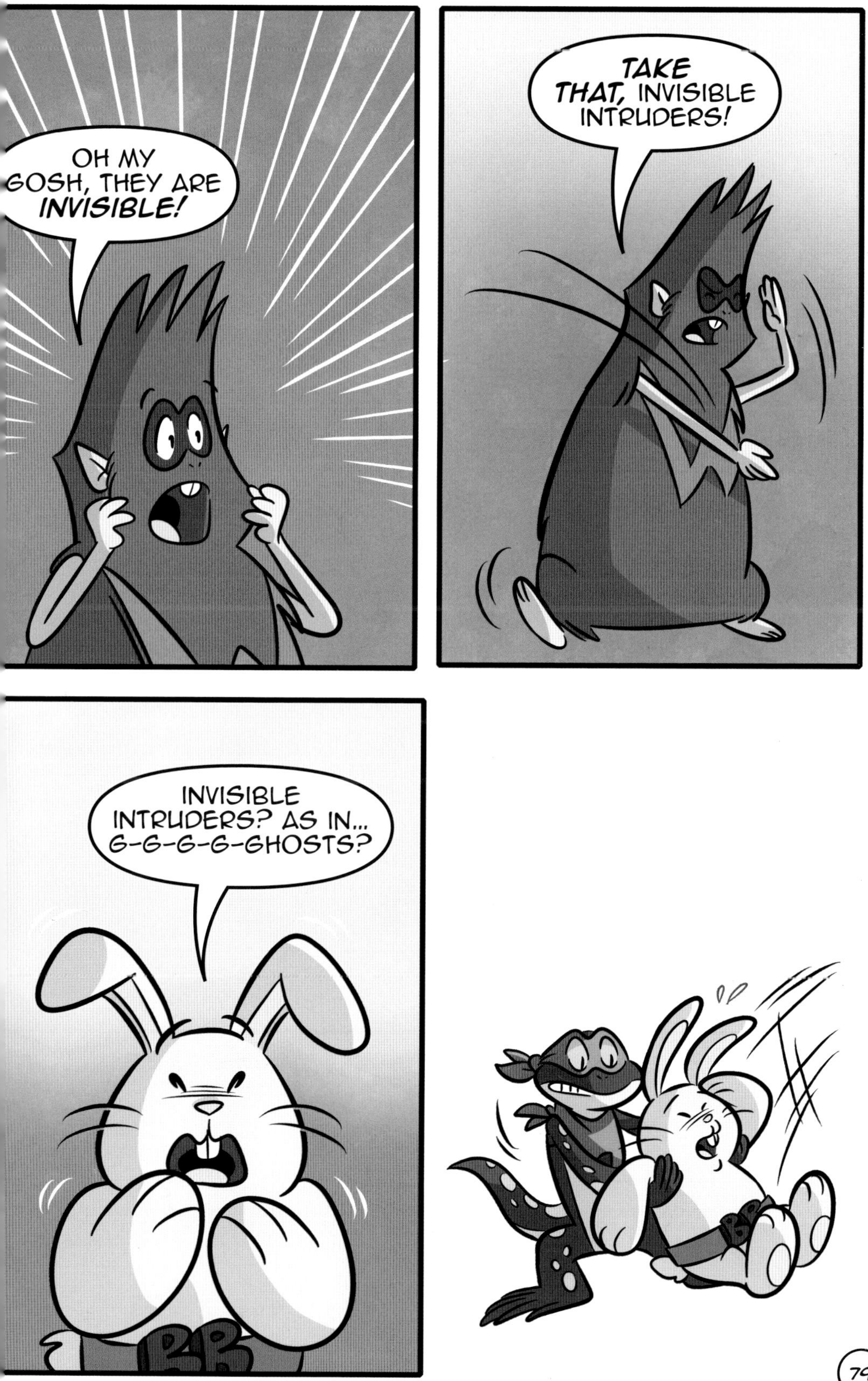
OH MY GOSH, THEY ARE *INVISIBLE!*
TAKE THAT, INVISIBLE INTRUDERS!
INVISIBLE INTRUDERS? AS IN... G-G-G-G-GHOSTS?

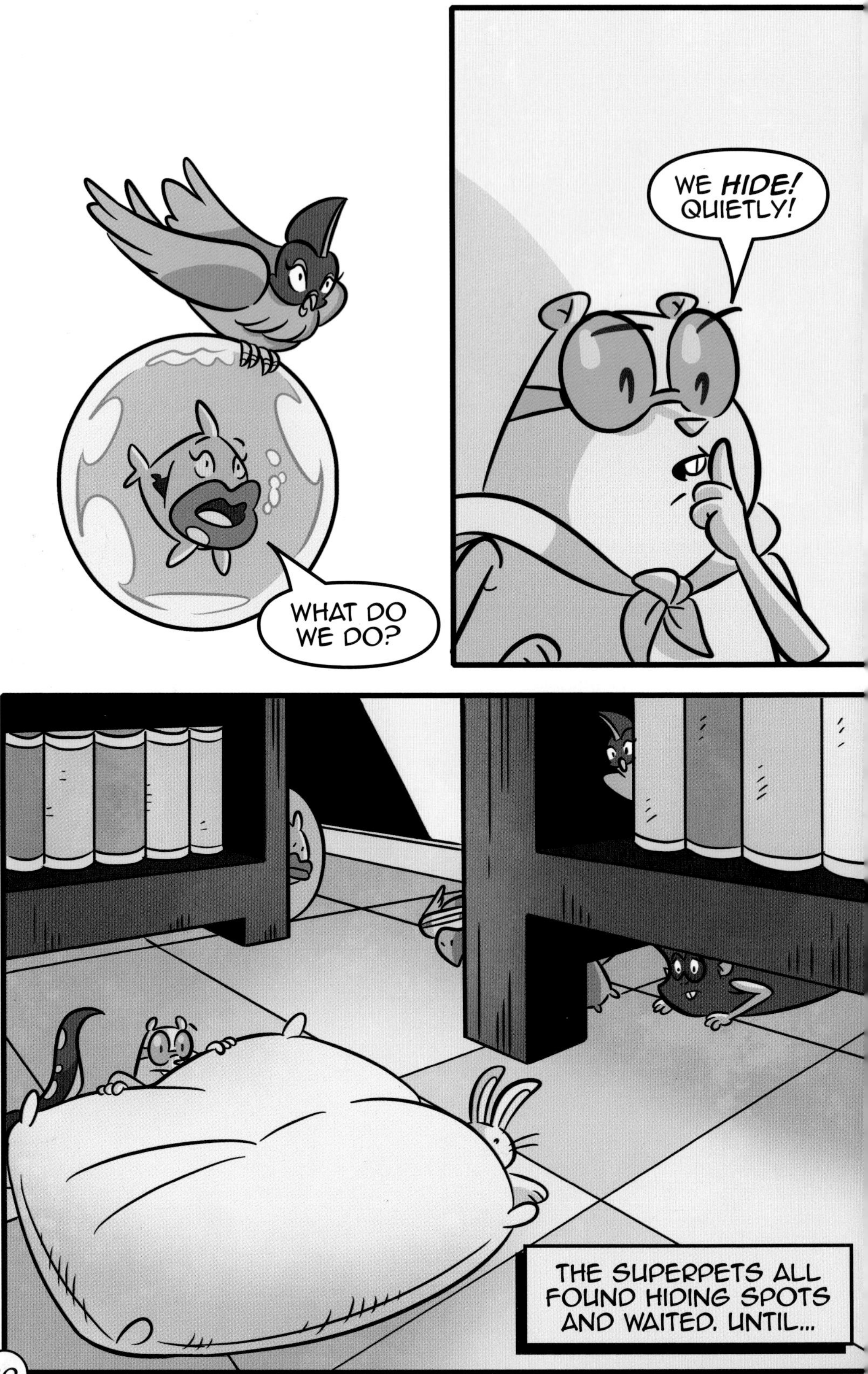
WHAT DO WE DO?
WE *HIDE!* QUIETLY!
THE SUPERPETS ALL FOUND HIDING SPOTS AND WAITED. UNTIL...

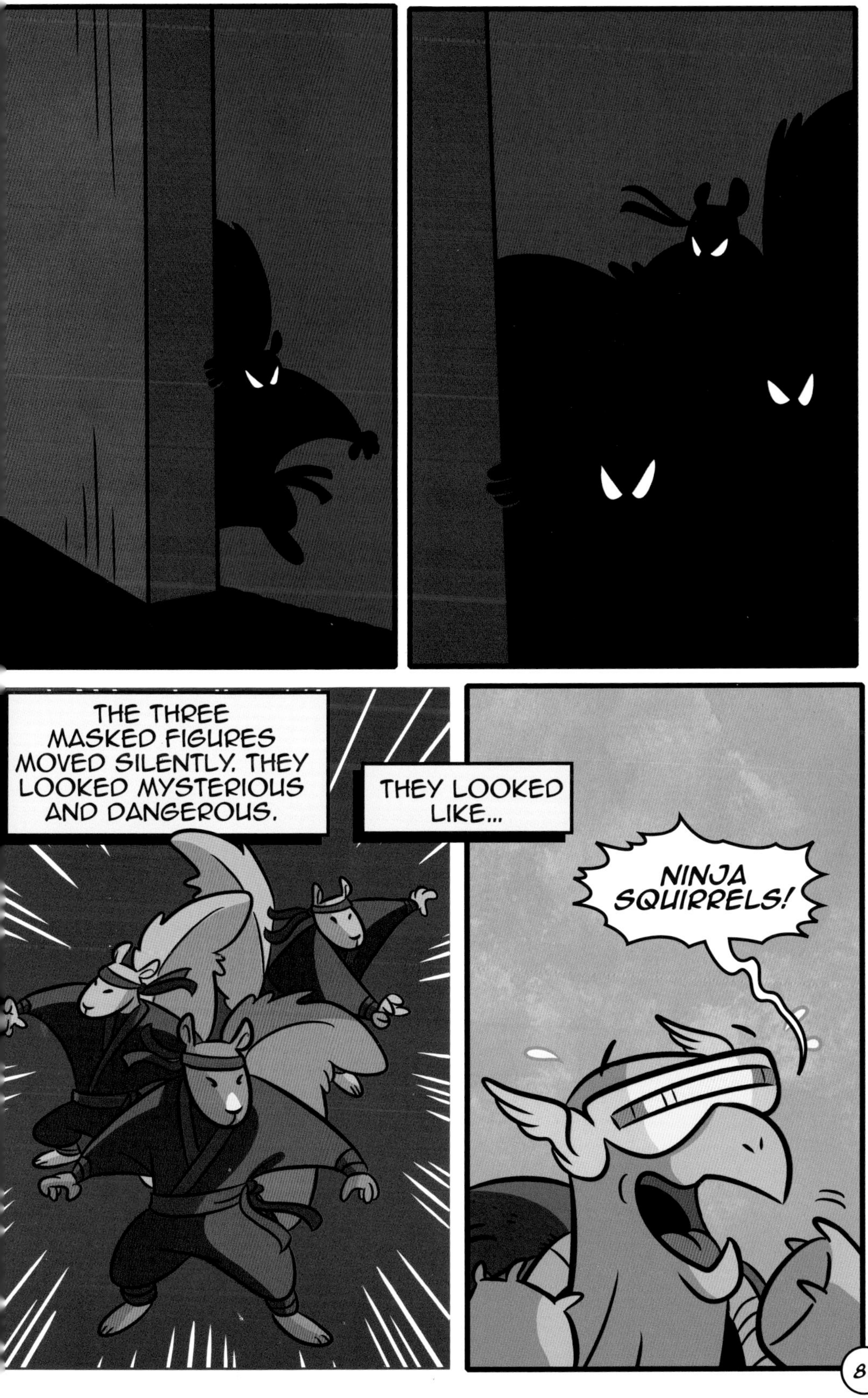
THE THREE MASKED FIGURES MOVED SILENTLY. THEY LOOKED MYSTERIOUS AND DANGEROUS.
THEY LOOKED LIKE...
NINJA SQUIRRELS!

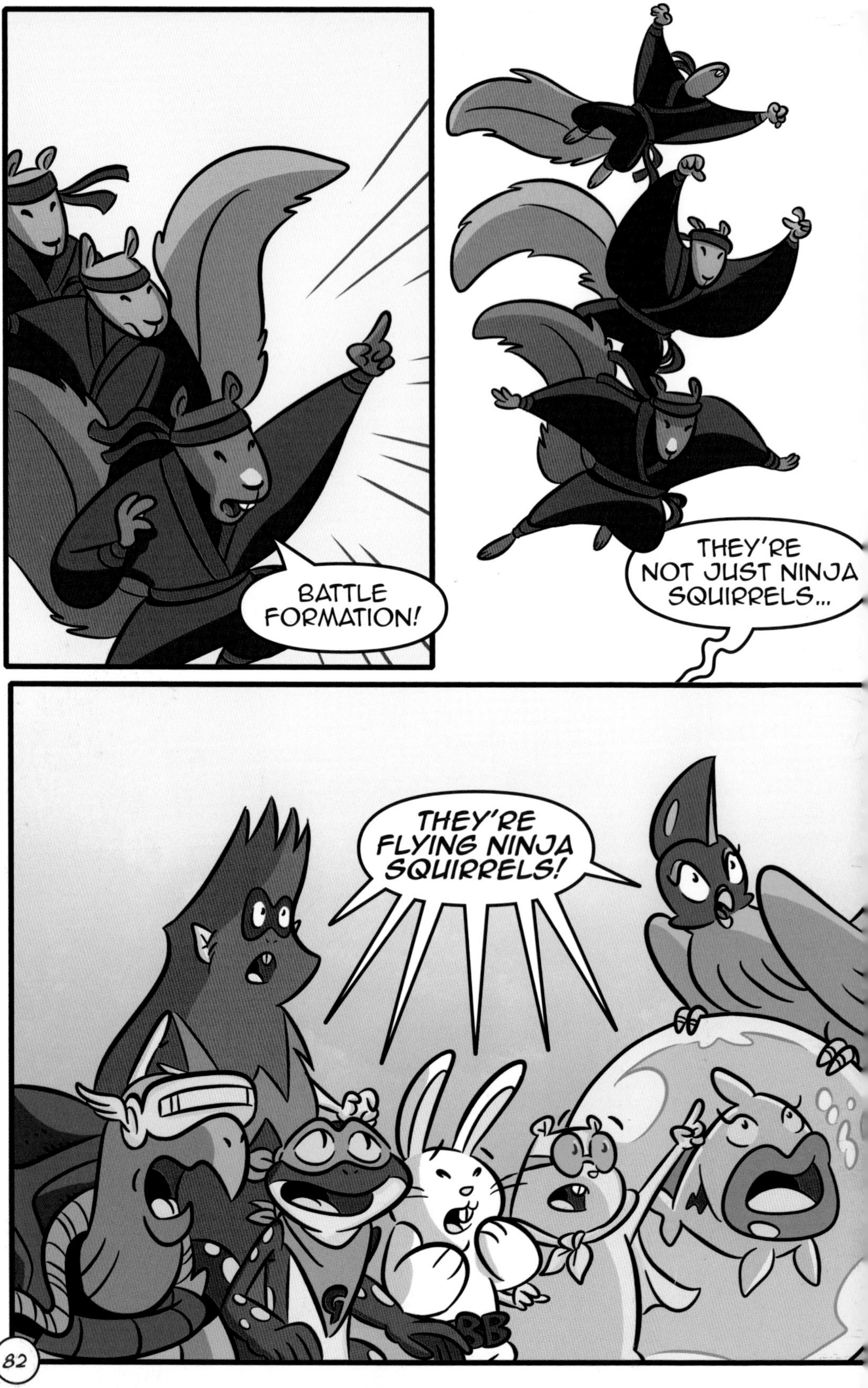
BATTLE FORMATION!
THEY'RE NOT JUST NINJA SQUIRRELS...
THEY'RE FLYING NINJA SQUIRRELS!

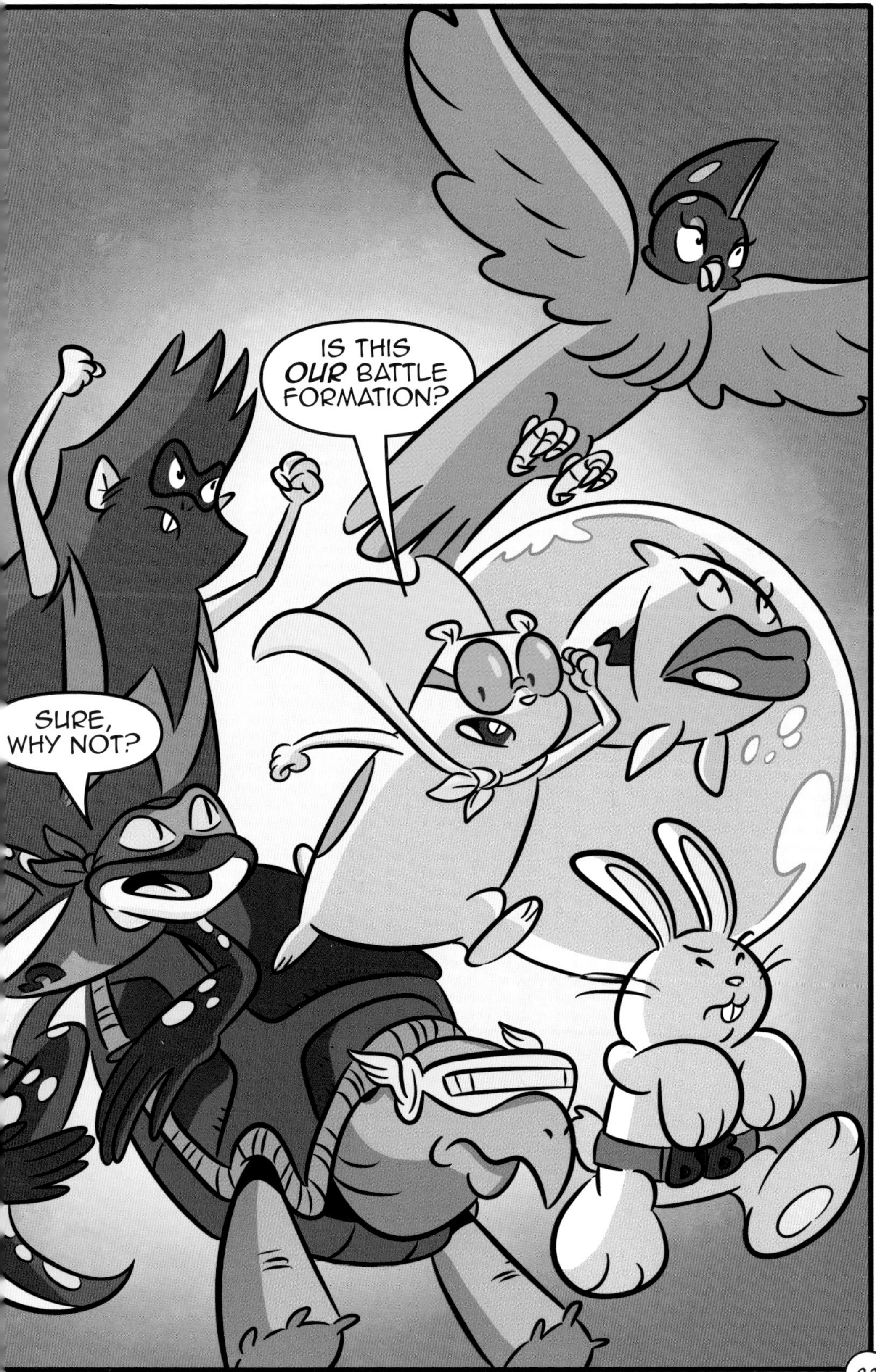
IS THIS OUR BATTLE FORMATION?
SURE, WHY NOT?

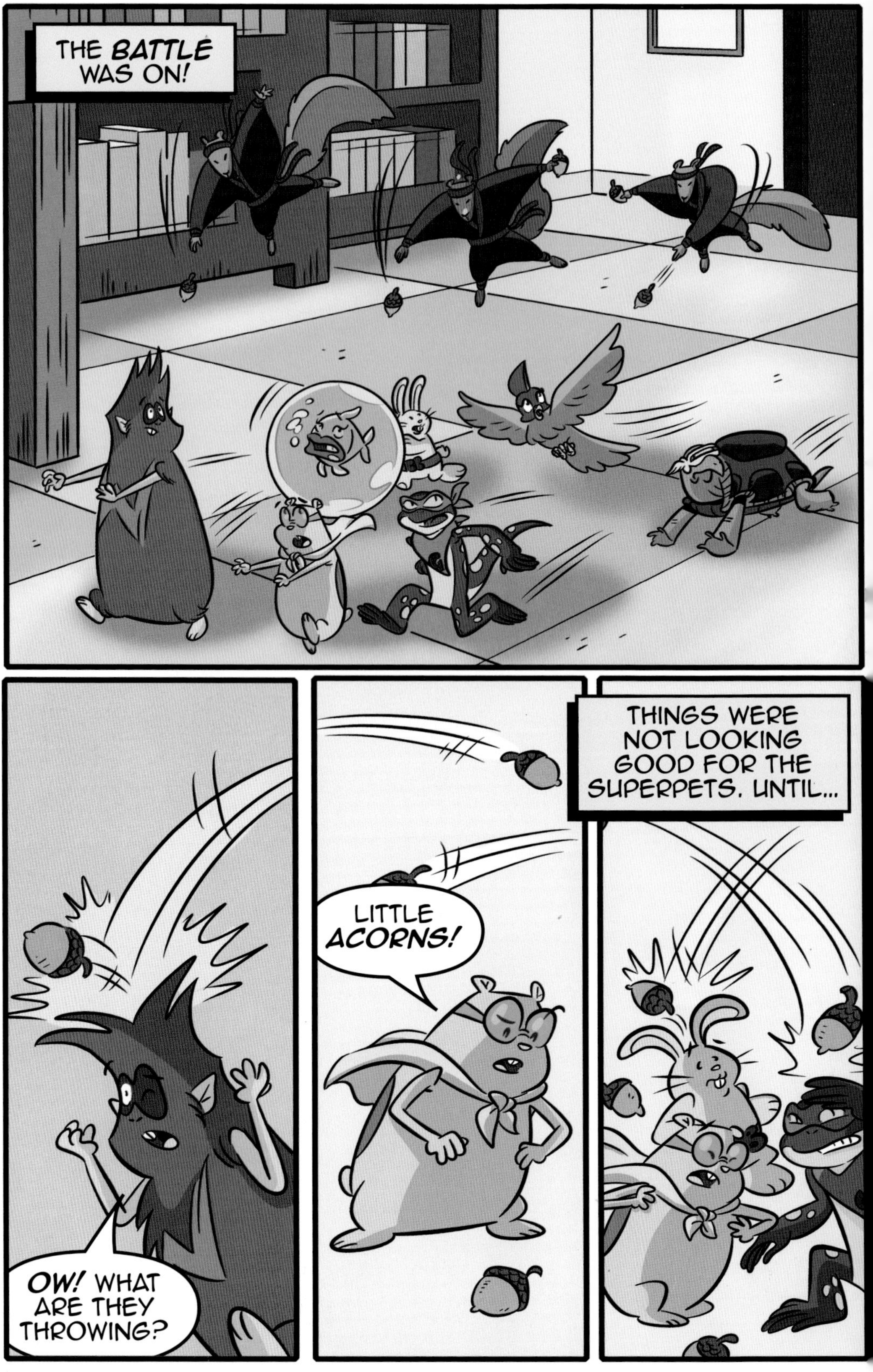
THE *BATTLE* WAS ON!
OW! WHAT ARE THEY THROWING?
LITTLE *ACORNS!*
THINGS WERE NOT LOOKING GOOD FOR THE SUPERPETS. UNTIL...

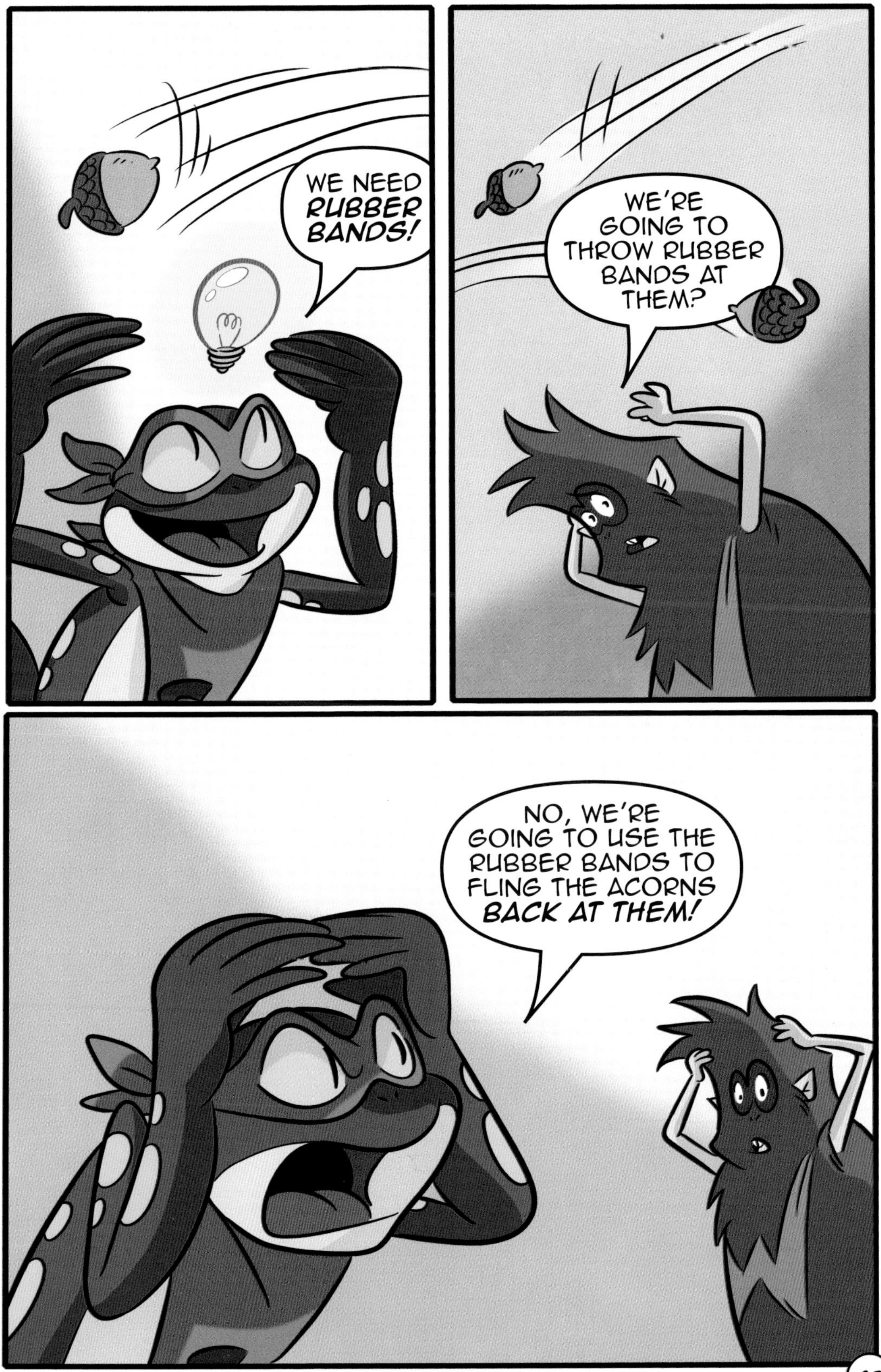
WE NEED RUBBER BANDS!
WE'RE GOING TO THROW RUBBER BANDS AT THEM?
NO, WE'RE GOING TO USE THE RUBBER BANDS TO FLING THE ACORNS BACK AT THEM!

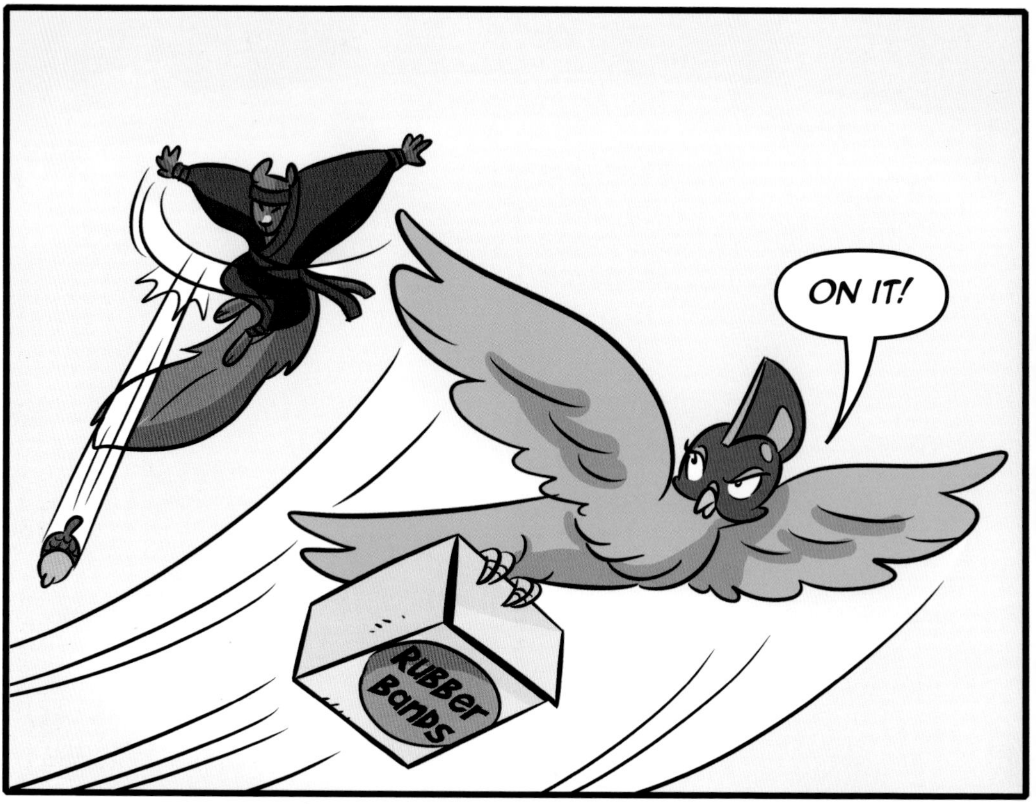
ON IT!
RUBBER BANDS

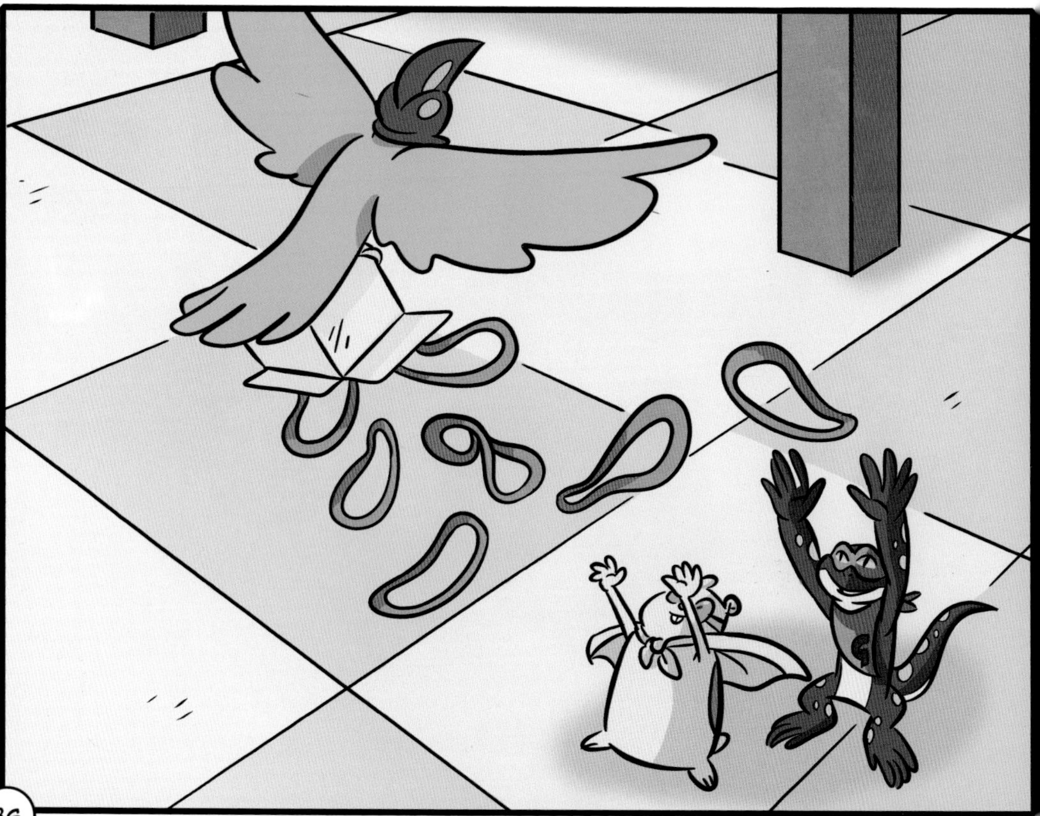

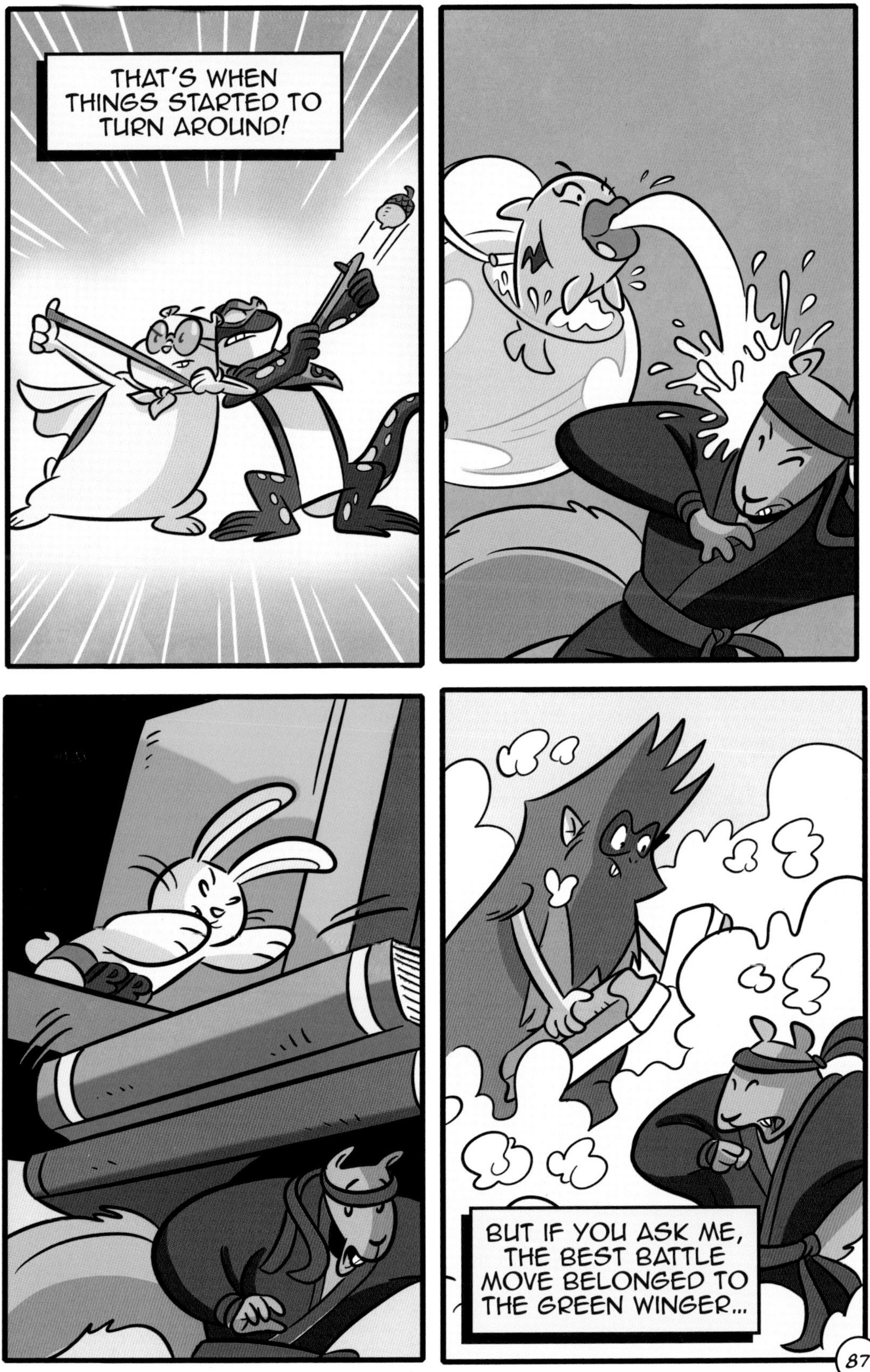
THAT'S WHEN THINGS STARTED TO TURN AROUND!
BUT IF YOU ASK ME, THE BEST BATTLE MOVE BELONGED TO THE GREEN WINGER...

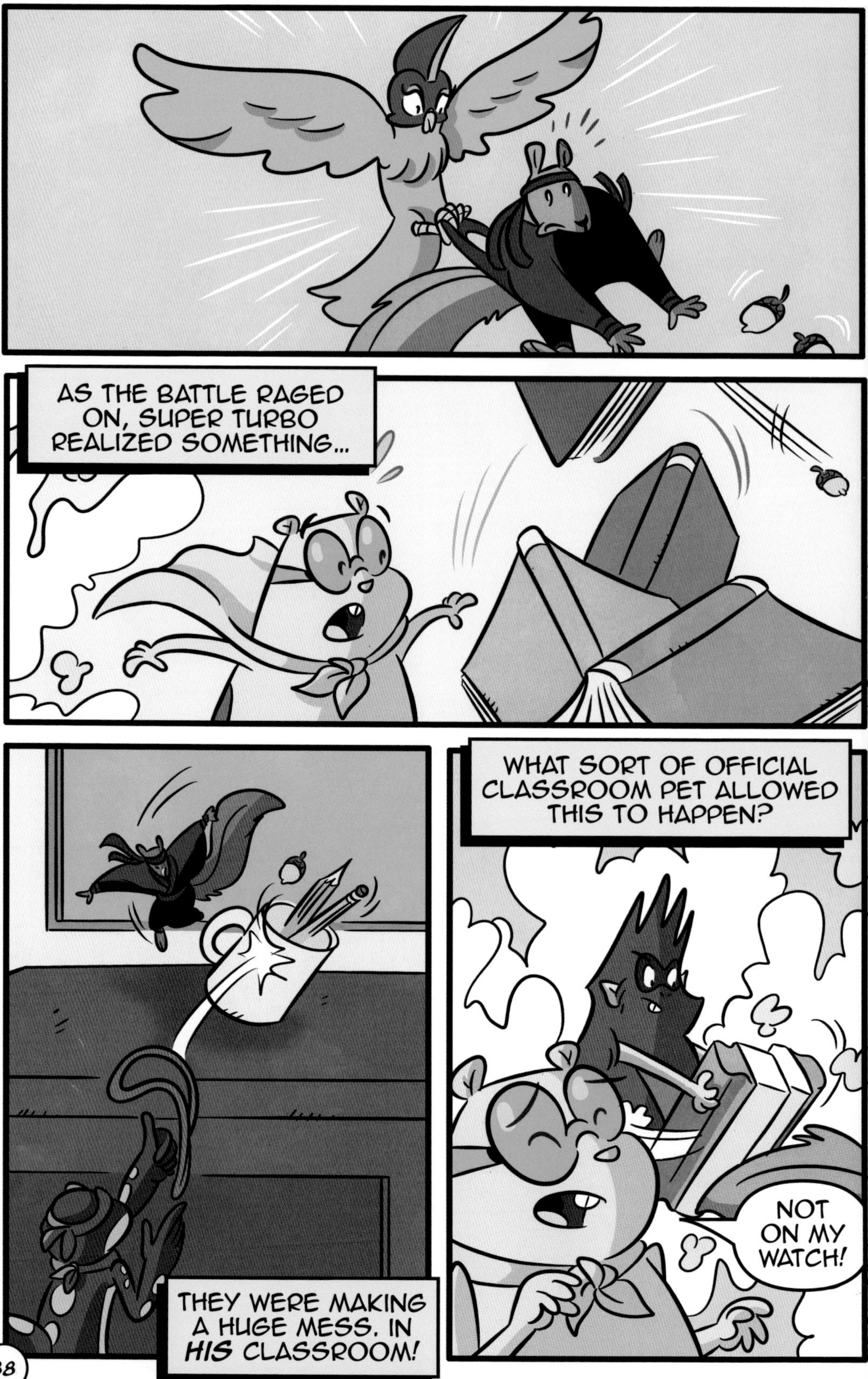
AS THE BATTLE RAGED ON, SUPER TURBO REALIZED SOMETHING...
THEY WERE MAKING A HUGE MESS. IN *HIS* CLASSROOM!
WHAT SORT OF OFFICIAL CLASSROOM PET ALLOWED THIS TO HAPPEN?
NOT ON MY WATCH!

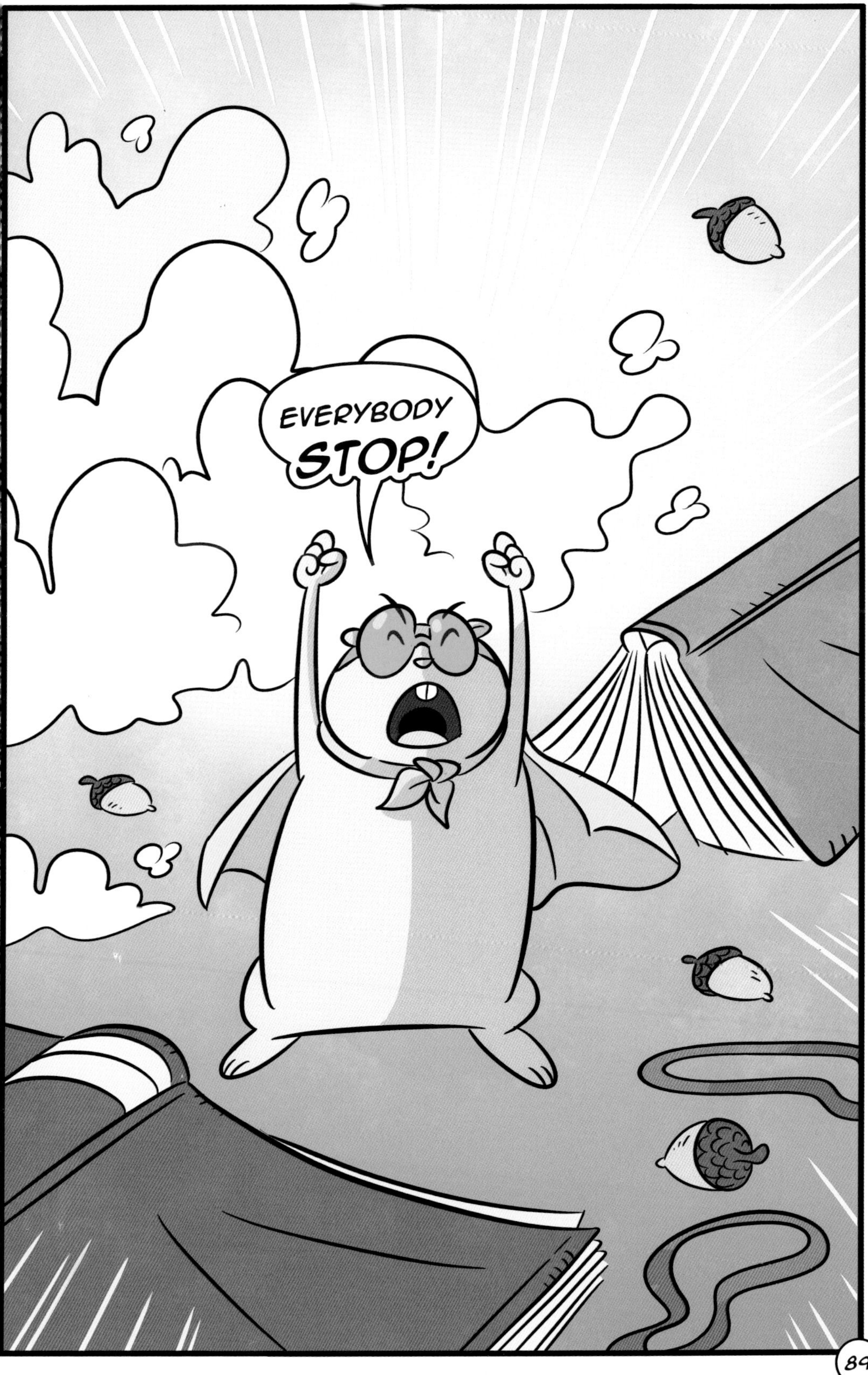
EVERYBODY STOP!

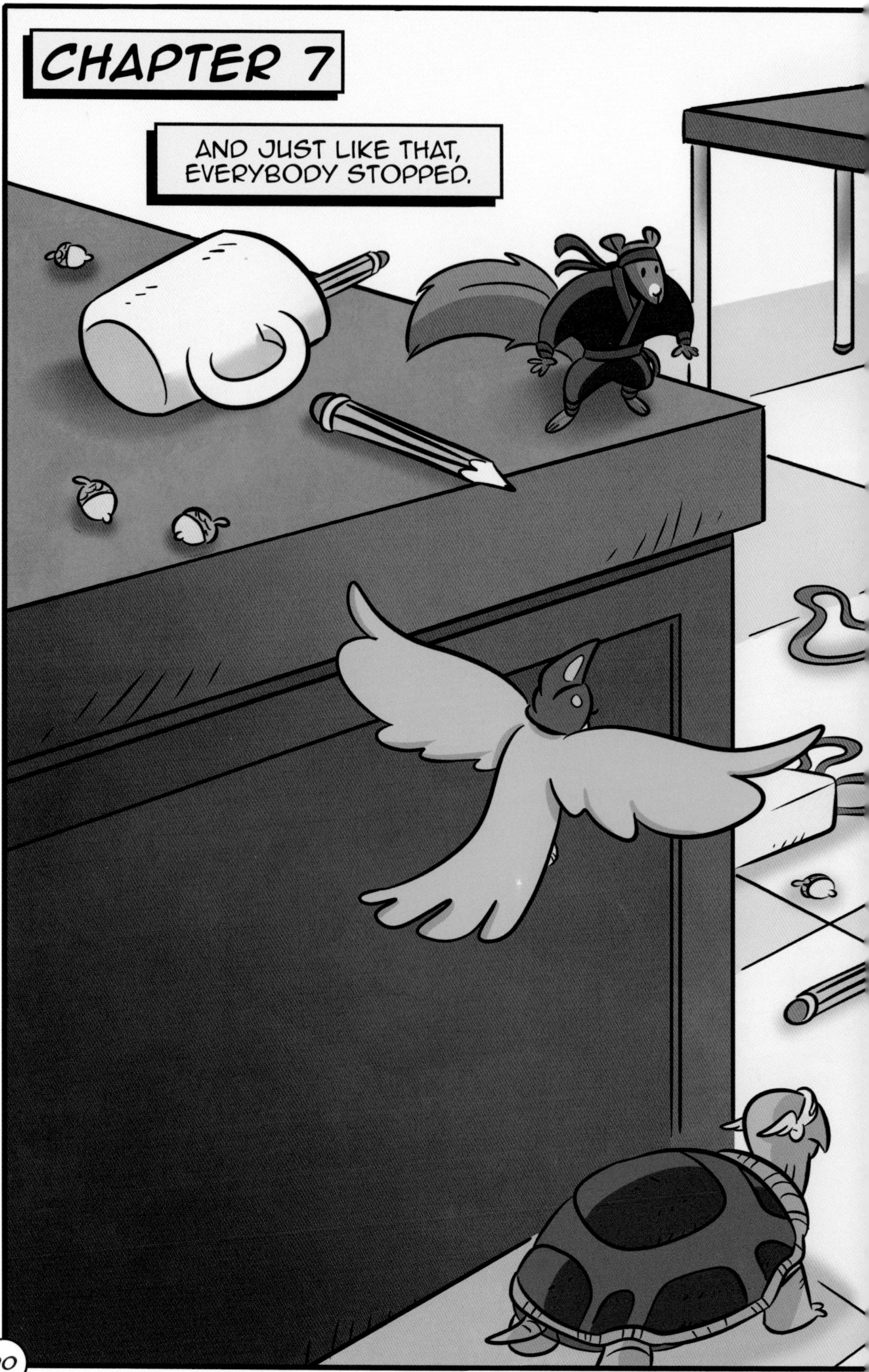
CHAPTER 7
AND JUST LIKE THAT, EVERYBODY STOPPED.

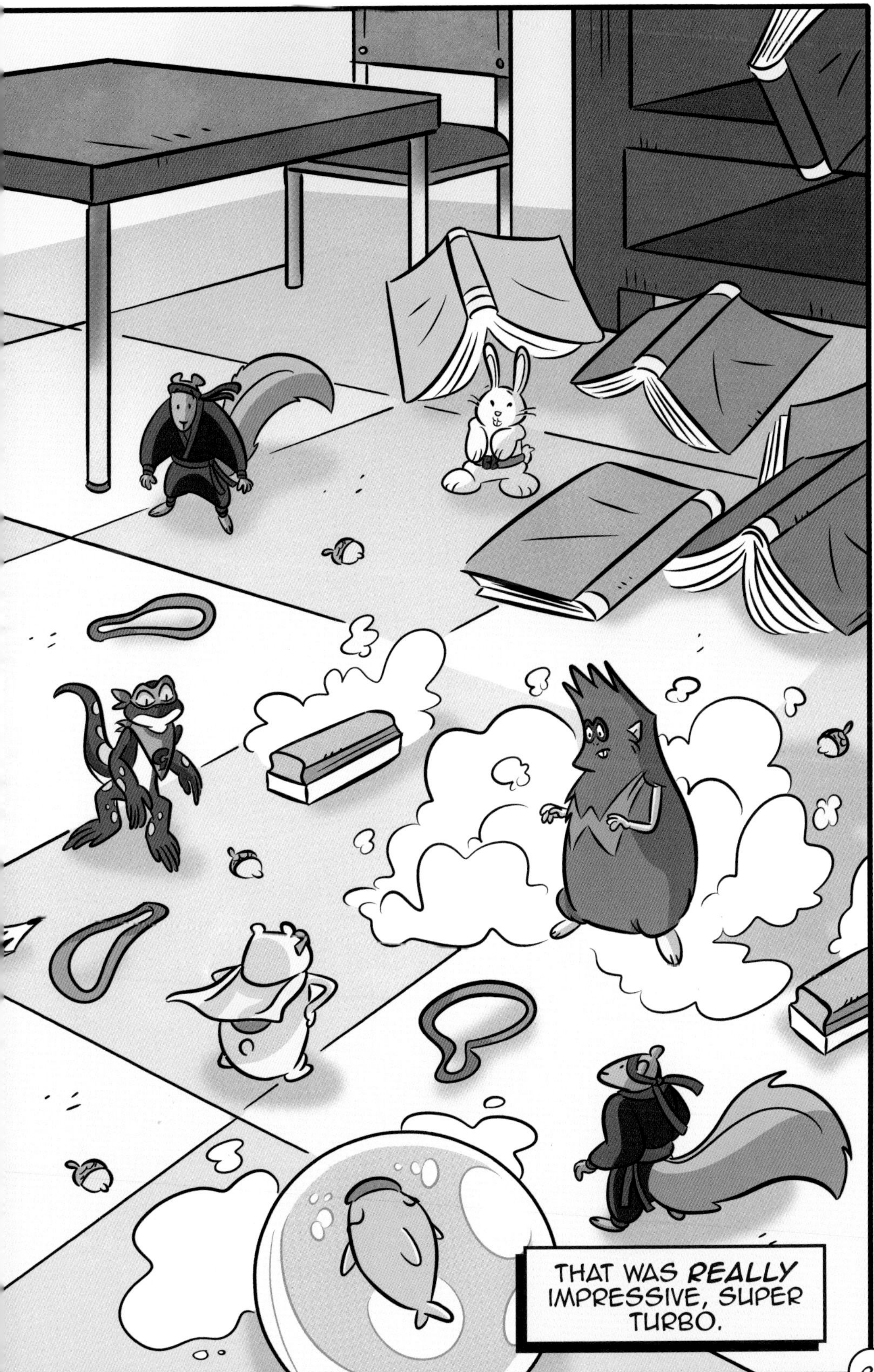
THAT WAS REALLY IMPRESSIVE, SUPER TURBO.

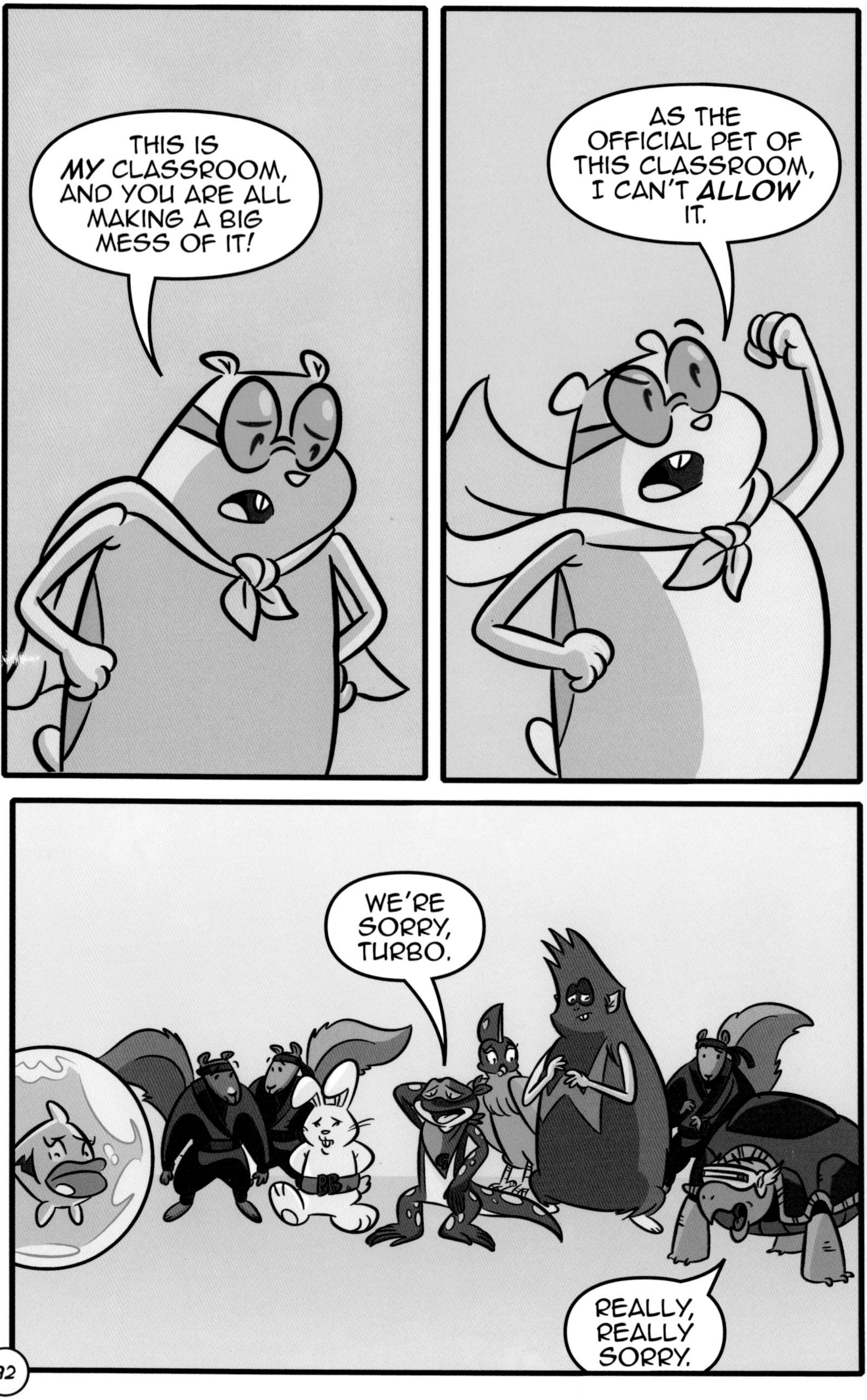
THIS IS *MY* CLASSROOM, AND YOU ARE ALL MAKING A BIG MESS OF IT!
AS THE OFFICIAL PET OF THIS CLASSROOM, I CAN'T *ALLOW* IT.
WE'RE SORRY, TURBO.
REALLY, REALLY SORRY.

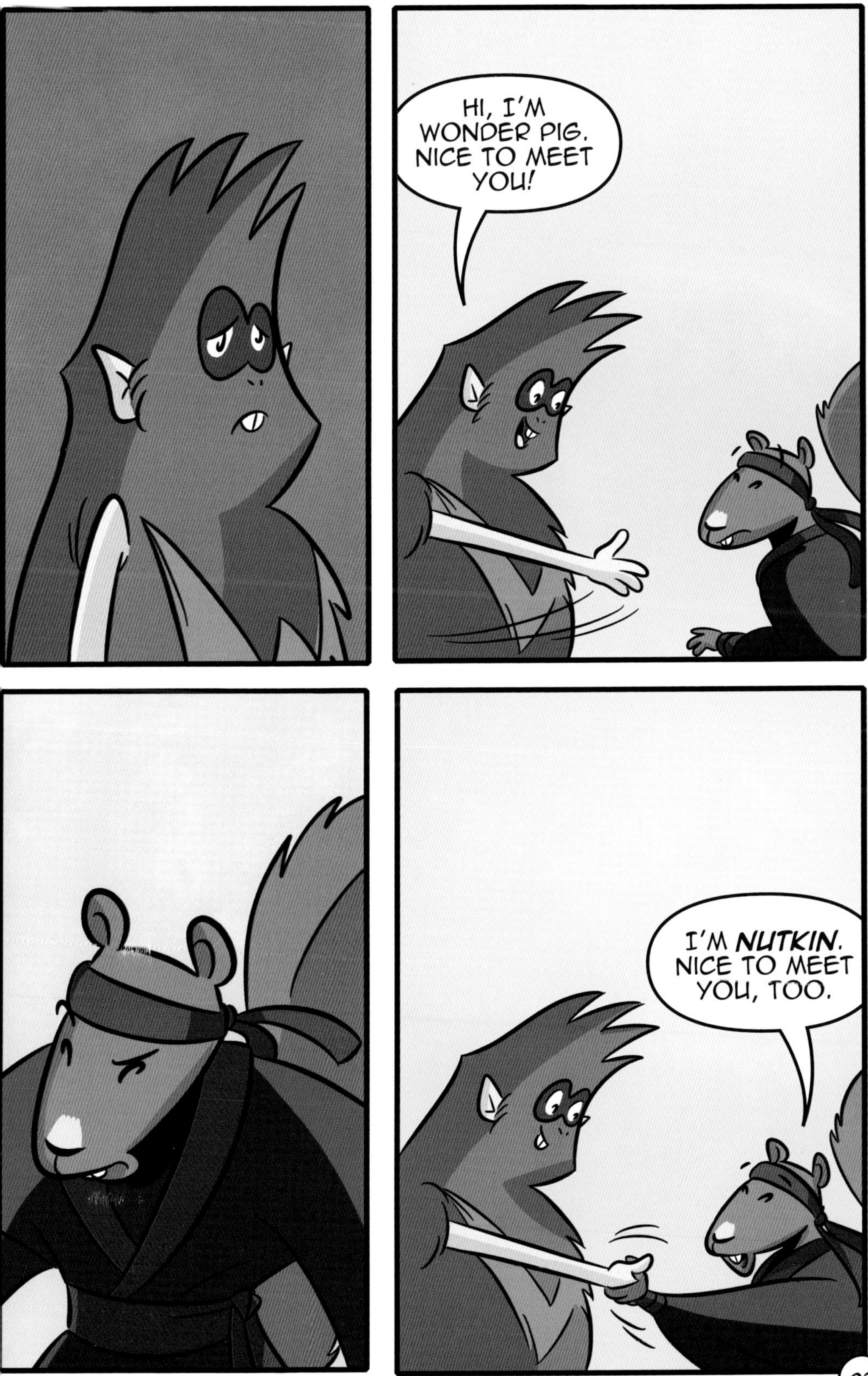
HI, I'M WONDER PIG. NICE TO MEET YOU!
I'M NUTKIN. NICE TO MEET YOU, TOO.

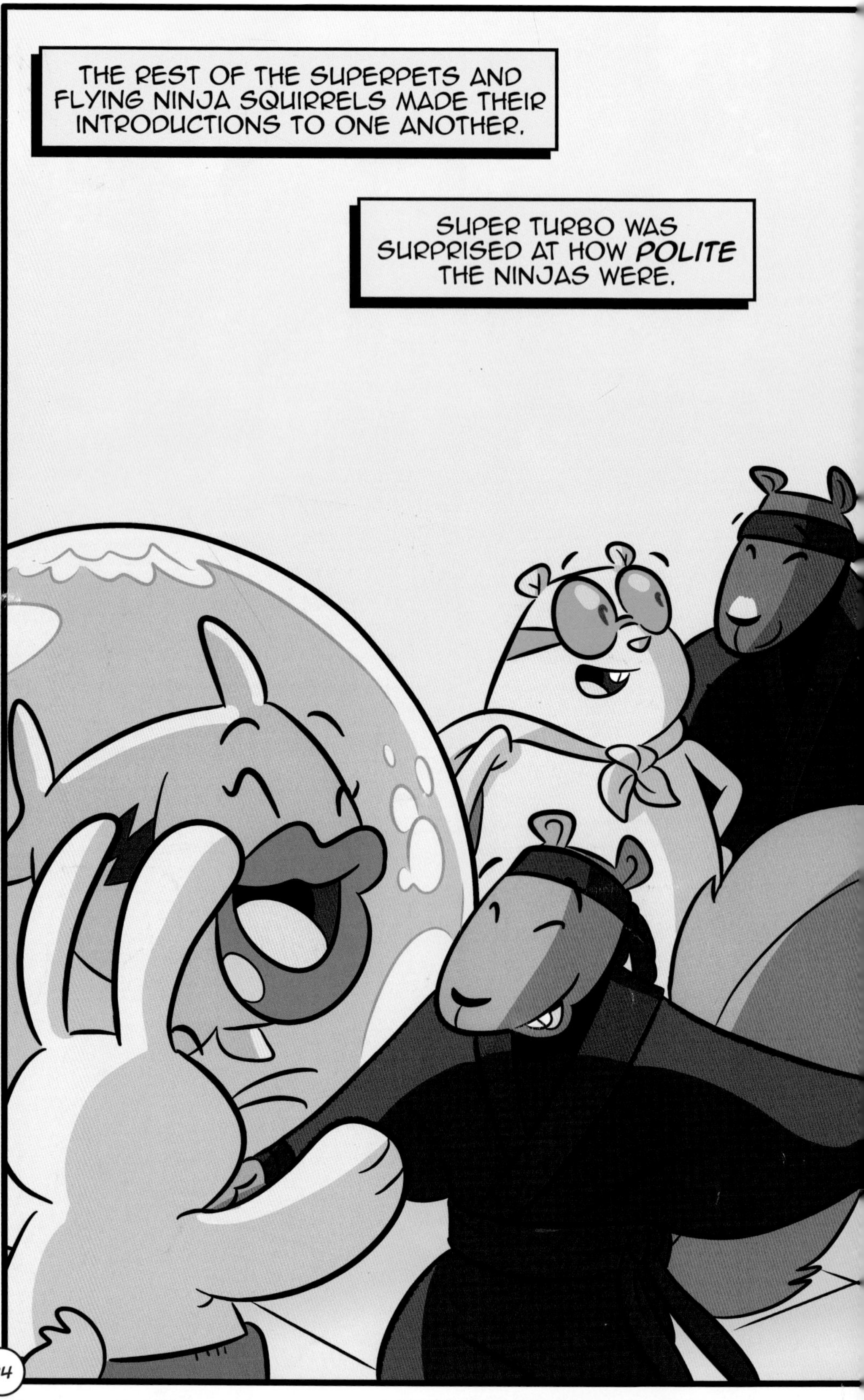
THE REST OF THE SUPERPETS AND FLYING NINJA SQUIRRELS MADE THEIR INTRODUCTIONS TO ONE ANOTHER.
SUPER TURBO WAS SURPRISED AT HOW *POLITE* THE NINJAS WERE.

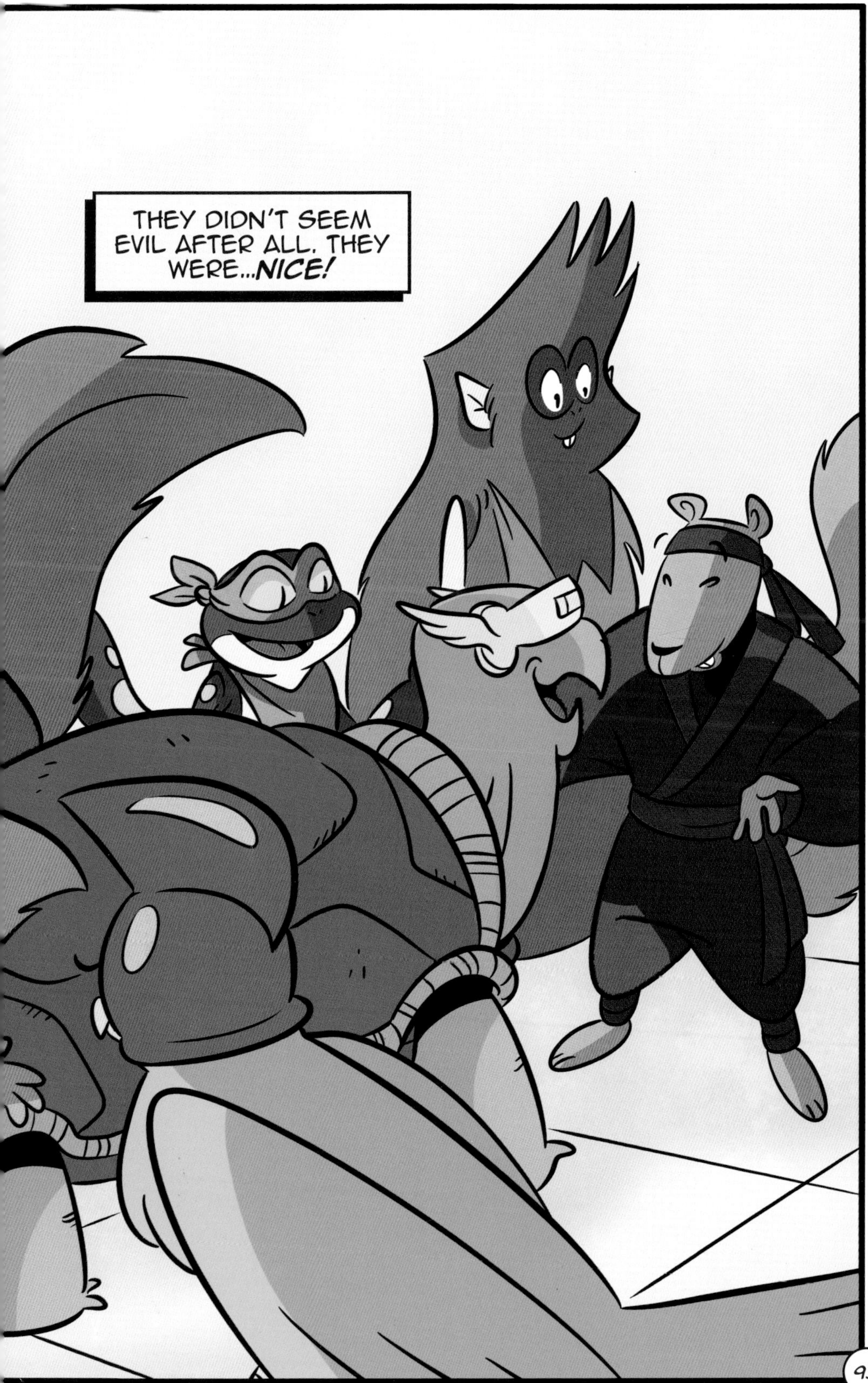
THEY DIDN'T SEEM EVIL AFTER ALL. THEY WERE...*NICE!*

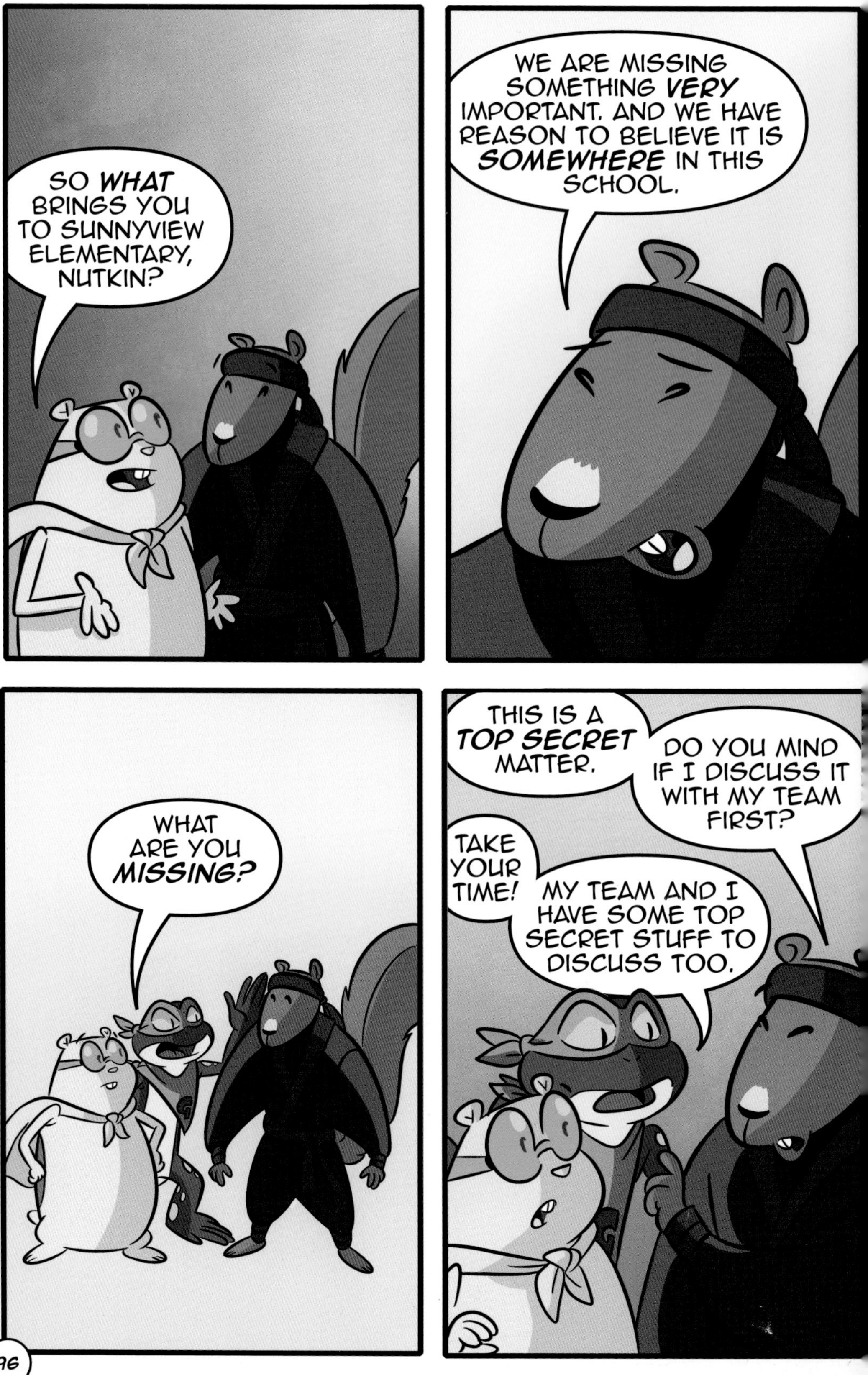
SO WHAT BRINGS YOU TO SUNNYVIEW ELEMENTARY, NUTKIN?
WE ARE MISSING SOMETHING VERY IMPORTANT. AND WE HAVE REASON TO BELIEVE IT IS SOMEWHERE IN THIS SCHOOL.
WHAT ARE YOU MISSING?
THIS IS A TOP SECRET MATTER.
DO YOU MIND IF I DISCUSS IT WITH MY TEAM FIRST?
TAKE YOUR TIME!
MY TEAM AND I HAVE SOME TOP SECRET STUFF TO DISCUSS TOO.

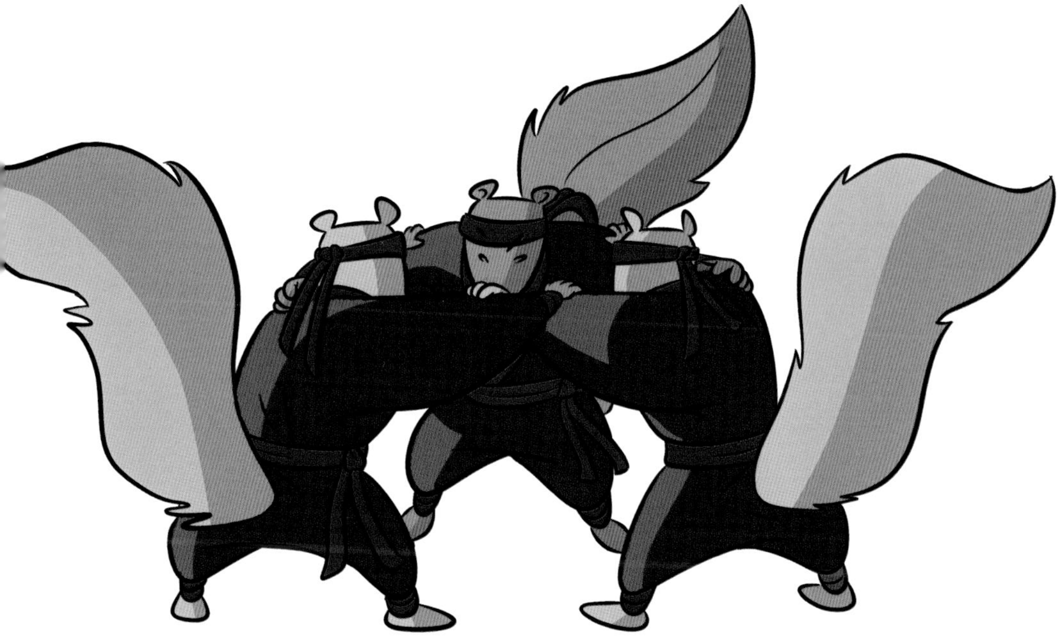

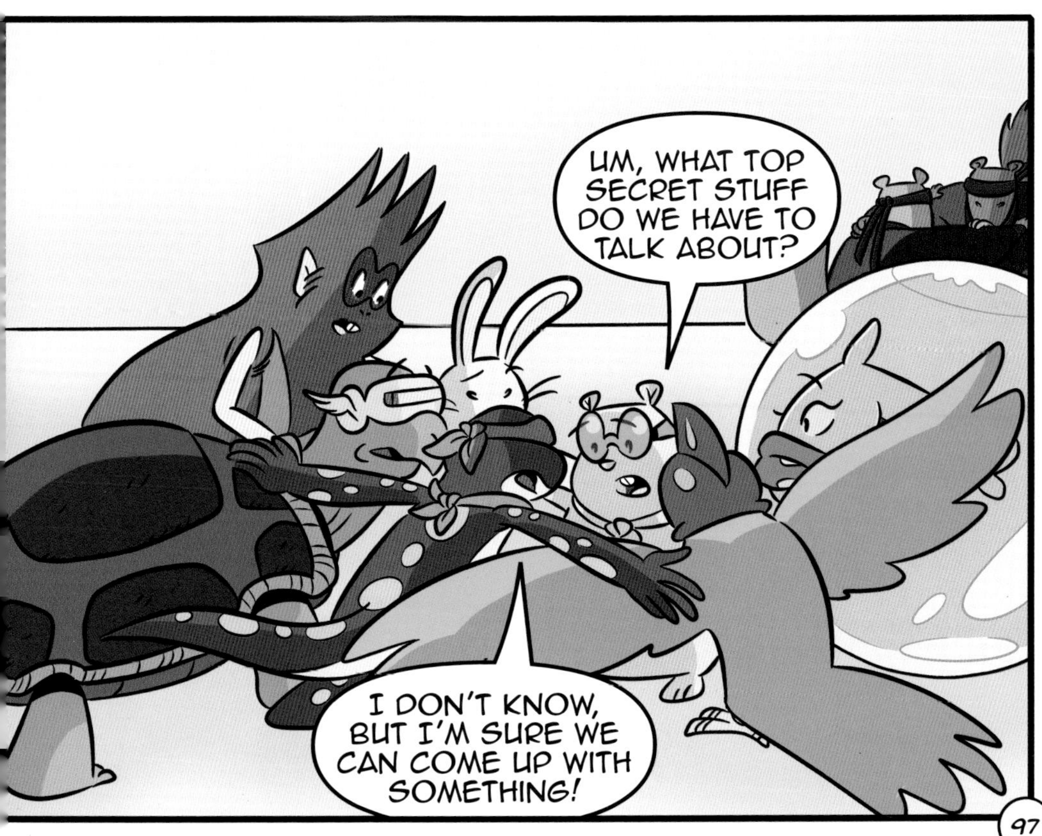
UM, WHAT TOP SECRET STUFF DO WE HAVE TO TALK ABOUT?
I DON'T KNOW, BUT I'M SURE WE CAN COME UP WITH SOMETHING!

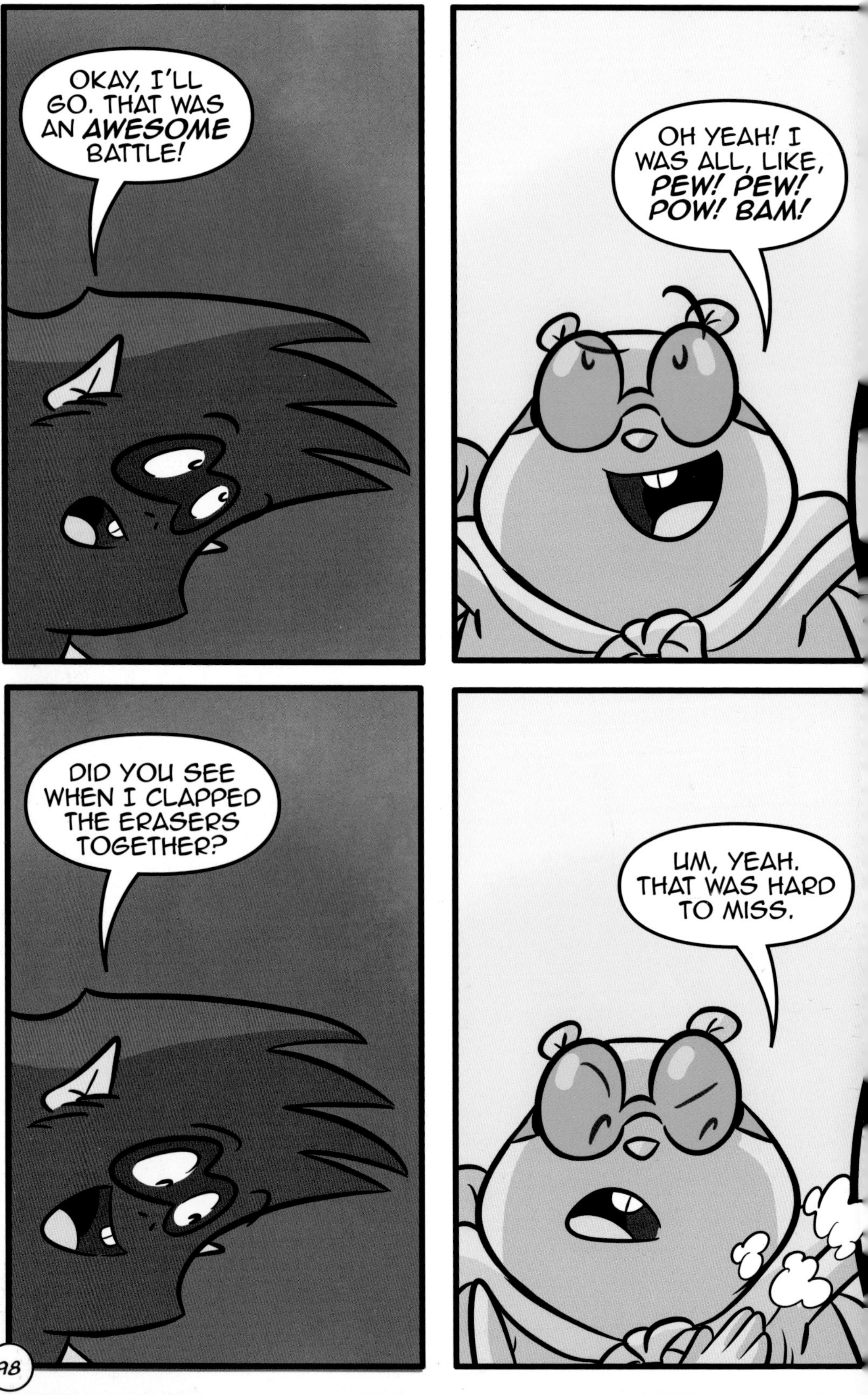
OKAY, I'LL GO. THAT WAS AN AWESOME BATTLE!
OH YEAH! I WAS ALL, LIKE, PEW! PEW! POW! BAM!
DID YOU SEE WHEN I CLAPPED THE ERASERS TOGETHER?
UM, YEAH. THAT WAS HARD TO MISS.

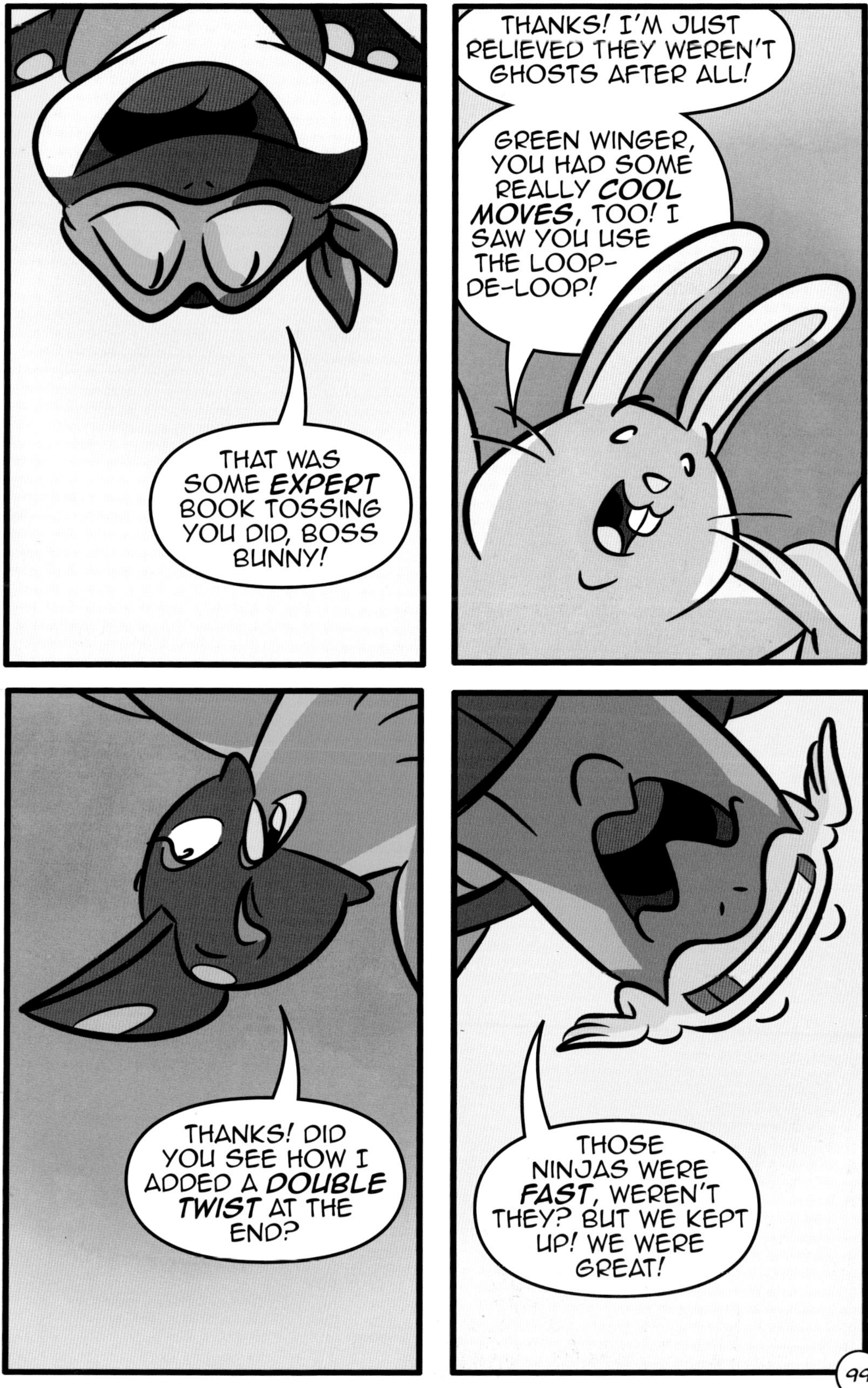
THAT WAS SOME EXPERT BOOK TOSSING YOU DID, BOSS BUNNY!
THANKS! I'M JUST RELIEVED THEY WEREN'T GHOSTS AFTER ALL!
GREEN WINGER, YOU HAD SOME REALLY COOL MOVES, TOO! I SAW YOU USE THE LOOP-DE-LOOP!
THANKS! DID YOU SEE HOW I ADDED A DOUBLE TWIST AT THE END?
THOSE NINJAS WERE FAST, WEREN'T THEY? BUT WE KEPT UP! WE WERE GREAT!

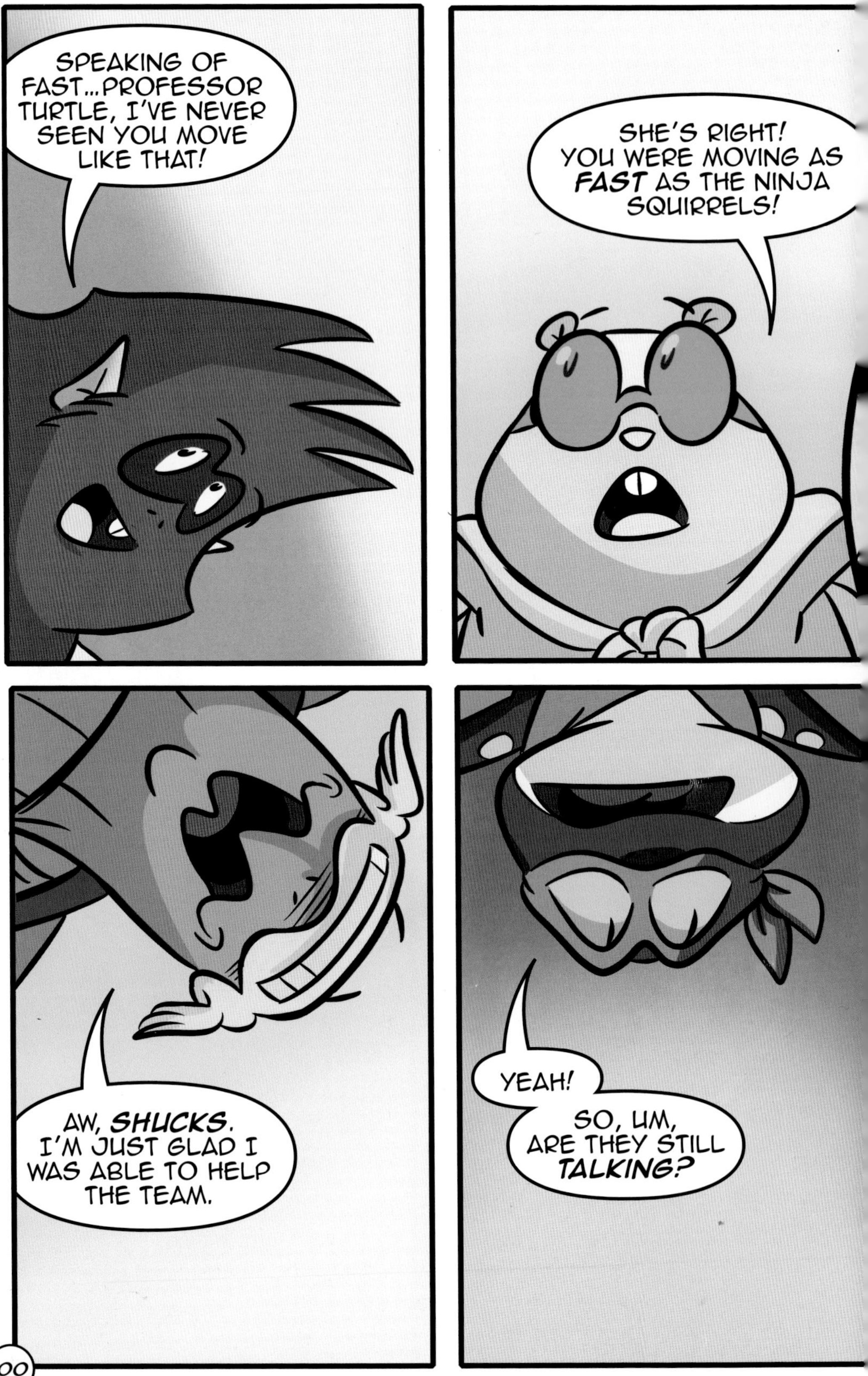
SPEAKING OF FAST...PROFESSOR TURTLE, I'VE NEVER SEEN YOU MOVE LIKE THAT!
SHE'S RIGHT! YOU WERE MOVING AS FAST AS THE NINJA SQUIRRELS!
AW, SHUCKS. I'M JUST GLAD I WAS ABLE TO HELP THE TEAM.
YEAH!
SO, UM, ARE THEY STILL TALKING?

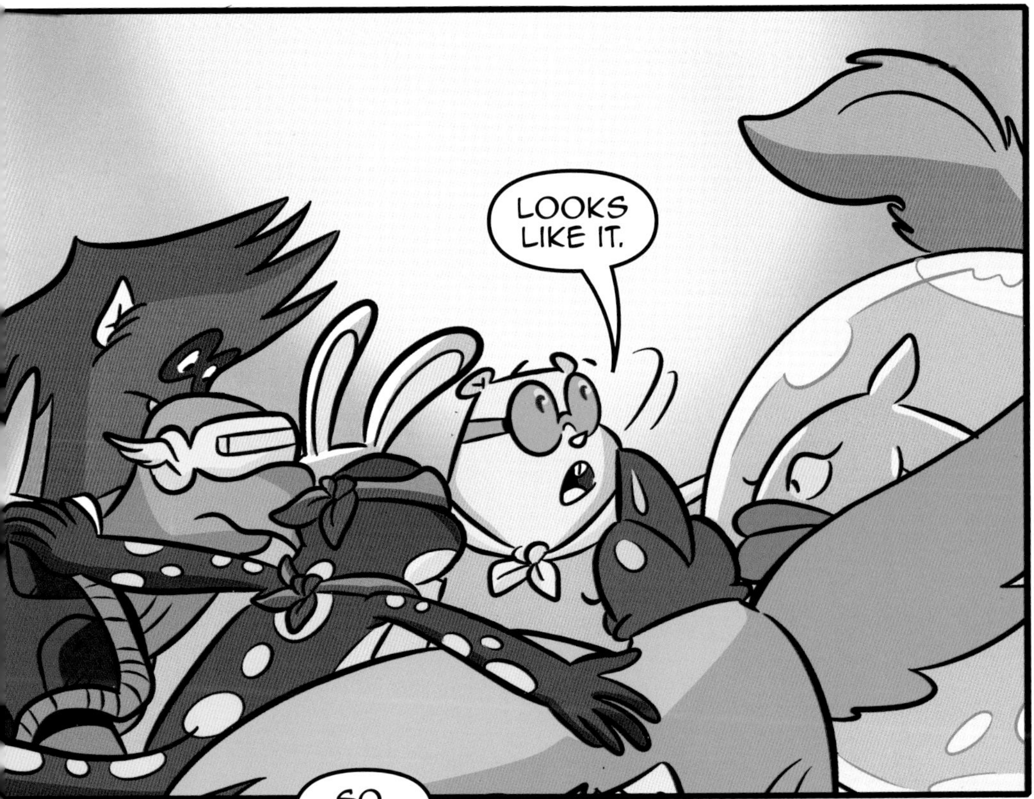
LOOKS LIKE IT.

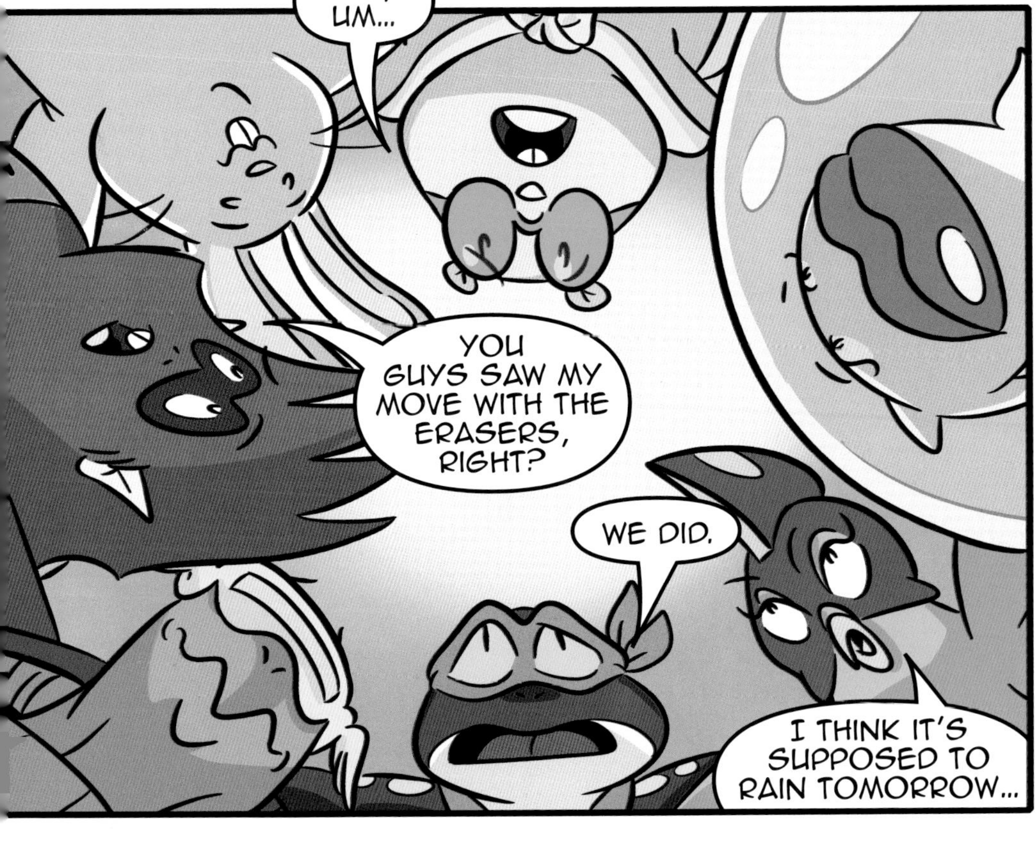
SO, UM...
YOU GUYS SAW MY MOVE WITH THE ERASERS, RIGHT?
WE DID.
I THINK IT'S SUPPOSED TO RAIN TOMORROW...

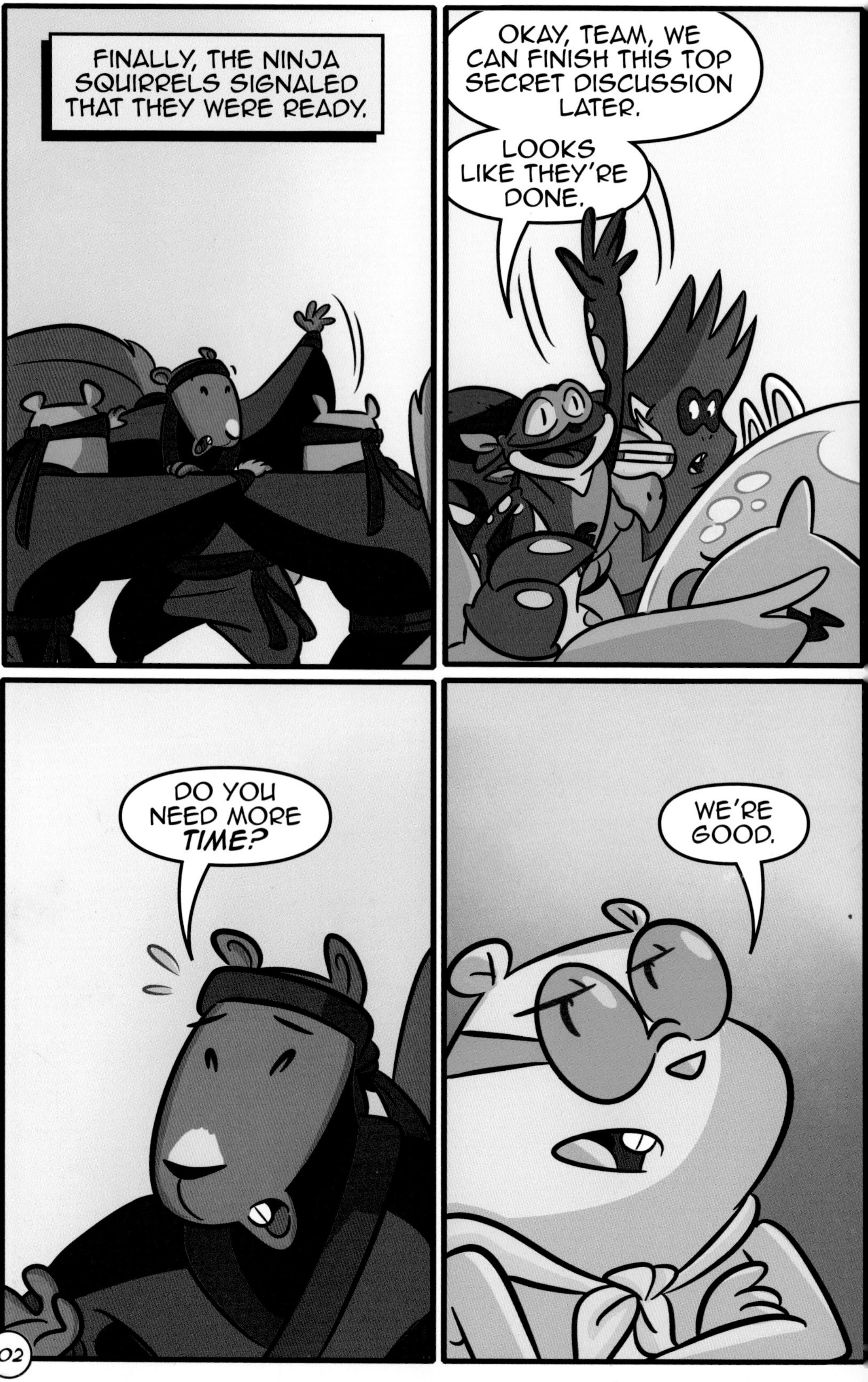
FINALLY, THE NINJA SQUIRRELS SIGNALED THAT THEY WERE READY.
OKAY, TEAM, WE CAN FINISH THIS TOP SECRET DISCUSSION LATER.
LOOKS LIKE THEY'RE DONE.
DO YOU NEED MORE *TIME?*
WE'RE GOOD.

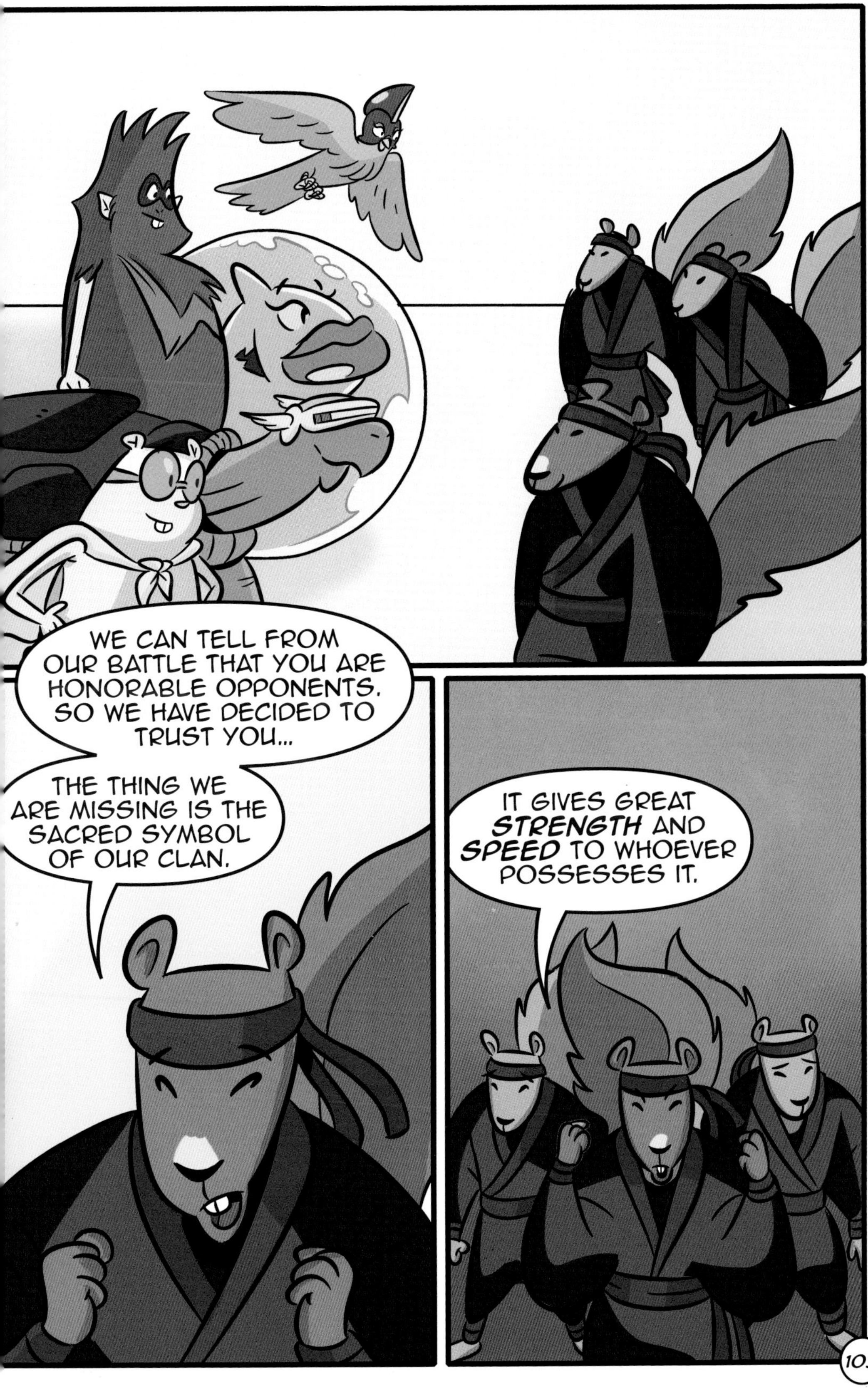
WE CAN TELL FROM OUR BATTLE THAT YOU ARE HONORABLE OPPONENTS. SO WE HAVE DECIDED TO TRUST YOU...
THE THING WE ARE MISSING IS THE SACRED SYMBOL OF OUR CLAN.
IT GIVES GREAT **STRENGTH** AND **SPEED** TO WHOEVER POSSESSES IT.

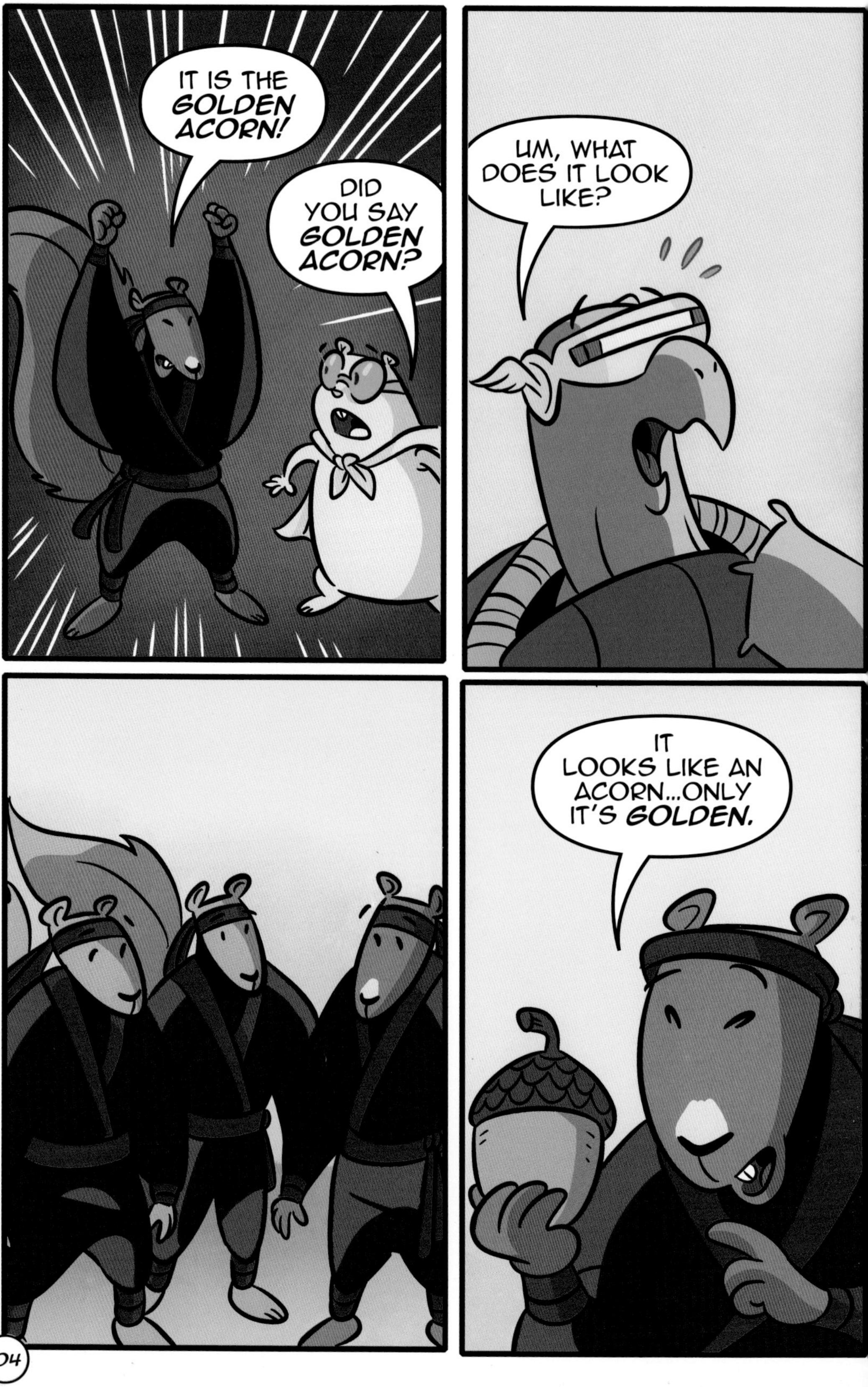
IT IS THE GOLDEN ACORN!
DID YOU SAY GOLDEN ACORN?
UM, WHAT DOES IT LOOK LIKE?
IT LOOKS LIKE AN ACORN...ONLY IT'S GOLDEN.

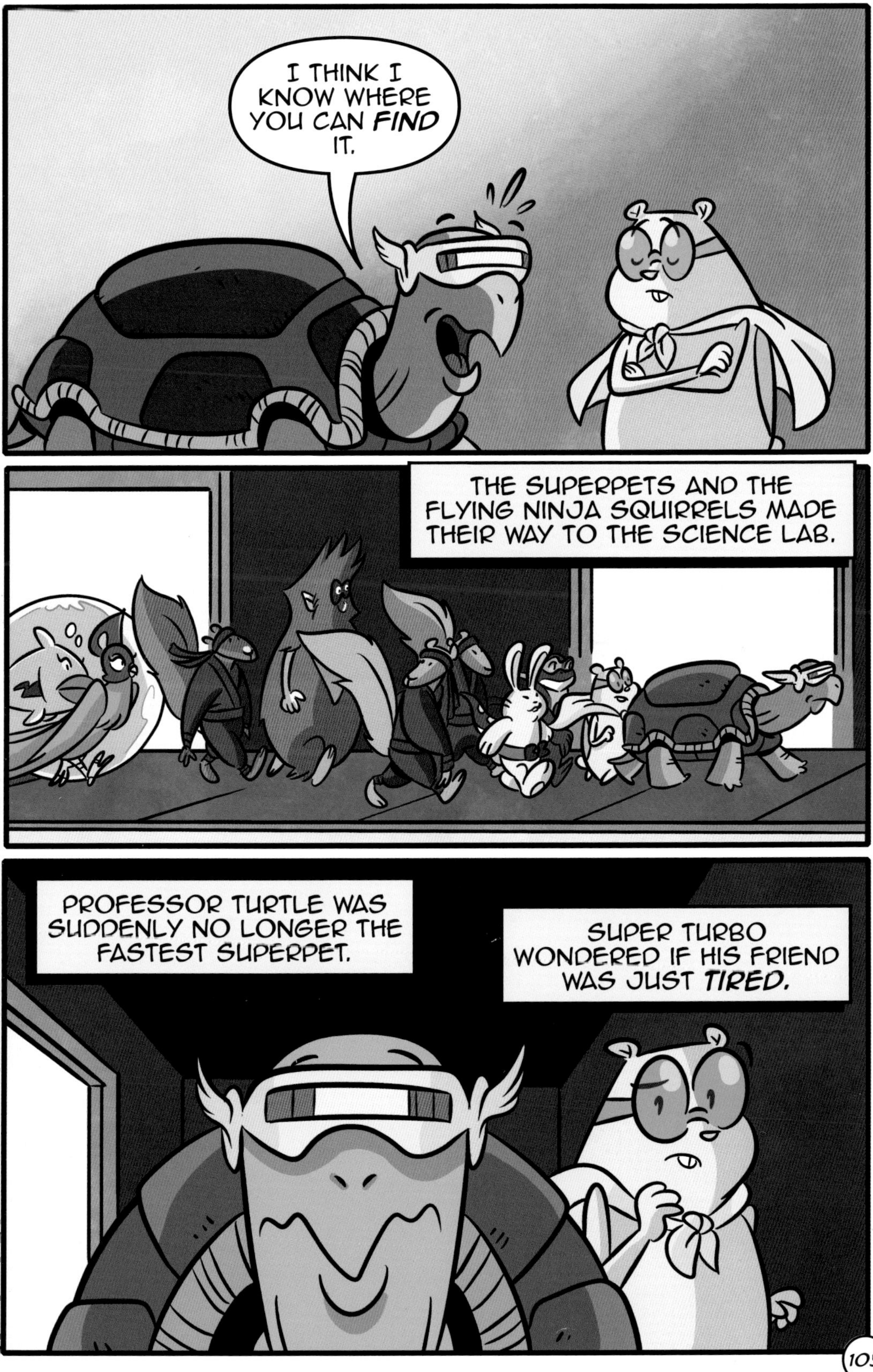
I THINK I KNOW WHERE YOU CAN *FIND* IT.
THE SUPERPETS AND THE FLYING NINJA SQUIRRELS MADE THEIR WAY TO THE SCIENCE LAB.
PROFESSOR TURTLE WAS SUDDENLY NO LONGER THE FASTEST SUPERPET.
SUPER TURBO WONDERED IF HIS FRIEND WAS JUST *TIRED.*

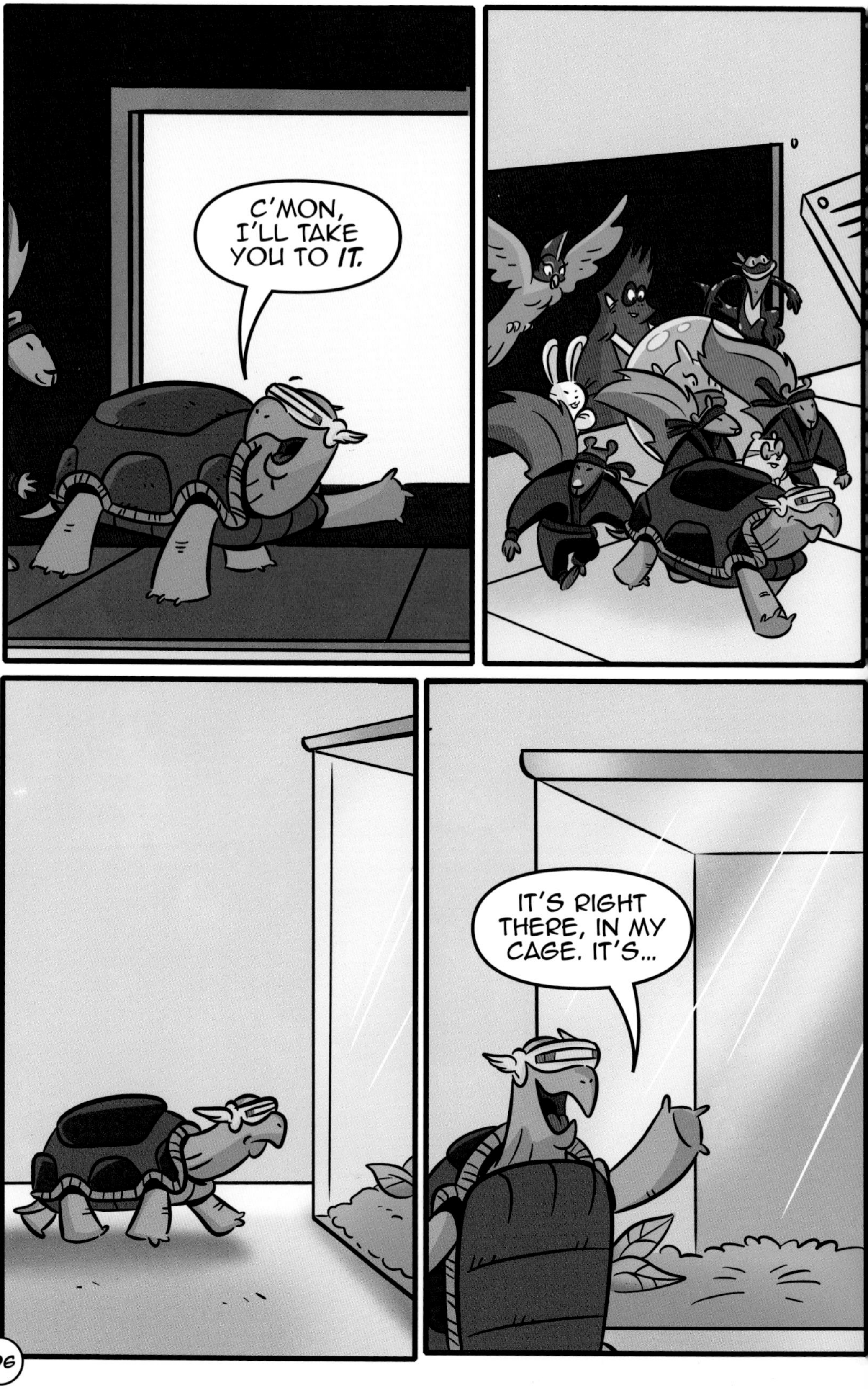
C'MON, I'LL TAKE YOU TO IT.
IT'S RIGHT THERE, IN MY CAGE. IT'S...

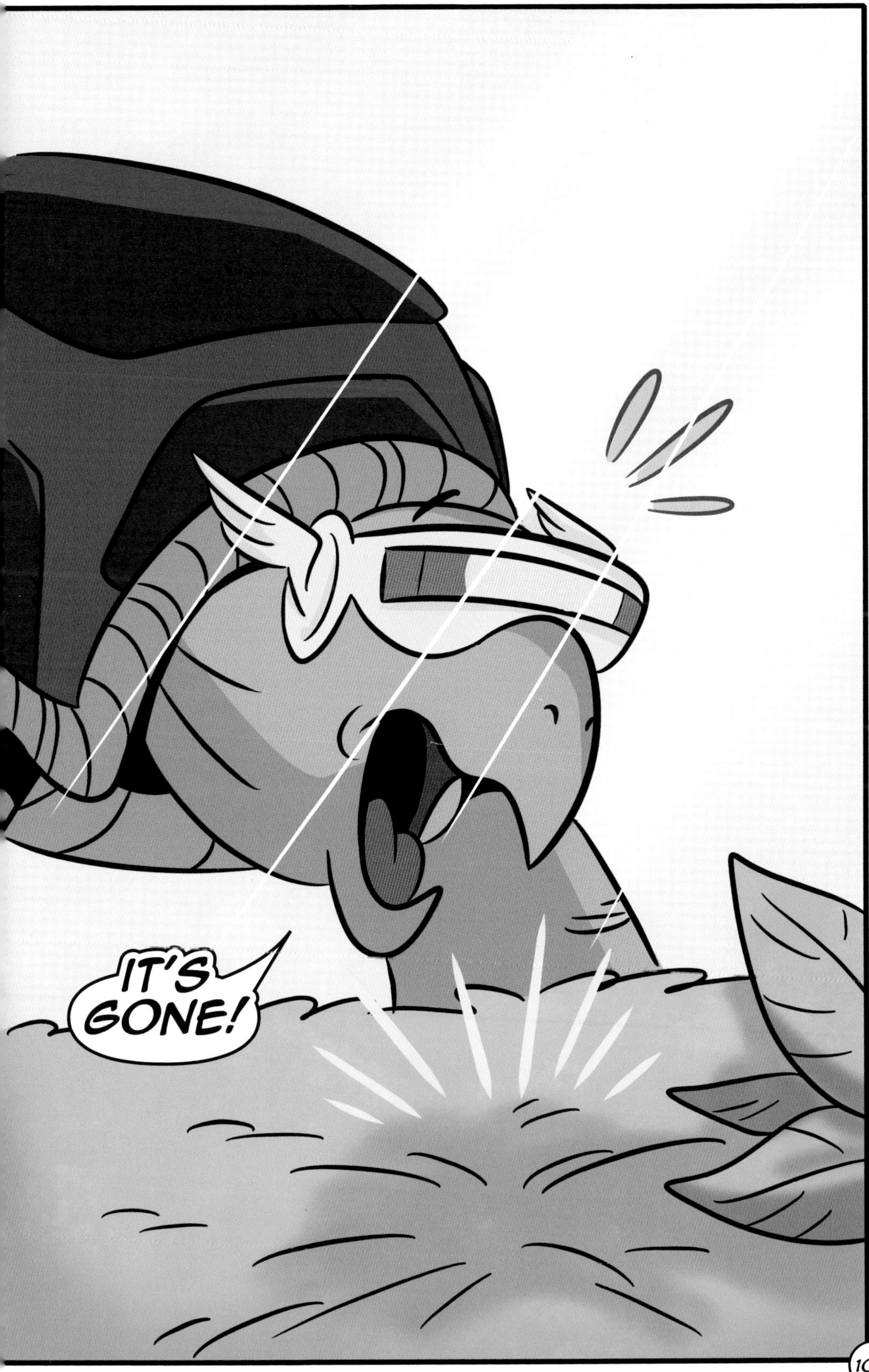
IT'S GONE!

CHAPTER 8

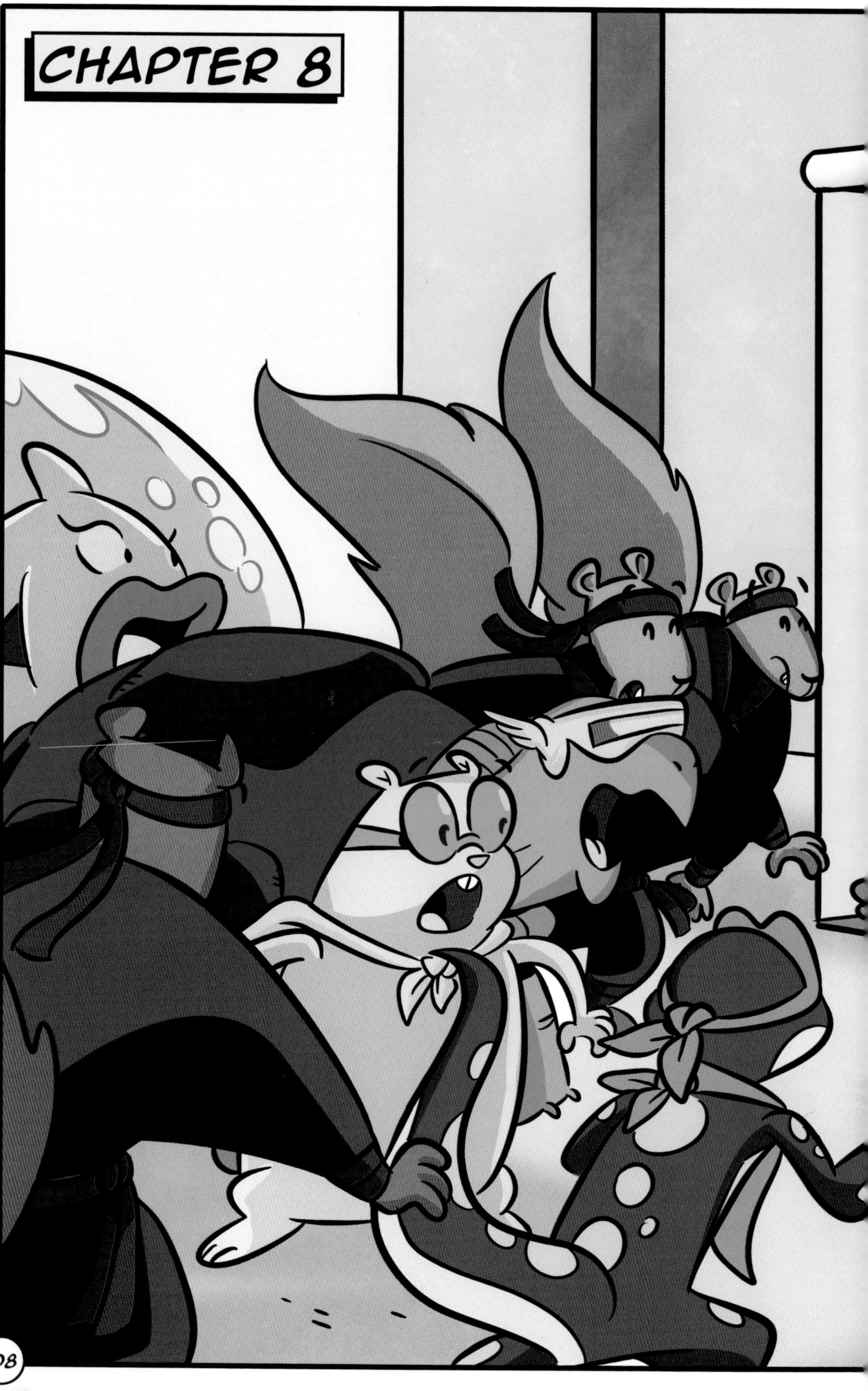

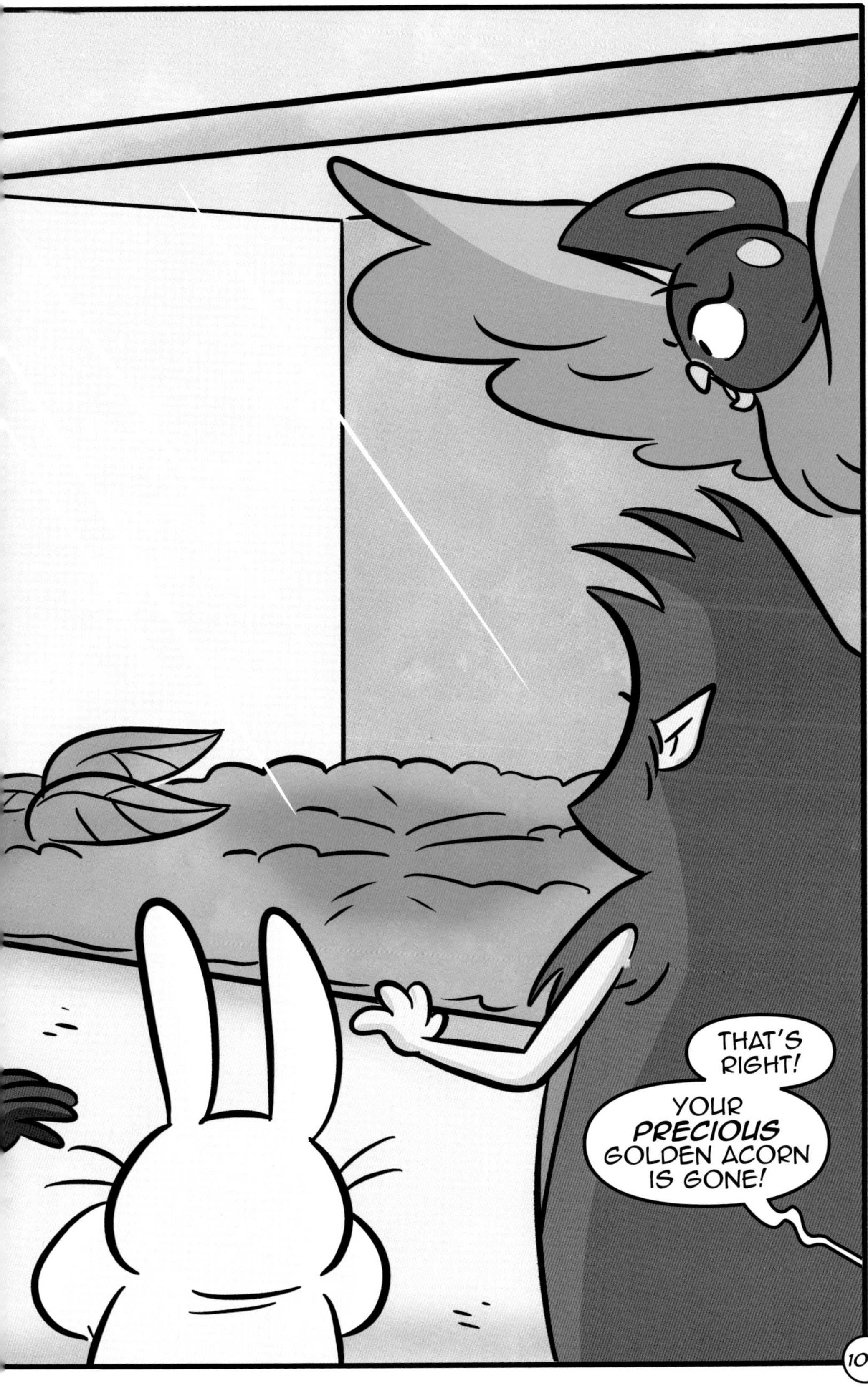
THAT'S RIGHT!
YOUR *PRECIOUS* GOLDEN ACORN IS GONE!

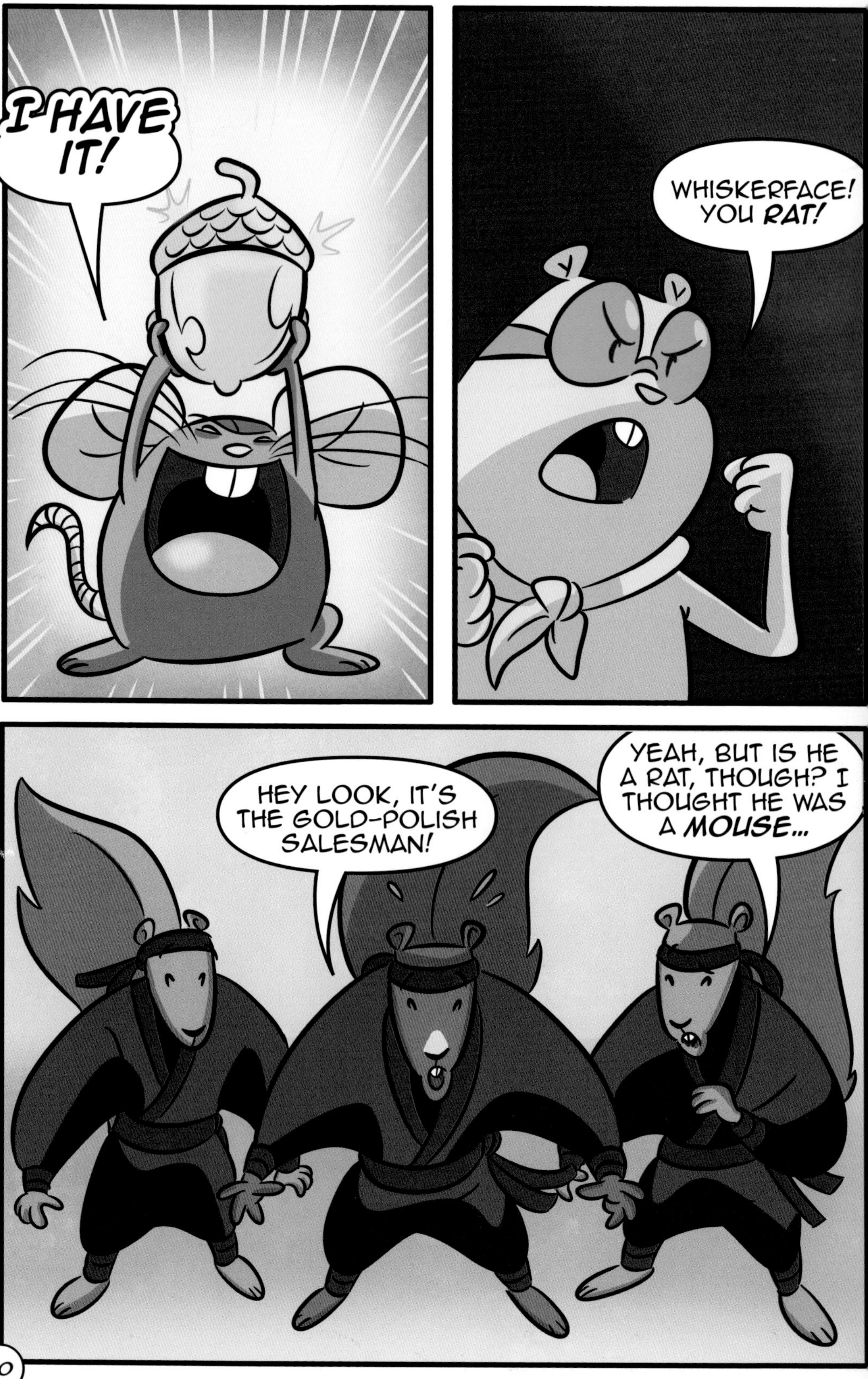
I HAVE IT!
WHISKERFACE! YOU RAT!
HEY LOOK, IT'S THE GOLD-POLISH SALESMAN!
YEAH, BUT IS HE A RAT, THOUGH? I THOUGHT HE WAS A MOUSE...

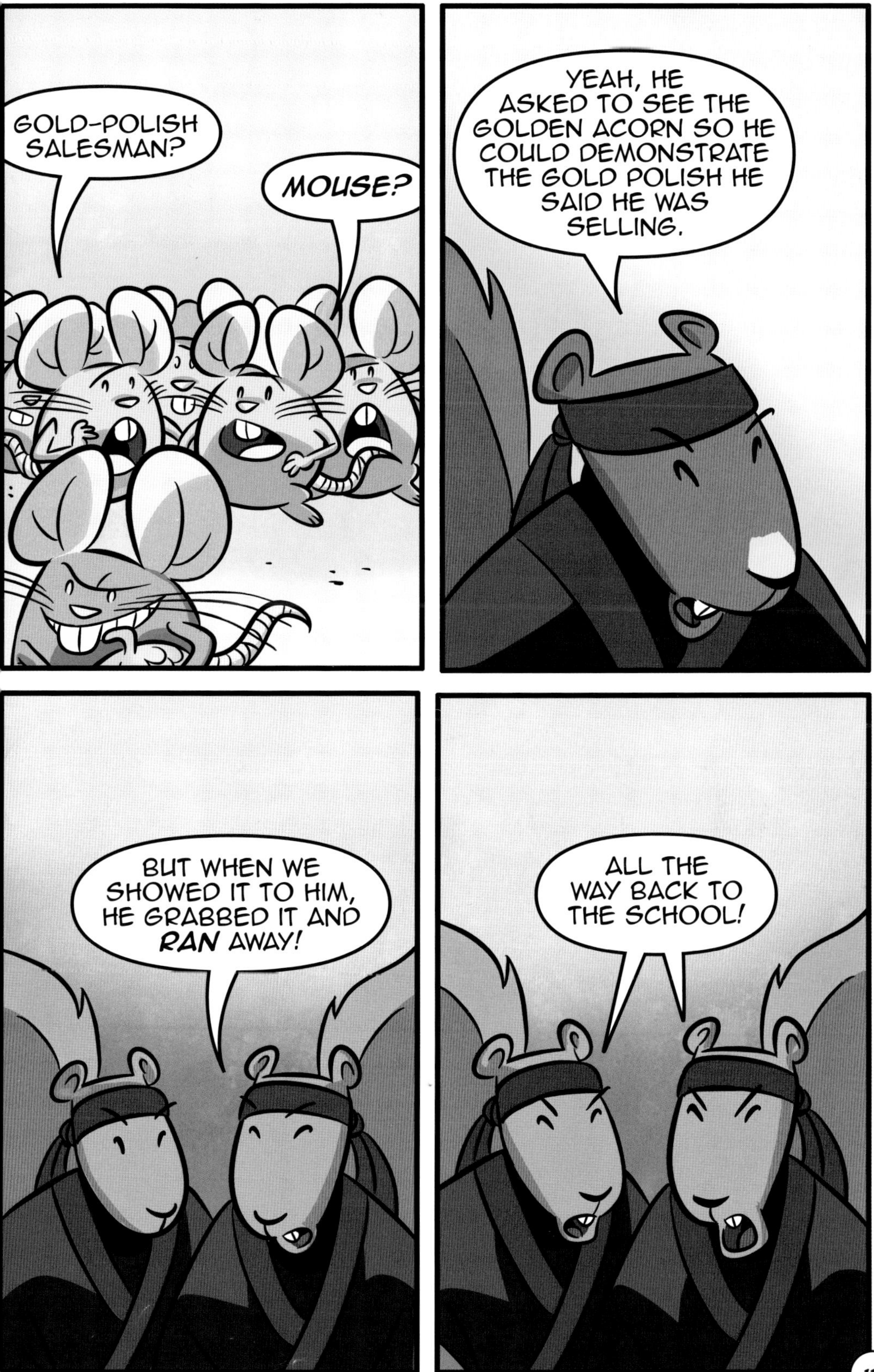
GOLD-POLISH SALESMAN?
MOUSE?
YEAH, HE ASKED TO SEE THE GOLDEN ACORN SO HE COULD DEMONSTRATE THE GOLD POLISH HE SAID HE WAS SELLING.
BUT WHEN WE SHOWED IT TO HIM, HE GRABBED IT AND RAN AWAY!
ALL THE WAY BACK TO THE SCHOOL!

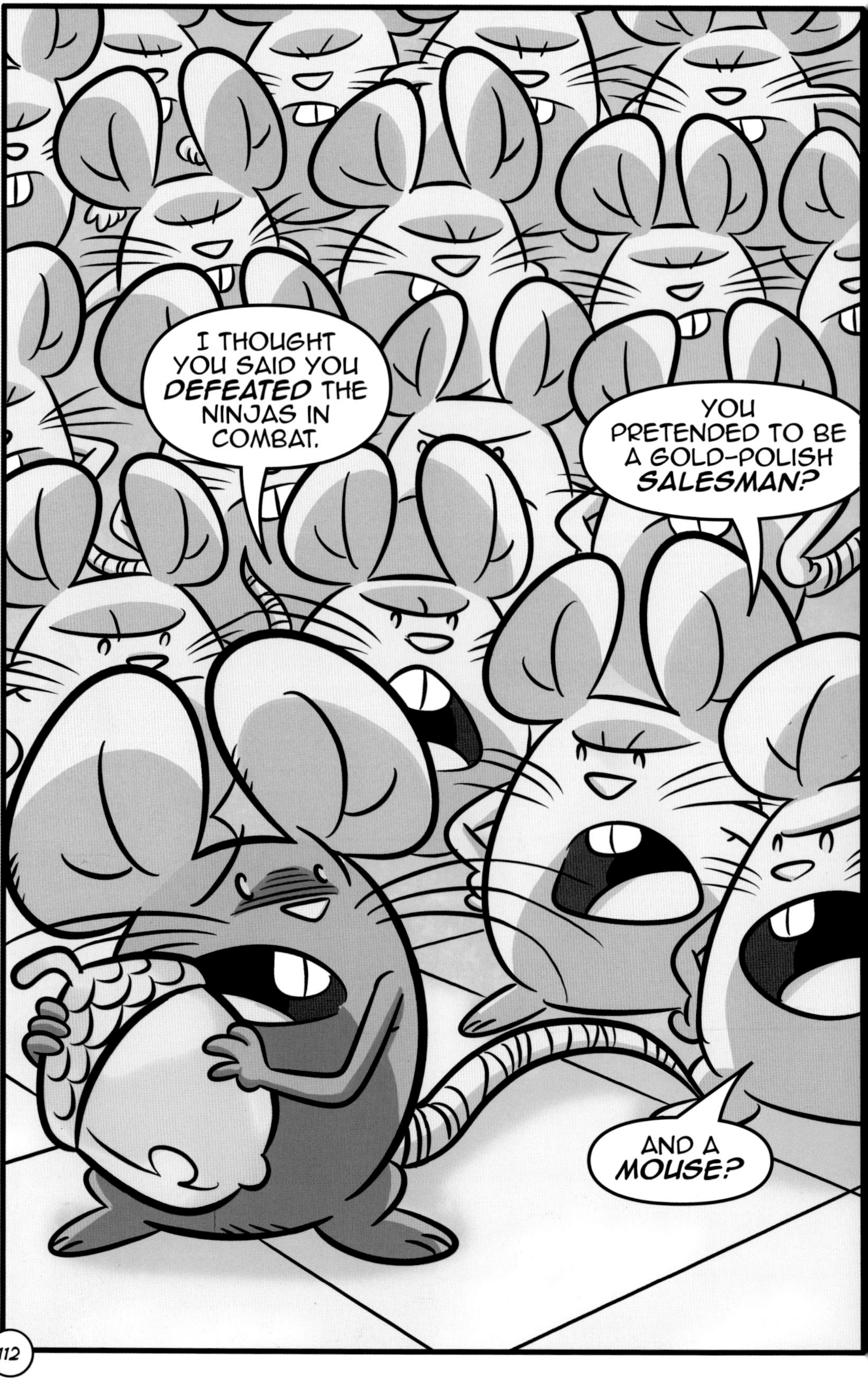
I THOUGHT YOU SAID YOU *DEFEATED* THE NINJAS IN COMBAT.
YOU PRETENDED TO BE A GOLD-POLISH *SALESMAN?*
AND A *MOUSE?*

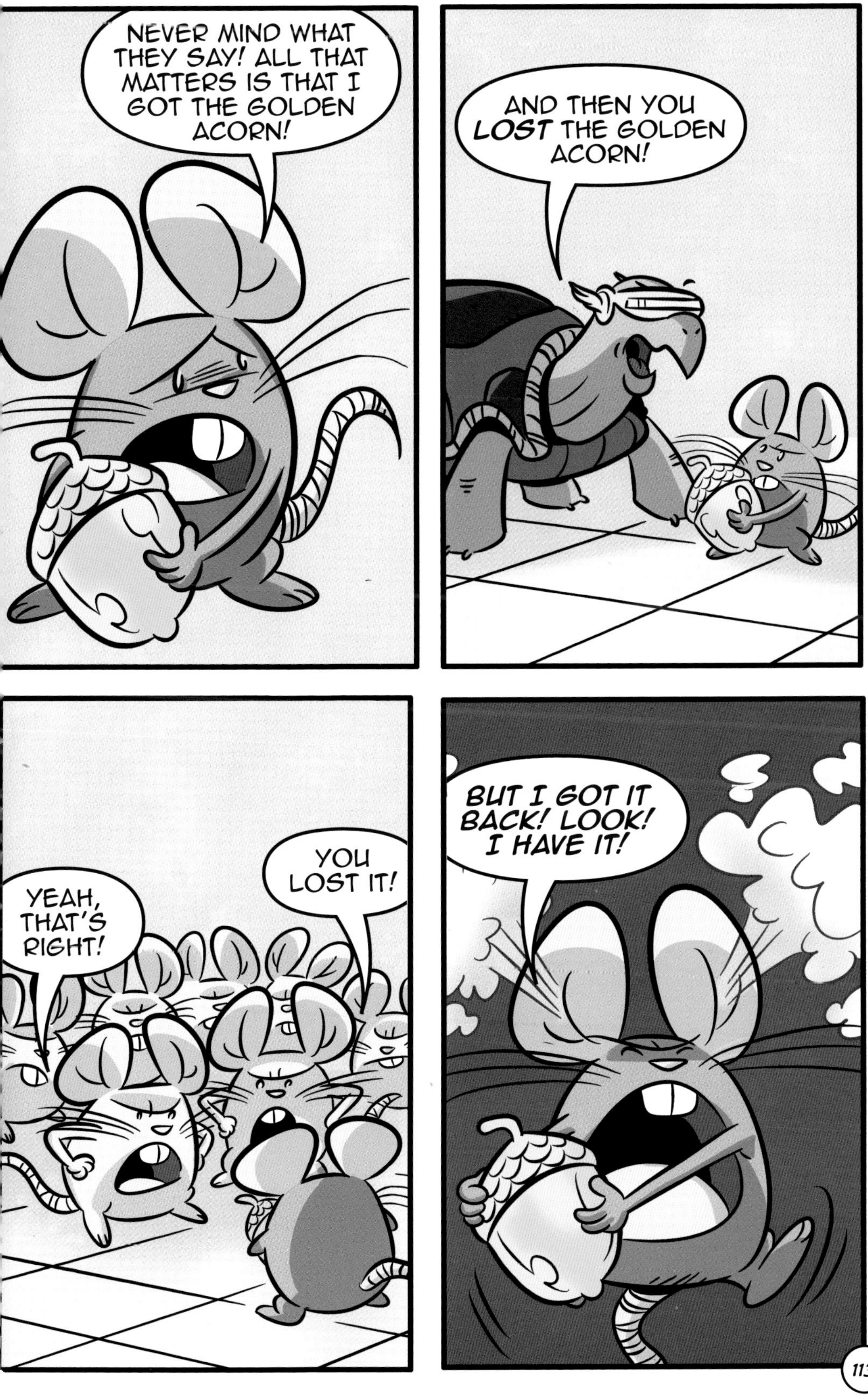
NEVER MIND WHAT THEY SAY! ALL THAT MATTERS IS THAT I GOT THE GOLDEN ACORN!
AND THEN YOU LOST THE GOLDEN ACORN!
YEAH, THAT'S RIGHT!
YOU LOST IT!
BUT I GOT IT BACK! LOOK! I HAVE IT!

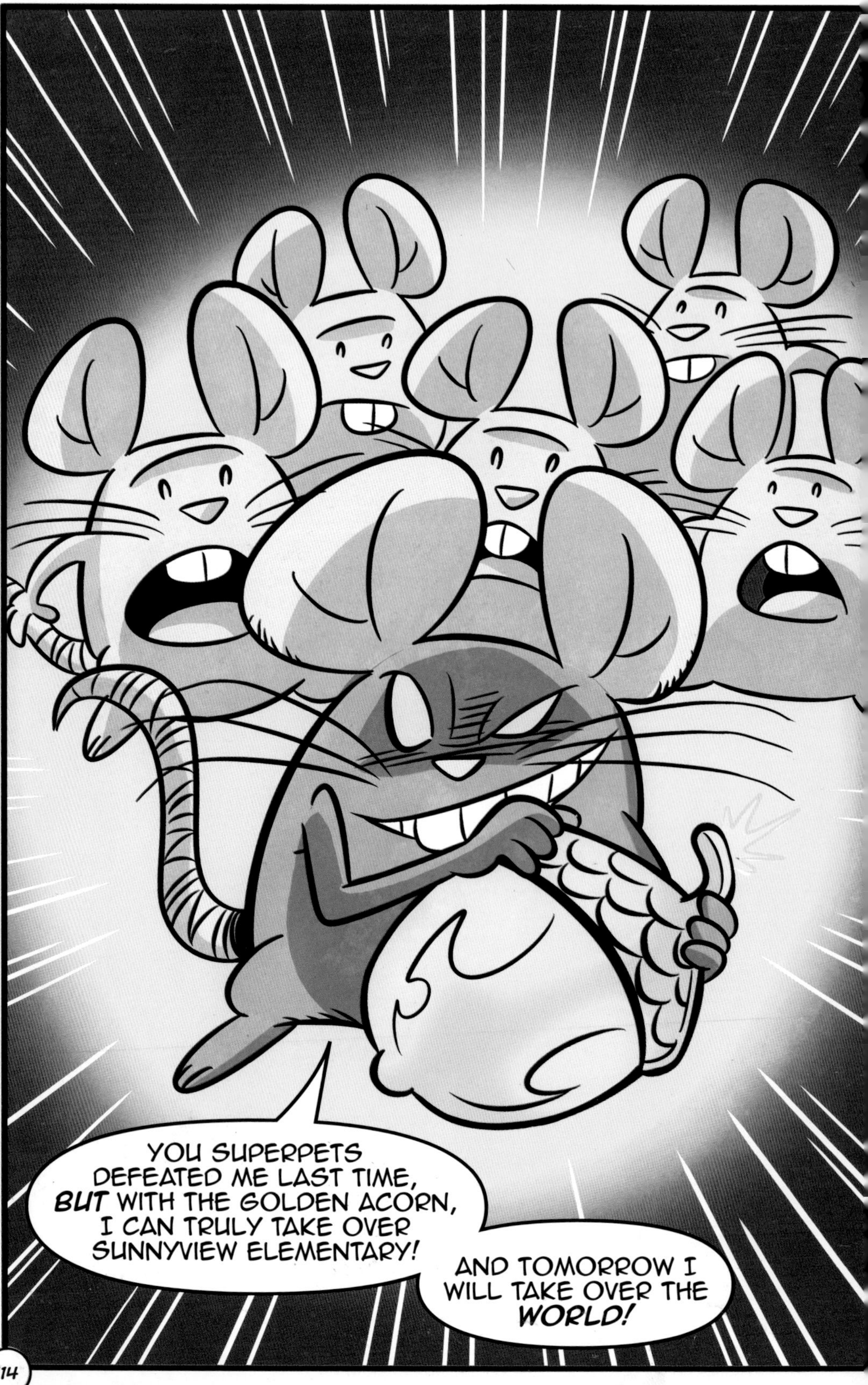
YOU SUPERPETS DEFEATED ME LAST TIME, BUT WITH THE GOLDEN ACORN, I CAN TRULY TAKE OVER SUNNYVIEW ELEMENTARY!
AND TOMORROW I WILL TAKE OVER THE WORLD!

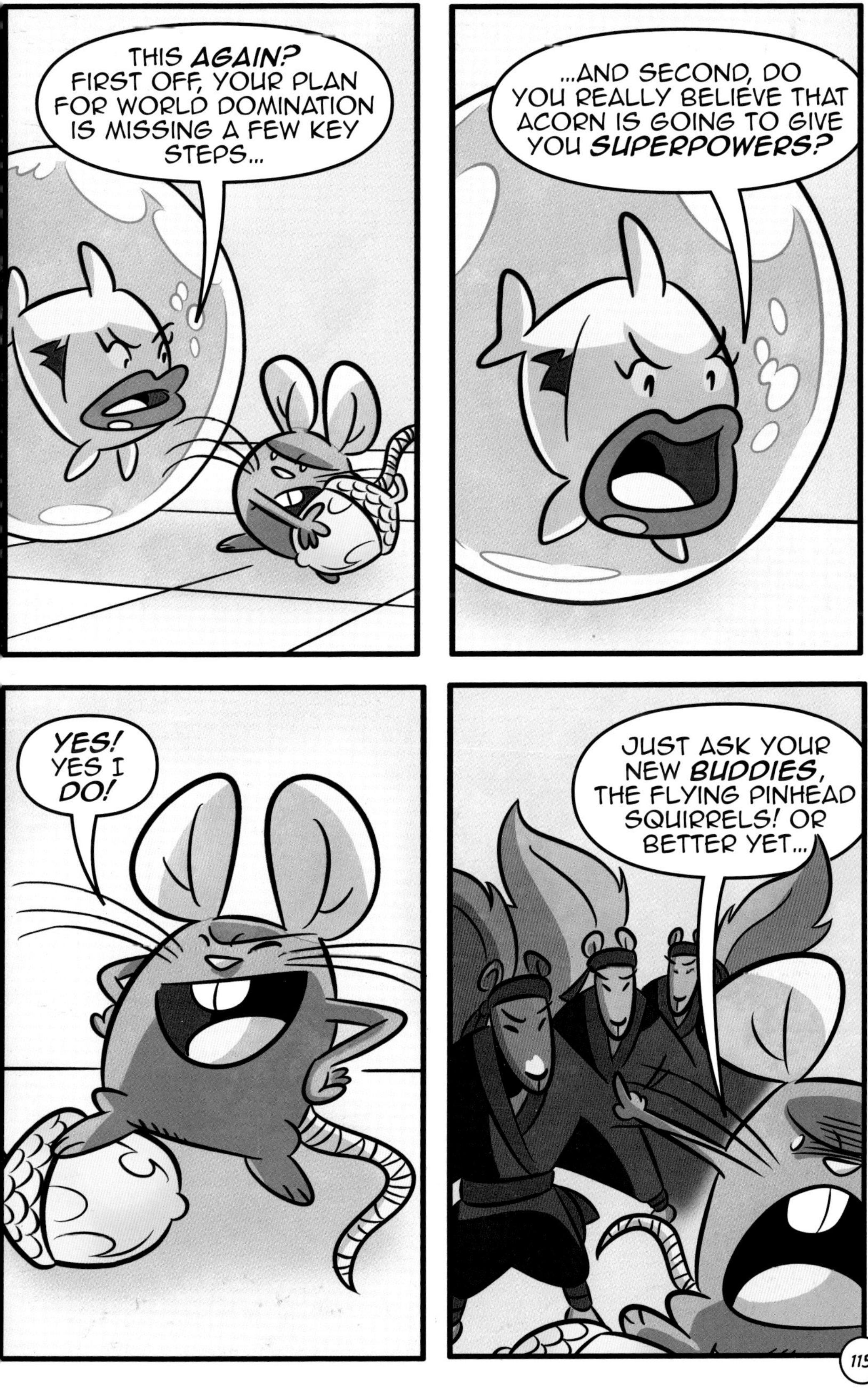
THIS AGAIN? FIRST OFF, YOUR PLAN FOR WORLD DOMINATION IS MISSING A FEW KEY STEPS...
...AND SECOND, DO YOU REALLY BELIEVE THAT ACORN IS GOING TO GIVE YOU SUPERPOWERS?
YES! YES I DO!
JUST ASK YOUR NEW BUDDIES, THE FLYING PINHEAD SQUIRRELS! OR BETTER YET...

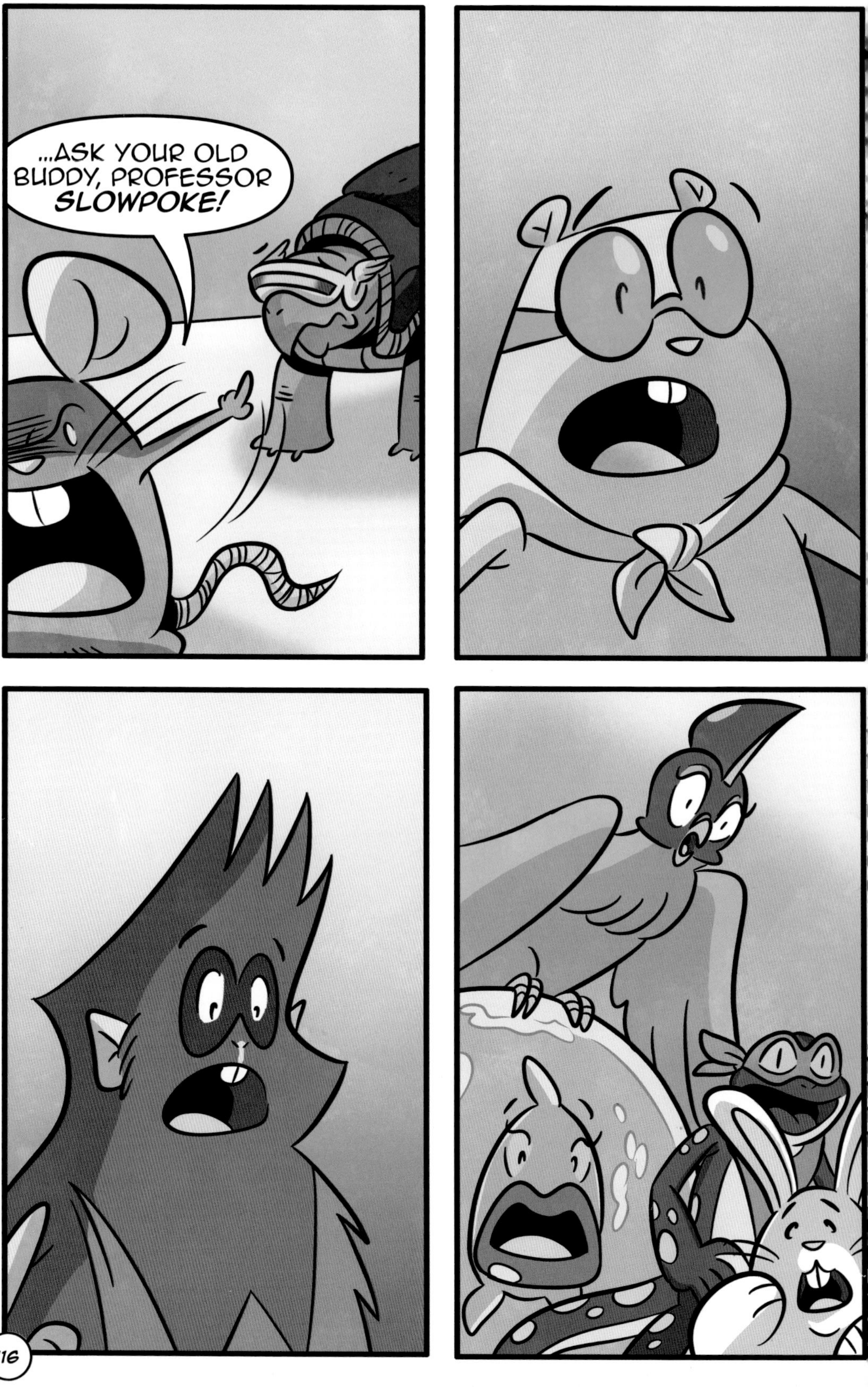
...ASK YOUR OLD BUDDY, PROFESSOR SLOWPOKE!

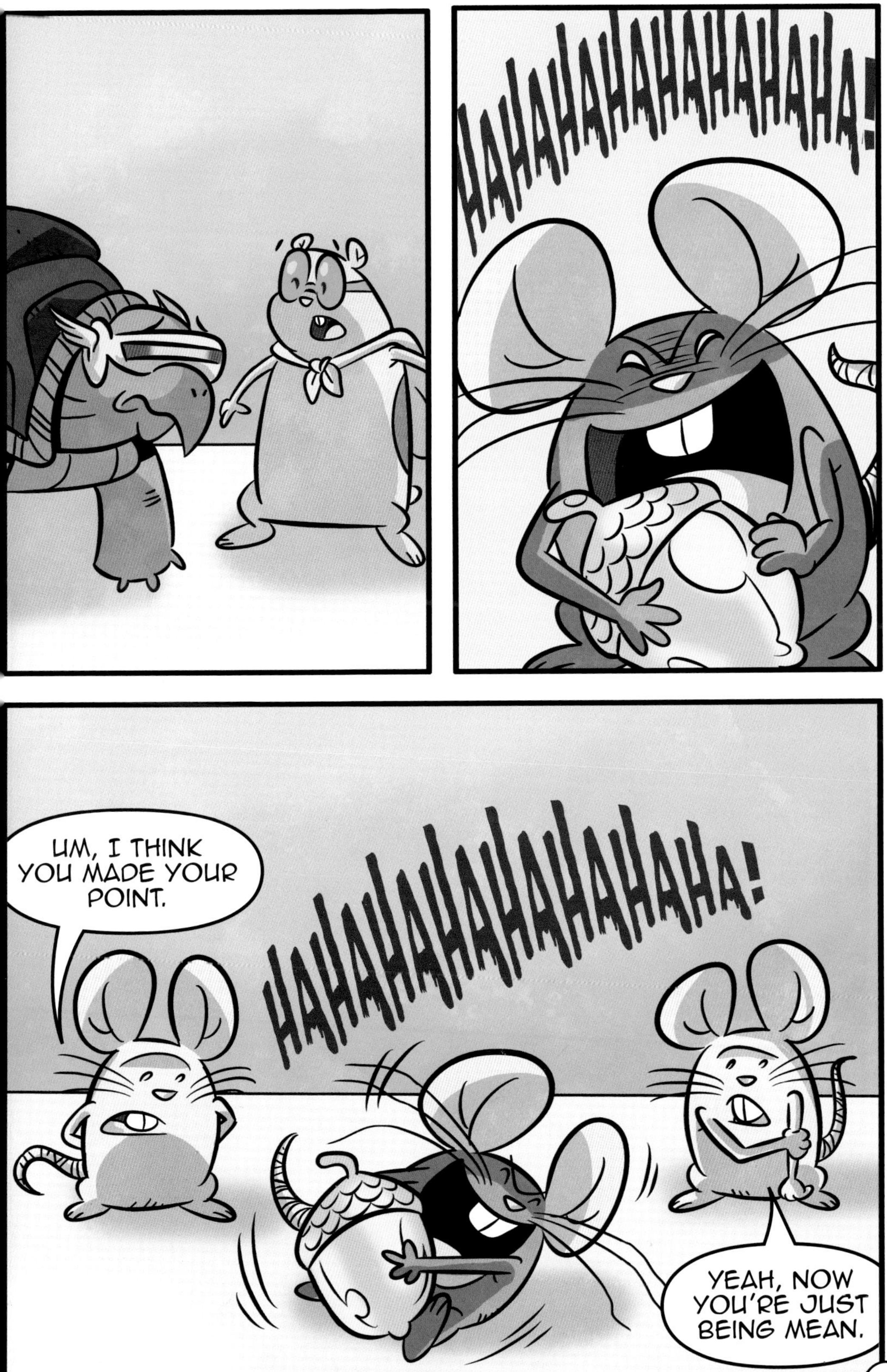
HAHAHAHAHAHAHAHAHA!
UM, I THINK YOU MADE YOUR POINT.
HAHAHAHAHAHAHAHAHAHA!
YEAH, NOW YOU'RE JUST BEING MEAN.

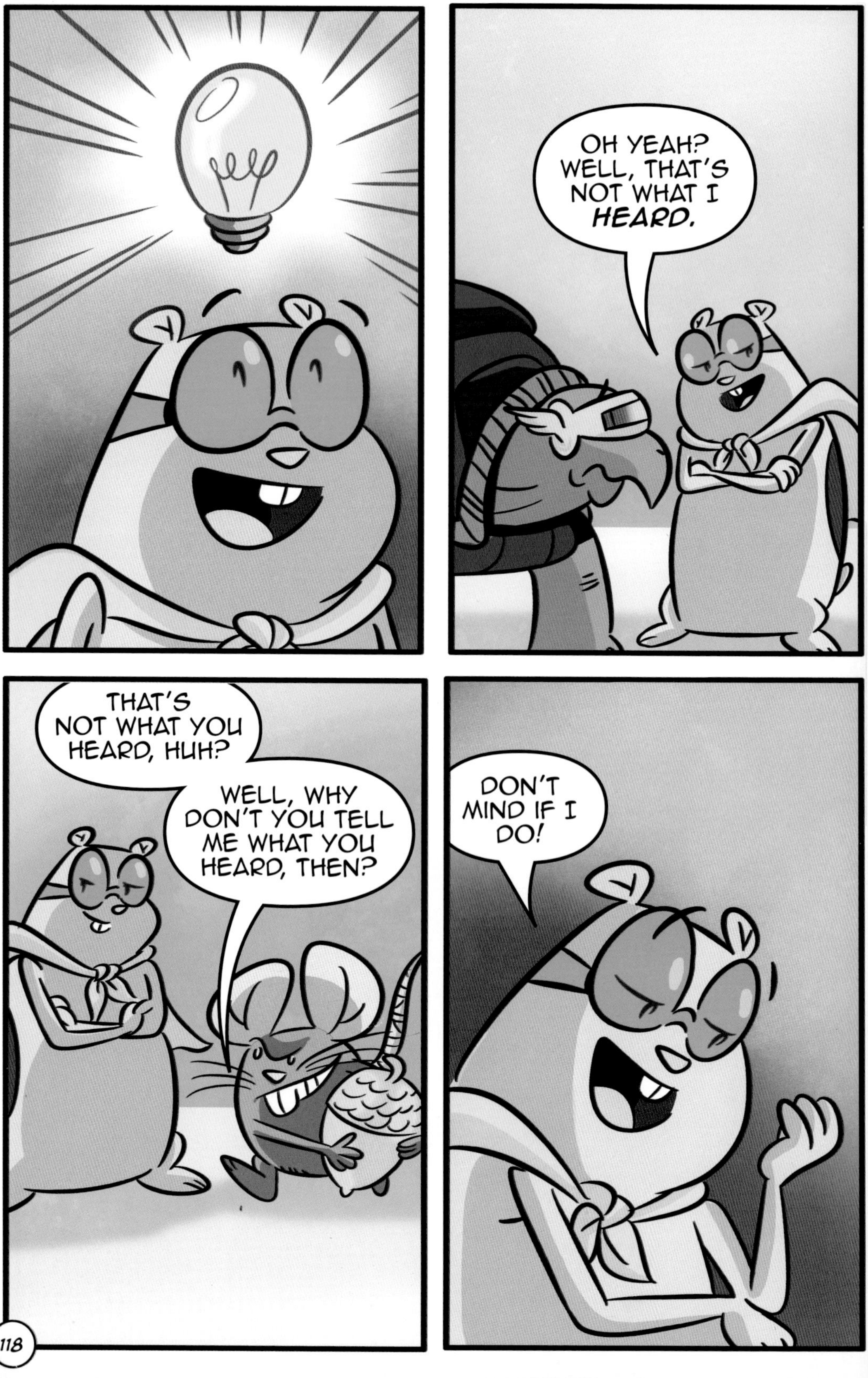
OH YEAH? WELL, THAT'S NOT WHAT I *HEARD.*
THAT'S NOT WHAT YOU HEARD, HUH?
WELL, WHY DON'T YOU TELL ME WHAT YOU HEARD, THEN?
DON'T MIND IF I DO!

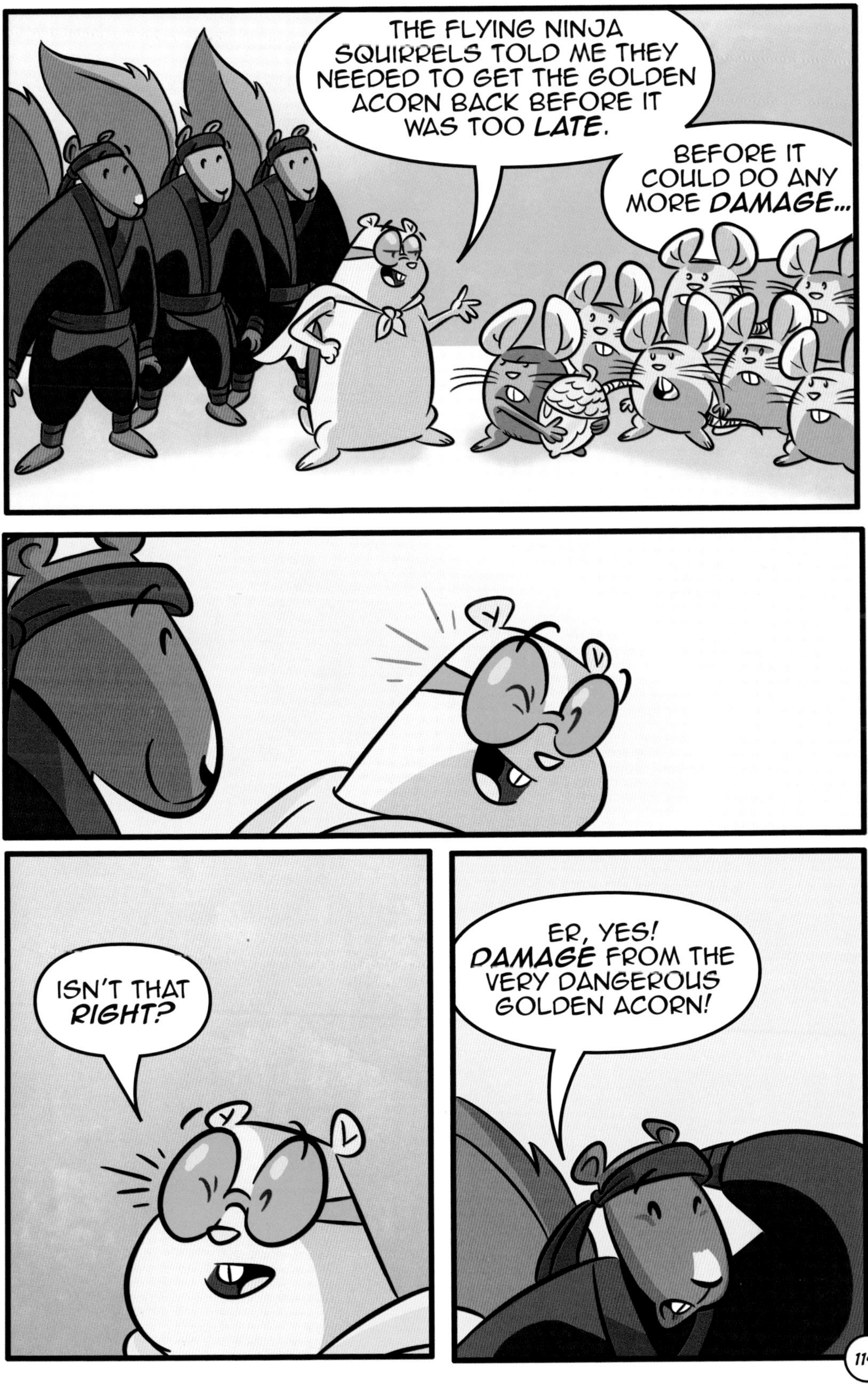
THE FLYING NINJA SQUIRRELS TOLD ME THEY NEEDED TO GET THE GOLDEN ACORN BACK BEFORE IT WAS TOO LATE.
BEFORE IT COULD DO ANY MORE DAMAGE...
ISN'T THAT RIGHT?
ER, YES! DAMAGE FROM THE VERY DANGEROUS GOLDEN ACORN!

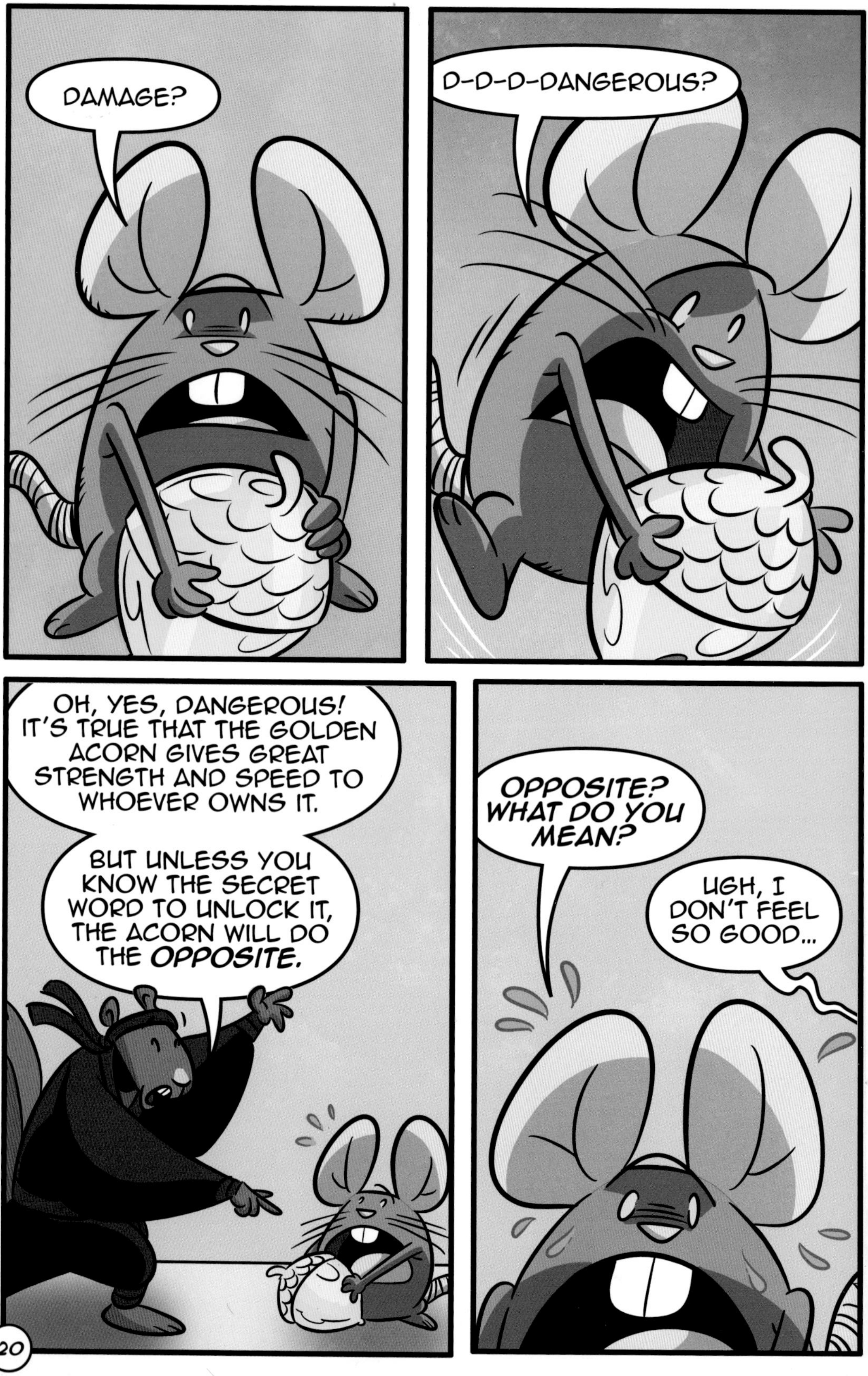
DAMAGE?
D-D-D-DANGEROUS?
OH, YES, DANGEROUS! IT'S TRUE THAT THE GOLDEN ACORN GIVES GREAT STRENGTH AND SPEED TO WHOEVER OWNS IT.
BUT UNLESS YOU KNOW THE SECRET WORD TO UNLOCK IT, THE ACORN WILL DO THE *OPPOSITE.*
OPPOSITE? WHAT DO YOU MEAN?
UGH, I DON'T FEEL SO GOOD...

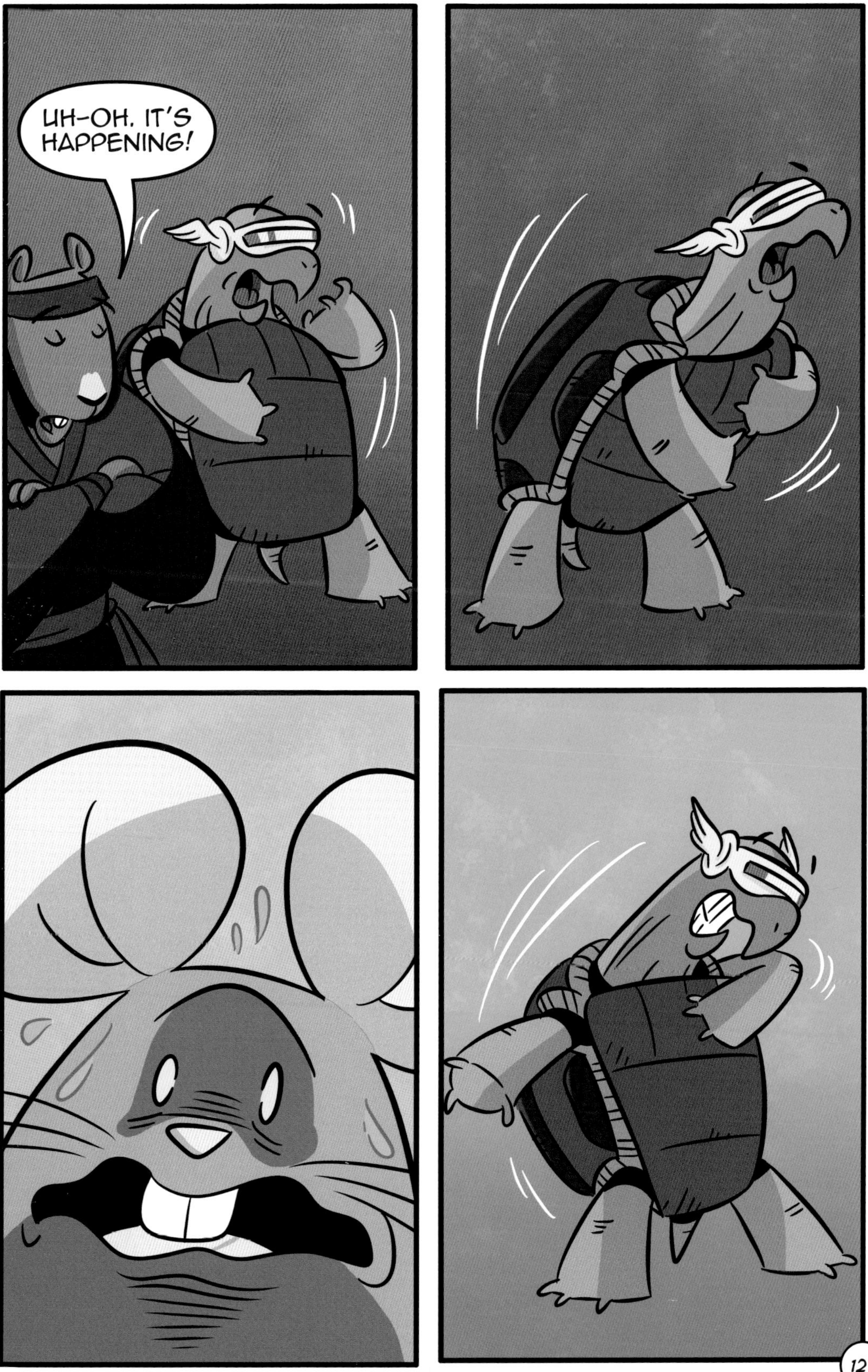
UH-OH. IT'S HAPPENING!

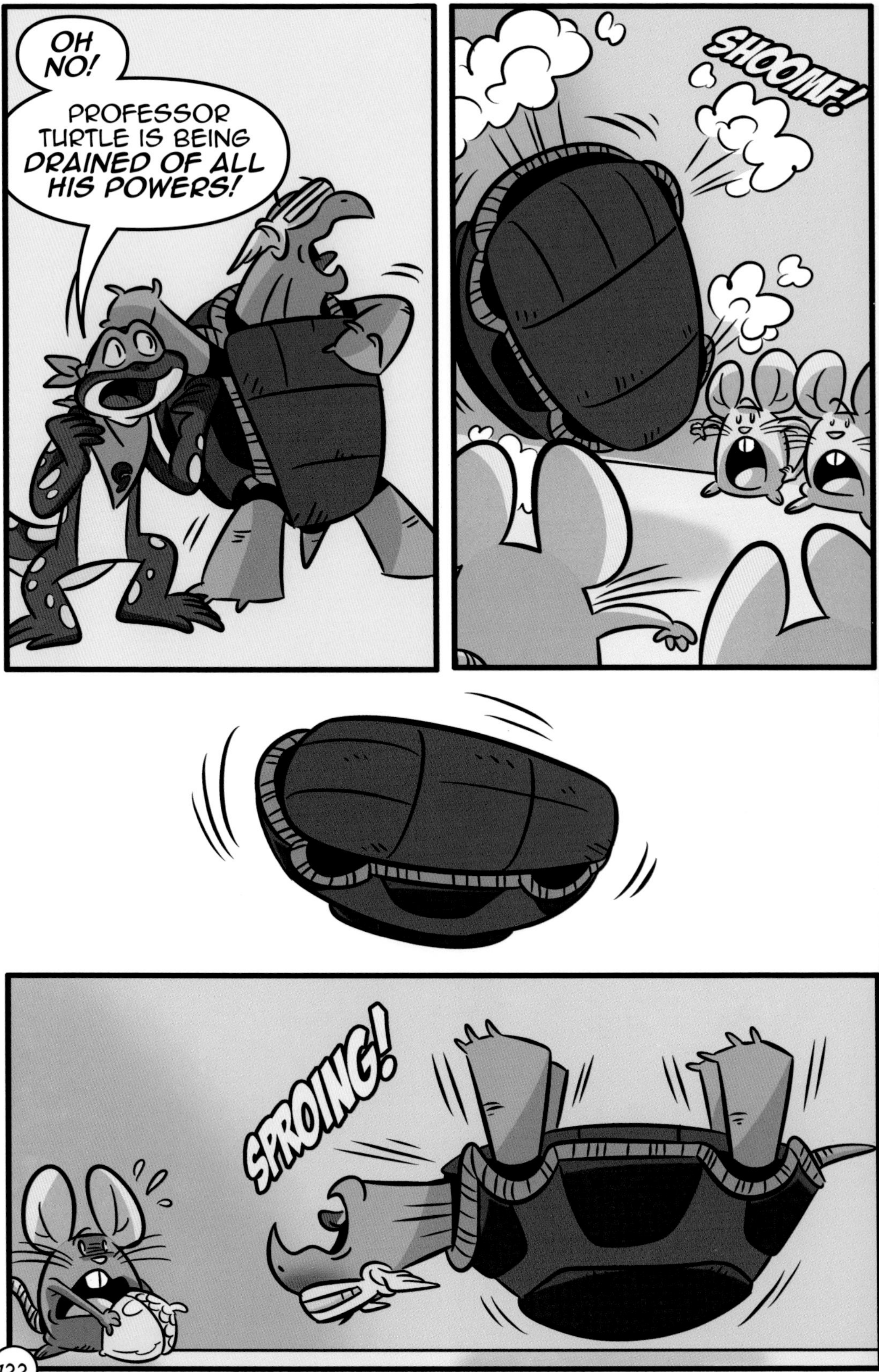
OH NO!
PROFESSOR TURTLE IS BEING DRAINED OF ALL HIS POWERS!
SHOOMF!
SPROING!

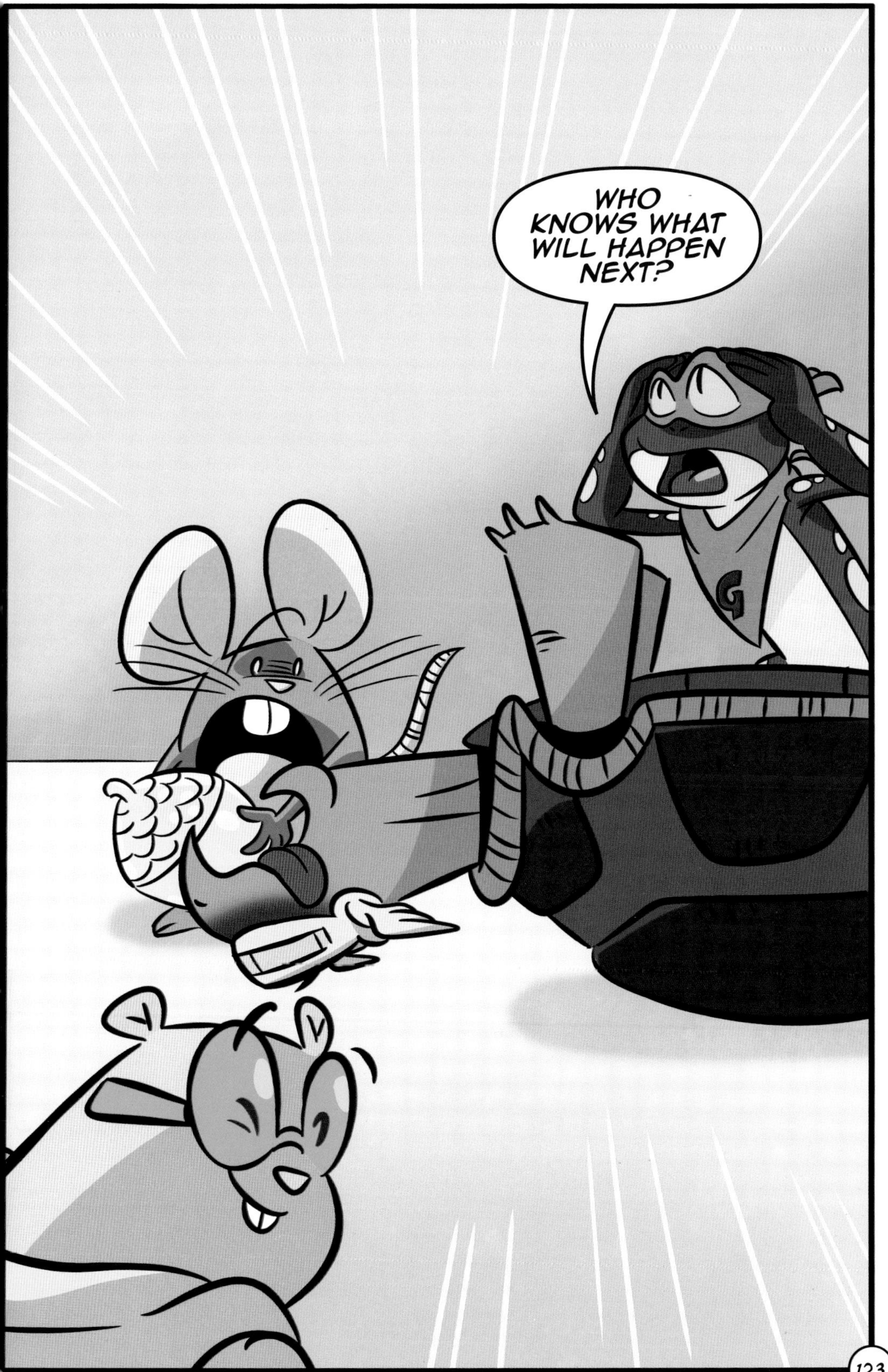
WHO KNOWS WHAT WILL HAPPEN NEXT?

CHAPTER 9

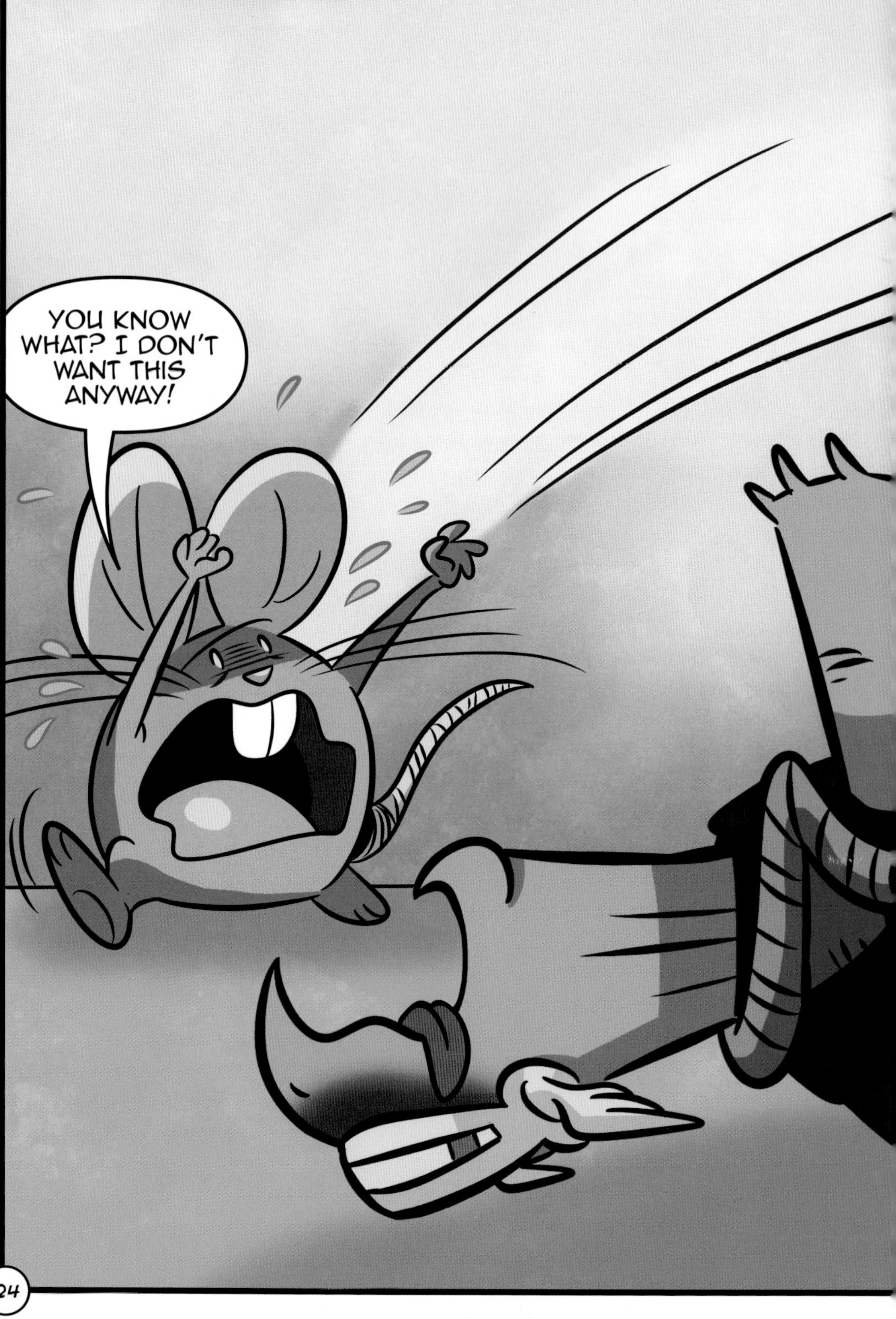
YOU KNOW WHAT? I DON'T WANT THIS ANYWAY!

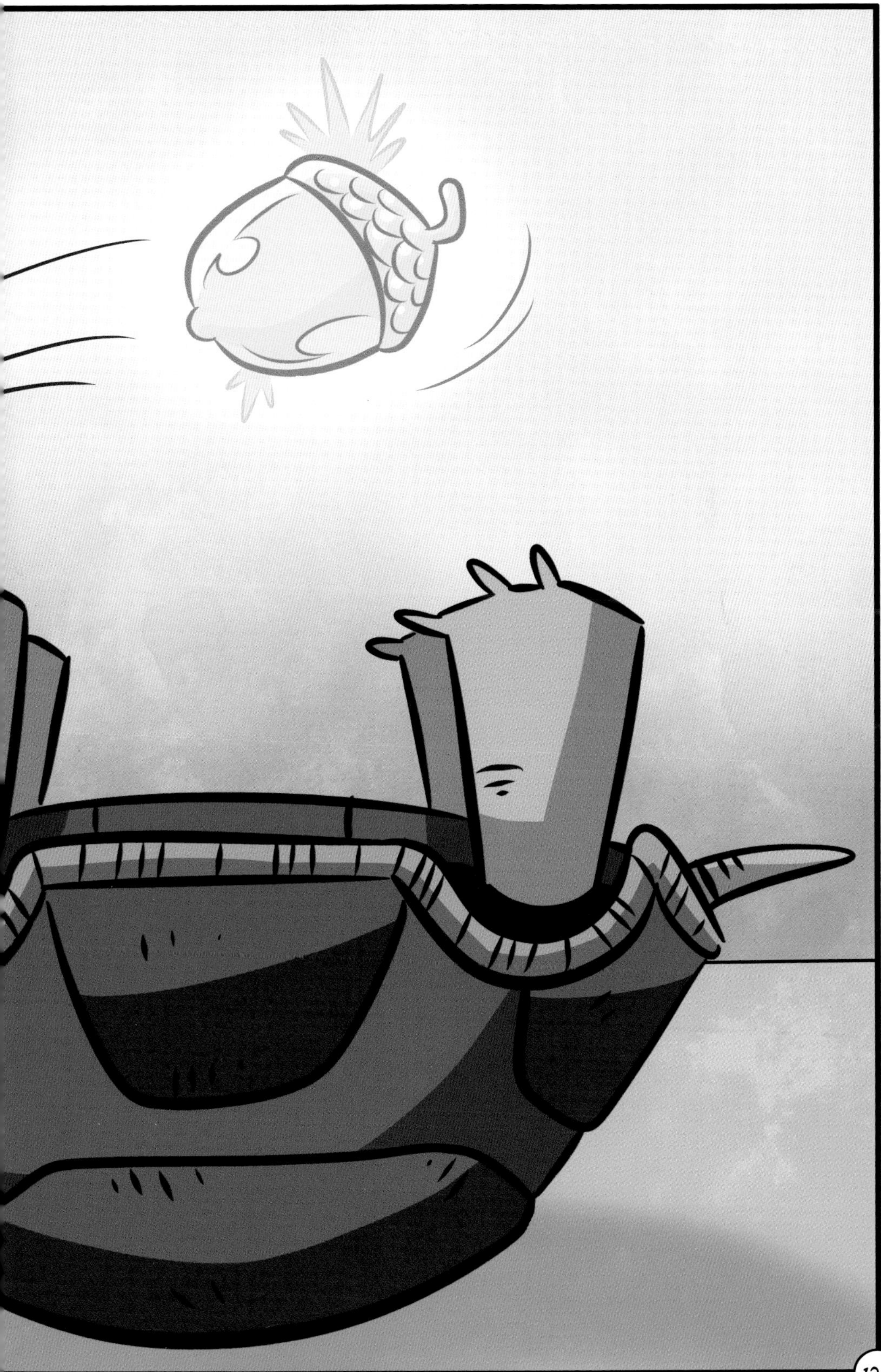

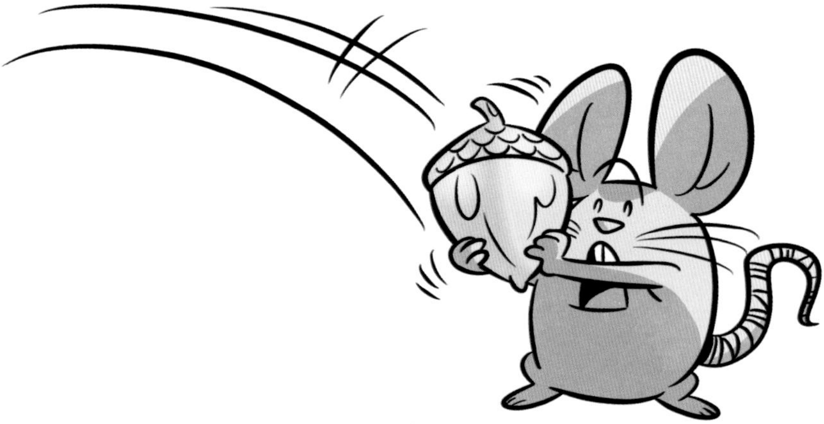

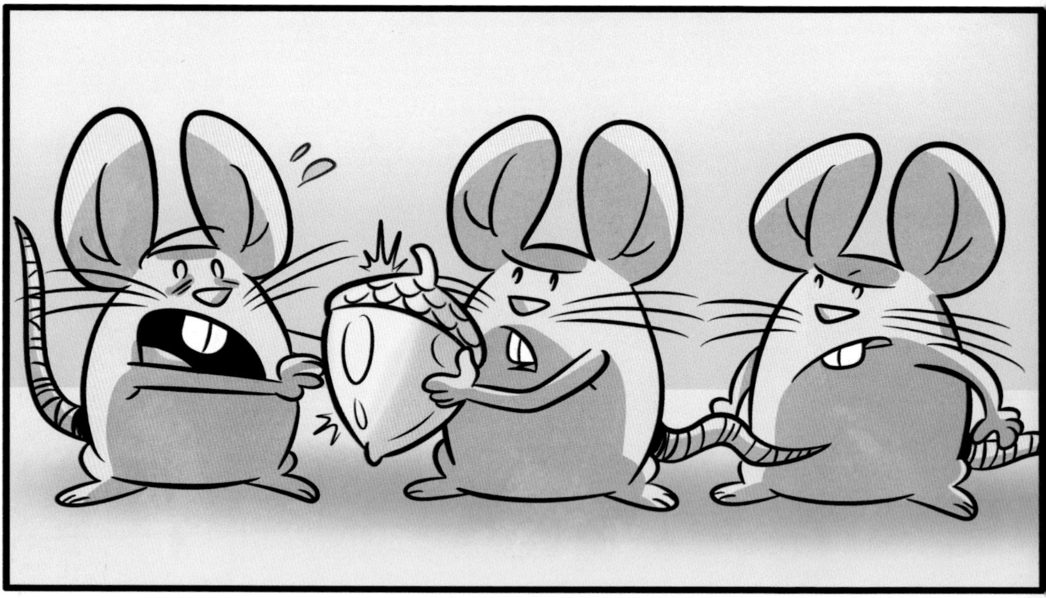

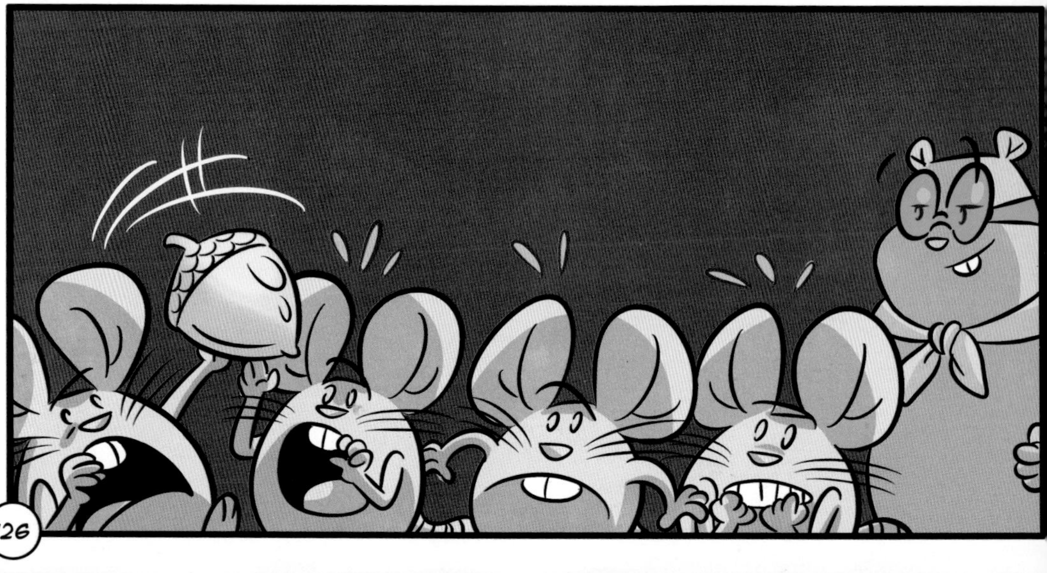

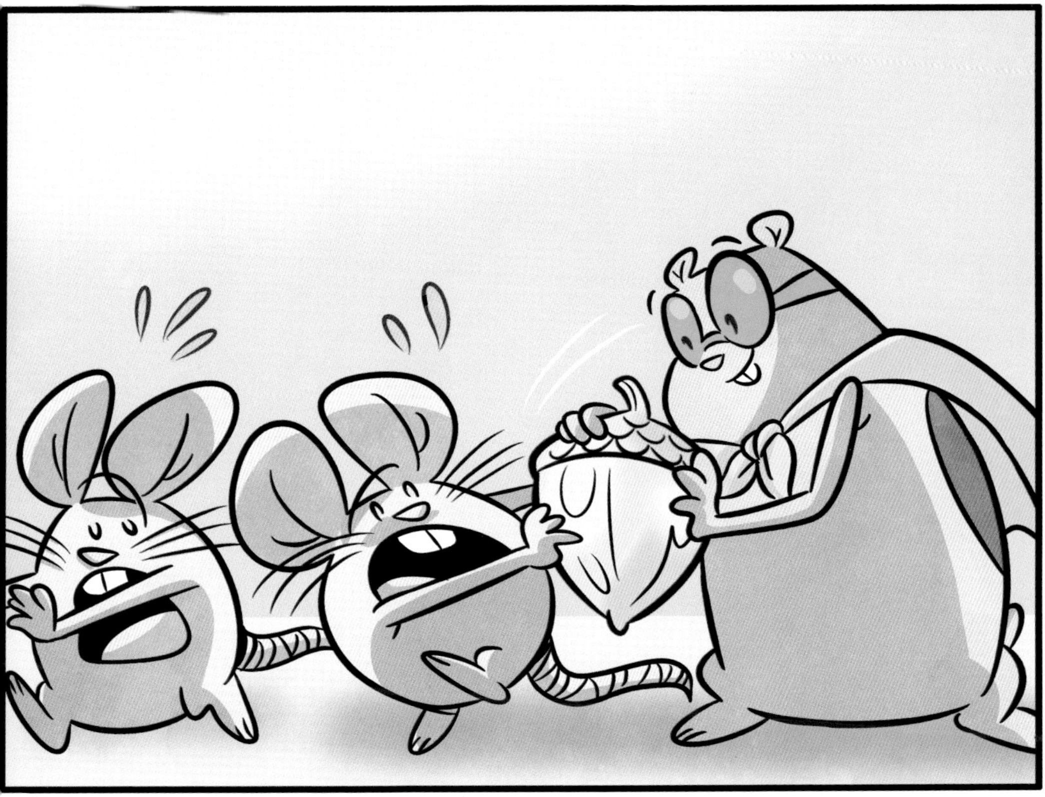

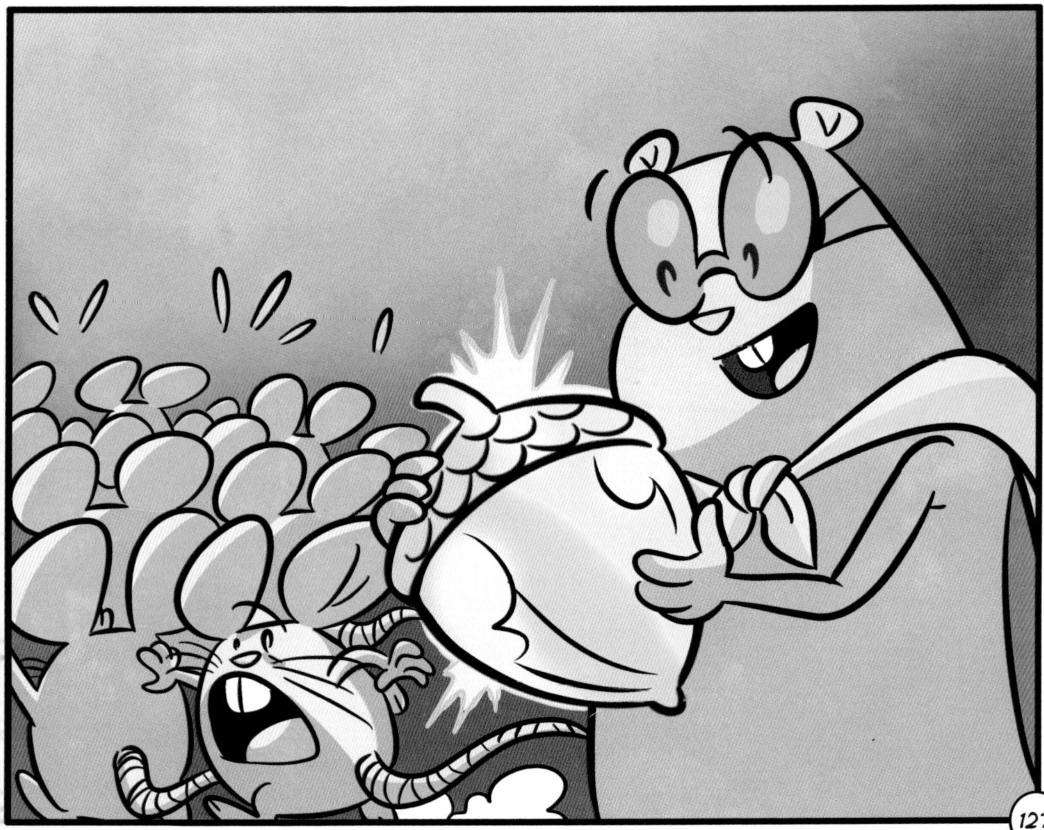

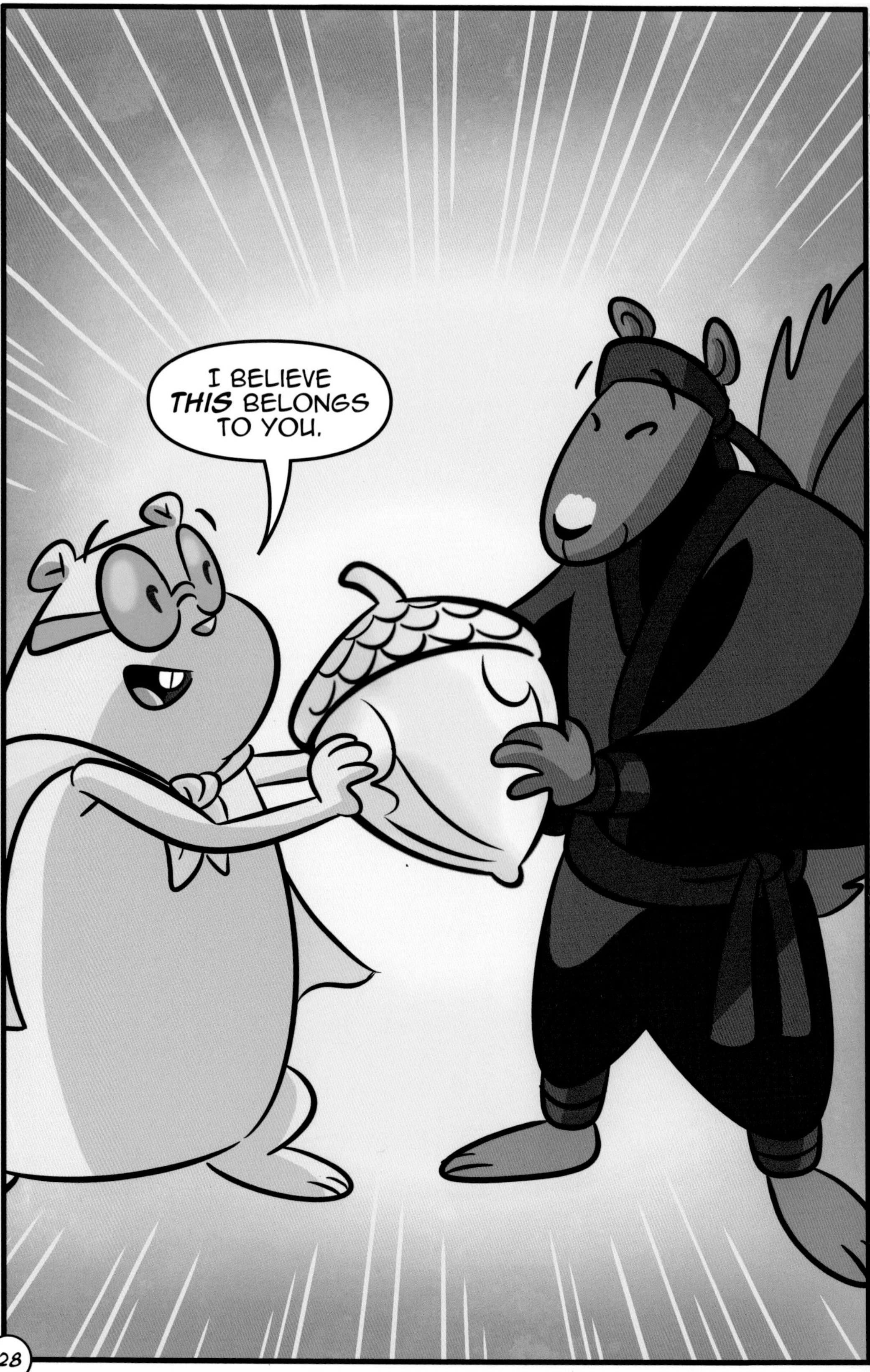
I BELIEVE THIS BELONGS TO YOU.

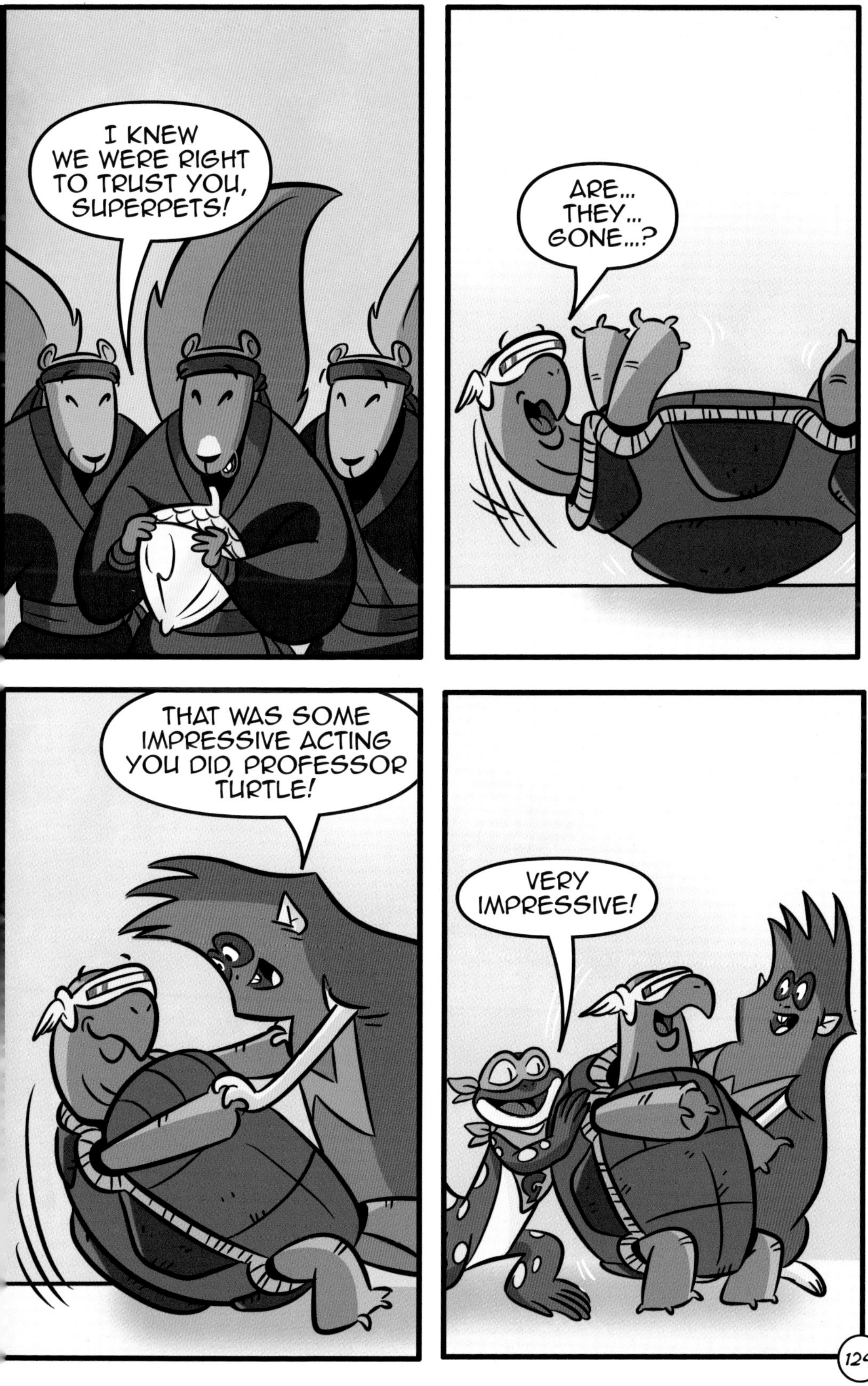
I KNEW WE WERE RIGHT TO TRUST YOU, SUPERPETS!
ARE... THEY... GONE...?
THAT WAS SOME IMPRESSIVE ACTING YOU DID, PROFESSOR TURTLE!
VERY IMPRESSIVE!

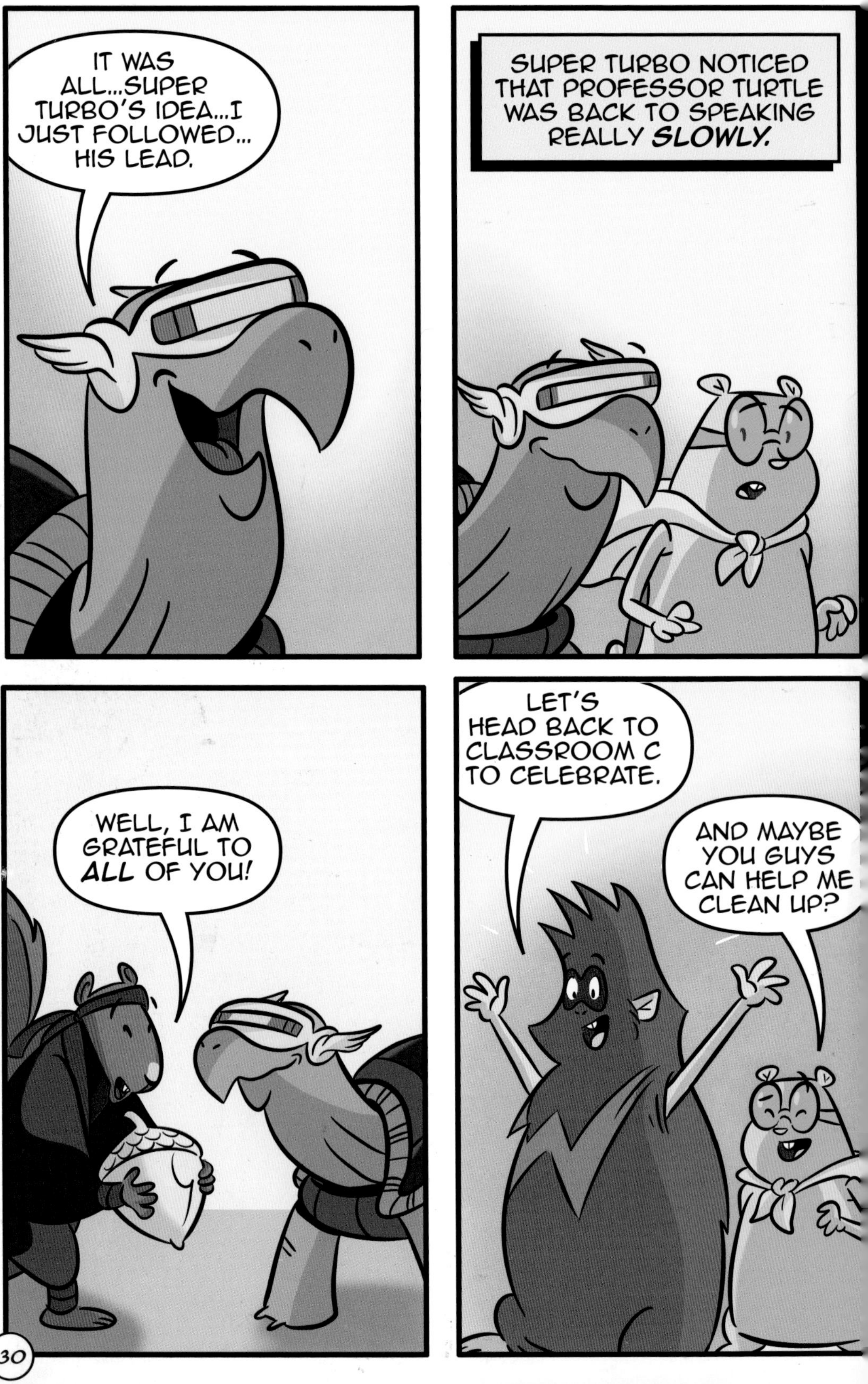
IT WAS ALL...SUPER TURBO'S IDEA...I JUST FOLLOWED... HIS LEAD.
SUPER TURBO NOTICED THAT PROFESSOR TURTLE WAS BACK TO SPEAKING REALLY **SLOWLY.**
WELL, I AM GRATEFUL TO **ALL** OF YOU!
LET'S HEAD BACK TO CLASSROOM C TO CELEBRATE.
AND MAYBE YOU GUYS CAN HELP ME CLEAN UP?

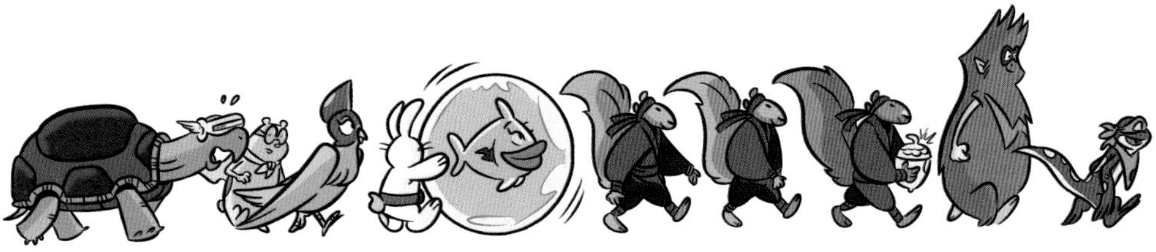

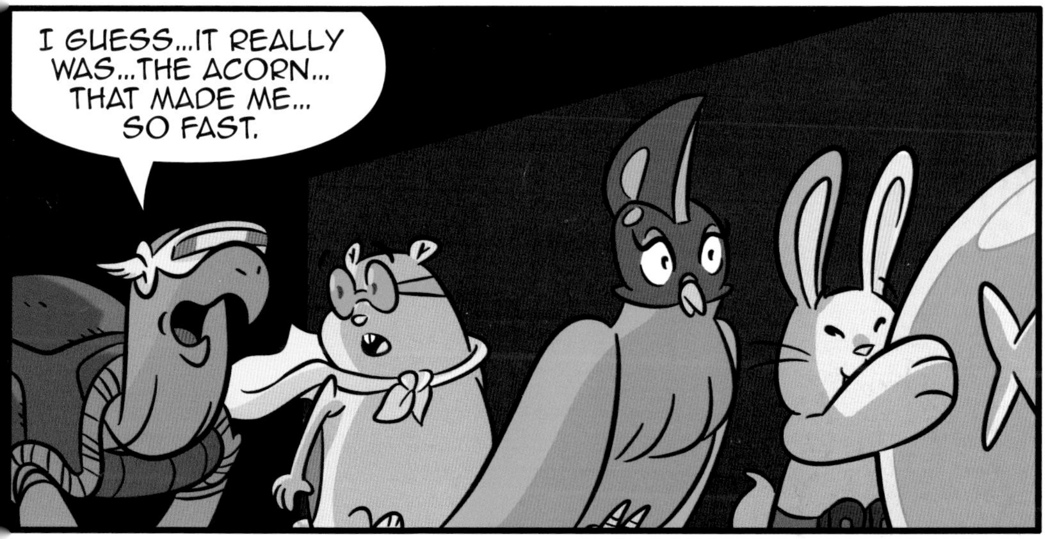
I GUESS...IT REALLY WAS...THE ACORN... THAT MADE ME... SO FAST.

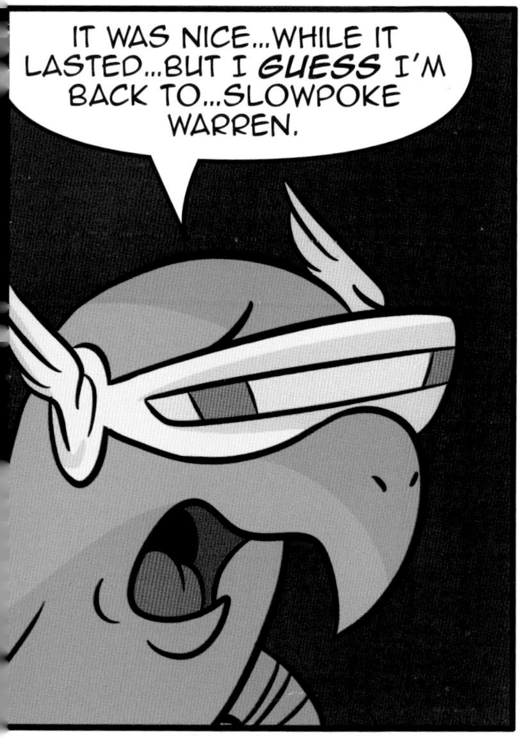
IT WAS NICE...WHILE IT LASTED...BUT I GUESS I'M BACK TO...SLOWPOKE WARREN.

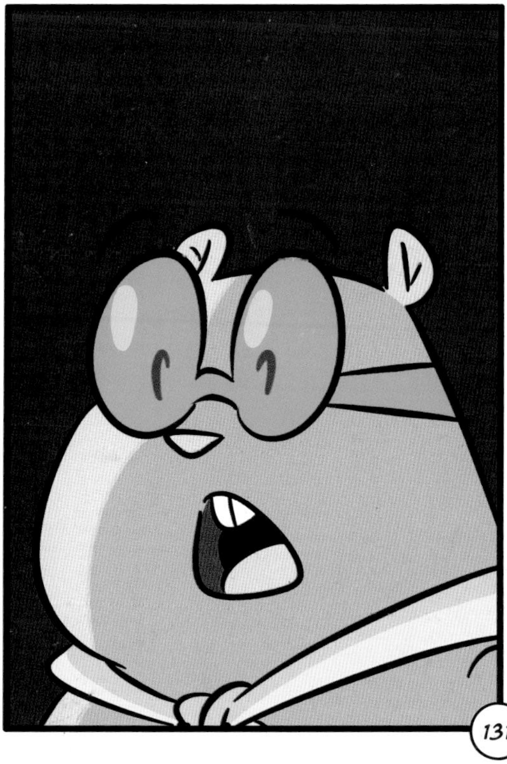

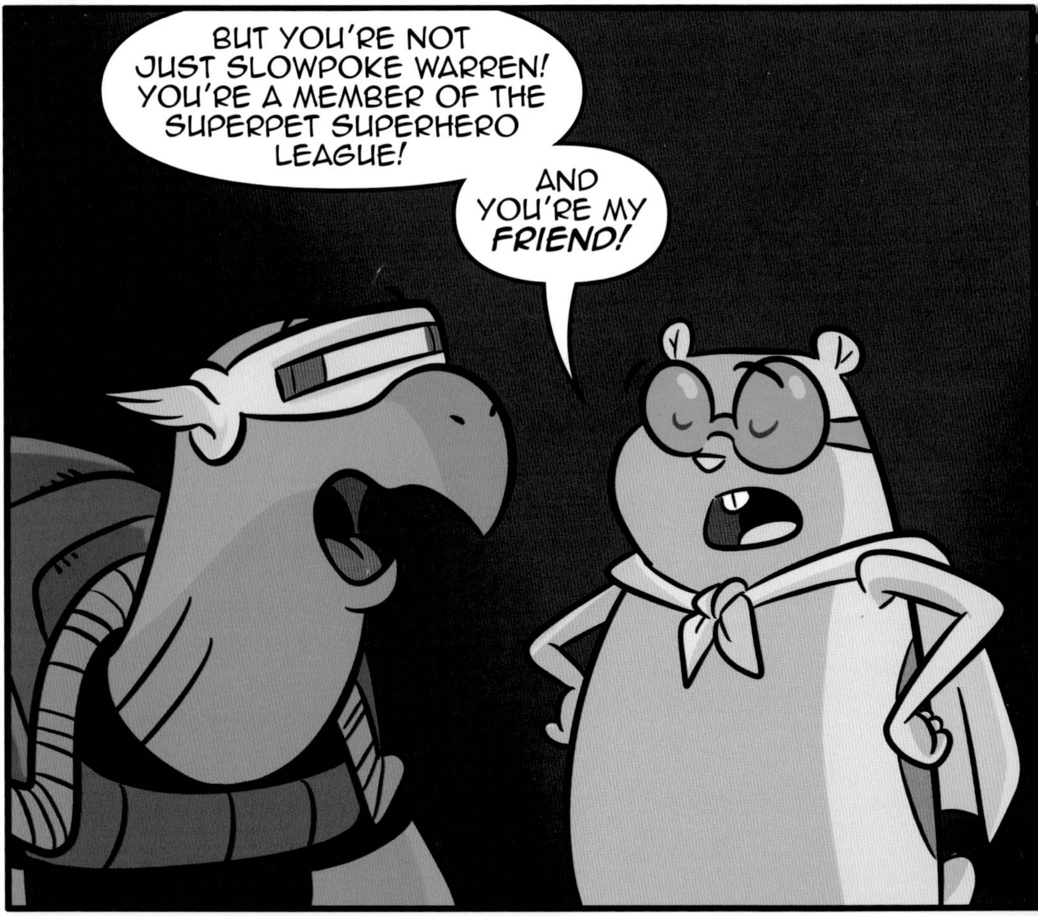
BUT YOU'RE NOT JUST SLOWPOKE WARREN! YOU'RE A MEMBER OF THE SUPERPET SUPERHERO LEAGUE!
AND YOU'RE MY *FRIEND!*

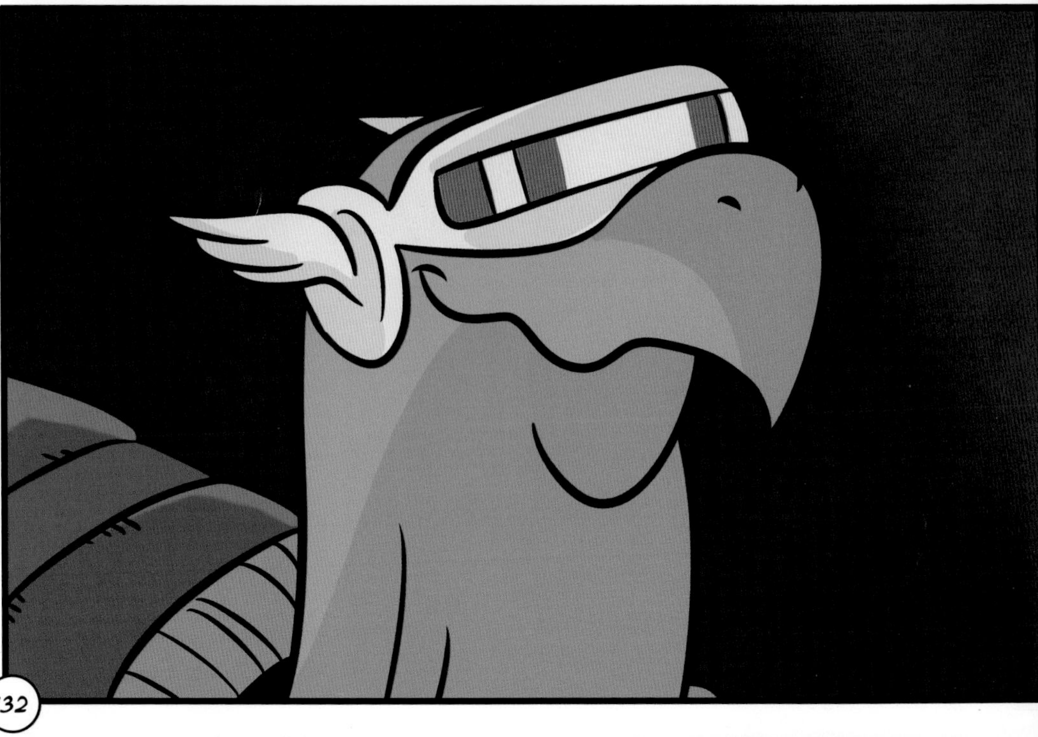

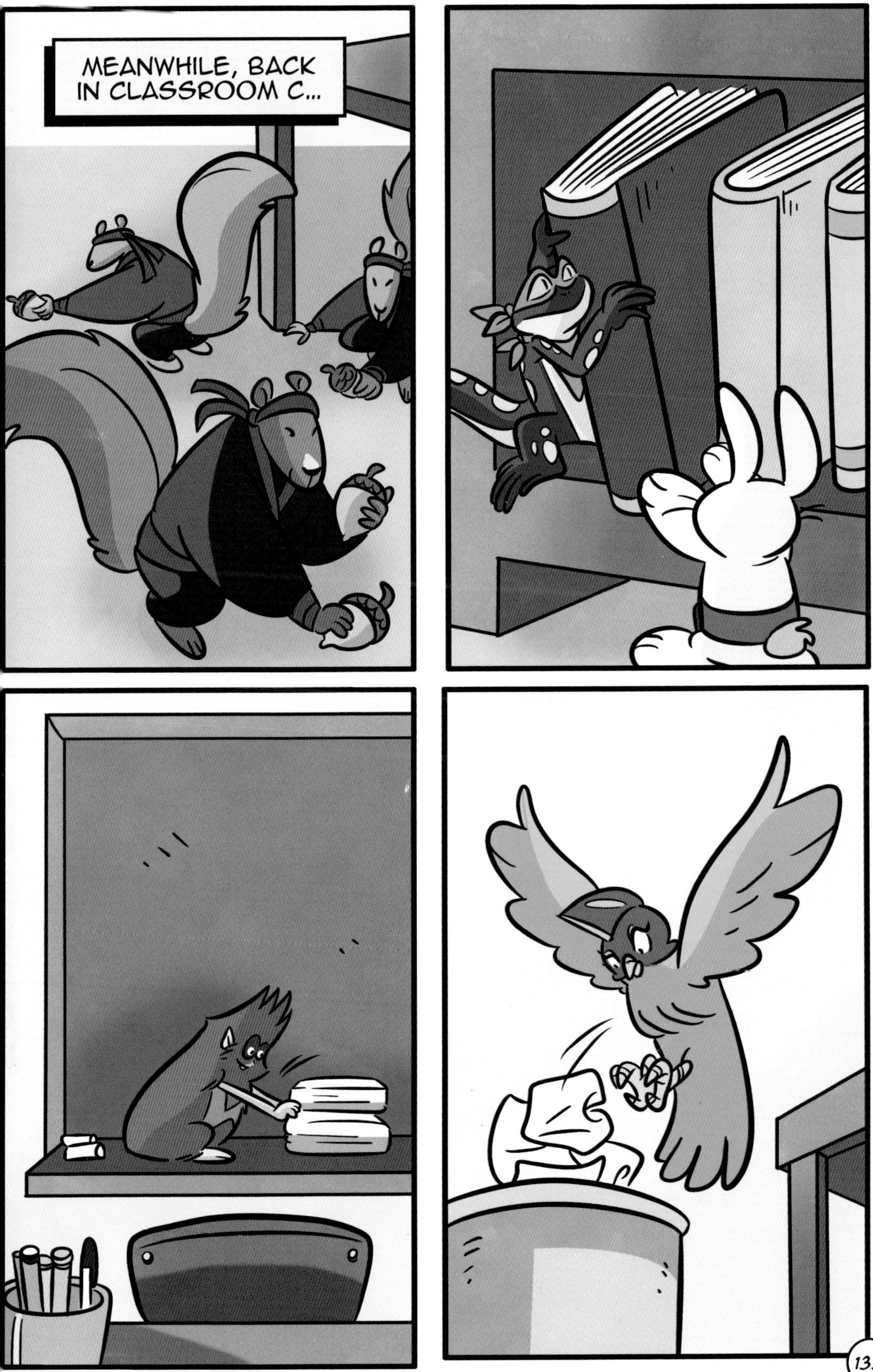
MEANWHILE, BACK IN CLASSROOM C...

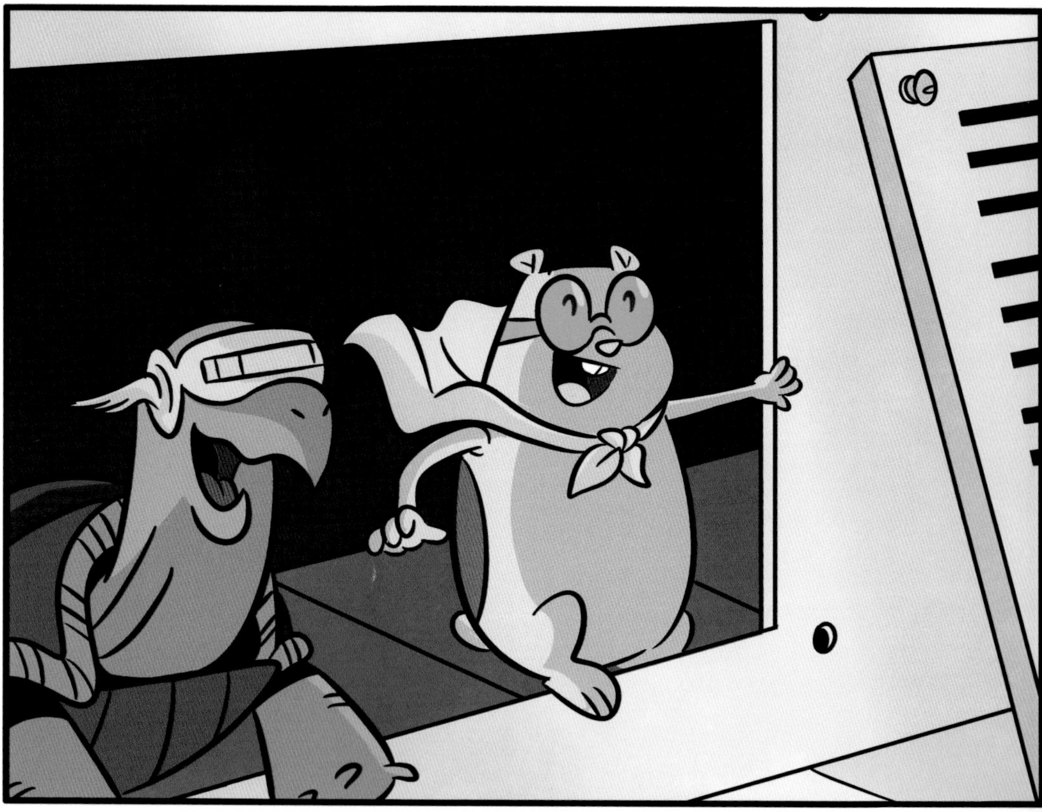

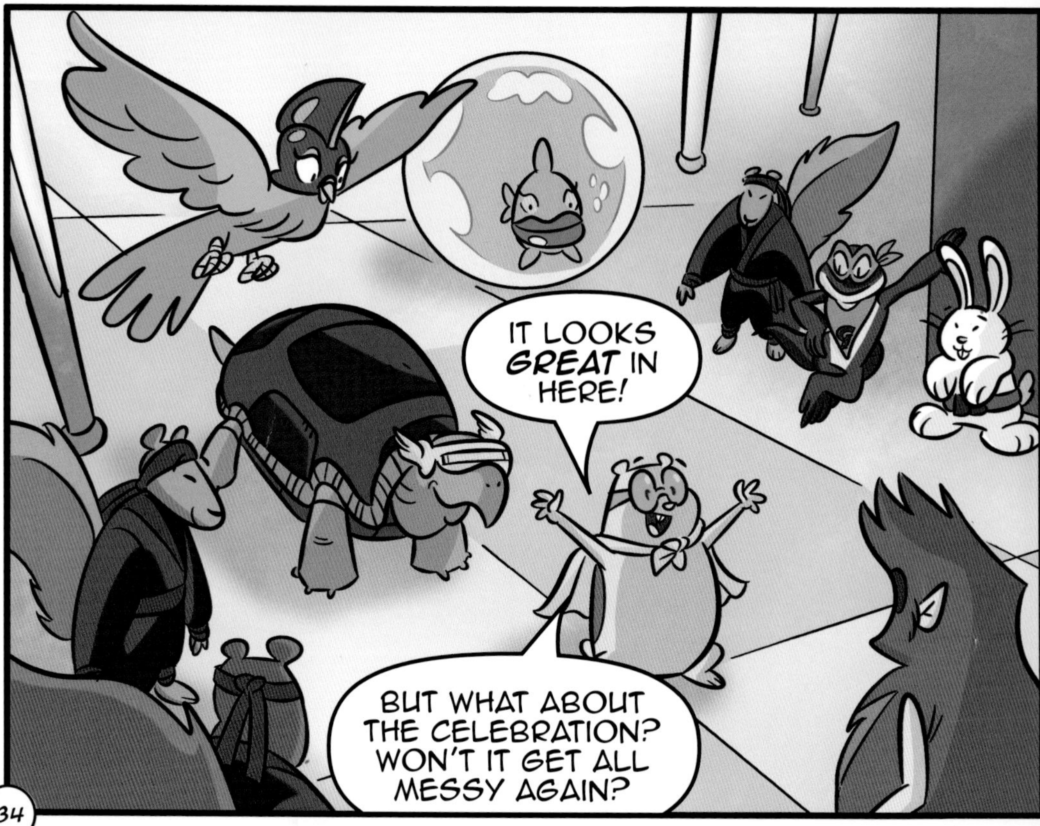
IT LOOKS GREAT IN HERE!
BUT WHAT ABOUT THE CELEBRATION? WON'T IT GET ALL MESSY AGAIN?

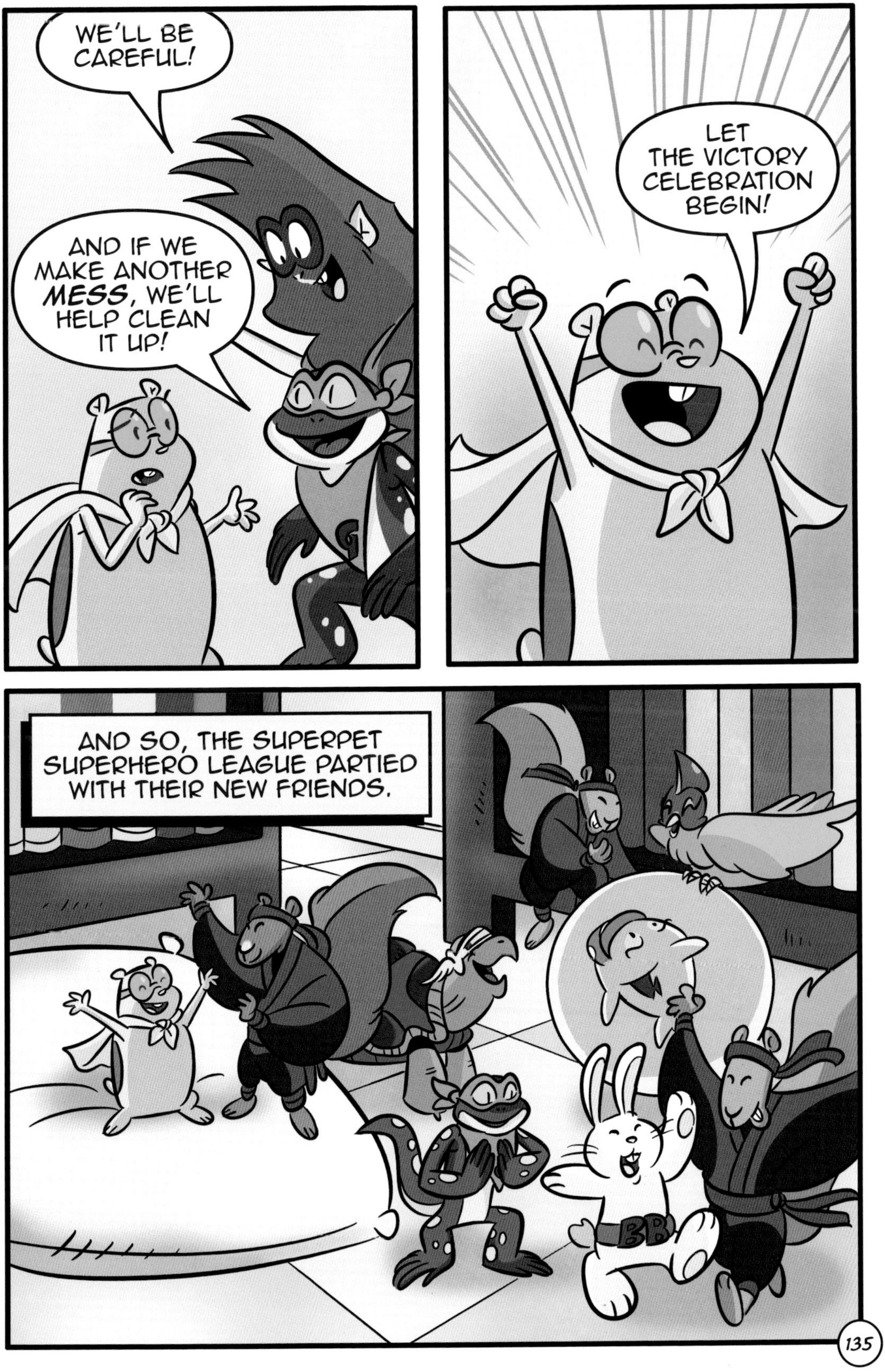
WE'LL BE CAREFUL!
AND IF WE MAKE ANOTHER *MESS*, WE'LL HELP CLEAN IT UP!
LET THE VICTORY CELEBRATION BEGIN!
AND SO, THE SUPERPET SUPERHERO LEAGUE PARTIED WITH THEIR NEW FRIENDS.
BB

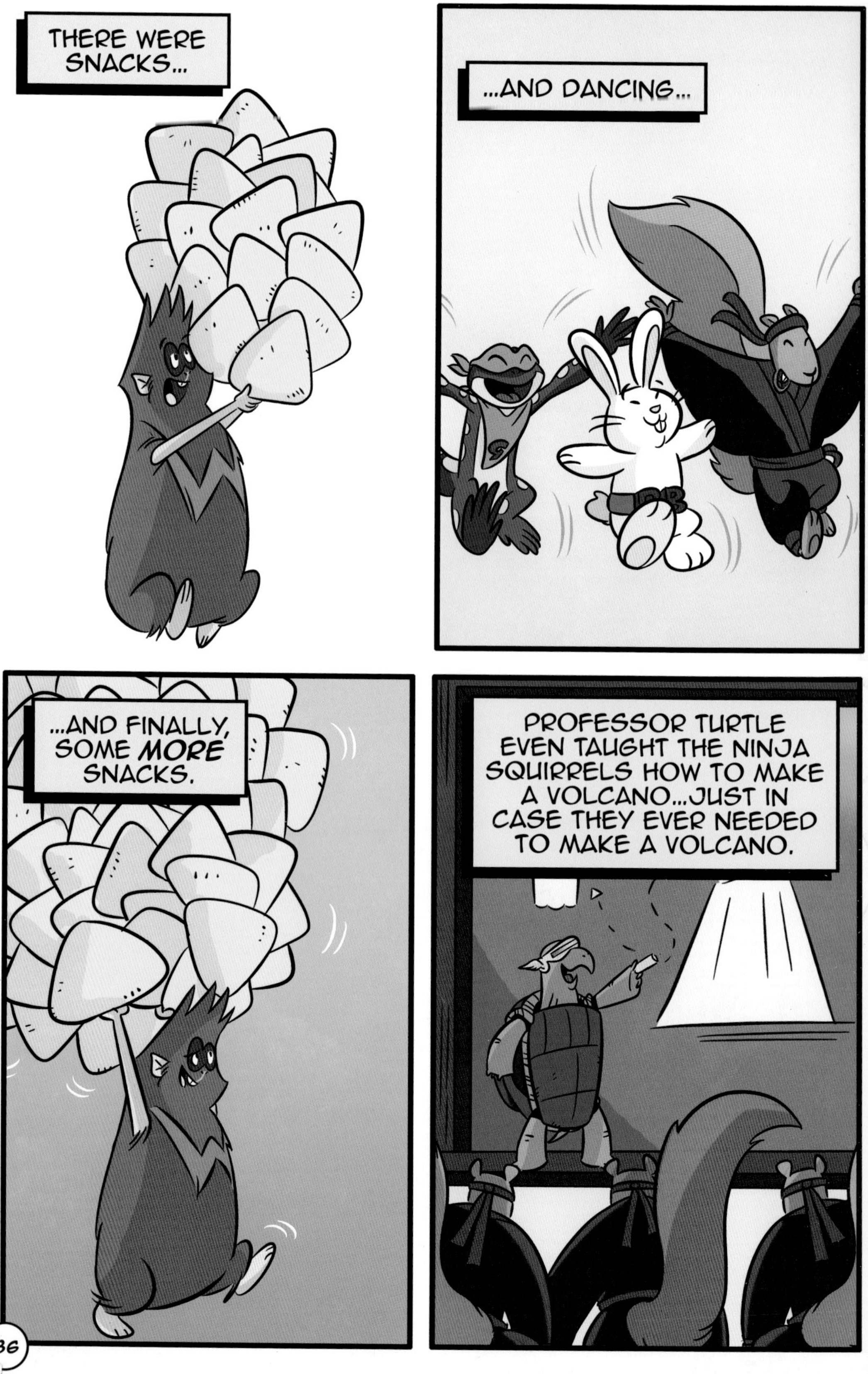
THERE WERE SNACKS...
...AND DANCING...
...AND FINALLY, SOME *MORE* SNACKS.
PROFESSOR TURTLE EVEN TAUGHT THE NINJA SQUIRRELS HOW TO MAKE A VOLCANO...JUST IN CASE THEY EVER NEEDED TO MAKE A VOLCANO.

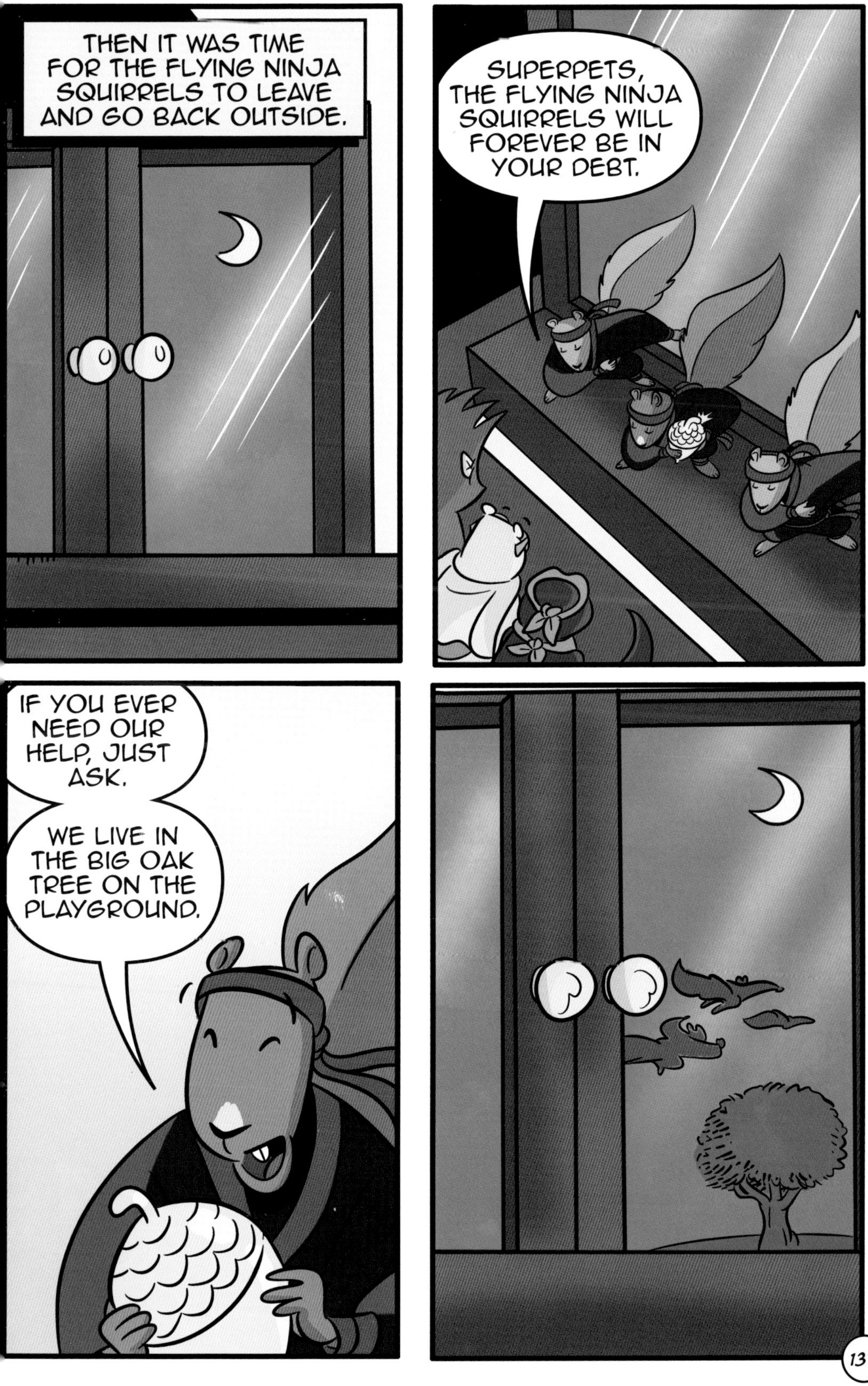
THEN IT WAS TIME FOR THE FLYING NINJA SQUIRRELS TO LEAVE AND GO BACK OUTSIDE.
SUPERPETS, THE FLYING NINJA SQUIRRELS WILL FOREVER BE IN YOUR DEBT.
IF YOU EVER NEED OUR HELP, JUST ASK.
WE LIVE IN THE BIG OAK TREE ON THE PLAYGROUND.

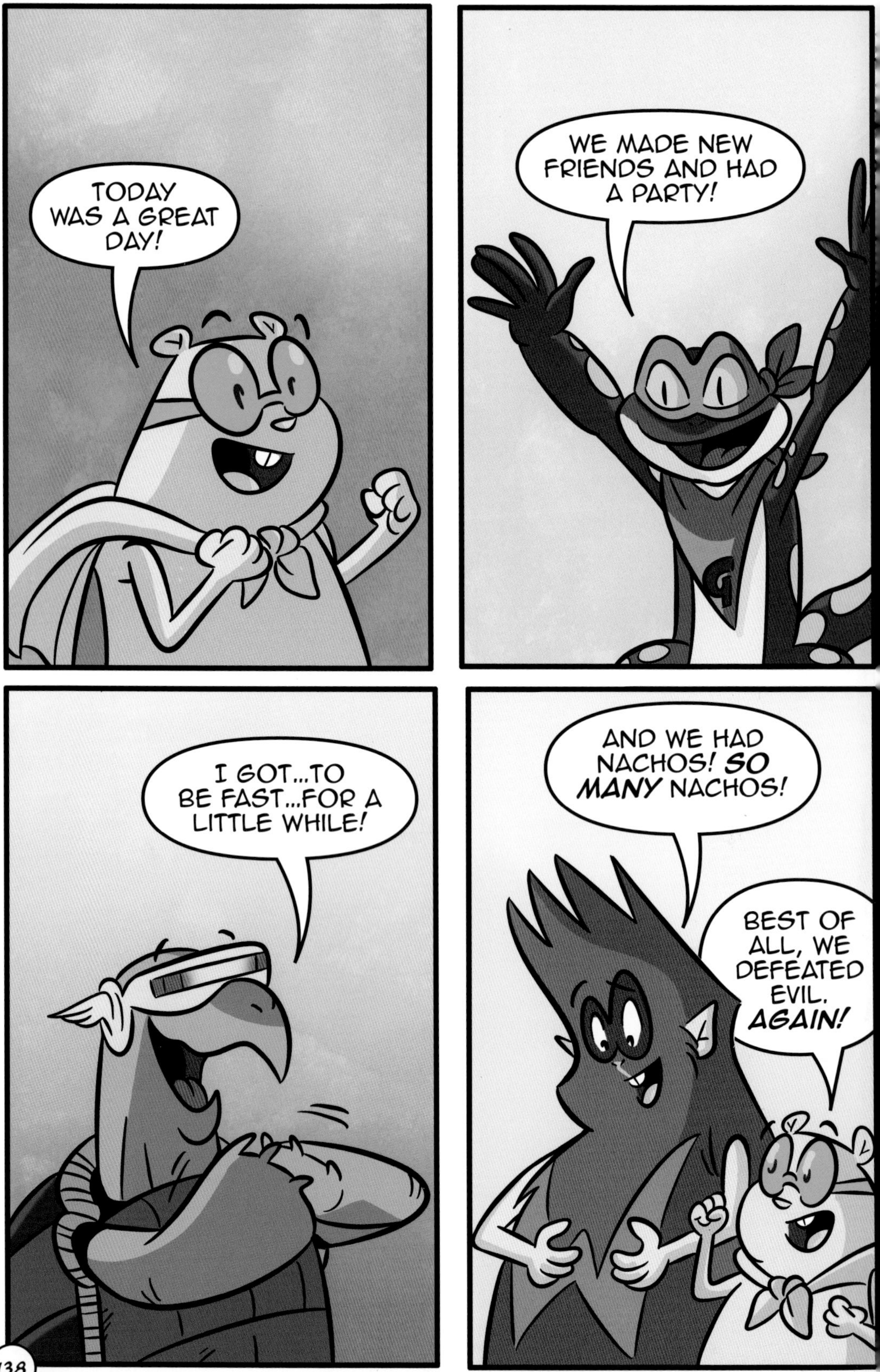
TODAY WAS A GREAT DAY!
WE MADE NEW FRIENDS AND HAD A PARTY!
I GOT...TO BE FAST...FOR A LITTLE WHILE!
AND WE HAD NACHOS! *SO MANY* NACHOS!
BEST OF ALL, WE DEFEATED EVIL. *AGAIN!*

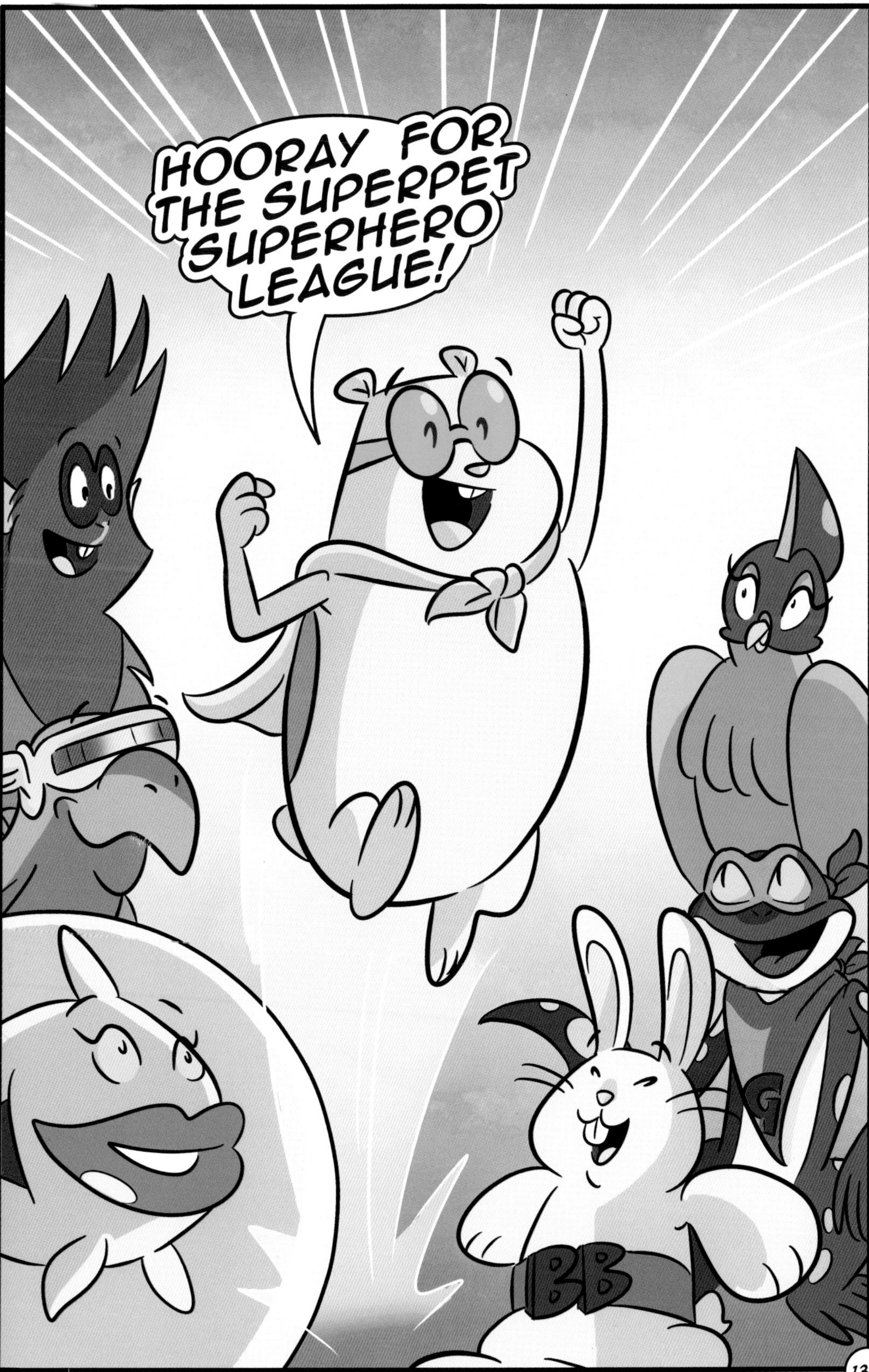
HOORAY FOR THE SUPERPET SUPERHERO LEAGUE!
BB
G

CAN'T GET ENOUGH OF THE **SUPERPET SUPERHERO LEAGUE?** CHECK OUT THEIR NEXT ADVENTURE...

Graphic Novel
SUPER TURBO
VS. THE PENCIL POINTER

TURN THE PAGE FOR A SNEAK PEEK...

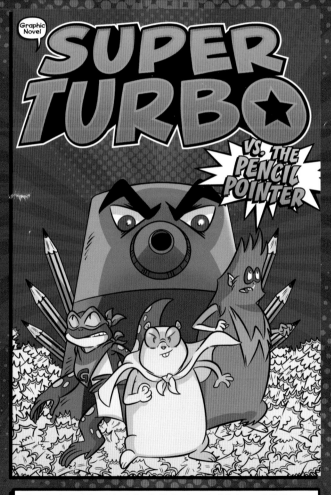

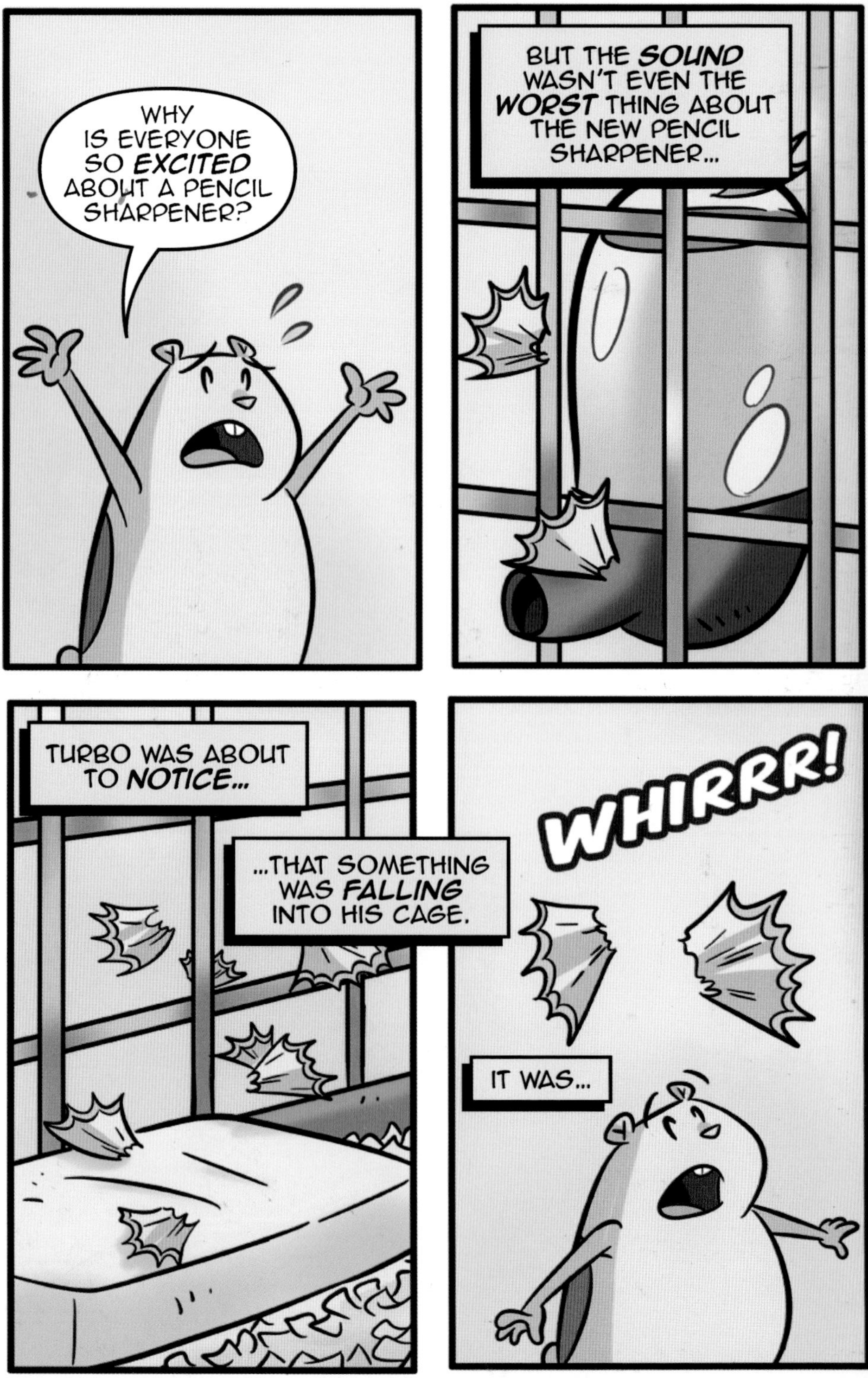

WHY IS EVERYONE SO EXCITED ABOUT A PENCIL SHARPENER?
BUT THE SOUND WASN'T EVEN THE WORST THING ABOUT THE NEW PENCIL SHARPENER...
TURBO WAS ABOUT TO NOTICE...
...THAT SOMETHING WAS FALLING INTO HIS CAGE.
WHIRRR!
IT WAS...

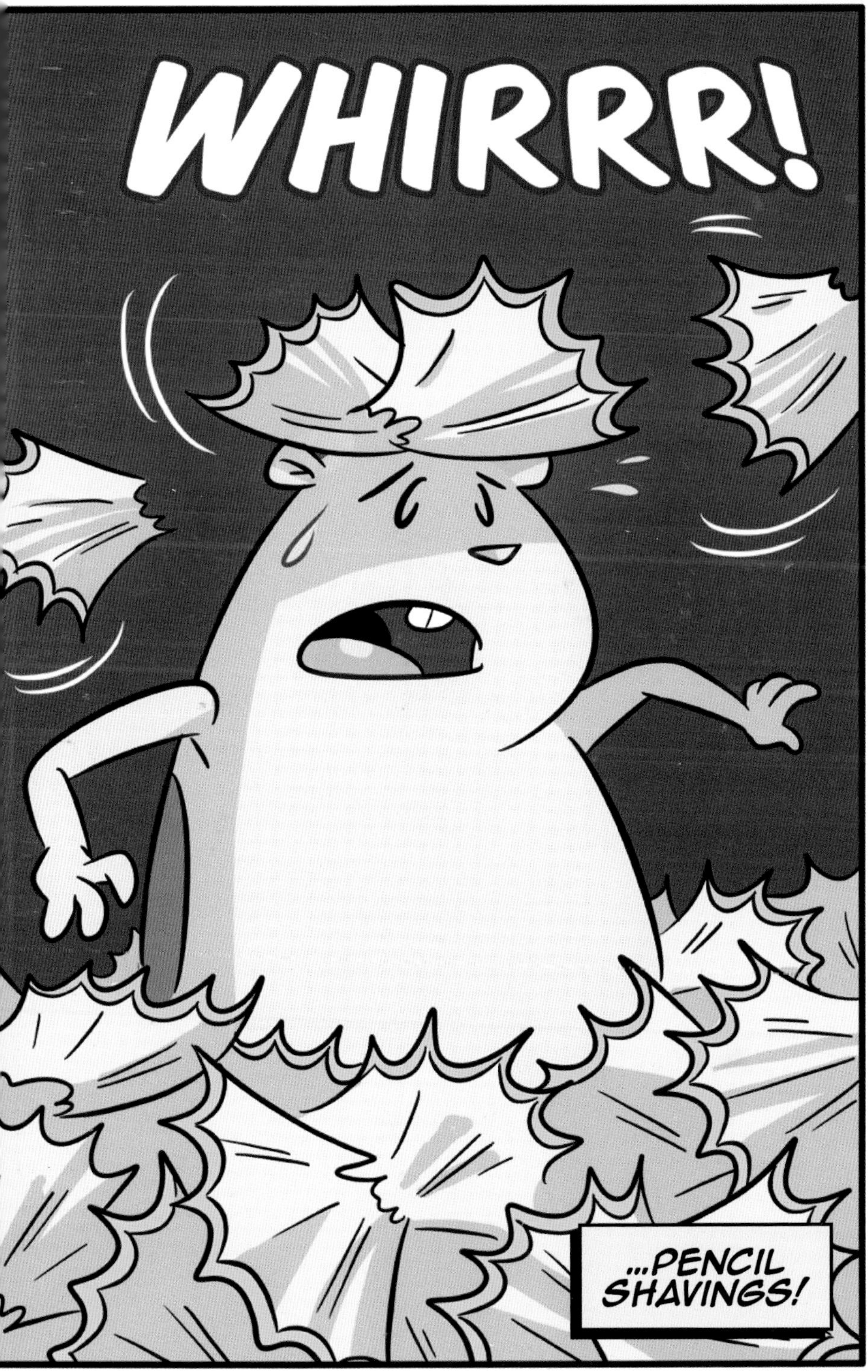
WHIRRR!
...PENCIL SHAVINGS!